Legends from China
THREE KINGDOMS

Three Kingdoms

Many centuries ago, China was made up of several provinces that frequently waged war with one another for regional supremacy. In 221 BC, the Qin Dynasty succeeded in uniting the warring provinces under a single banner, but the unity was short-lived, only lasting fifteen years. After the collapse of the Qin Dynasty, the Han Dynasty was established in 206 BC, and unity was restored. The Han Dynasty would last for hundreds of years, until the Post-Han Era, when the unified nation once again began to unravel. As rebellion and chaos gripped the land, three men came forward to take control of the nation: Bei Liu, Cao Cao, and Ce Sun. The three men each established separate kingdoms, Shu, Wei, and Wu, and for a century they contended for supremacy. This was known as the Age of the Three Kingdoms.

Written more than six hundred years ago, *Three Kingdoms* is one of the oldest and most seminal works in all of Eastern literature. An epic story spanning decades and featuring hundreds of characters, it remains a definitive tale of desperate heroism, political treachery, and the bonds of brotherhood.

Wei Dong Chen and Xiao Long Liang have chosen to draw this adaptation of *Three Kingdoms* in a manner reminiscent of the ancient Chinese printing technique. It is our hope that the historical look of *Three Kingdoms* will amplify the timelessness of its themes, which are just as relevant today as they were thousands of years ago.

THREE KINGDOMS
Vol. 02

The Family Plot

Created by *WEI DONG CHEN*

Wei Dong Chen, a highly acclaimed and beloved artist, and an influential leader in the "New Chinese Cartoon" trend, is the founder of Creator World in Tianjin, the largest comics studio in China. Recently the Chinese government entrusted him with the role of general manager of the Beijing Book Fair, and his reputation as a pillar of Chinese comics has brought him many students. He has published more than three hundred cartoons, which have been recognized for their strong literary value not only in Korea, but in Europe and Japan as well. Free spirited and energetic, Wei Dong Chen's positivist philosophy is reflected in the wisdom of his work. He is published serially in numerous publications while continuing to conceive projects that explore new dimensions of the form.

Illustrated by *XIAO LONG LIANG*

Xiao Long Liang is considered one of Wei Dong Chen's greatest students. One of the most highly regarded cartoonists in China today, Xiao Long's fantastic technique and expression of Chinese culture have won him the acclaim of cartoon lovers throughout China. His other works include "Outlaws of the Marsh" and "A Story on the Motorbike".

Original Story
"The Romance of the Three Kingdoms" by Luo, GuanZhong

Editing & Designing
Design Hongs, Jonathan Evans, KH Lee, YK Kim,
HJ Lee, JS Kim, Lampin, Qing Shao, Xiao Nan Li, Ke Hu

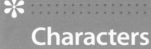

BEI LIU, YU GUAN, AND FEI ZHANG

Bei Liu, Yu Guan, and Fei Zhang are three men from the rural provinces who have sworn a blood oath to defend each other and restore the nation. They come to the aid of Zan GongSun when his army is under heavy attack during the battle for Ji Province. There they meet Yun Zhao, a young warrior who will likely factor into their future, especially Bei Liu's.

SHAO YUAN

Shao Yuan is one of the most ambitious and cunning of the 18 feudal lords who created the coalition army. After the coalition falls apart, Shao Yuan sets his sights on conquering Ji Province. He enlists the help of Zan GongSun to carry out the attack, but when the governor of Ji abandons the province Shao Yuan claims the land for himself.

ZAN GONGSUN

Zan GongSun was persuaded by Shao Yuan to help him conquer Ji Province, but when the province falls Yuan refuses to share it. GongSun goes to war against his former ally, and when the battle goes badly he turns to Bei Liu and his sworn brothers for aid.

YUN ZHAO

Yun Zhao is a young and extremely powerful soldier who served under the banner of Shao Yuan until he defected to Zan GongSun's side. Following the battle for Ji Province, Zhao grows frustrated serving under GongSun and asks to join Bei Liu and his brothers.

JIAN SUN

Jian Sun, known as the "Tiger of the East," is a famous warrior who was defeated in battle by Biao Liu. Soon after, he is persuaded by Shao Yuan's brother, Shu, to attack Biao Liu's palace. But the attack costs Jian Sun many tactical advantages, and the slightest lapse in judgment could lead to deadly consequences.

CE SUN

Ce, Jian Sun's eldest son, admires his father's legendary abilities in battle, yet is fundamentally different from his idol. When an unexpected situation forces Ce to decide the course of his family's future, he will learn just how dissimilar they truly are.

ZHUO DONG

Zhuo Dong is the de facto ruler of China, who ordered the death of the previous emperor so that the crown would fall to his weaker sibling. Zhuo then faced off against the coalition of 18 lords, only managing to escape by burning the capital city of LuoYang and relocating to ChangAn. He has a tendency for vanity and gluttony, as well as callousness towards the feelings of others. This self-indulgent view means that he has great capacity for terror, yet by the same token reveals the precariousness of his situation. This weakness is exploited by Yun Wang, who uses his daughter Diao Chan to set a trap that ensnares Zhuo Dong, endangering his reign.

BU LU

Bu Lu, a greatly feared warrior, is the sworn man of Zhuo Dong, who considers him a son. When Bu Lu is introduced to Diao Chan, he falls in love with her almost instantly. However, Diao Chan is then introduced to Zhuo Dong as part of an elaborate revenge plot, setting a series of events into motion that will strain the relationship.

YUN WANG

Yun Wang is a civil minister serving under Zhuo Dong. When Yun Wang witnesses Zhuo Dong commit a horrifying act of cruelty, he pledges to do whatever he can to destroy the despot's reign. Yun Wang understands that the greatest threat to Zhuo Dong isn't an enemy force, but one of his closest allies. Using his daughter Diao Chan as bait, Yun Wang sets a trap that pits Zhuo Dong against Bu Lu, which could prove to be deadly for either man.

DIAO CHAN

Diao Chan is Yun Wang's daughter. Though she possesses a delicate beauty and grace stunningly exhibited in the art of song and dance, Diao Chan's beauty disguises a ruthless and cunning heart. It is her mind for cunning that allows her father's plan to have such deadly consequences.

Chapter 1

Bei Liu Meets Yun Zhao ^{AD 192}

Summary

After the coalition army of the 18 feudal lords falls apart, Shao Yuan sets his sights on conquering the Ji Province. He convinces Zan GongSun to assist him in the battle, but when the governor of Ji Province flees before any battle could begin, Shao Yuan claims the land for himself. Now, Zan GongSun's army does battle with their former allies. When the battle turns against him, Zan GongSun calls on Bei Liu and his sworn brothers, who meet a promising young warrior named Yun Zhao while aiding the lord.

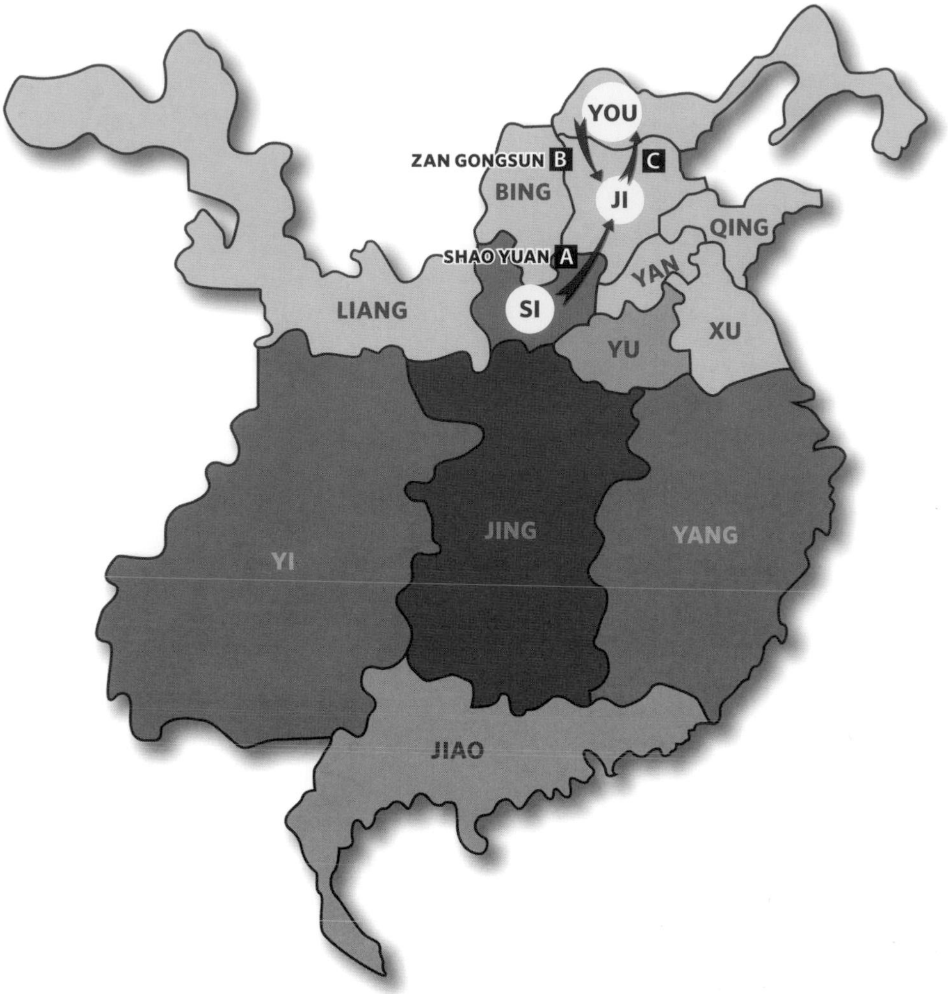
YOU
ZAN GONGSUN B
C
BING
JI
QING
SHAO YUAN A
YAN
SI
LIANG
XU
YU
JING
YANG
YI
JIAO

A Shao Yuan's Scheme

When word spreads that Shao Yuan and Zan GongSun have joined forces to conquer Ji Province, the governor of the province flees before any fighting begins.

B C Zan GongSun's Flight

After Shao Yuan double crosses his ally and claims Ji for his own, Zan GongSun declares war on Yuan. The battle quickly turns against GongSun, and he retreats from Ji Province.

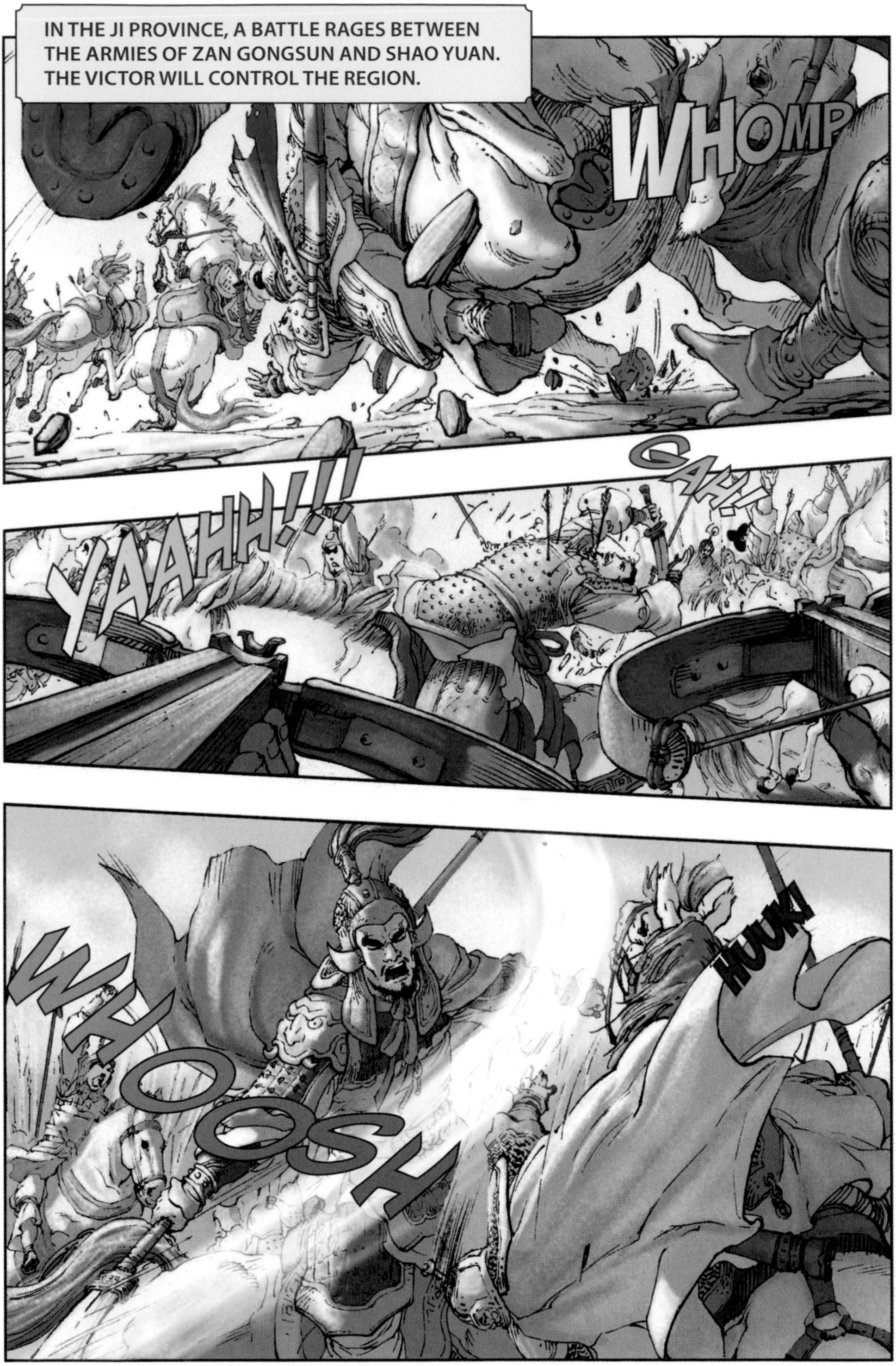
IN THE JI PROVINCE, A BATTLE RAGES BETWEEN THE ARMIES OF ZAN GONGSUN AND SHAO YUAN. THE VICTOR WILL CONTROL THE REGION.
WHOMP
GAH!
YAAHH!!!
WHOOOSH
HUUK!

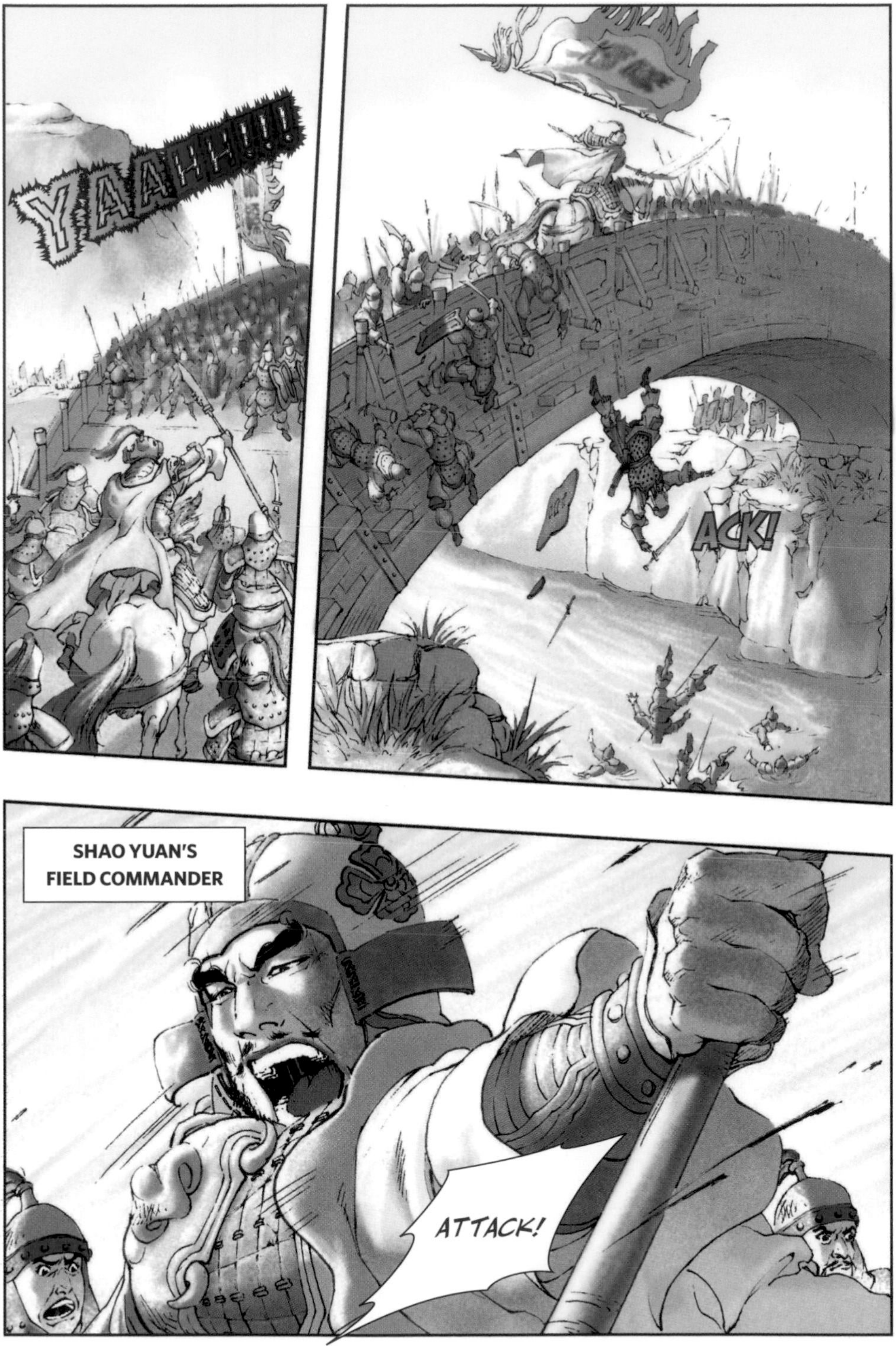
YAAHH!!!
ACK!
SHAO YUAN'S FIELD COMMANDER
ATTACK!

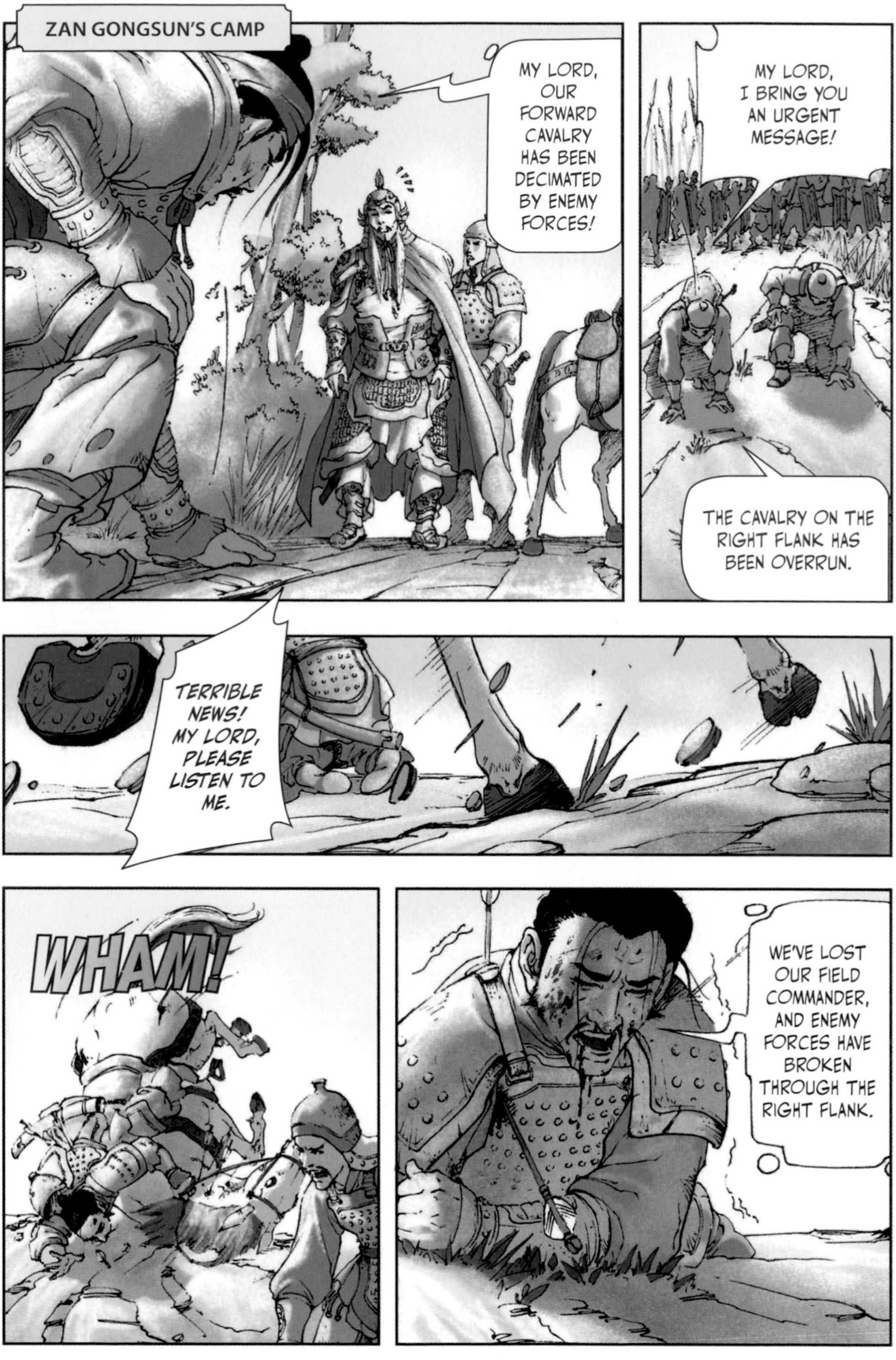
ZAN GONGSUN'S CAMP
MY LORD, OUR FORWARD CAVALRY HAS BEEN DECIMATED BY ENEMY FORCES!
MY LORD, I BRING YOU AN URGENT MESSAGE!
THE CAVALRY ON THE RIGHT FLANK HAS BEEN OVERRUN.
TERRIBLE NEWS! MY LORD, PLEASE LISTEN TO ME.
WHAM!
WE'VE LOST OUR FIELD COMMANDER, AND ENEMY FORCES HAVE BROKEN THROUGH THE RIGHT FLANK.

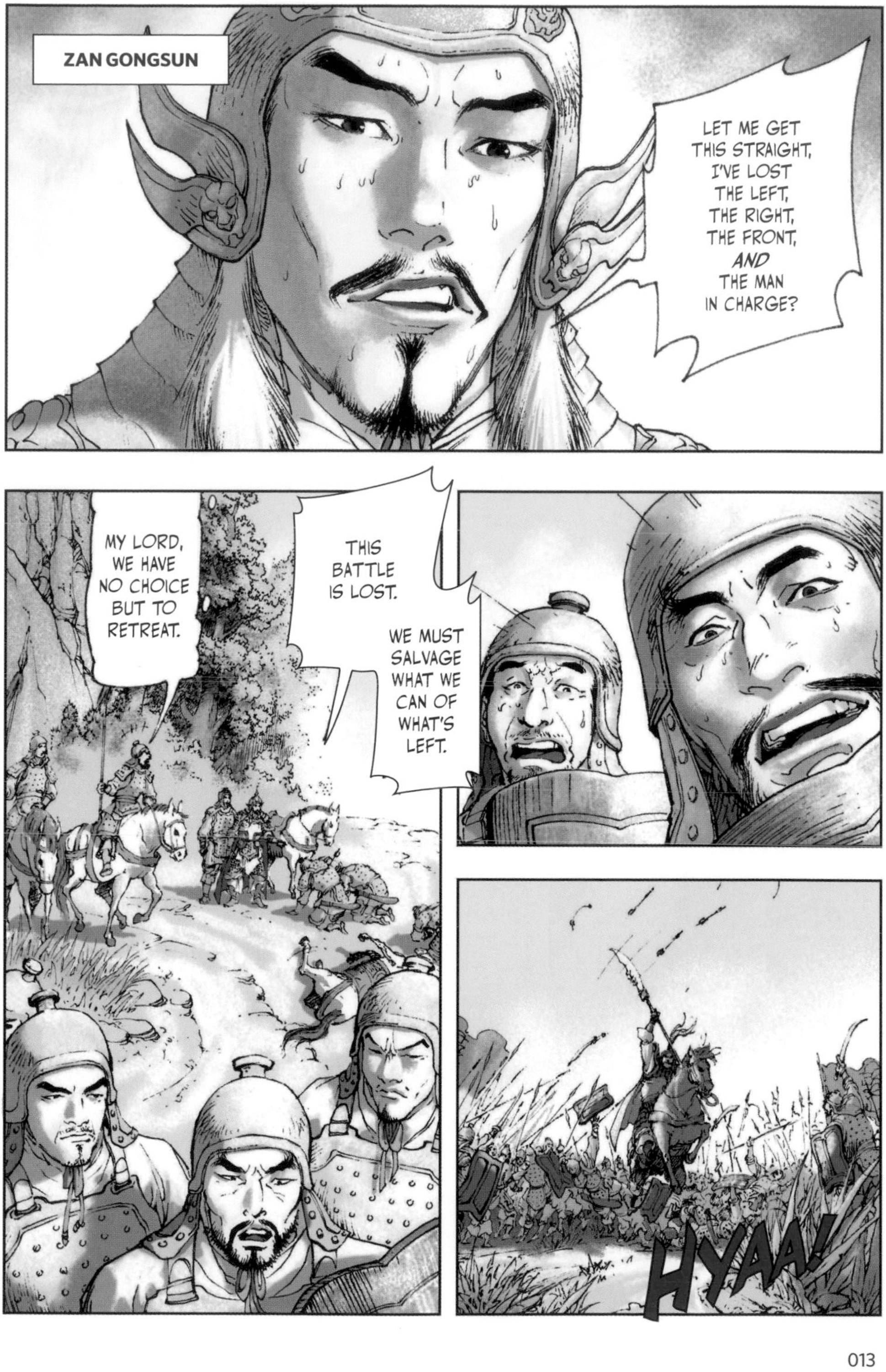
ZAN GONGSUN
LET ME GET THIS STRAIGHT, I'VE LOST THE LEFT, THE RIGHT, THE FRONT, AND THE MAN IN CHARGE?
MY LORD, WE HAVE NO CHOICE BUT TO RETREAT.
THIS BATTLE IS LOST.
WE MUST SALVAGE WHAT WE CAN OF WHAT'S LEFT.
HYAA!

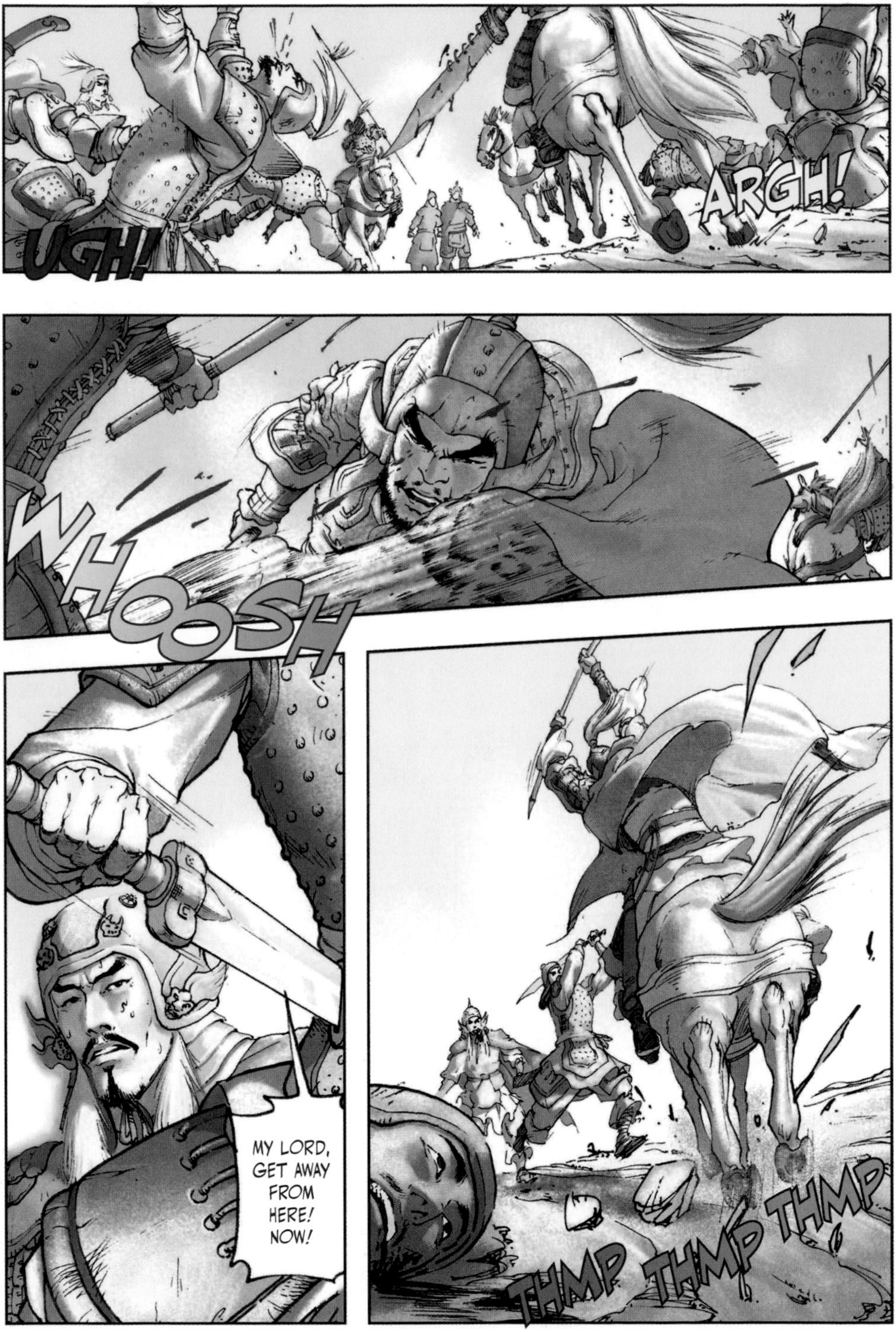
UGH!
ARGH!
WHOOSH
MY LORD, GET AWAY FROM HERE! NOW!
THMP THMP THMP

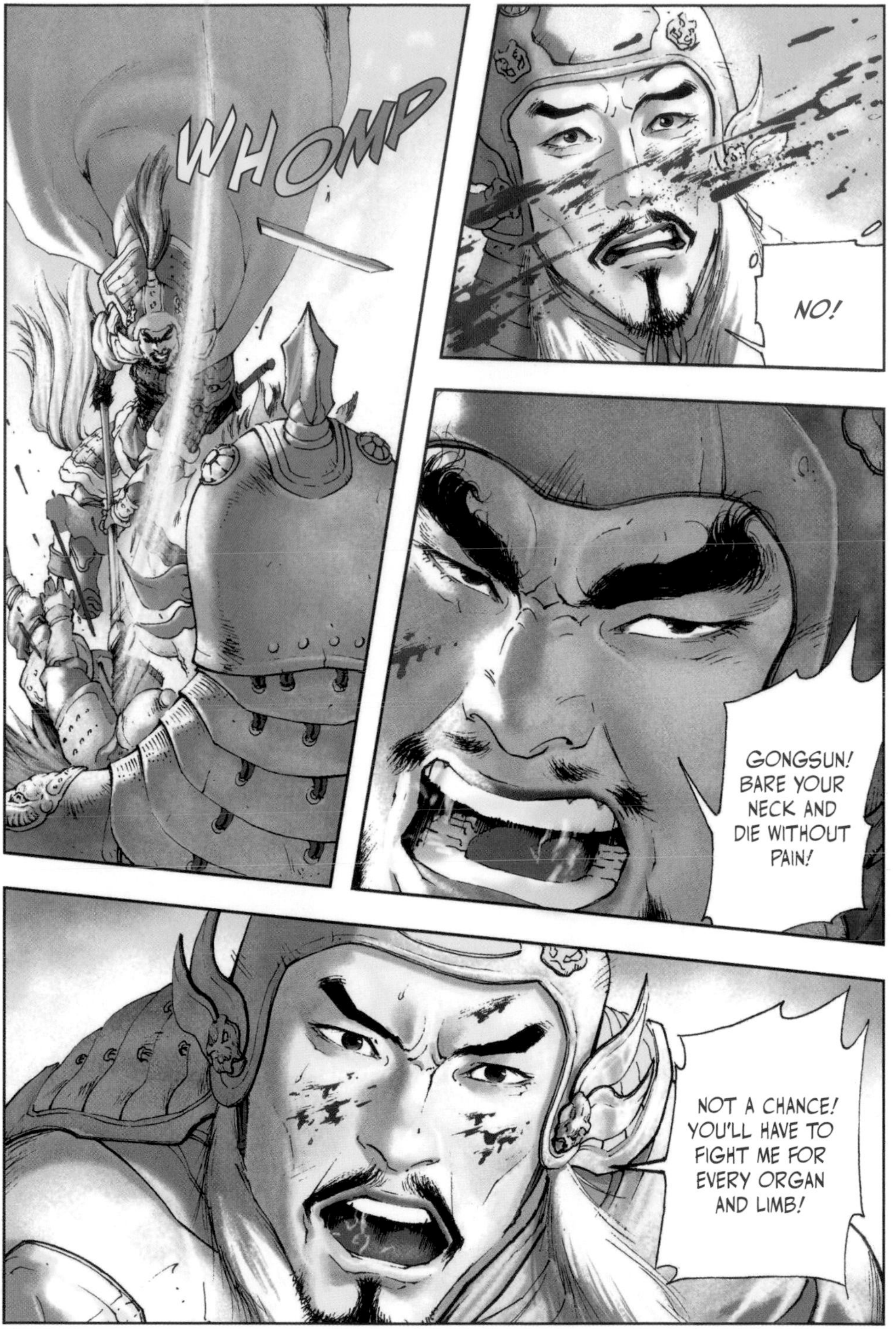
WHOMP
NO!
GONGSUN! BARE YOUR NECK AND DIE WITHOUT PAIN!
NOT A CHANCE! YOU'LL HAVE TO FIGHT ME FOR EVERY ORGAN AND LIMB!

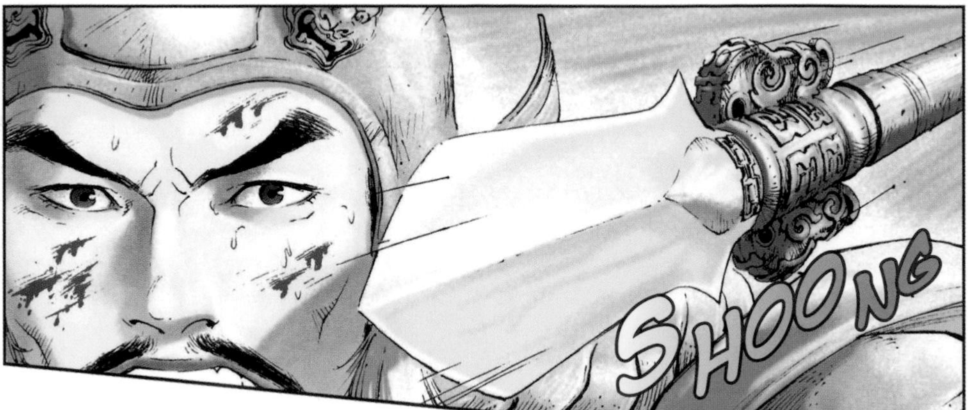
SHOOONG

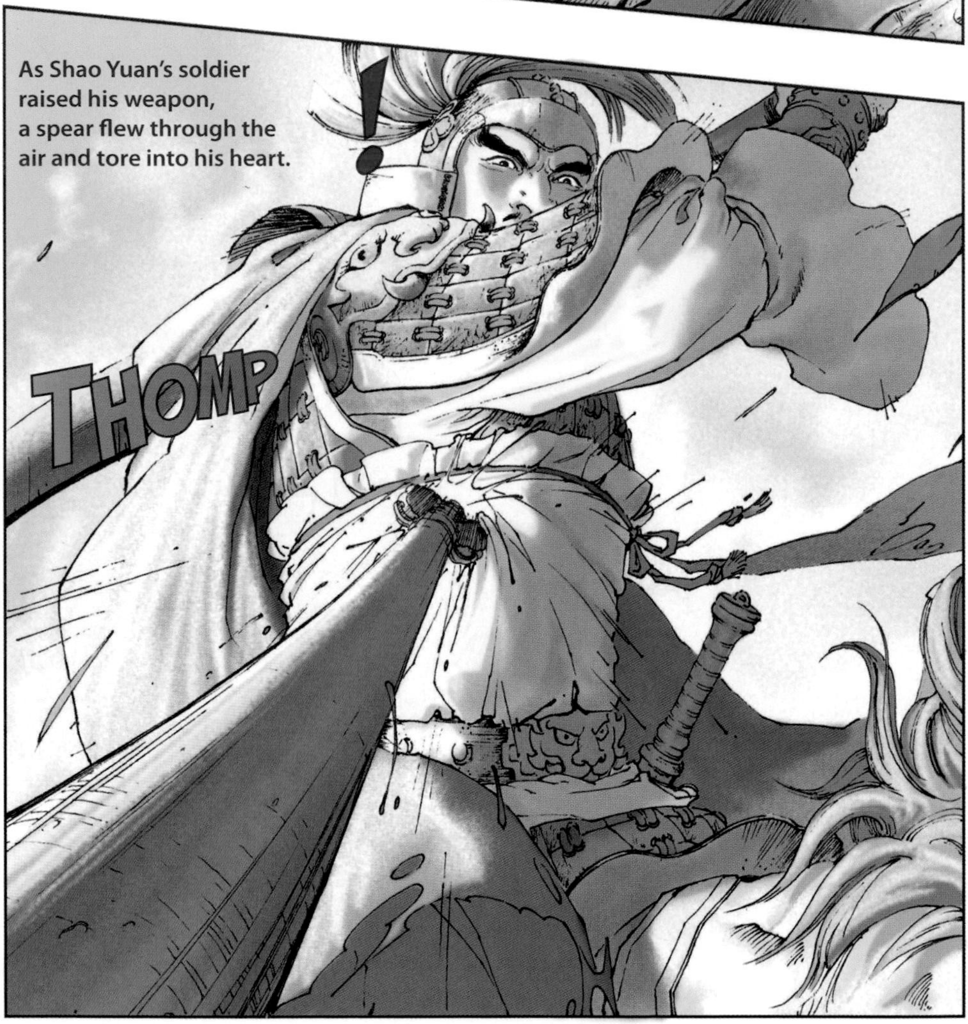
As Shao Yuan's soldier
raised his weapon,
a spear flew through the
air and tore into his heart.
!
THOMP

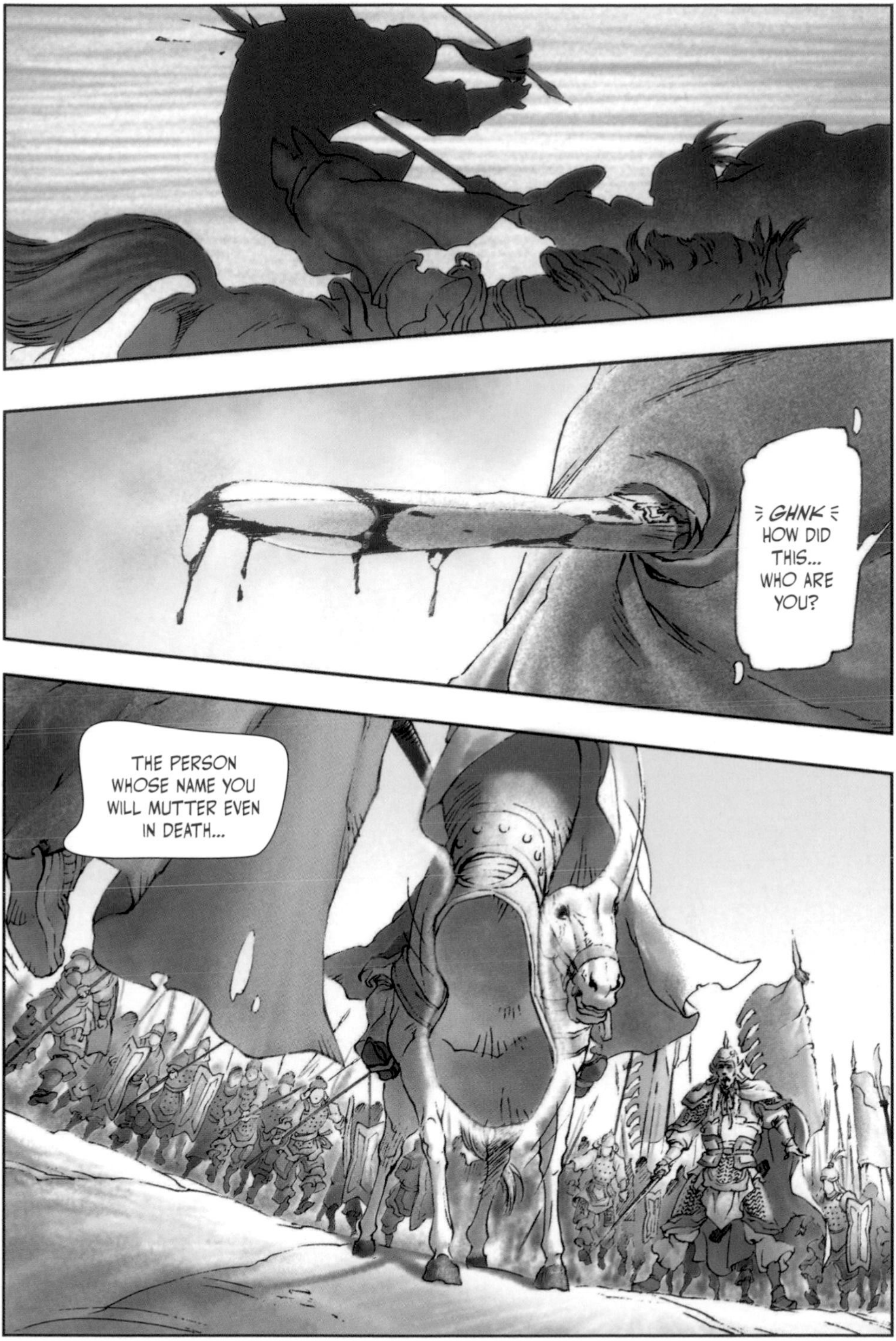
GHNK
HOW DID THIS... WHO ARE YOU?
THE PERSON WHOSE NAME YOU WILL MUTTER EVEN IN DEATH...

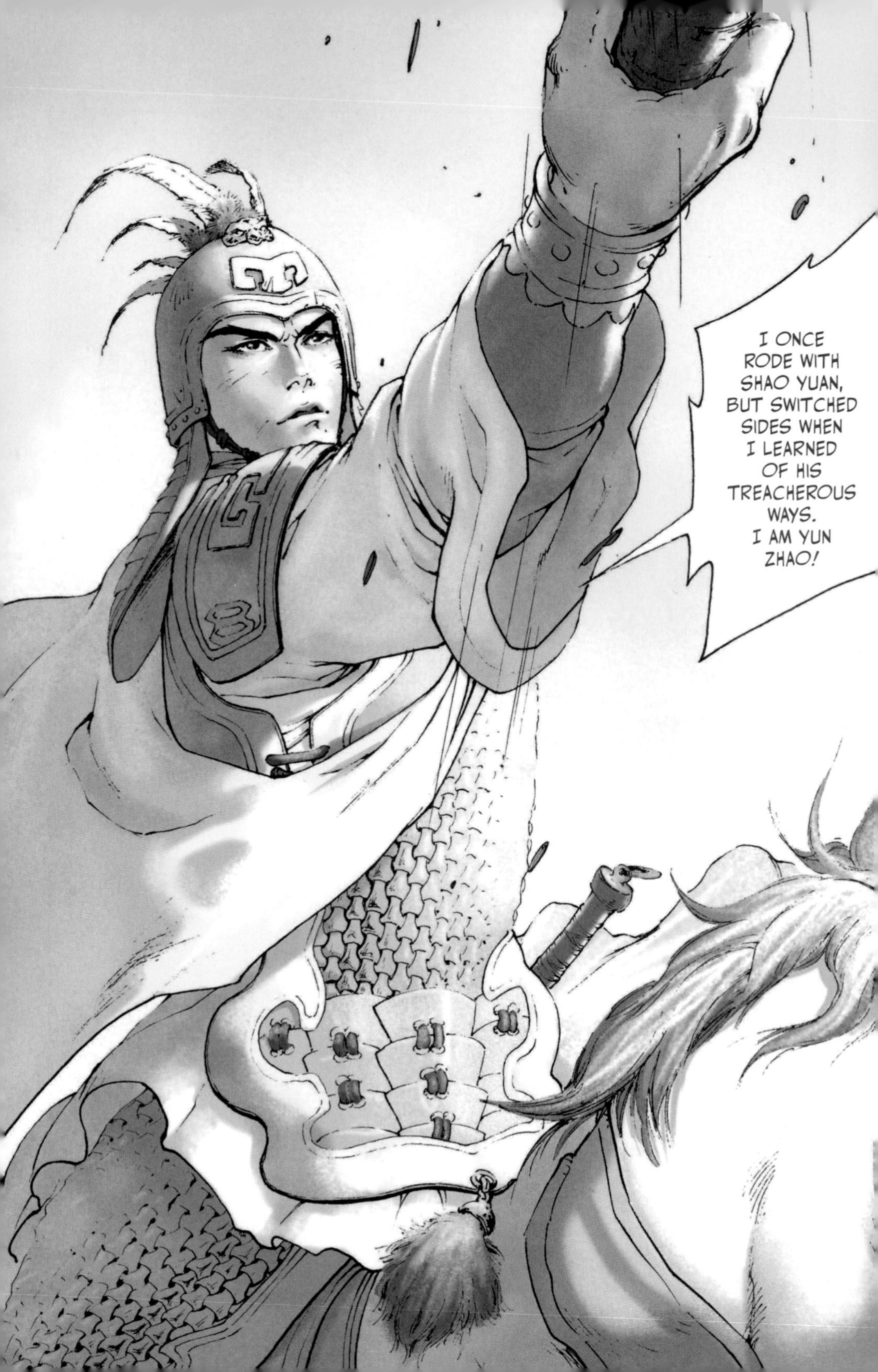
I ONCE RODE WITH SHAO YUAN, BUT SWITCHED SIDES WHEN I LEARNED OF HIS TREACHEROUS WAYS. I AM YUN ZHAO!

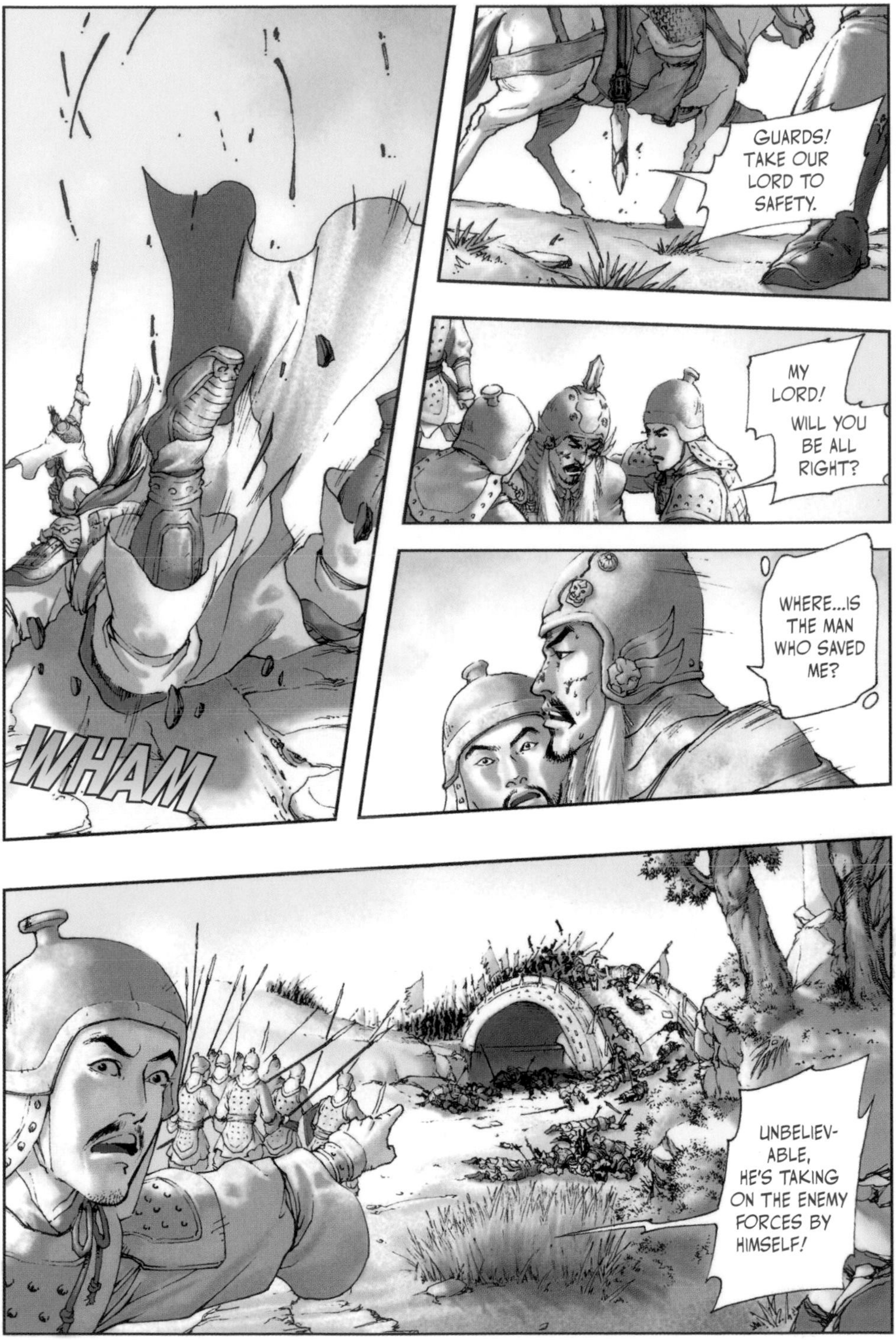
WHAM
GUARDS! TAKE OUR LORD TO SAFETY.
MY LORD! WILL YOU BE ALL RIGHT?
WHERE...IS THE MAN WHO SAVED ME?
UNBELIEV-ABLE, HE'S TAKING ON THE ENEMY FORCES BY HIMSELF!

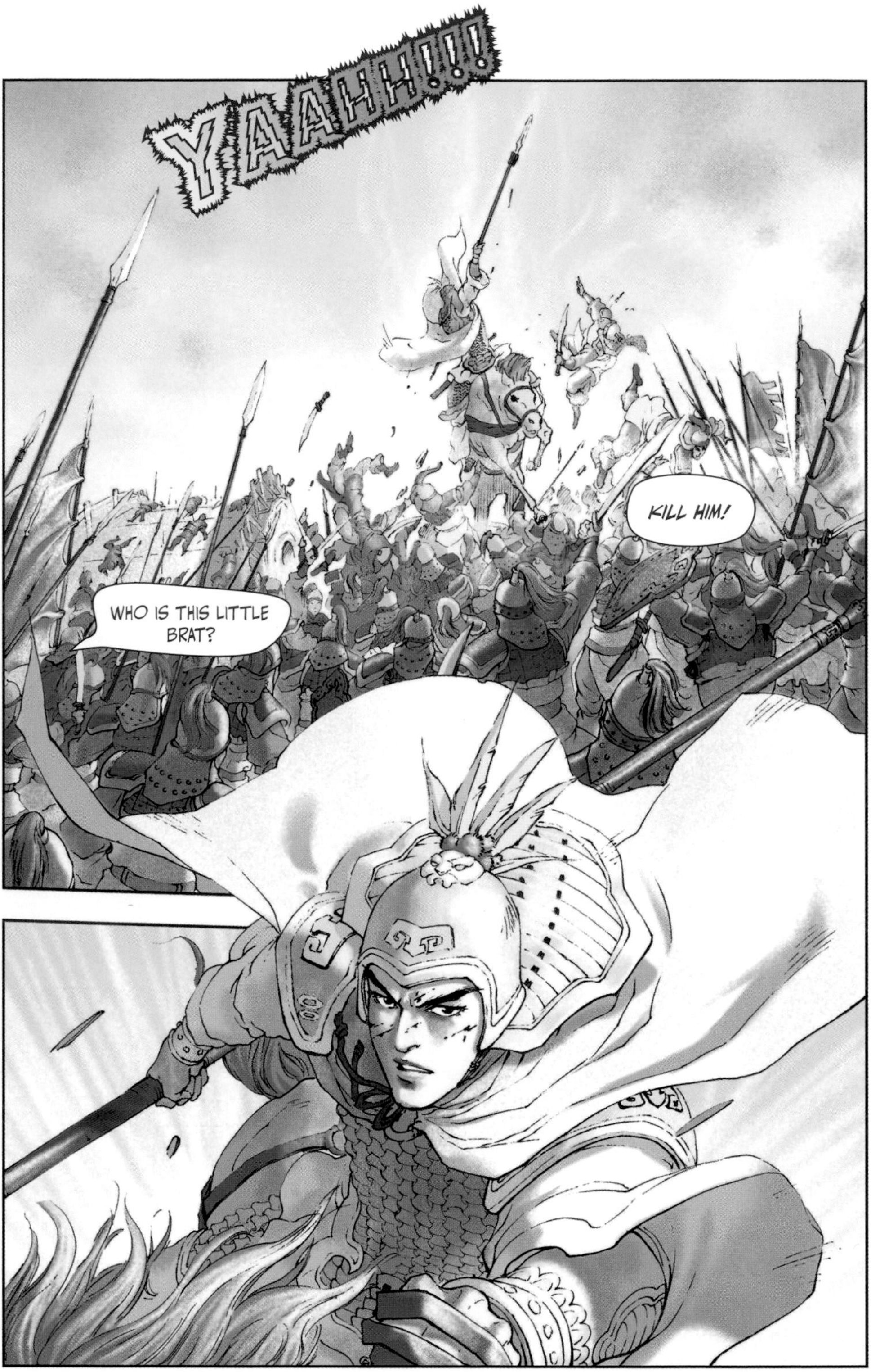
YAAHH!!!
KILL HIM!
WHO IS THIS LITTLE BRAT?

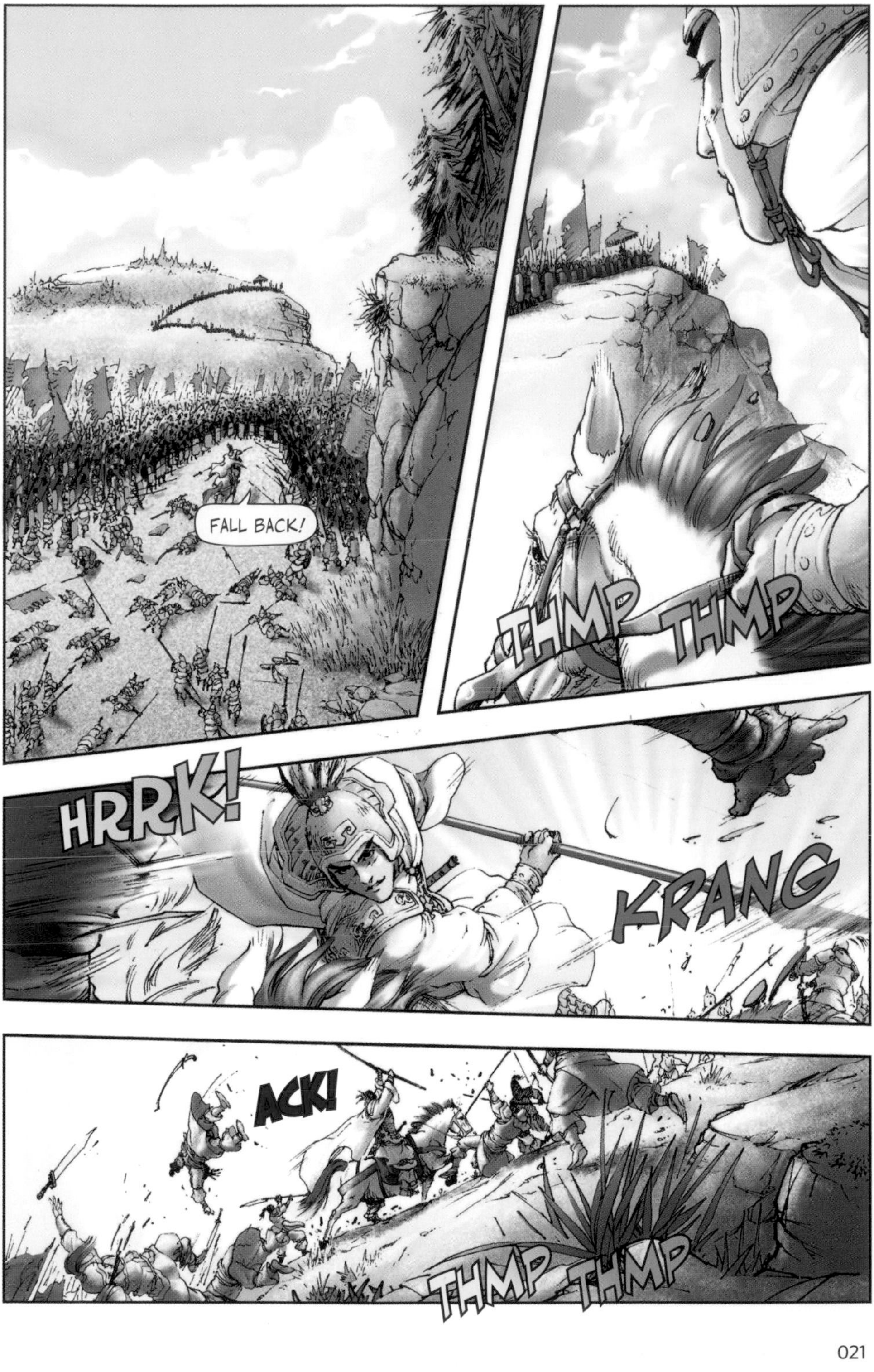
FALL BACK!
THMP THMP
HRRK!
KRANG
ACK!
THMP THMP

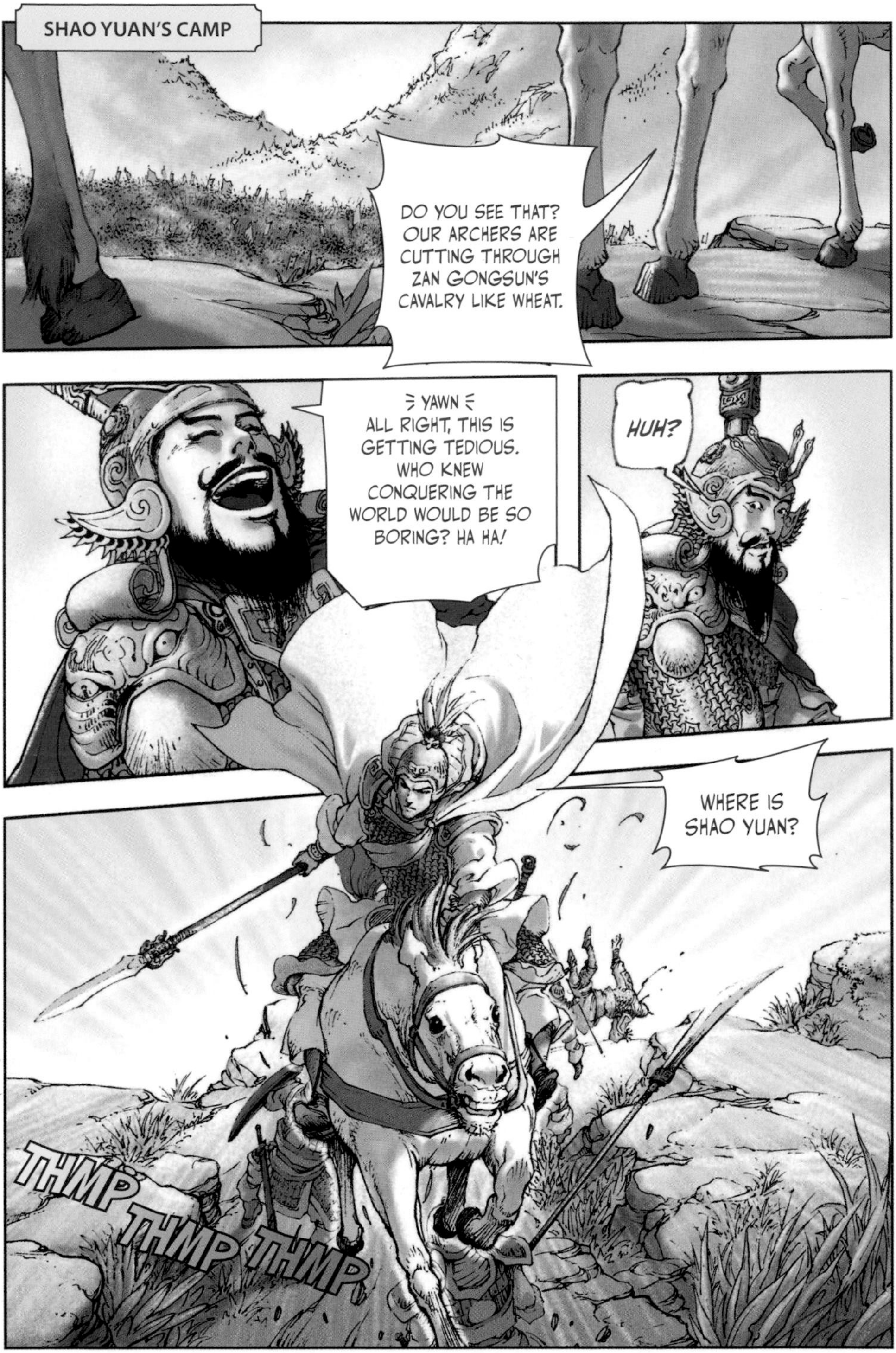
SHAO YUAN'S CAMP
DO YOU SEE THAT? OUR ARCHERS ARE CUTTING THROUGH ZAN GONGSUN'S CAVALRY LIKE WHEAT.
YAWN
ALL RIGHT, THIS IS GETTING TEDIOUS. WHO KNEW CONQUERING THE WORLD WOULD BE SO BORING? HA HA!
HUH?
WHERE IS SHAO YUAN?
THMP THMP THMP

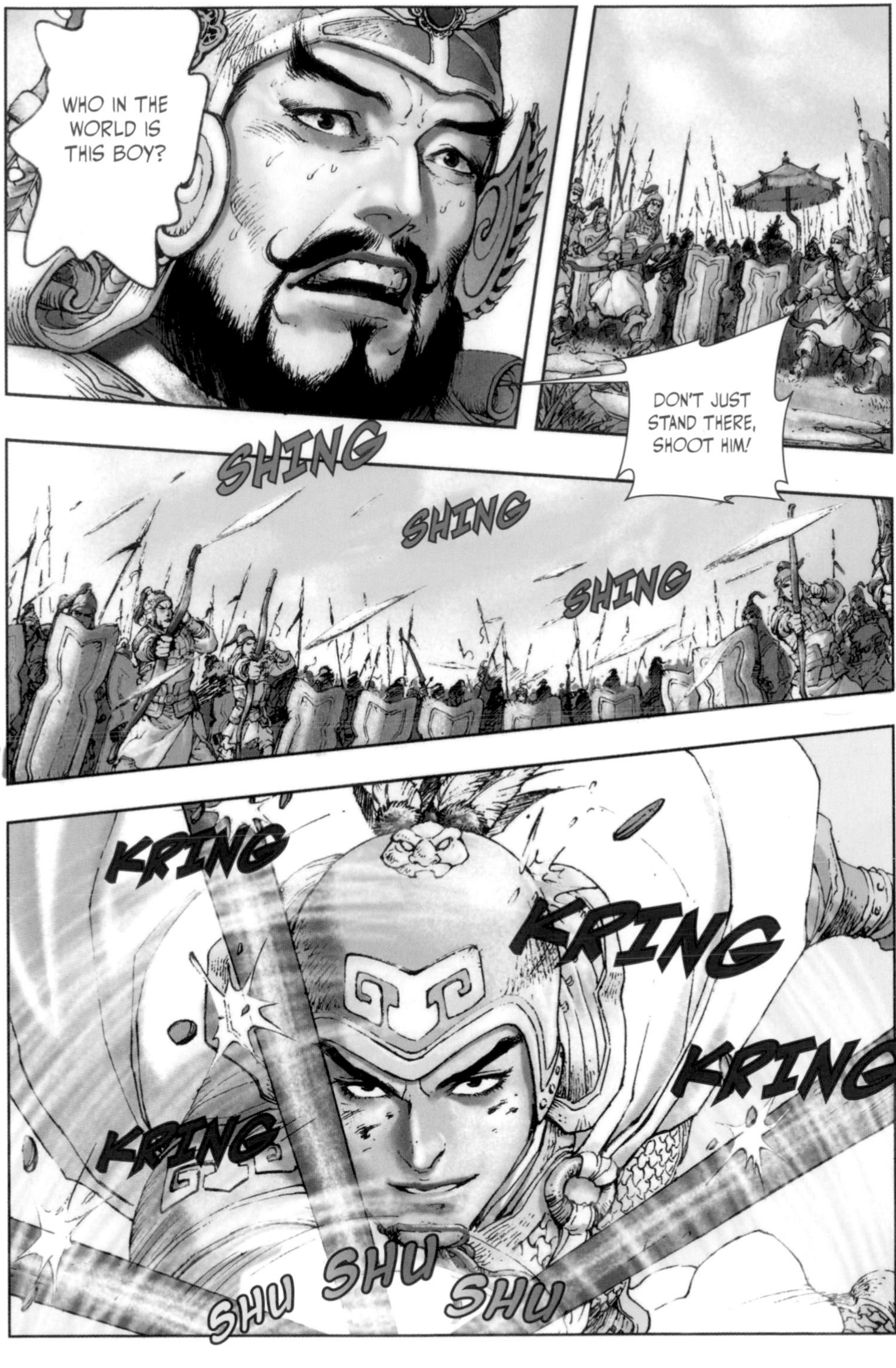
WHO IN THE WORLD IS THIS BOY?
DON'T JUST STAND THERE, SHOOT HIM!
SHING
SHING
SHING
KRING
KRING
KRING
KRING
SHU
SHU
SHU

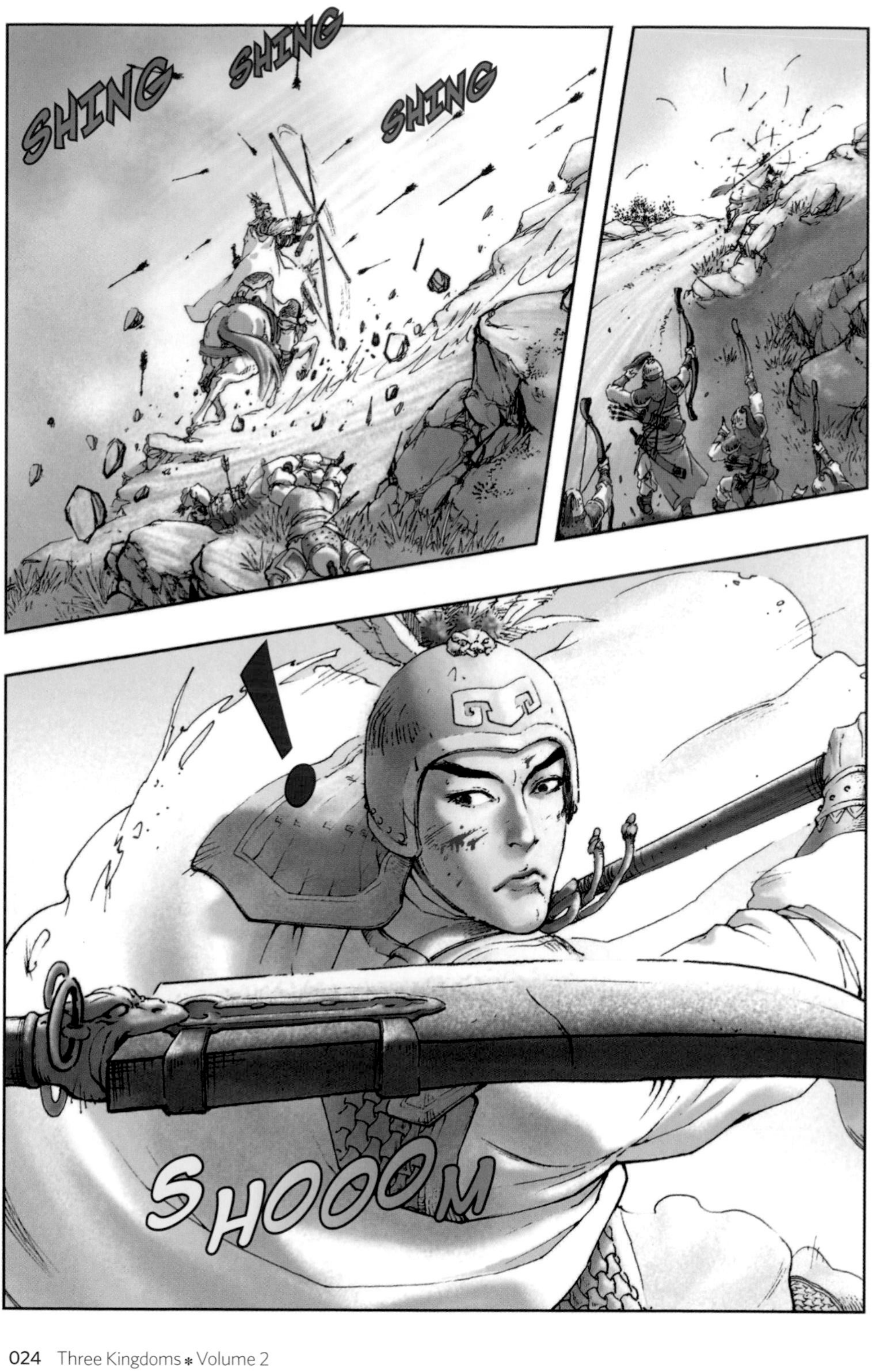
SHING
SHING
SHING
!
SHOOOM

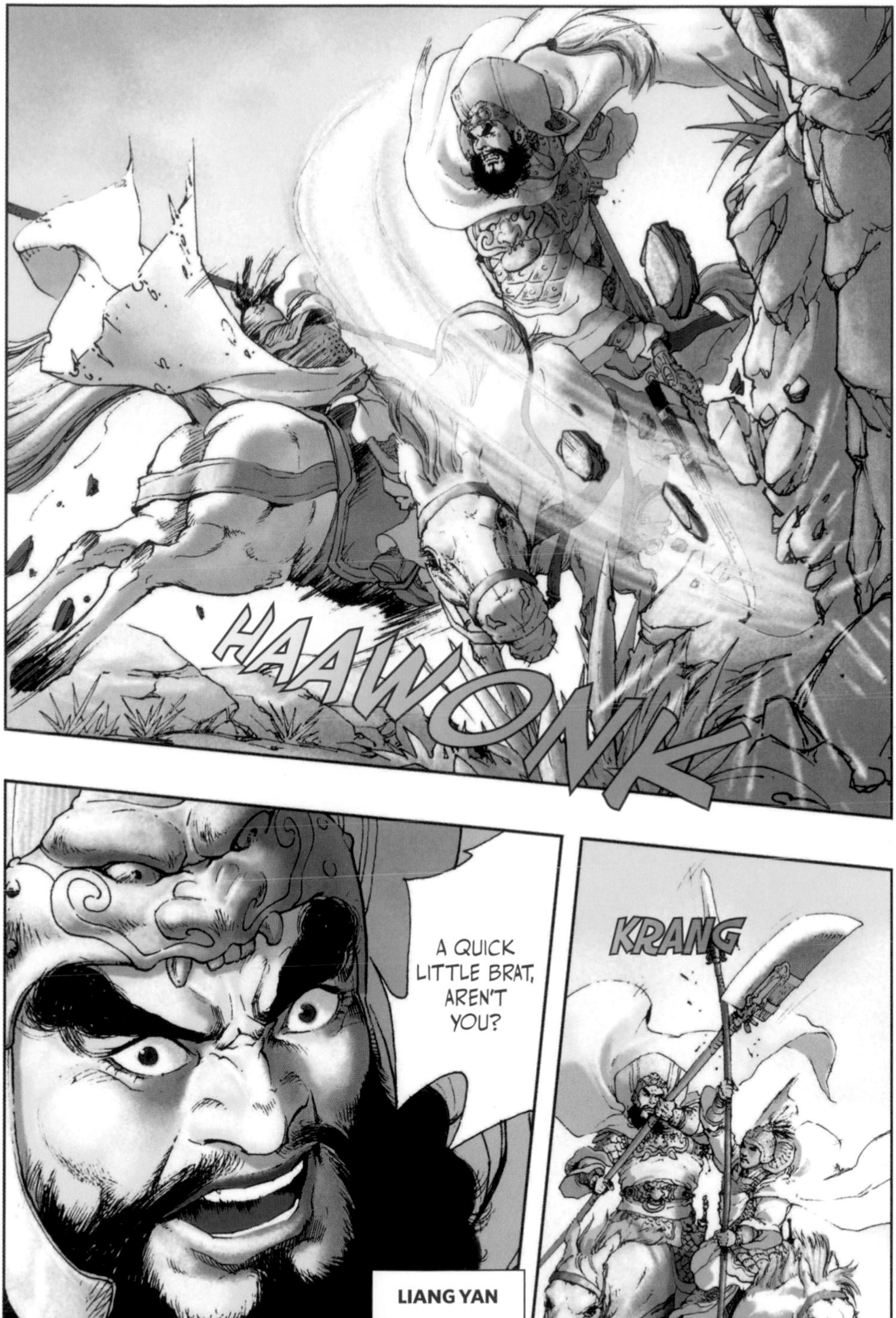
HAAWONK
A QUICK LITTLE BRAT, AREN'T YOU?
LIANG YAN
KRANG

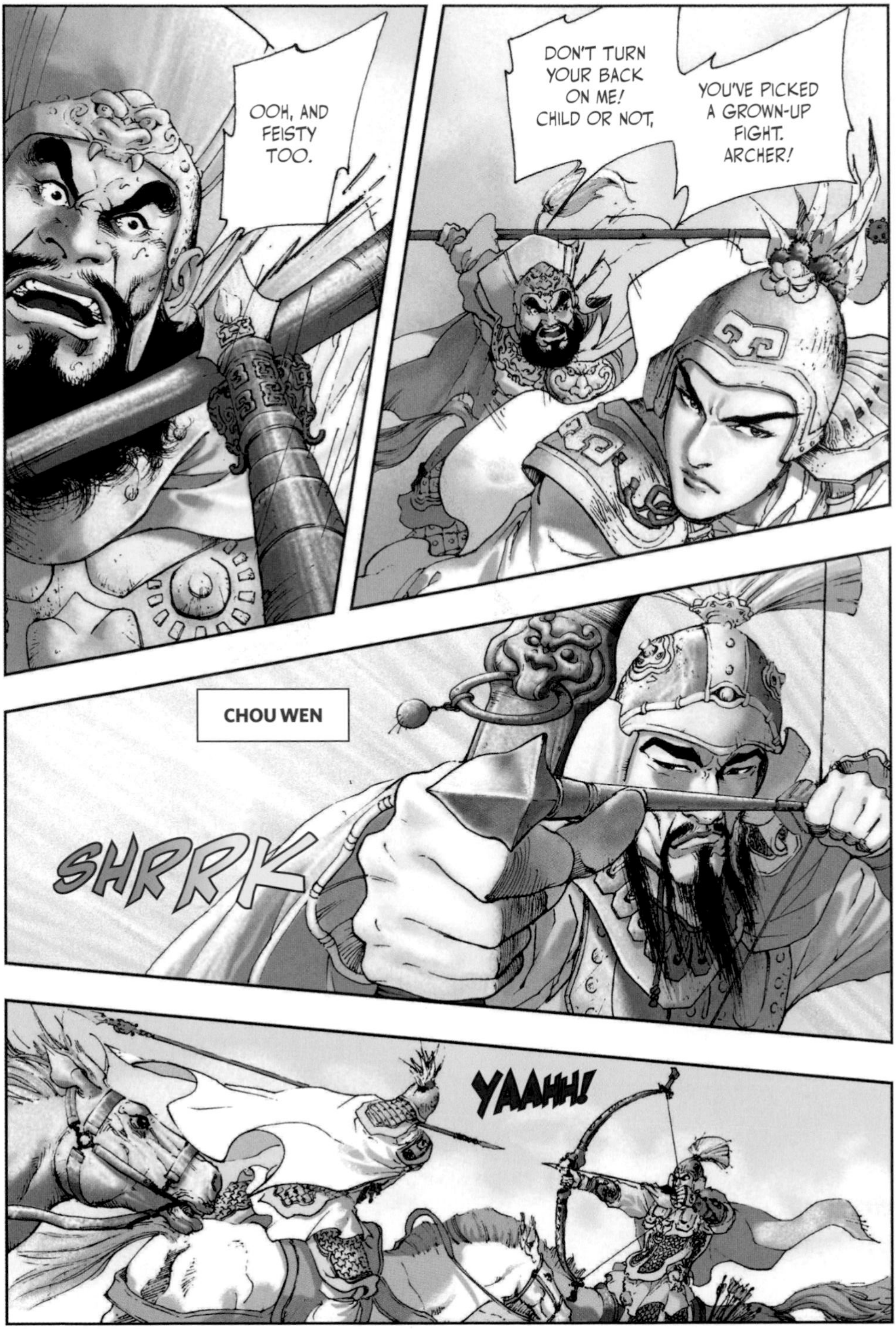
OOH, AND FEISTY TOO.
DON'T TURN YOUR BACK ON ME! CHILD OR NOT,
YOU'VE PICKED A GROWN-UP FIGHT. ARCHER!
CHOU WEN
SHRRK
YAAHH!

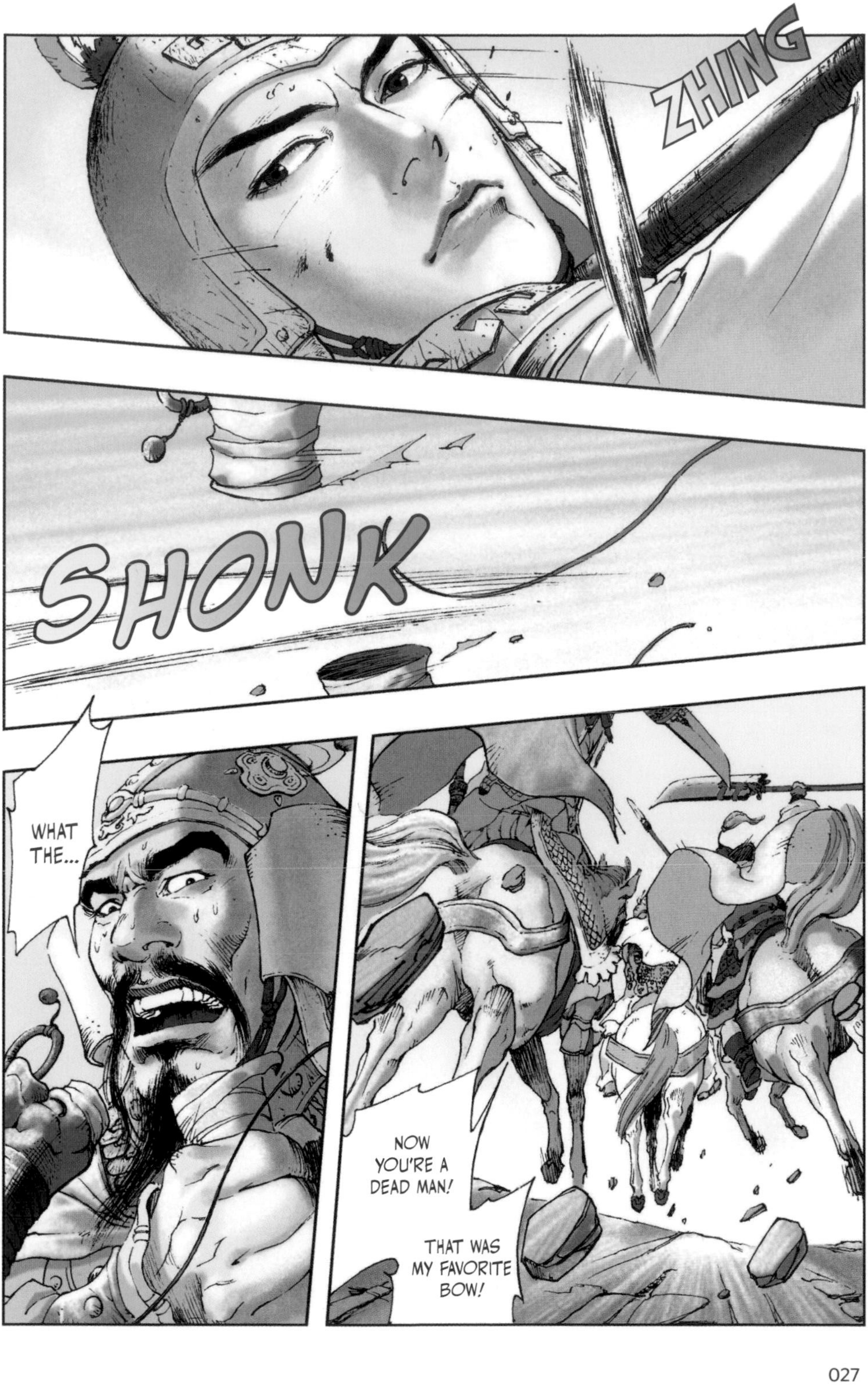
ZHING
SHONK
WHAT THE...
NOW YOU'RE A DEAD MAN!
THAT WAS MY FAVORITE BOW!

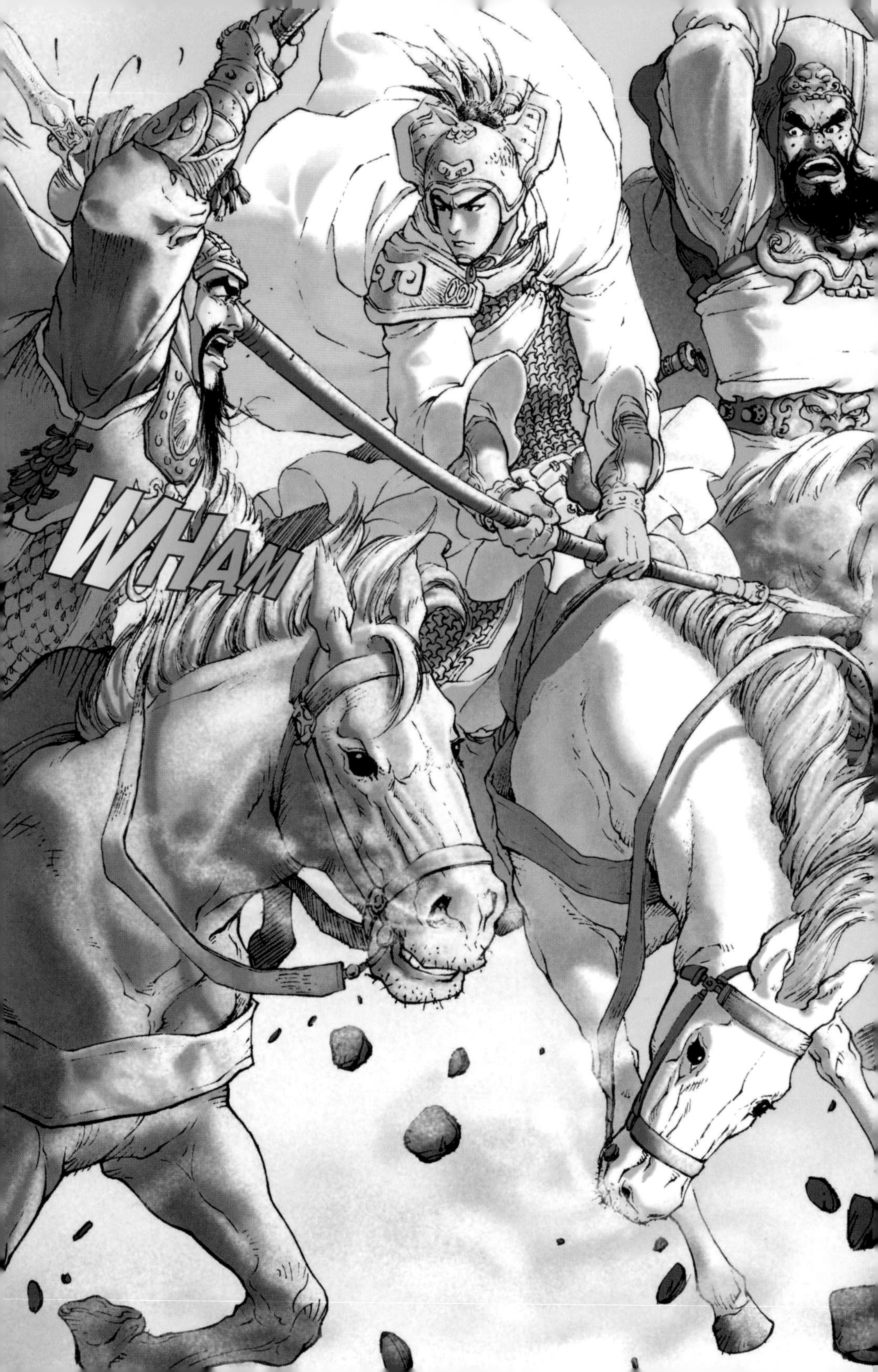
WHAM

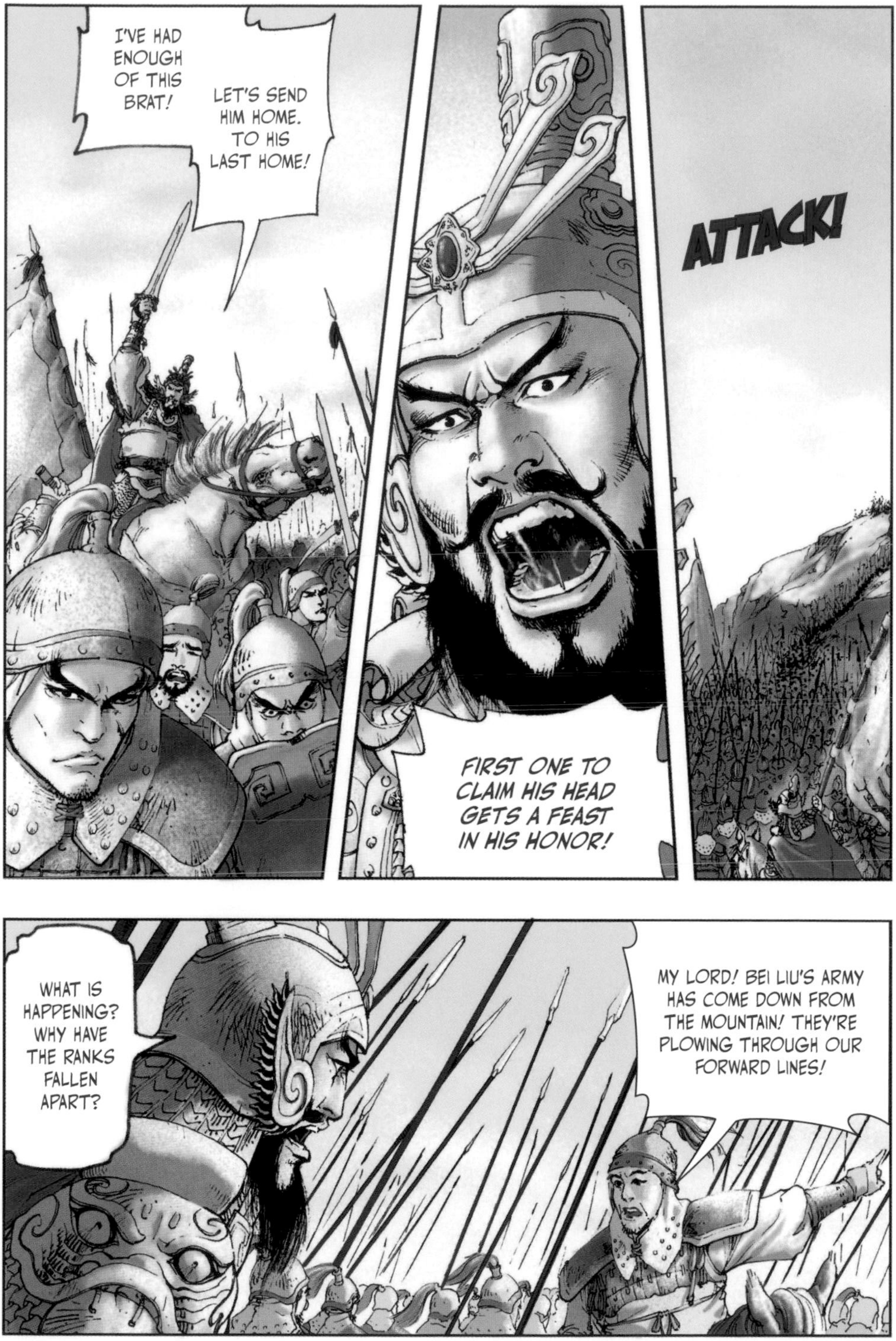
I'VE HAD ENOUGH OF THIS BRAT!
LET'S SEND HIM HOME. TO HIS LAST HOME!
FIRST ONE TO CLAIM HIS HEAD GETS A FEAST IN HIS HONOR!
ATTACK!
WHAT IS HAPPENING? WHY HAVE THE RANKS FALLEN APART?
MY LORD! BEI LIU'S ARMY HAS COME DOWN FROM THE MOUNTAIN! THEY'RE PLOWING THROUGH OUR FORWARD LINES!

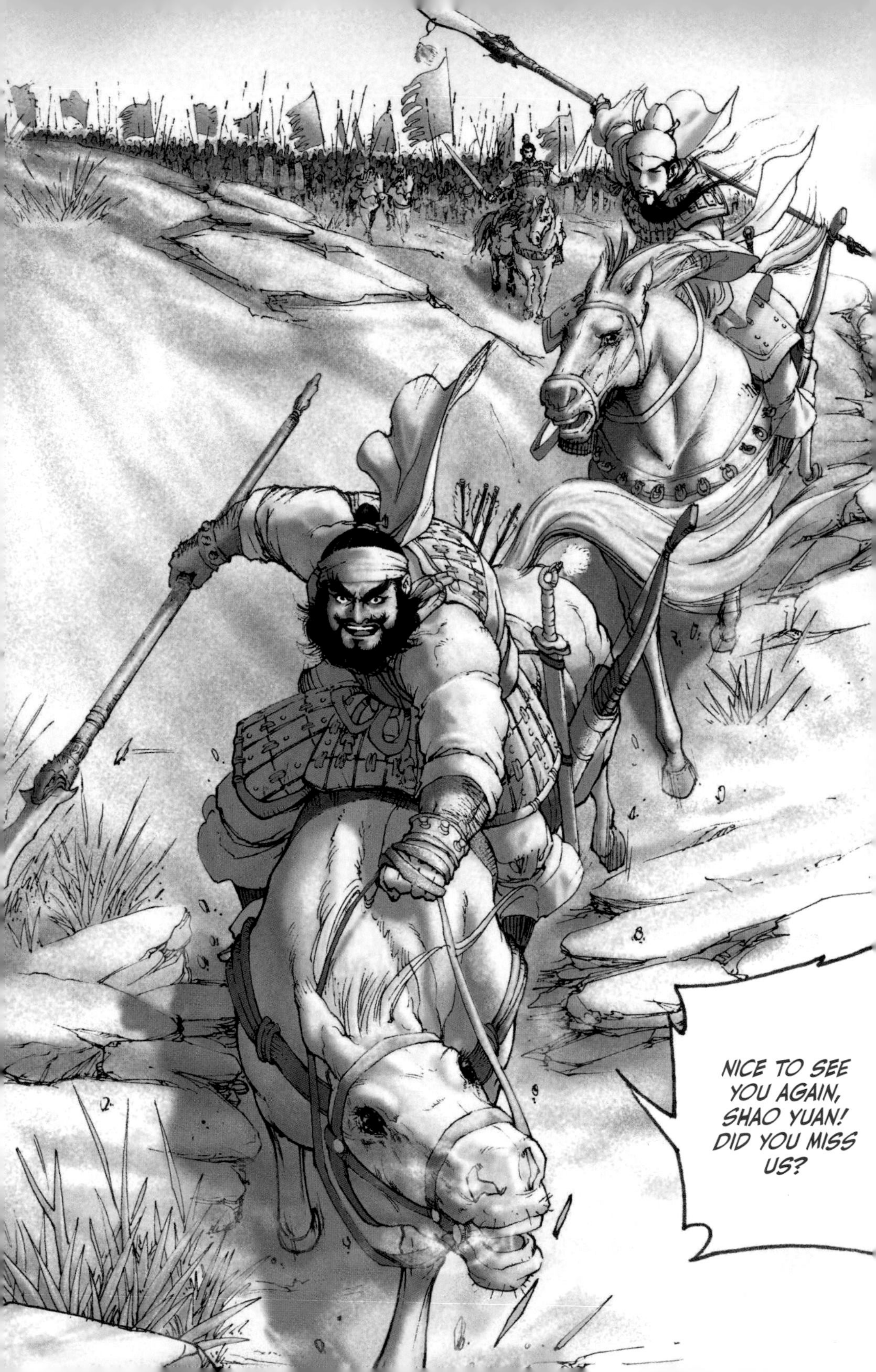
NICE TO SEE YOU AGAIN, SHAO YUAN! DID YOU MISS US?

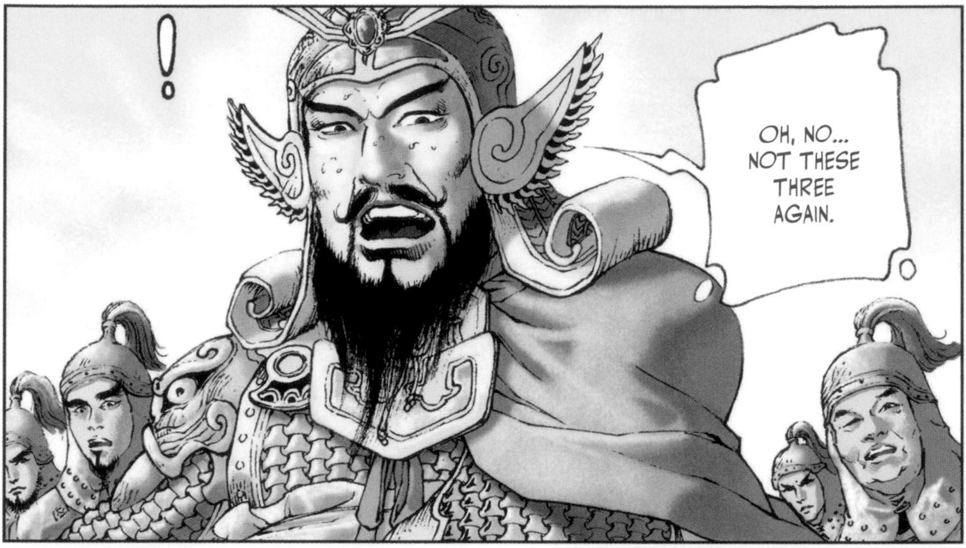
!
OH, NO... NOT THESE THREE AGAIN.

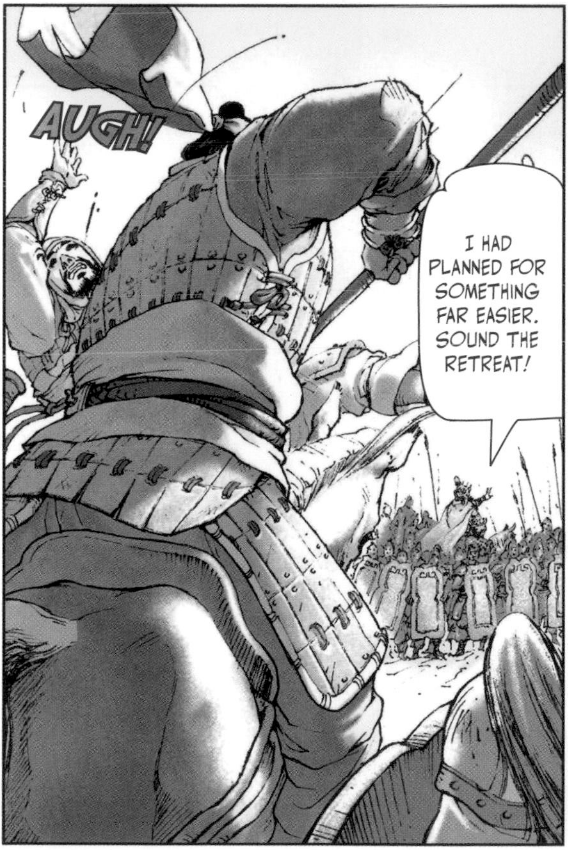
AUGH!
I HAD PLANNED FOR SOMETHING FAR EASIER. SOUND THE RETREAT!

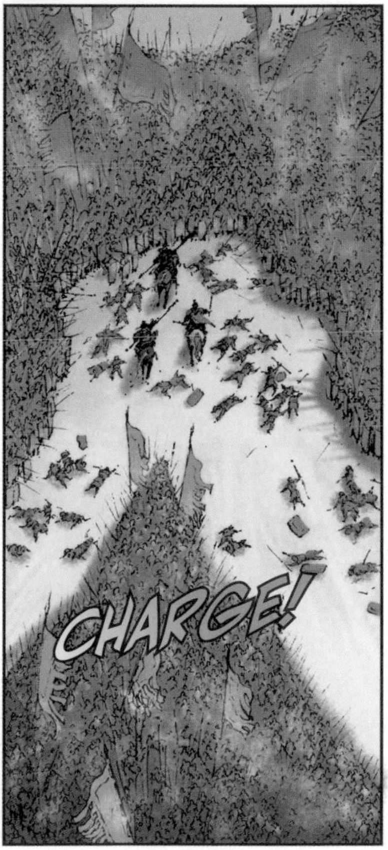
CHARGE!

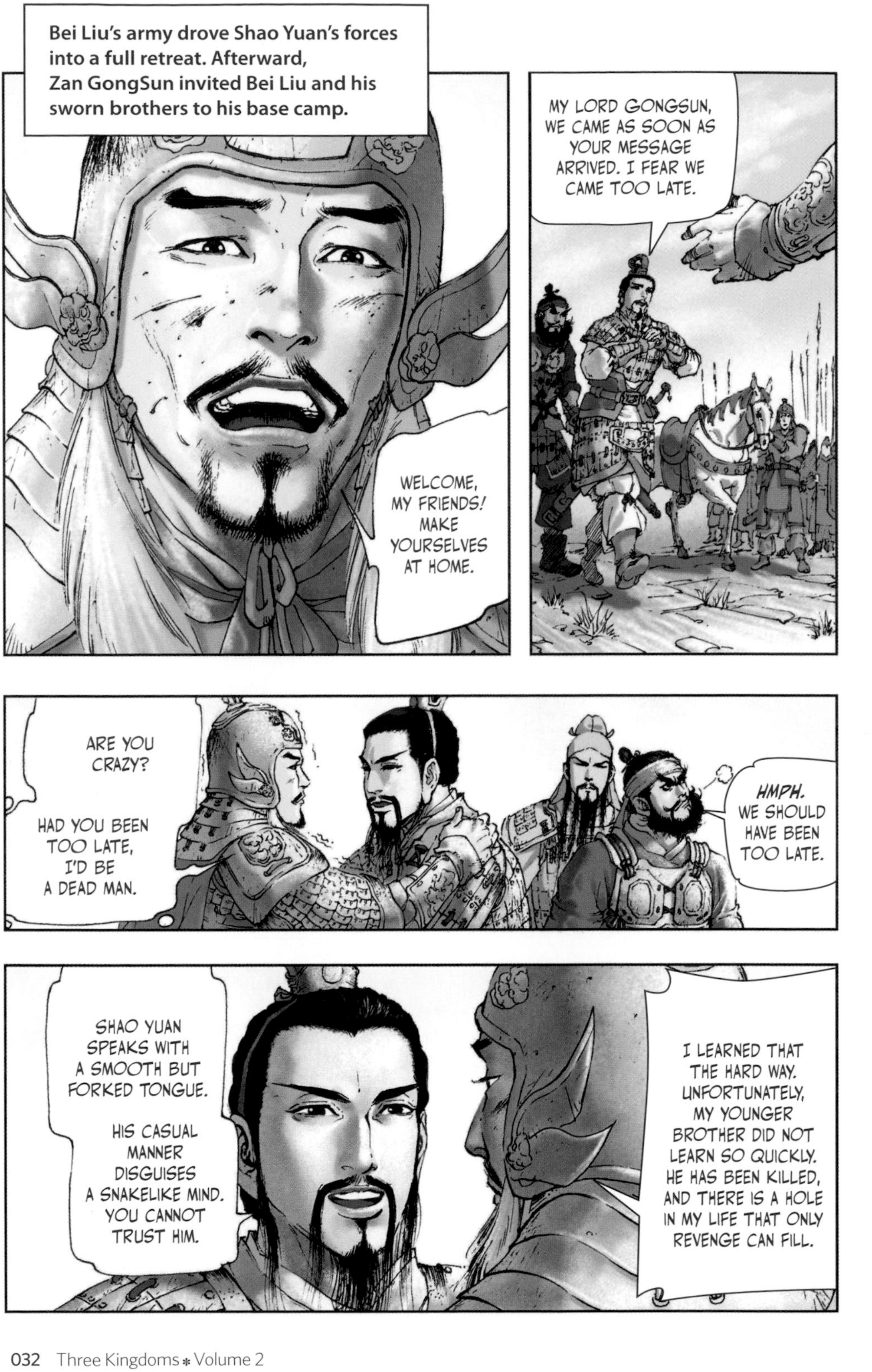
Bei Liu's army drove Shao Yuan's forces into a full retreat. Afterward, Zan GongSun invited Bei Liu and his sworn brothers to his base camp.
MY LORD GONGSUN, WE CAME AS SOON AS YOUR MESSAGE ARRIVED. I FEAR WE CAME TOO LATE.
WELCOME, MY FRIENDS! MAKE YOURSELVES AT HOME.
ARE YOU CRAZY?
HAD YOU BEEN TOO LATE, I'D BE A DEAD MAN.
HMPH. WE SHOULD HAVE BEEN TOO LATE.
SHAO YUAN SPEAKS WITH A SMOOTH BUT FORKED TONGUE.
HIS CASUAL MANNER DISGUISES A SNAKELIKE MIND. YOU CANNOT TRUST HIM.
I LEARNED THAT THE HARD WAY. UNFORTUNATELY, MY YOUNGER BROTHER DID NOT LEARN SO QUICKLY. HE HAS BEEN KILLED, AND THERE IS A HOLE IN MY LIFE THAT ONLY REVENGE CAN FILL.

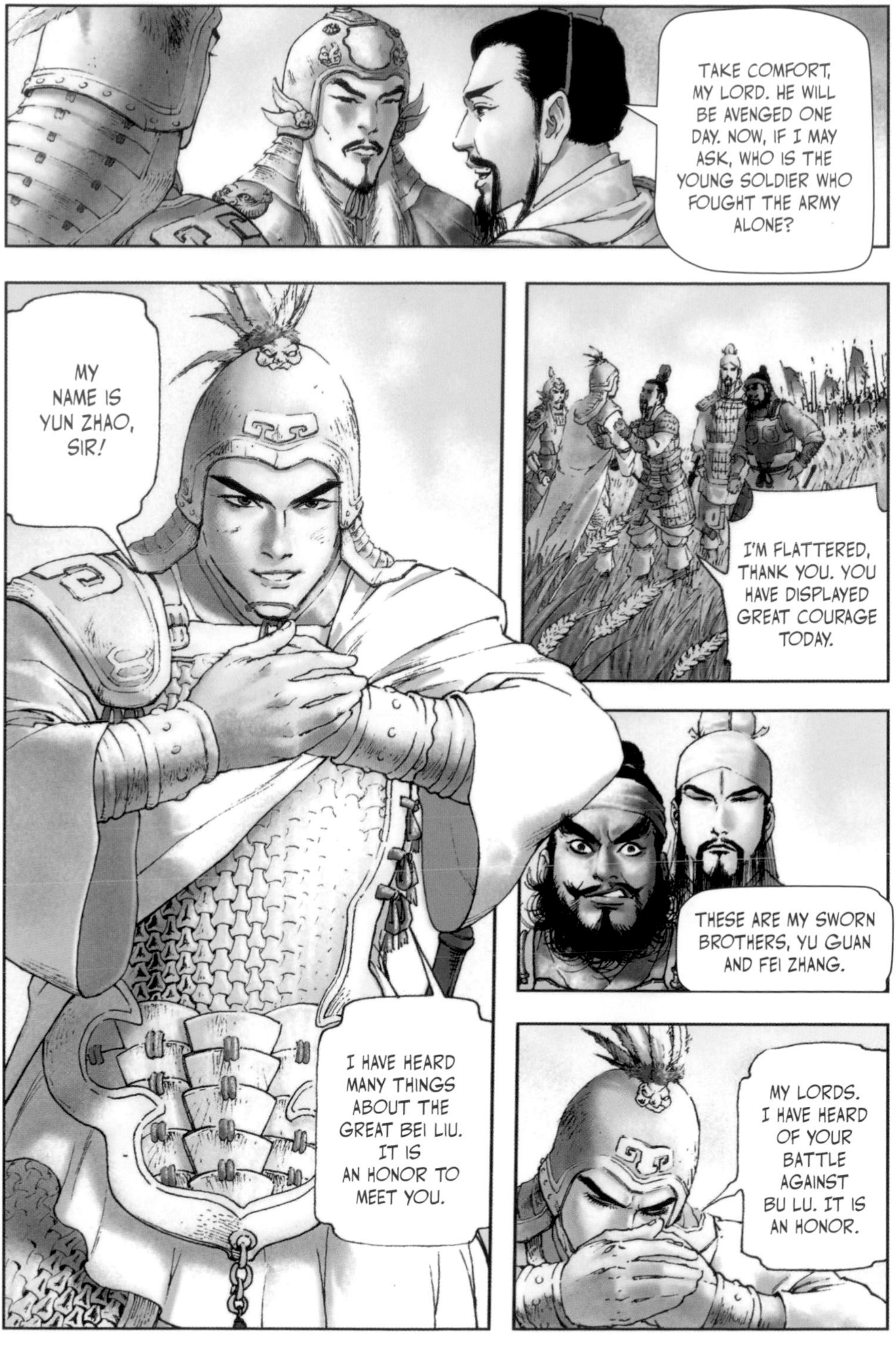
TAKE COMFORT, MY LORD. HE WILL BE AVENGED ONE DAY. NOW, IF I MAY ASK, WHO IS THE YOUNG SOLDIER WHO FOUGHT THE ARMY ALONE?
MY NAME IS YUN ZHAO, SIR!
I'M FLATTERED, THANK YOU. YOU HAVE DISPLAYED GREAT COURAGE TODAY.
THESE ARE MY SWORN BROTHERS, YU GUAN AND FEI ZHANG.
I HAVE HEARD MANY THINGS ABOUT THE GREAT BEI LIU. IT IS AN HONOR TO MEET YOU.
MY LORDS. I HAVE HEARD OF YOUR BATTLE AGAINST BU LU. IT IS AN HONOR.

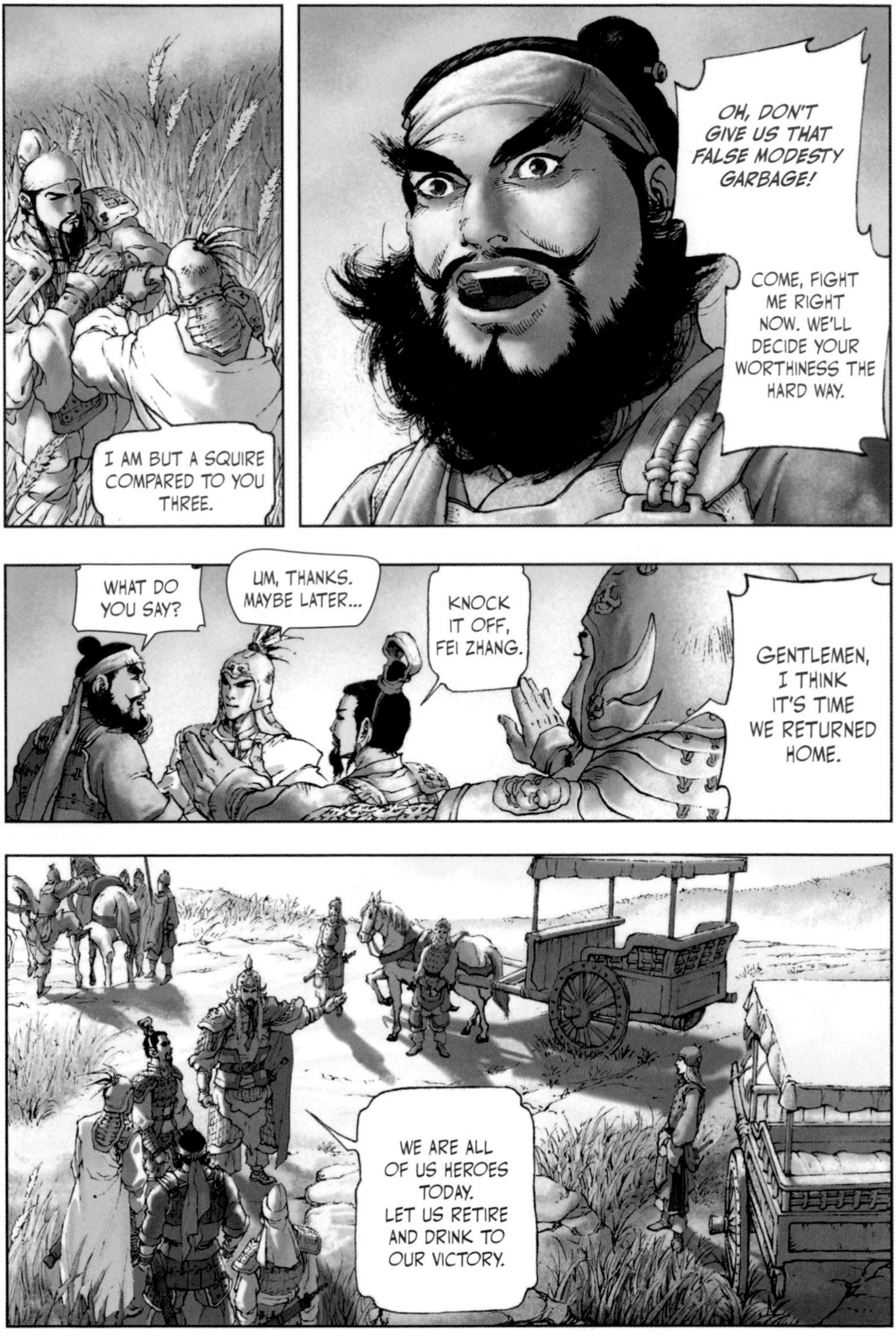
I AM BUT A SQUIRE COMPARED TO YOU THREE.
OH, DON'T GIVE US THAT FALSE MODESTY GARBAGE!
COME, FIGHT ME RIGHT NOW. WE'LL DECIDE YOUR WORTHINESS THE HARD WAY.
WHAT DO YOU SAY?
UM, THANKS. MAYBE LATER...
KNOCK IT OFF, FEI ZHANG.
GENTLEMEN, I THINK IT'S TIME WE RETURNED HOME.
WE ARE ALL OF US HEROES TODAY.
LET US RETIRE AND DRINK TO OUR VICTORY.

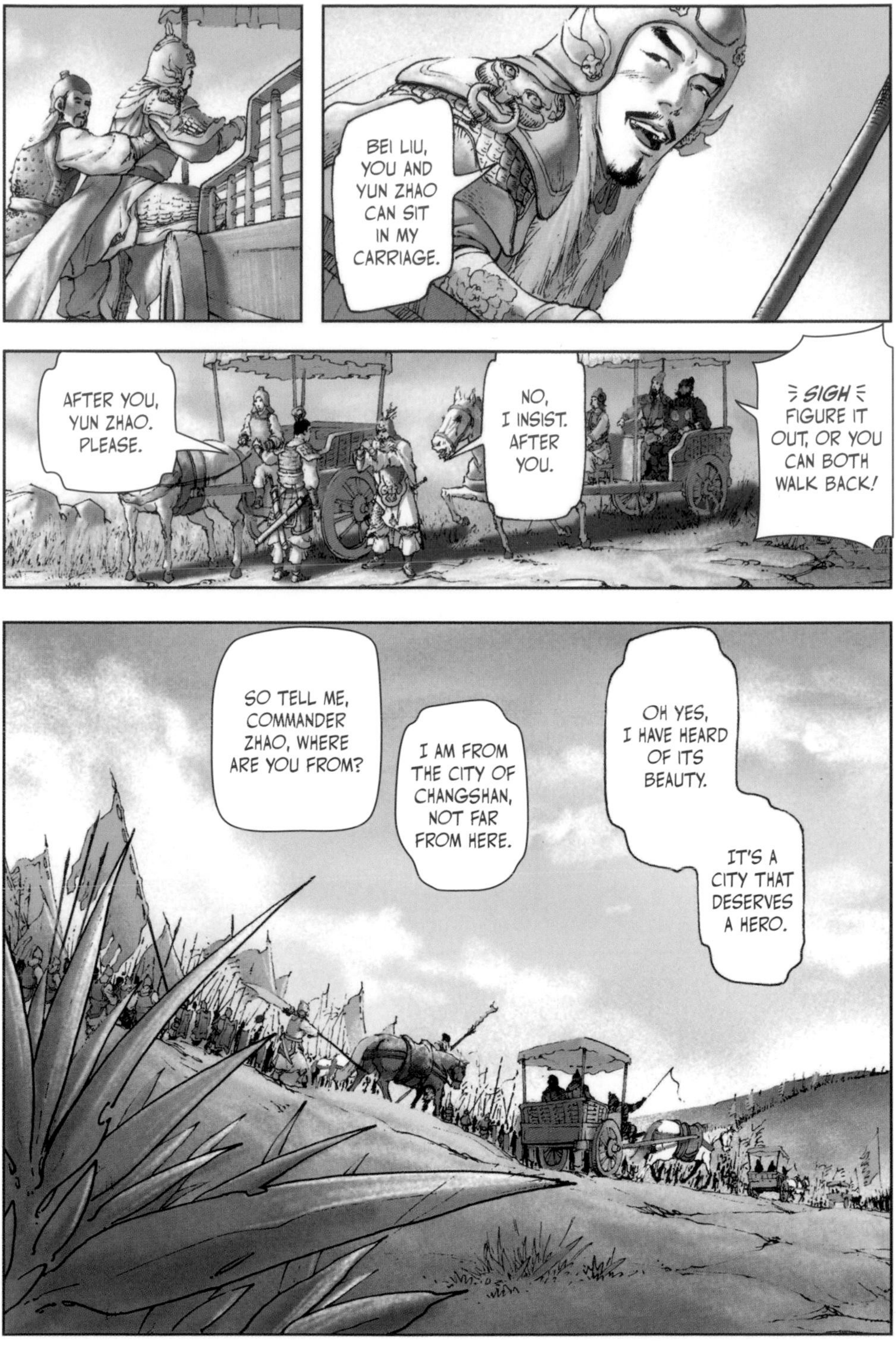
BEI LIU, YOU AND YUN ZHAO CAN SIT IN MY CARRIAGE.
AFTER YOU, YUN ZHAO. PLEASE.
NO, I INSIST. AFTER YOU.
SIGH
FIGURE IT OUT, OR YOU CAN BOTH WALK BACK!
SO TELL ME, COMMANDER ZHAO, WHERE ARE YOU FROM?
I AM FROM THE CITY OF CHANGSHAN, NOT FAR FROM HERE.
OH YES, I HAVE HEARD OF ITS BEAUTY.
IT'S A CITY THAT DESERVES A HERO.

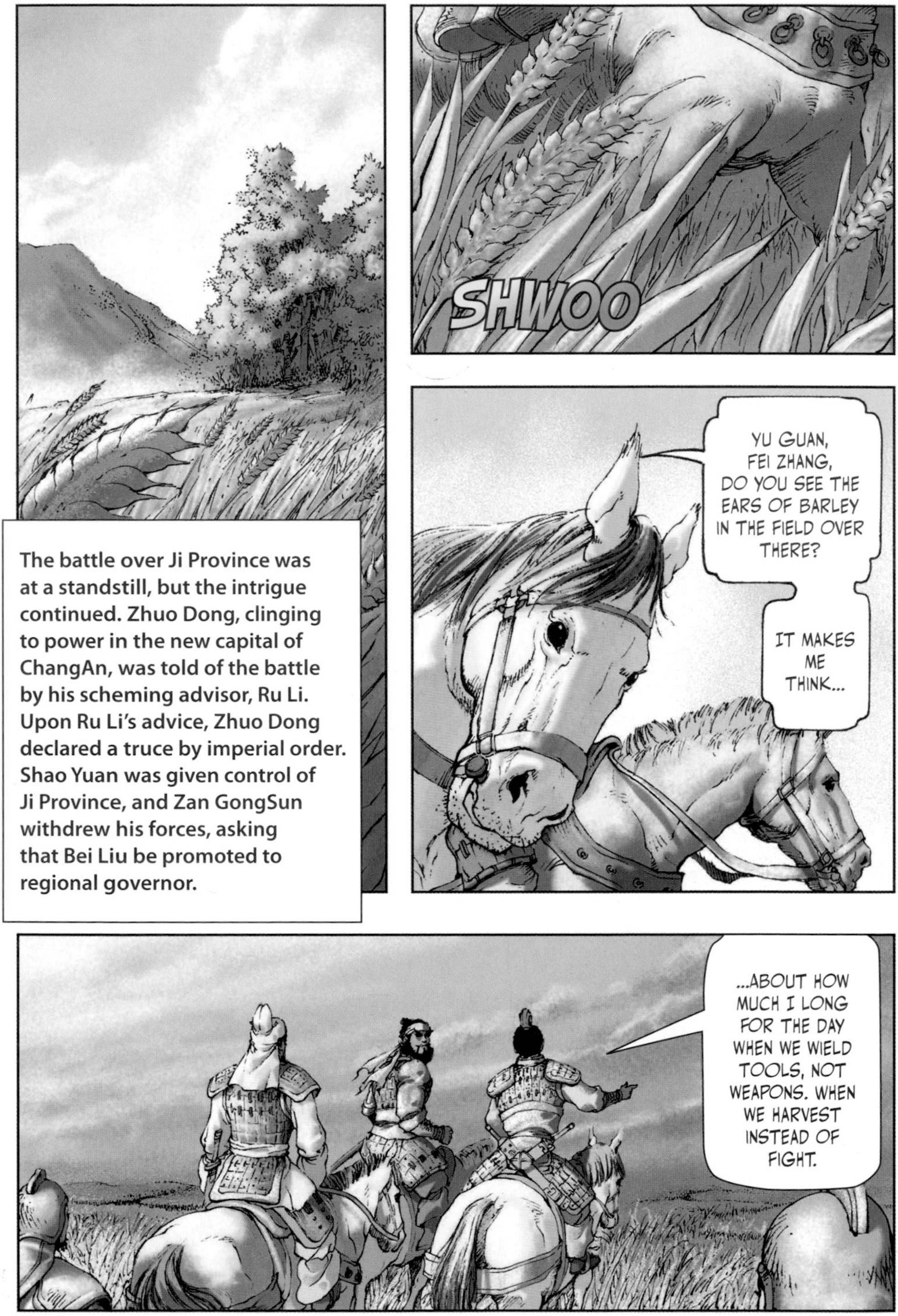
The battle over Ji Province was at a standstill, but the intrigue continued. Zhuo Dong, clinging to power in the new capital of ChangAn, was told of the battle by his scheming advisor, Ru Li. Upon Ru Li's advice, Zhuo Dong declared a truce by imperial order. Shao Yuan was given control of Ji Province, and Zan GongSun withdrew his forces, asking that Bei Liu be promoted to regional governor.
SHWOO
YU GUAN, FEI ZHANG, DO YOU SEE THE EARS OF BARLEY IN THE FIELD OVER THERE?
IT MAKES ME THINK...
...ABOUT HOW MUCH I LONG FOR THE DAY WHEN WE WIELD TOOLS, NOT WEAPONS. WHEN WE HARVEST INSTEAD OF FIGHT.

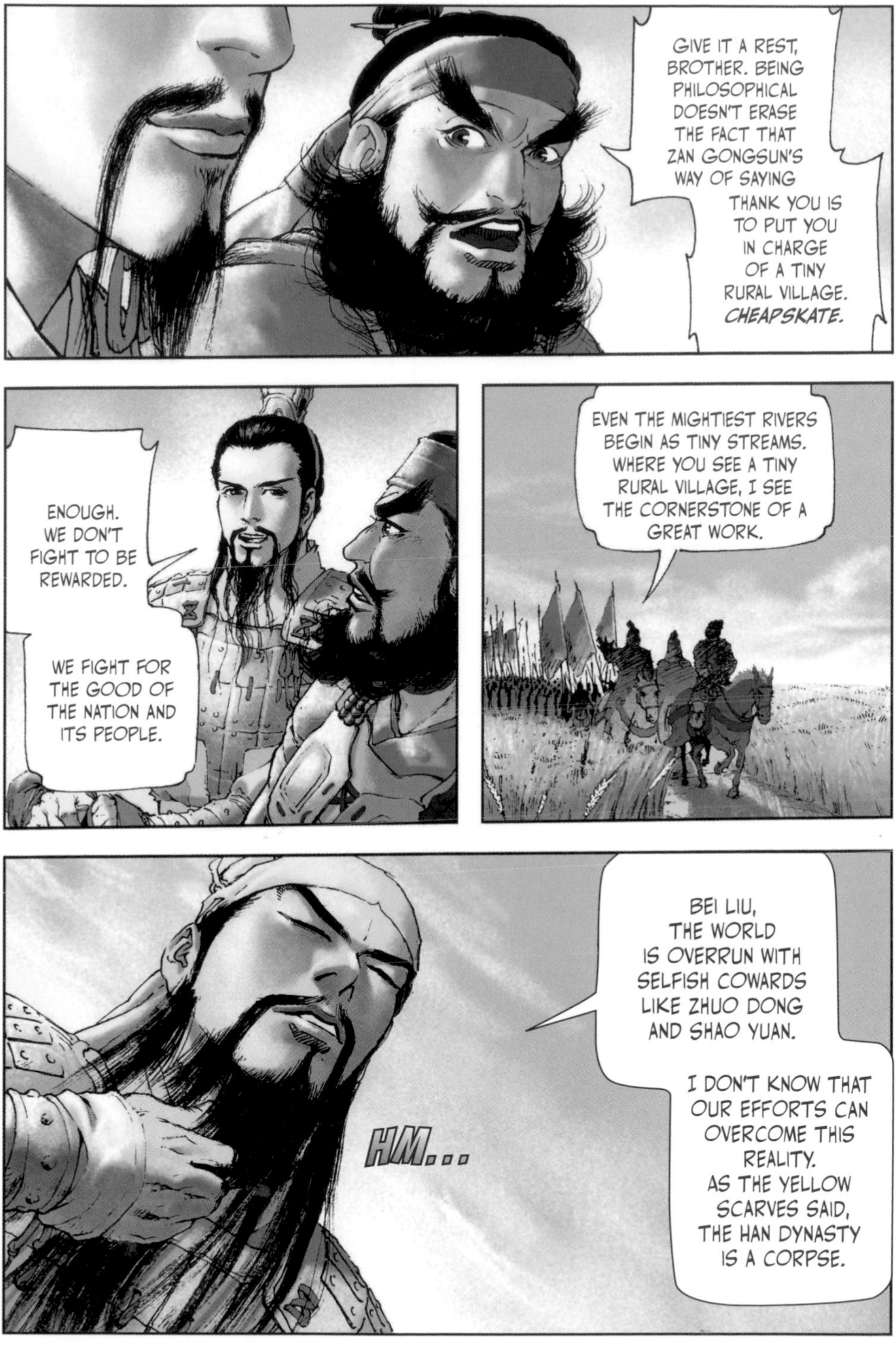
GIVE IT A REST, BROTHER. BEING PHILOSOPHICAL DOESN'T ERASE THE FACT THAT ZAN GONGSUN'S WAY OF SAYING THANK YOU IS TO PUT YOU IN CHARGE OF A TINY RURAL VILLAGE. *CHEAPSKATE.*
ENOUGH. WE DON'T FIGHT TO BE REWARDED.
WE FIGHT FOR THE GOOD OF THE NATION AND ITS PEOPLE.
EVEN THE MIGHTIEST RIVERS BEGIN AS TINY STREAMS. WHERE YOU SEE A TINY RURAL VILLAGE, I SEE THE CORNERSTONE OF A GREAT WORK.
BEI LIU, THE WORLD IS OVERRUN WITH SELFISH COWARDS LIKE ZHUO DONG AND SHAO YUAN.
HM...
I DON'T KNOW THAT OUR EFFORTS CAN OVERCOME THIS REALITY. AS THE YELLOW SCARVES SAID, THE HAN DYNASTY IS A CORPSE.

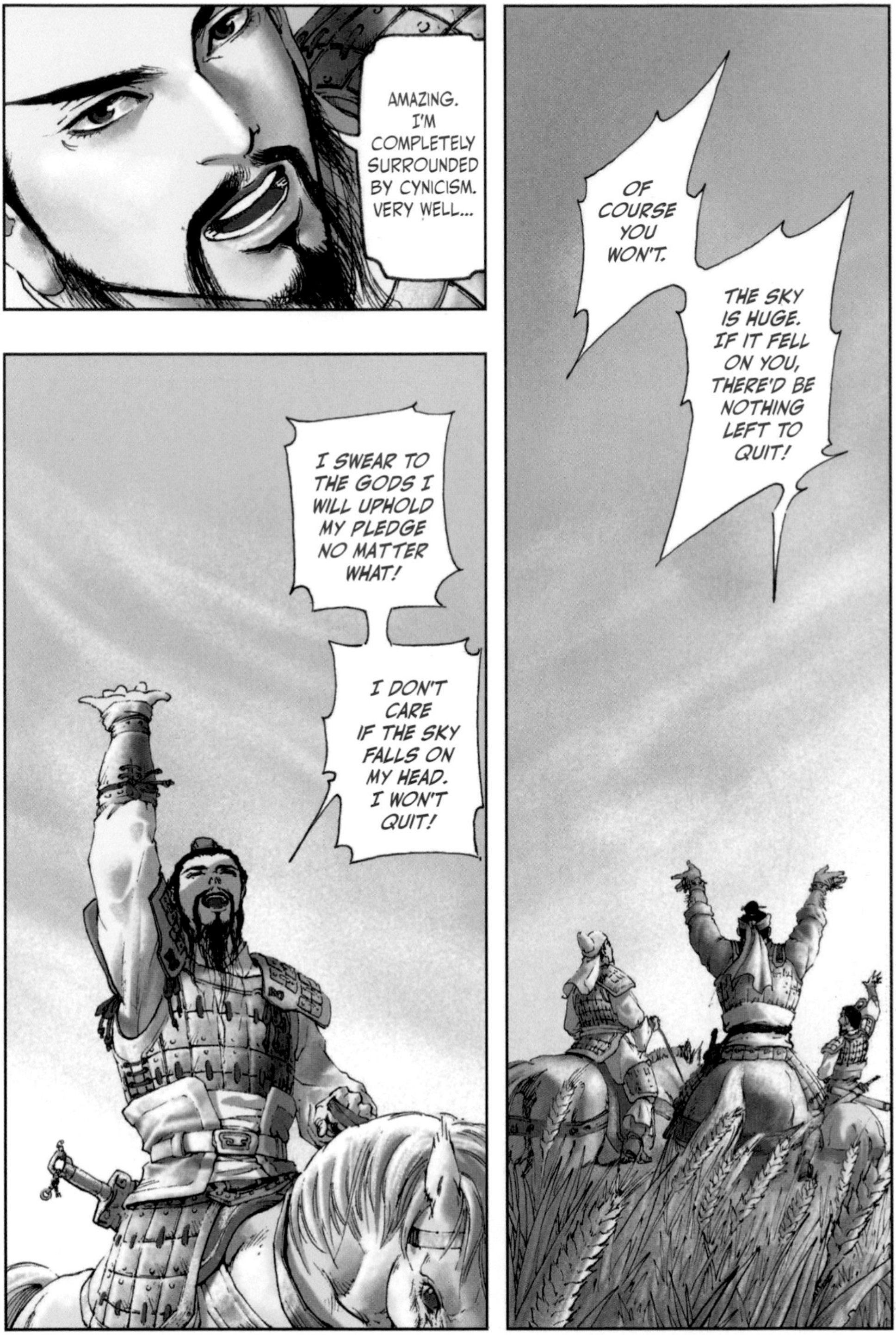
AMAZING. I'M COMPLETELY SURROUNDED BY CYNICISM. VERY WELL...
I SWEAR TO THE GODS I WILL UPHOLD MY PLEDGE NO MATTER WHAT!
I DON'T CARE IF THE SKY FALLS ON MY HEAD. I WON'T QUIT!
OF COURSE YOU WON'T.
THE SKY IS HUGE. IF IT FELL ON YOU, THERE'D BE NOTHING LEFT TO QUIT!

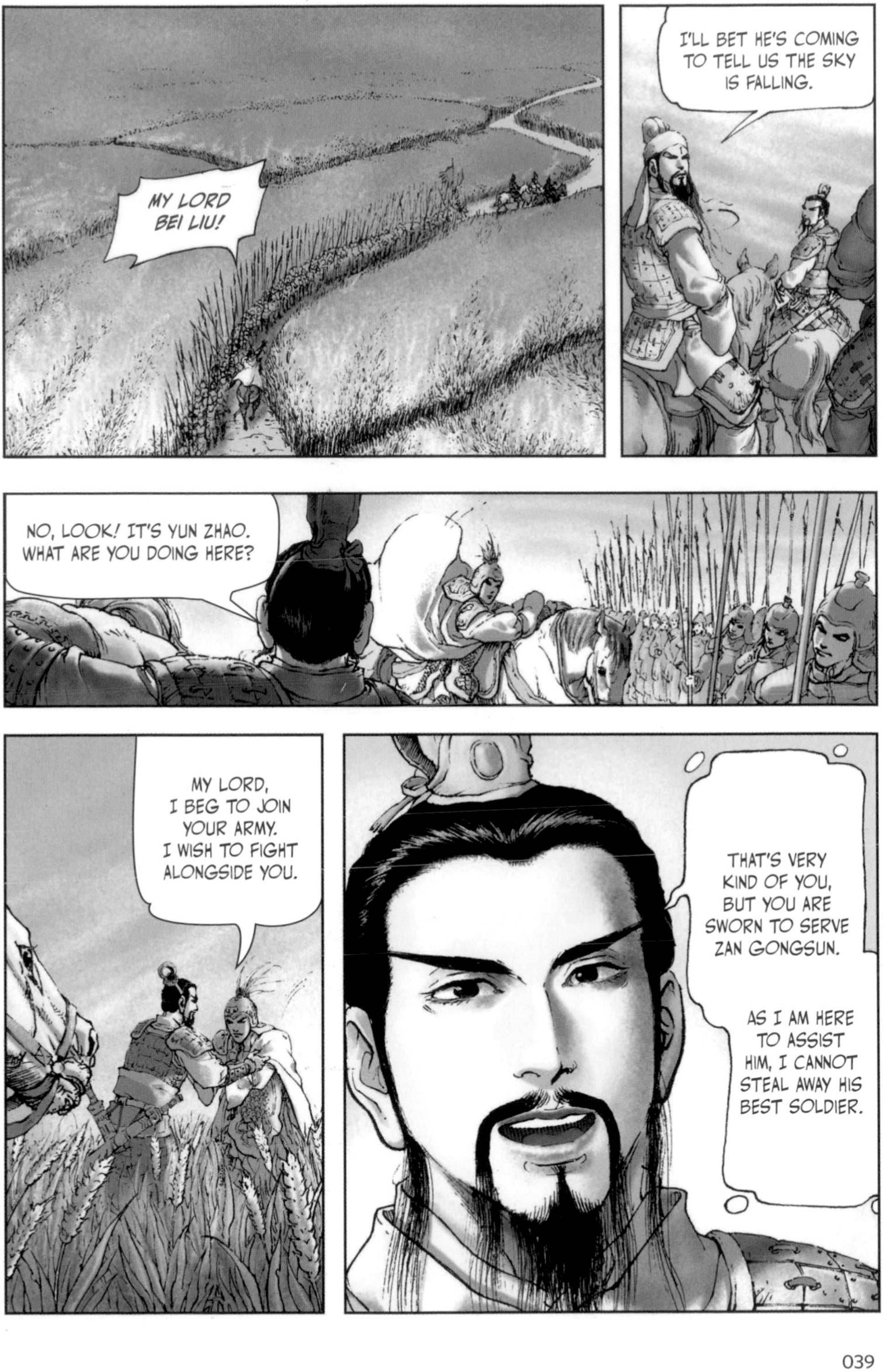
MY LORD BEI LIU!
I'LL BET HE'S COMING TO TELL US THE SKY IS FALLING.
NO, LOOK! IT'S YUN ZHAO. WHAT ARE YOU DOING HERE?
MY LORD, I BEG TO JOIN YOUR ARMY. I WISH TO FIGHT ALONGSIDE YOU.
THAT'S VERY KIND OF YOU, BUT YOU ARE SWORN TO SERVE ZAN GONGSUN.
AS I AM HERE TO ASSIST HIM, I CANNOT STEAL AWAY HIS BEST SOLDIER.

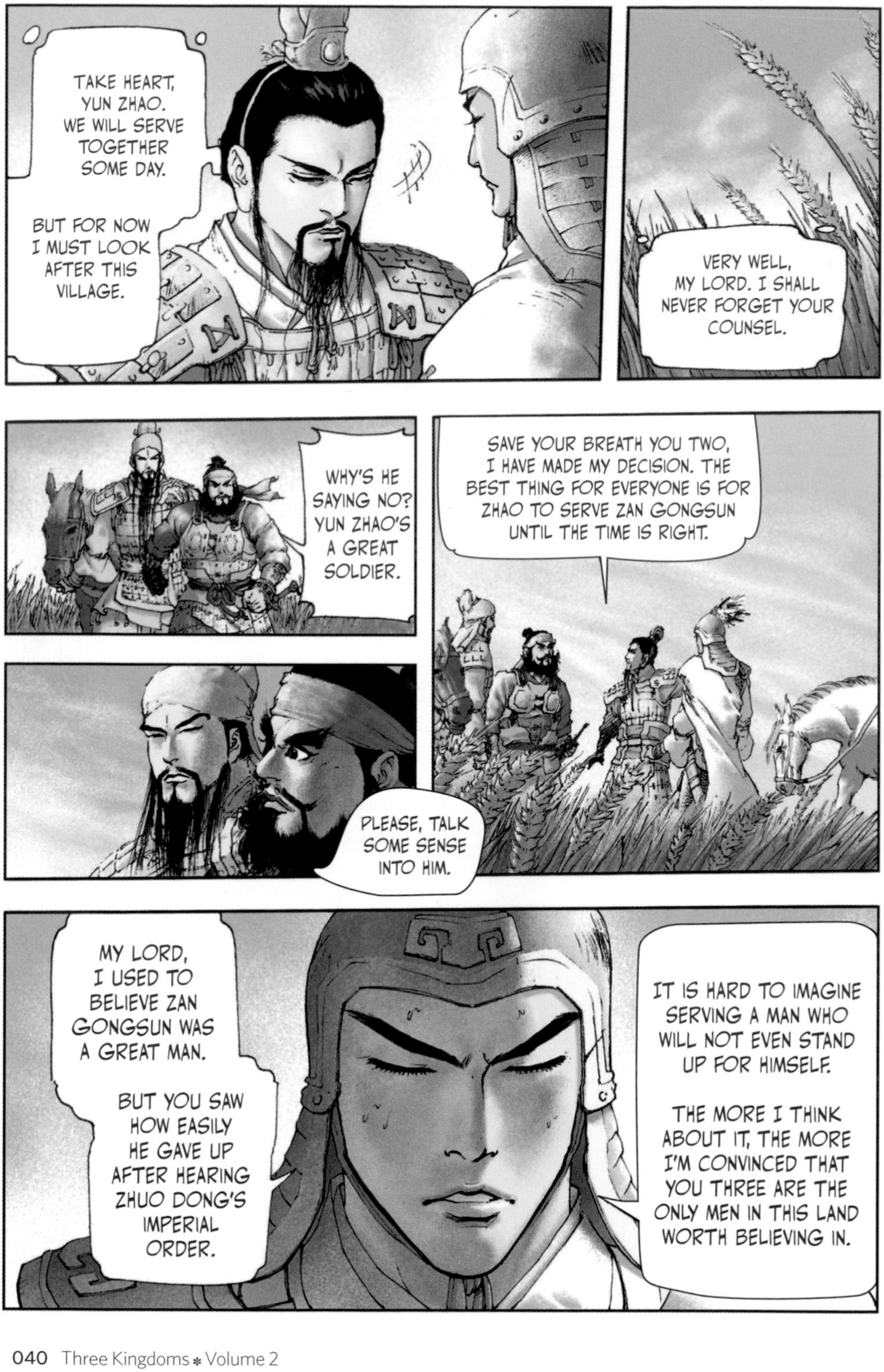
TAKE HEART, YUN ZHAO. WE WILL SERVE TOGETHER SOME DAY.
BUT FOR NOW I MUST LOOK AFTER THIS VILLAGE.
VERY WELL, MY LORD. I SHALL NEVER FORGET YOUR COUNSEL.
WHY'S HE SAYING NO? YUN ZHAO'S A GREAT SOLDIER.
PLEASE, TALK SOME SENSE INTO HIM.
SAVE YOUR BREATH YOU TWO, I HAVE MADE MY DECISION. THE BEST THING FOR EVERYONE IS FOR ZHAO TO SERVE ZAN GONGSUN UNTIL THE TIME IS RIGHT.
MY LORD, I USED TO BELIEVE ZAN GONGSUN WAS A GREAT MAN.
BUT YOU SAW HOW EASILY HE GAVE UP AFTER HEARING ZHUO DONG'S IMPERIAL ORDER.
IT IS HARD TO IMAGINE SERVING A MAN WHO WILL NOT EVEN STAND UP FOR HIMSELF.
THE MORE I THINK ABOUT IT, THE MORE I'M CONVINCED THAT YOU THREE ARE THE ONLY MEN IN THIS LAND WORTH BELIEVING IN.

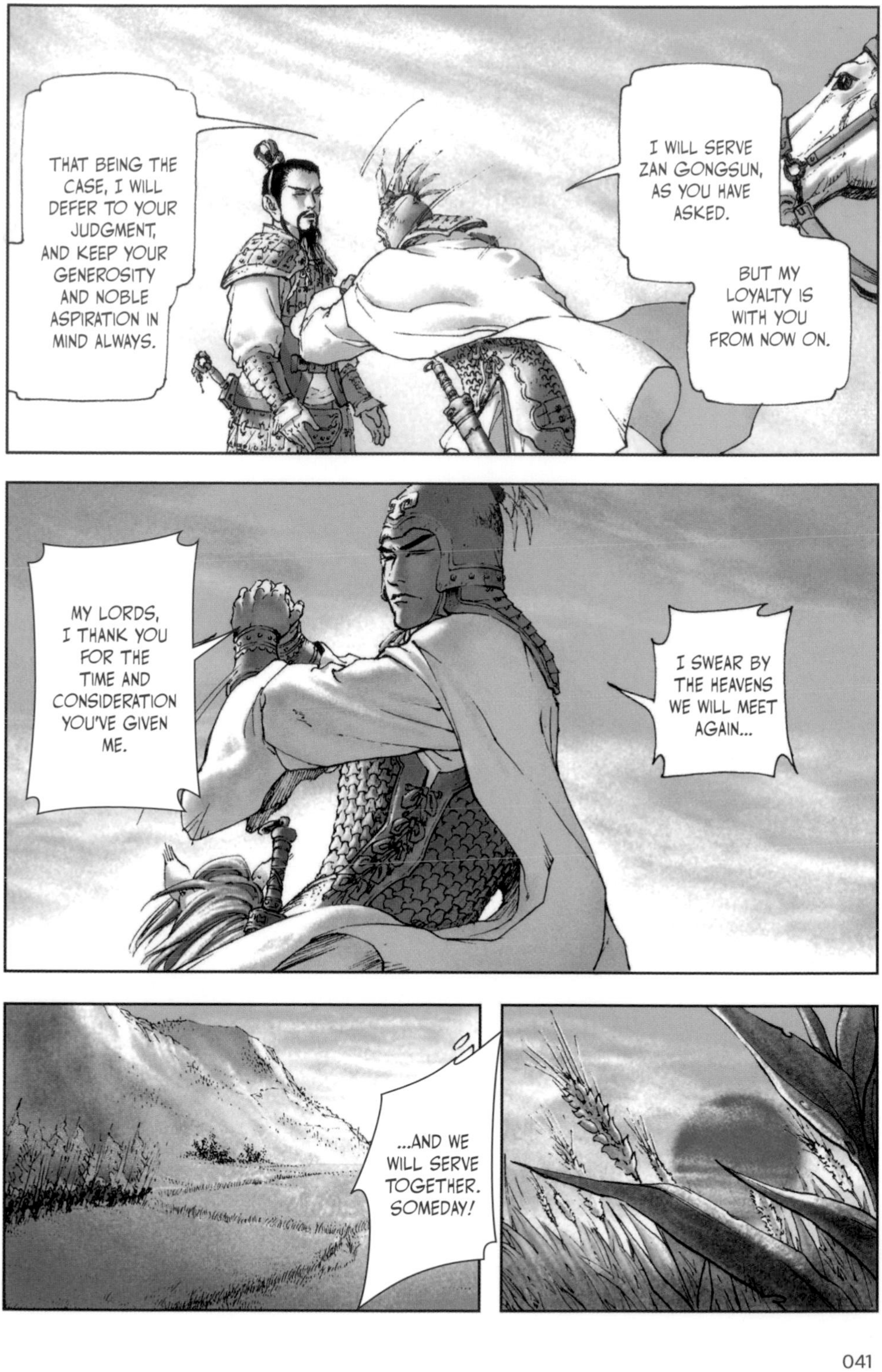
THAT BEING THE CASE, I WILL DEFER TO YOUR JUDGMENT, AND KEEP YOUR GENEROSITY AND NOBLE ASPIRATION IN MIND ALWAYS.
I WILL SERVE ZAN GONGSUN, AS YOU HAVE ASKED.
BUT MY LOYALTY IS WITH YOU FROM NOW ON.
MY LORDS, I THANK YOU FOR THE TIME AND CONSIDERATION YOU'VE GIVEN ME.
I SWEAR BY THE HEAVENS WE WILL MEET AGAIN...
...AND WE WILL SERVE TOGETHER. SOMEDAY!

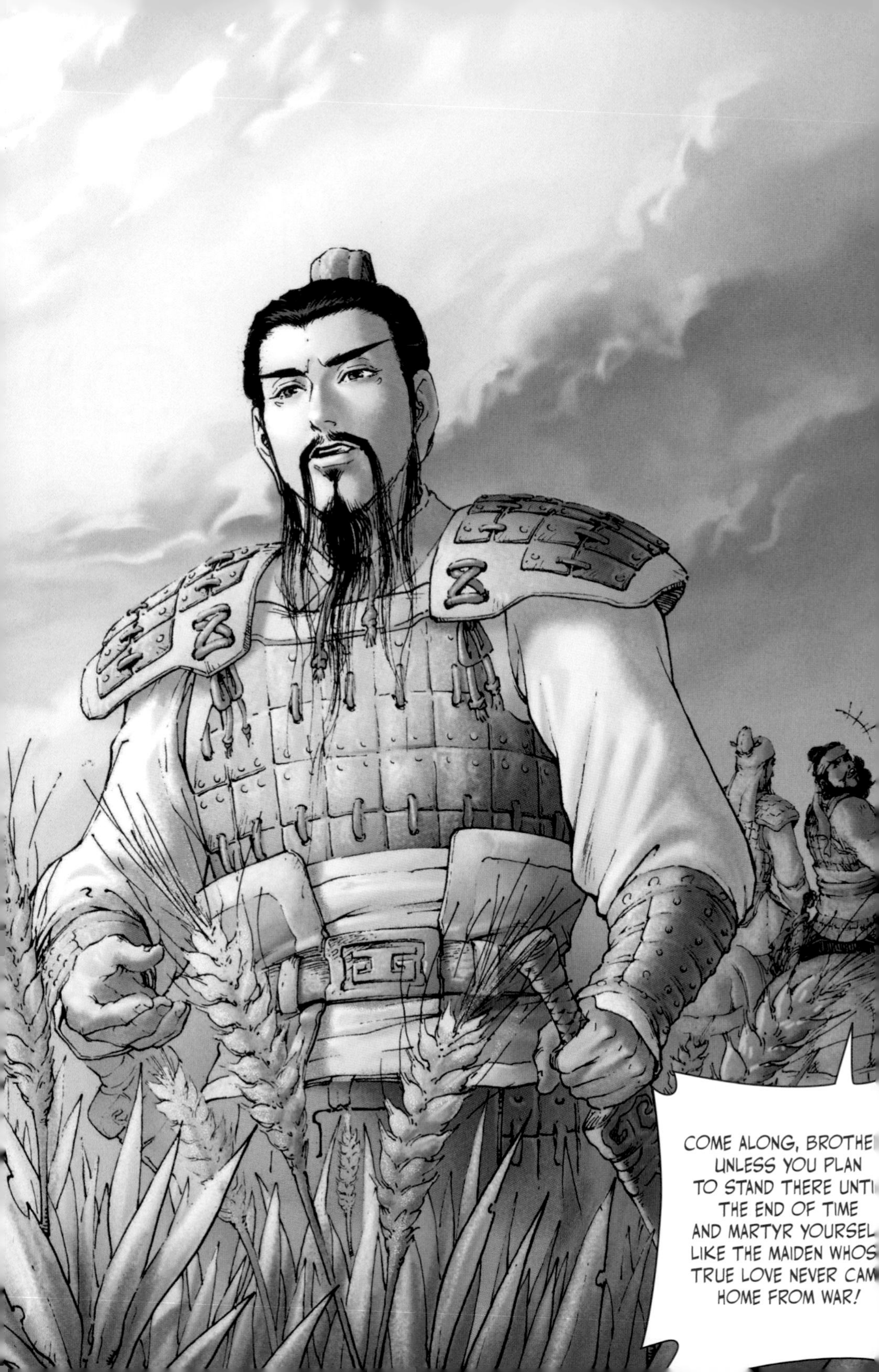
COME ALONG, BROTHE
UNLESS YOU PLAN
TO STAND THERE UNTI
THE END OF TIME
AND MARTYR YOURSEL
LIKE THE MAIDEN WHOS
TRUE LOVE NEVER CAM
HOME FROM WAR!

BEI LIU

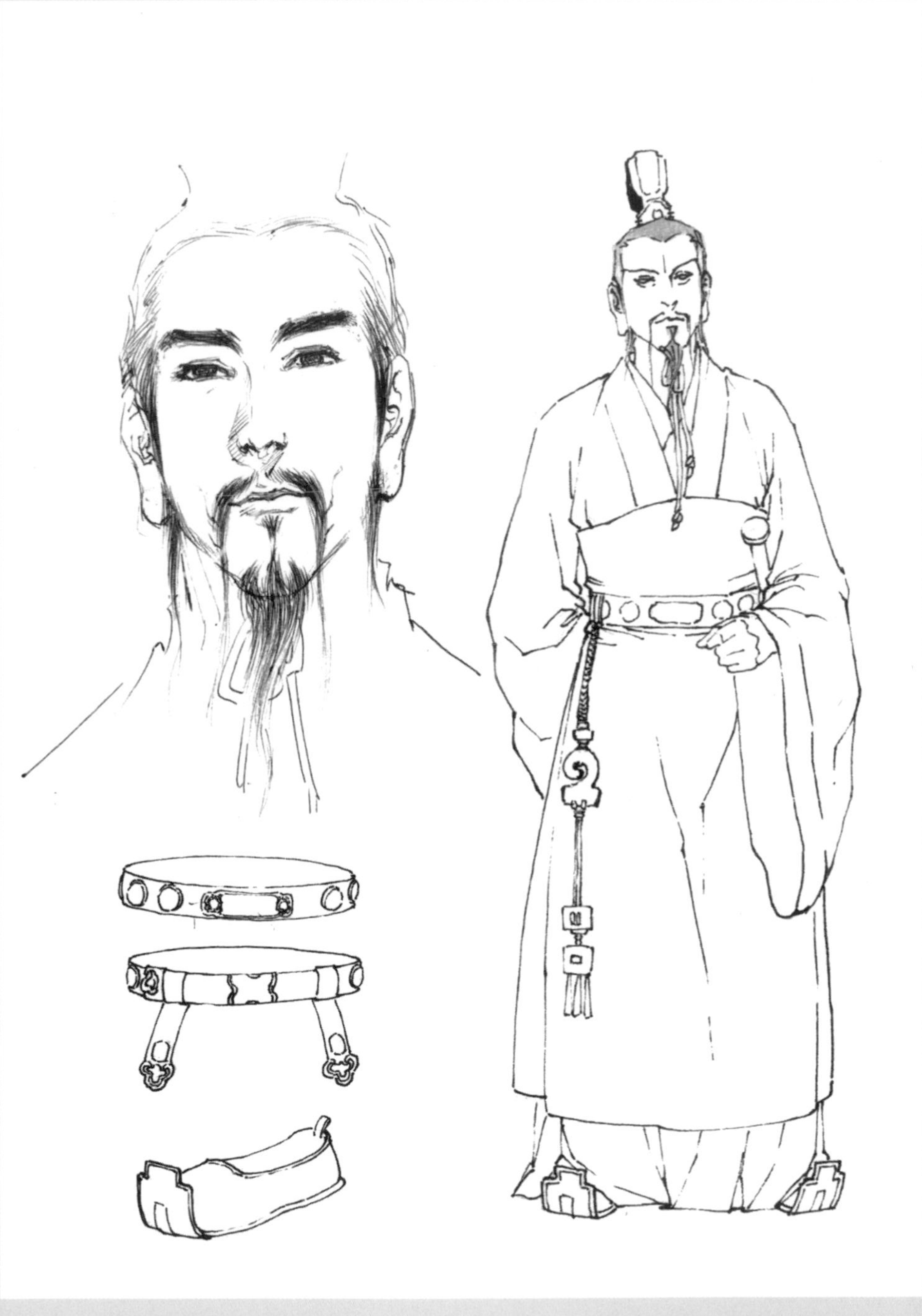

Chapter 2

The Dangerous Hubris of Jian Sun AD 191

Summary

Having been humiliated in battle by Biao Liu, Jian Sun is persuaded by Shu Yuan to avenge his defeat by attacking Biao Liu's palace in Jing Province. When an emergency envoy is dispatched from the palace to seek help from a neighboring province, Jian Sun recklessly decides to pursue them. The envoy ambushes and kills Jian Sun, after which Ce Sun, Jian's son, inherits his father's title and negotiates a truce with Biao Liu.

XiLiang
Zhuo
ChangShan
BeiHai
PuYang
XiaoPei
GuanDu
XuZhou
XiaPi
LuoYang
XuDu
ChangAn
HanZhong
NanYang
YangZhou
ShouChun
River Huai
XiangYang
HeFei
Wu
A
ChengDu
NanJun
ChaiSang
KuaiJi
Red Cliffs
BoYang
YuZhang
ChangSha

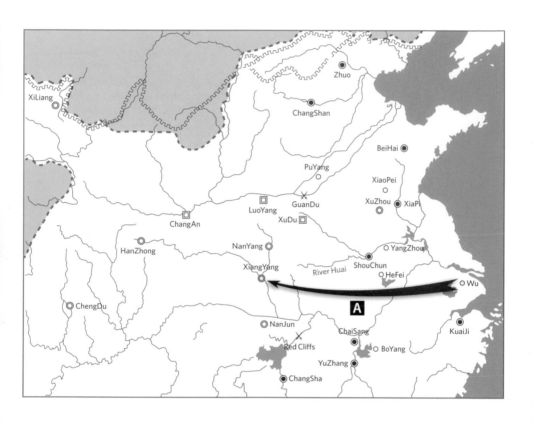

A Jian Sun Attacks Jing Province

Jian Sun decides to attack Biao Liu's palace at the urging of Shu Yuan, but in doing so he leads his army into a river valley and forfeits the tactical advantage of higher ground.

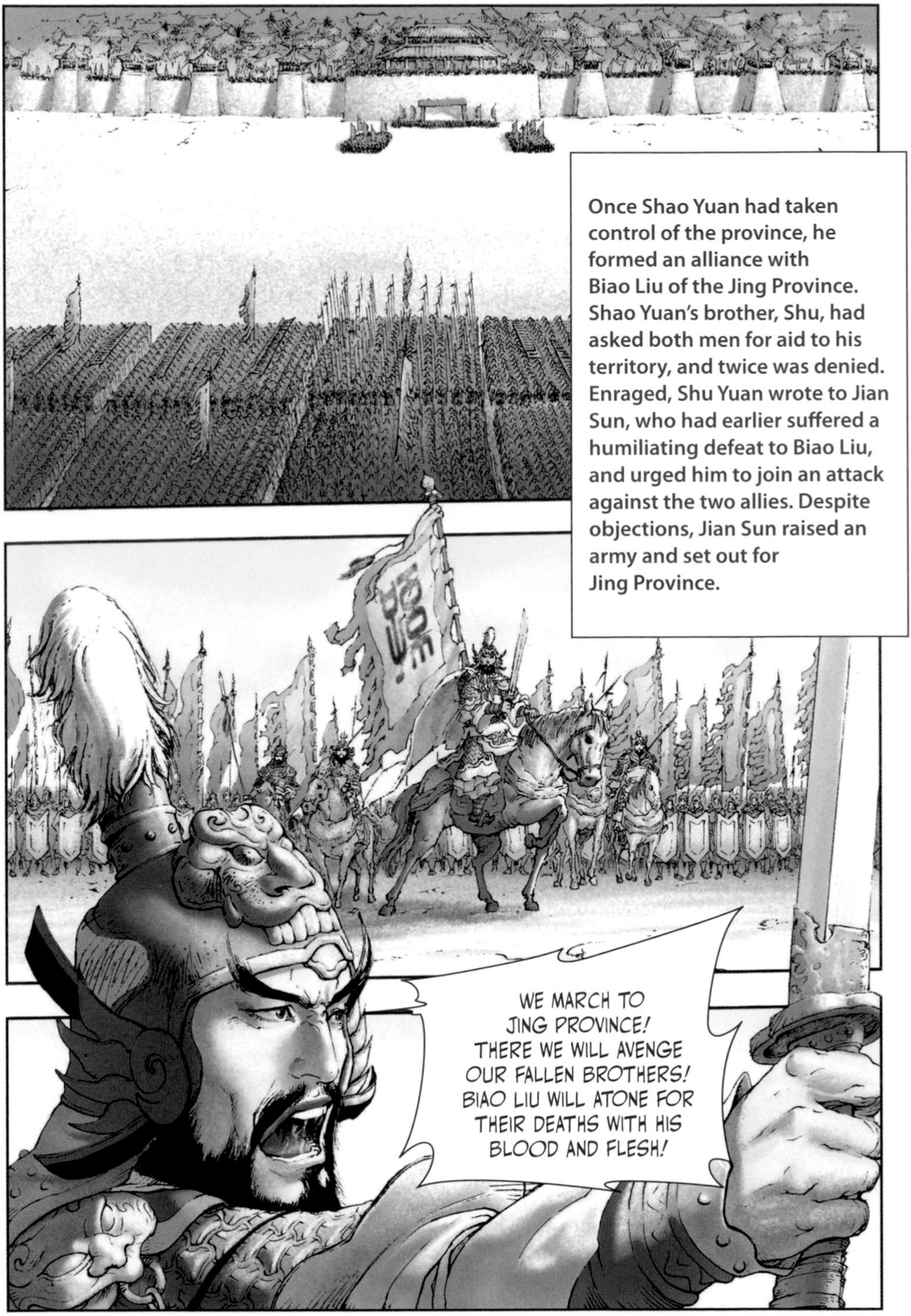
Once Shao Yuan had taken control of the province, he formed an alliance with Biao Liu of the Jing Province. Shao Yuan's brother, Shu, had asked both men for aid to his territory, and twice was denied. Enraged, Shu Yuan wrote to Jian Sun, who had earlier suffered a humiliating defeat to Biao Liu, and urged him to join an attack against the two allies. Despite objections, Jian Sun raised an army and set out for Jing Province.
WE MARCH TO JING PROVINCE! THERE WE WILL AVENGE OUR FALLEN BROTHERS! BIAO LIU WILL ATONE FOR THEIR DEATHS WITH HIS BLOOD AND FLESH!

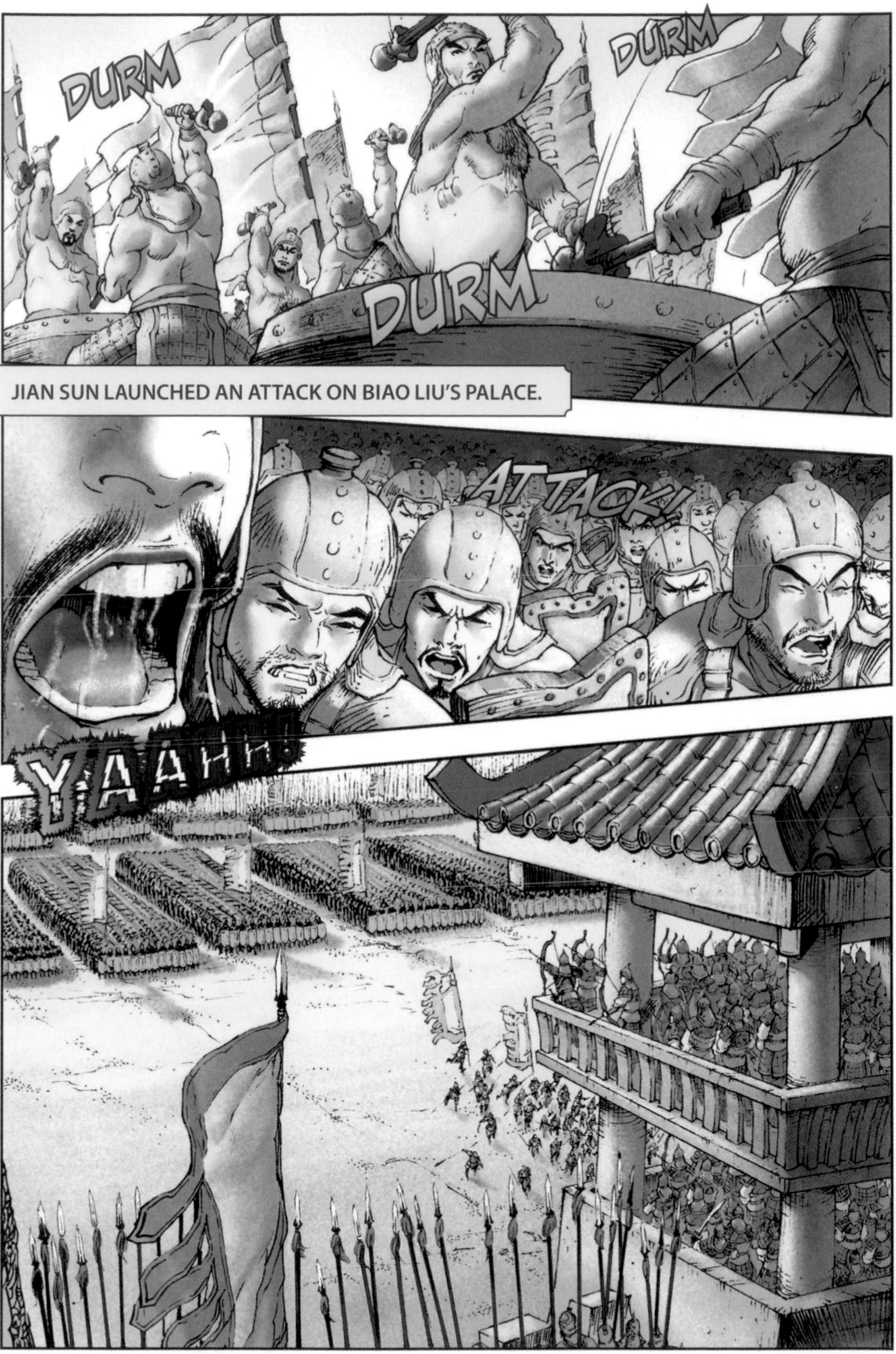
DURM
DURM
DURM
JIAN SUN LAUNCHED AN ATTACK ON BIAO LIU'S PALACE.
ATTACK!
YAAHH!

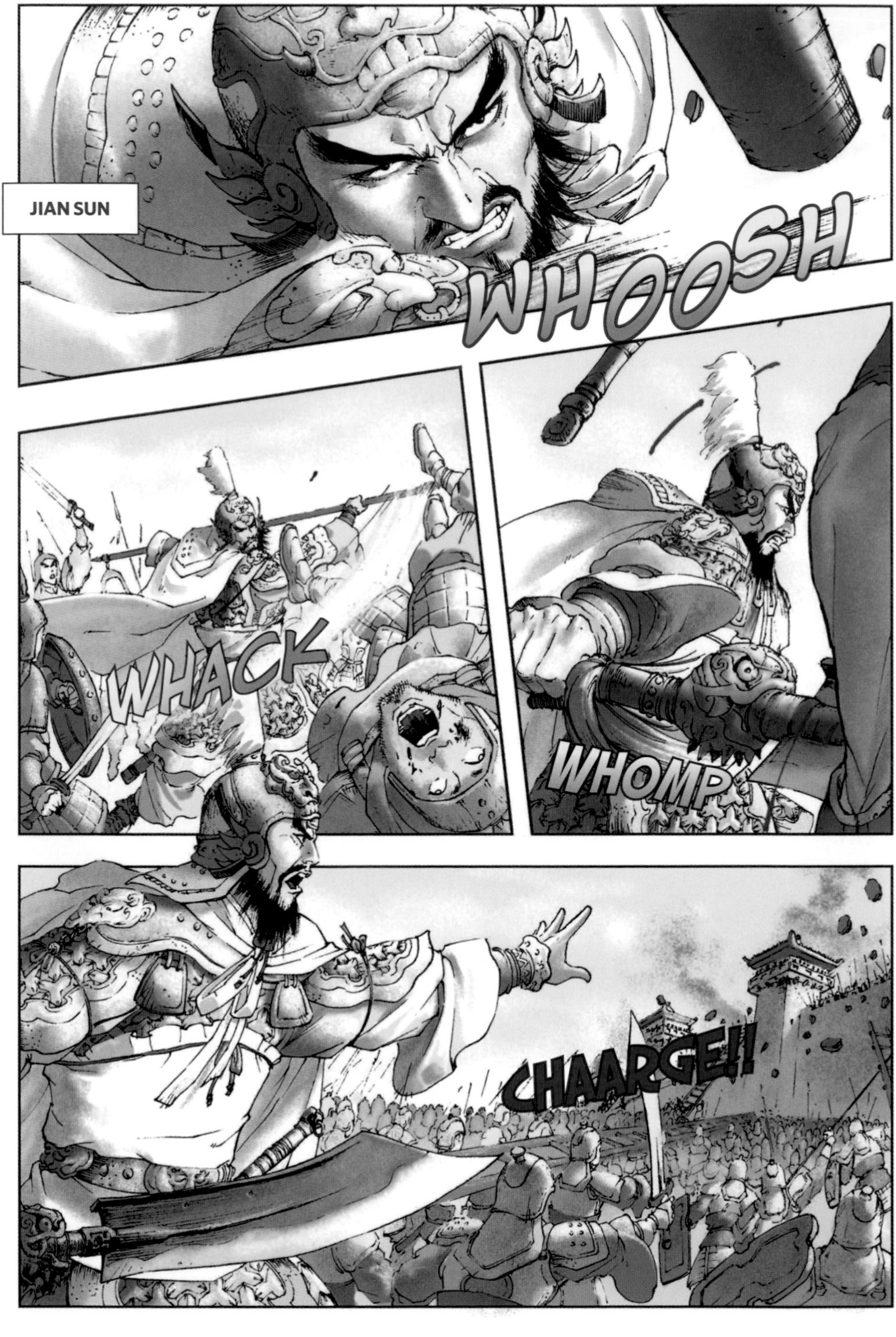
JIAN SUN
WHOOSH
WHACK
WHOMP
CHAARGE!!

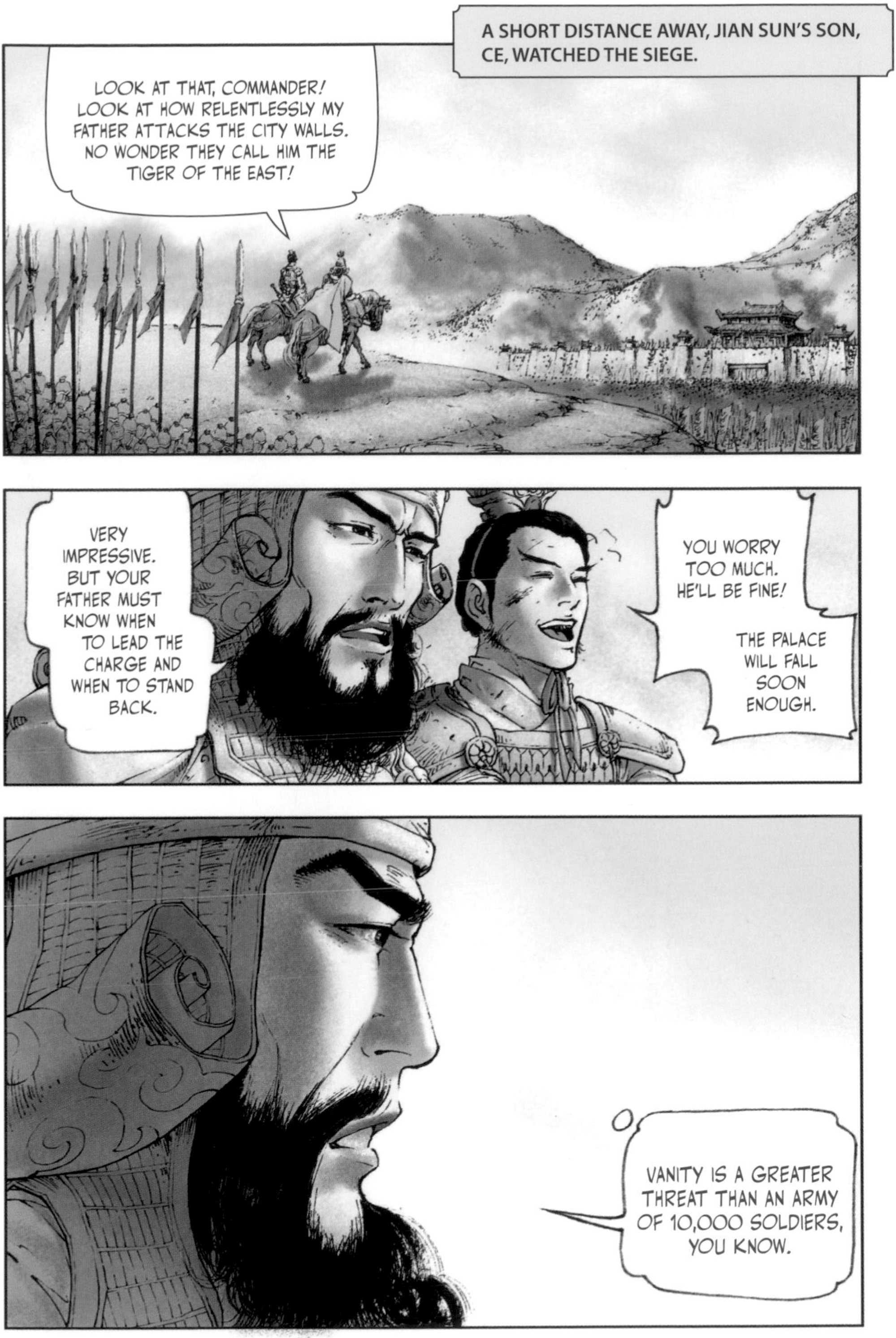
A SHORT DISTANCE AWAY, JIAN SUN'S SON, CE, WATCHED THE SIEGE.
LOOK AT THAT, COMMANDER! LOOK AT HOW RELENTLESSLY MY FATHER ATTACKS THE CITY WALLS. NO WONDER THEY CALL HIM THE TIGER OF THE EAST!
VERY IMPRESSIVE. BUT YOUR FATHER MUST KNOW WHEN TO LEAD THE CHARGE AND WHEN TO STAND BACK.
YOU WORRY TOO MUCH. HE'LL BE FINE!
THE PALACE WILL FALL SOON ENOUGH.
VANITY IS A GREATER THREAT THAN AN ARMY OF 10,000 SOLDIERS, YOU KNOW.

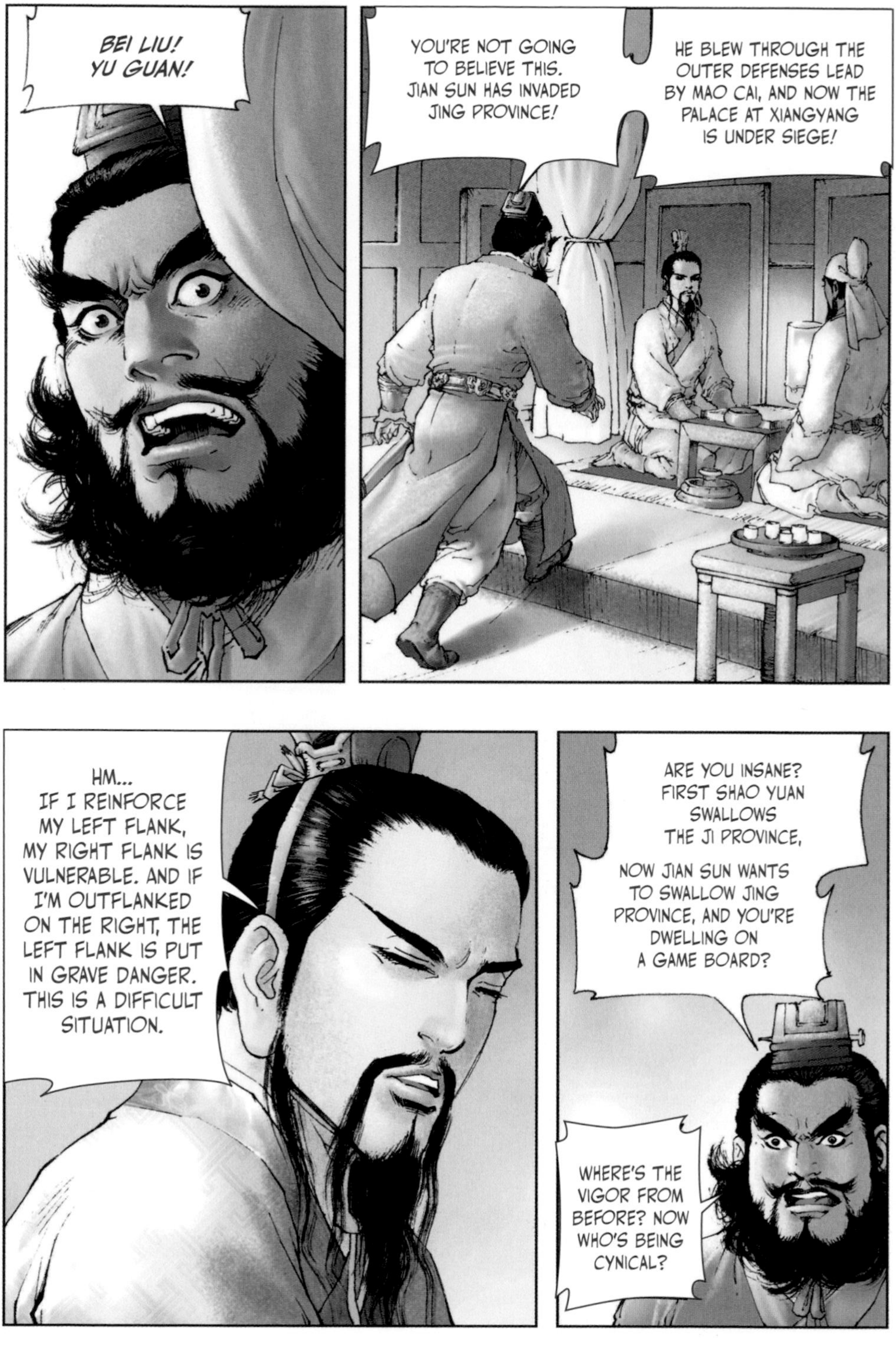
BEI LIU! YU GUAN!
YOU'RE NOT GOING TO BELIEVE THIS. JIAN SUN HAS INVADED JING PROVINCE!
HE BLEW THROUGH THE OUTER DEFENSES LEAD BY MAO CAI, AND NOW THE PALACE AT XIANGYANG IS UNDER SIEGE!
HM... IF I REINFORCE MY LEFT FLANK, MY RIGHT FLANK IS VULNERABLE. AND IF I'M OUTFLANKED ON THE RIGHT, THE LEFT FLANK IS PUT IN GRAVE DANGER. THIS IS A DIFFICULT SITUATION.
ARE YOU INSANE? FIRST SHAO YUAN SWALLOWS THE JI PROVINCE,
NOW JIAN SUN WANTS TO SWALLOW JING PROVINCE, AND YOU'RE DWELLING ON A GAME BOARD?
WHERE'S THE VIGOR FROM BEFORE? NOW WHO'S BEING CYNICAL?

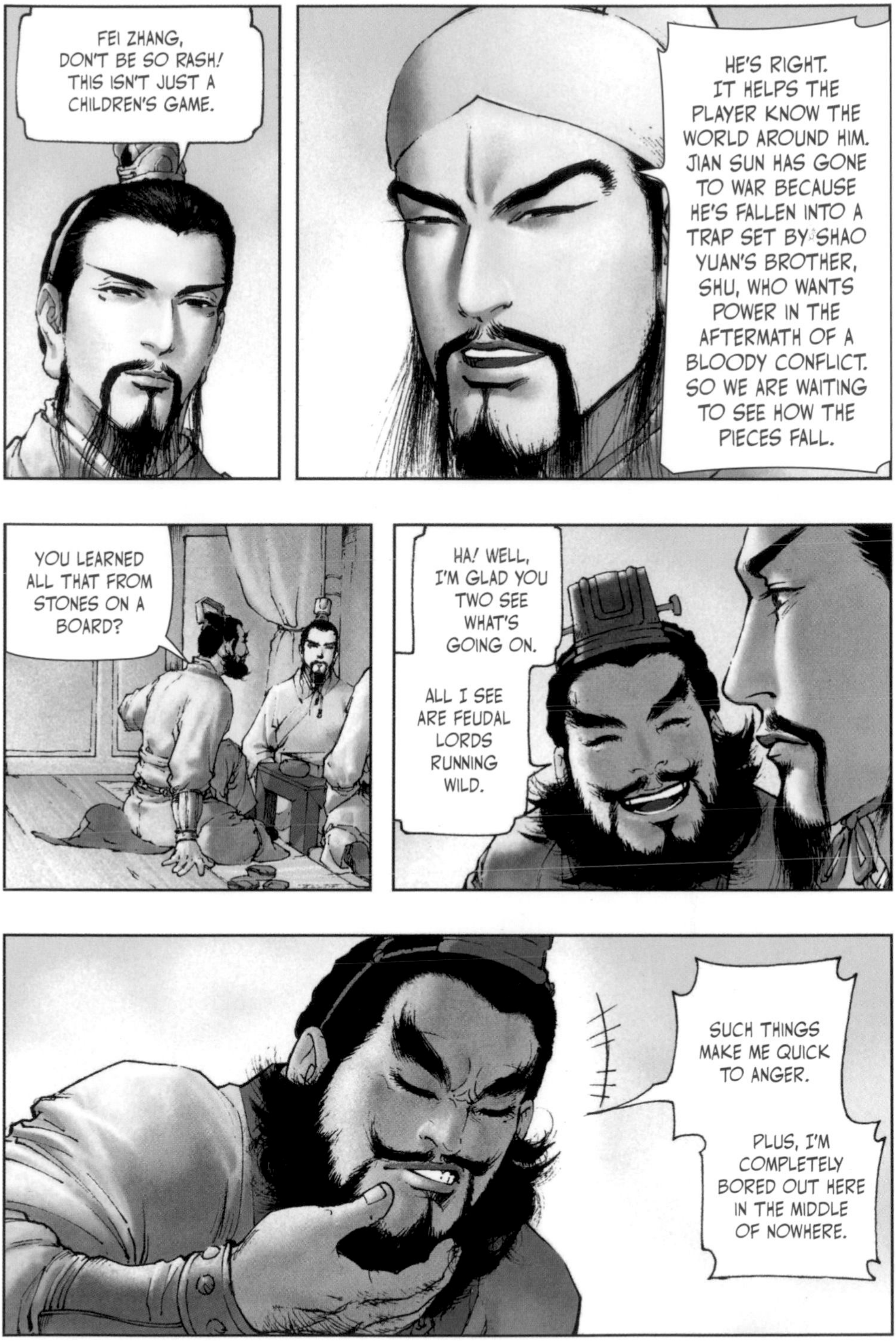
FEI ZHANG, DON'T BE SO RASH! THIS ISN'T JUST A CHILDREN'S GAME.
HE'S RIGHT. IT HELPS THE PLAYER KNOW THE WORLD AROUND HIM. JIAN SUN HAS GONE TO WAR BECAUSE HE'S FALLEN INTO A TRAP SET BY SHAO YUAN'S BROTHER, SHU, WHO WANTS POWER IN THE AFTERMATH OF A BLOODY CONFLICT. SO WE ARE WAITING TO SEE HOW THE PIECES FALL.
YOU LEARNED ALL THAT FROM STONES ON A BOARD?
HA! WELL, I'M GLAD YOU TWO SEE WHAT'S GOING ON.
ALL I SEE ARE FEUDAL LORDS RUNNING WILD.
SUCH THINGS MAKE ME QUICK TO ANGER.
PLUS, I'M COMPLETELY BORED OUT HERE IN THE MIDDLE OF NOWHERE.

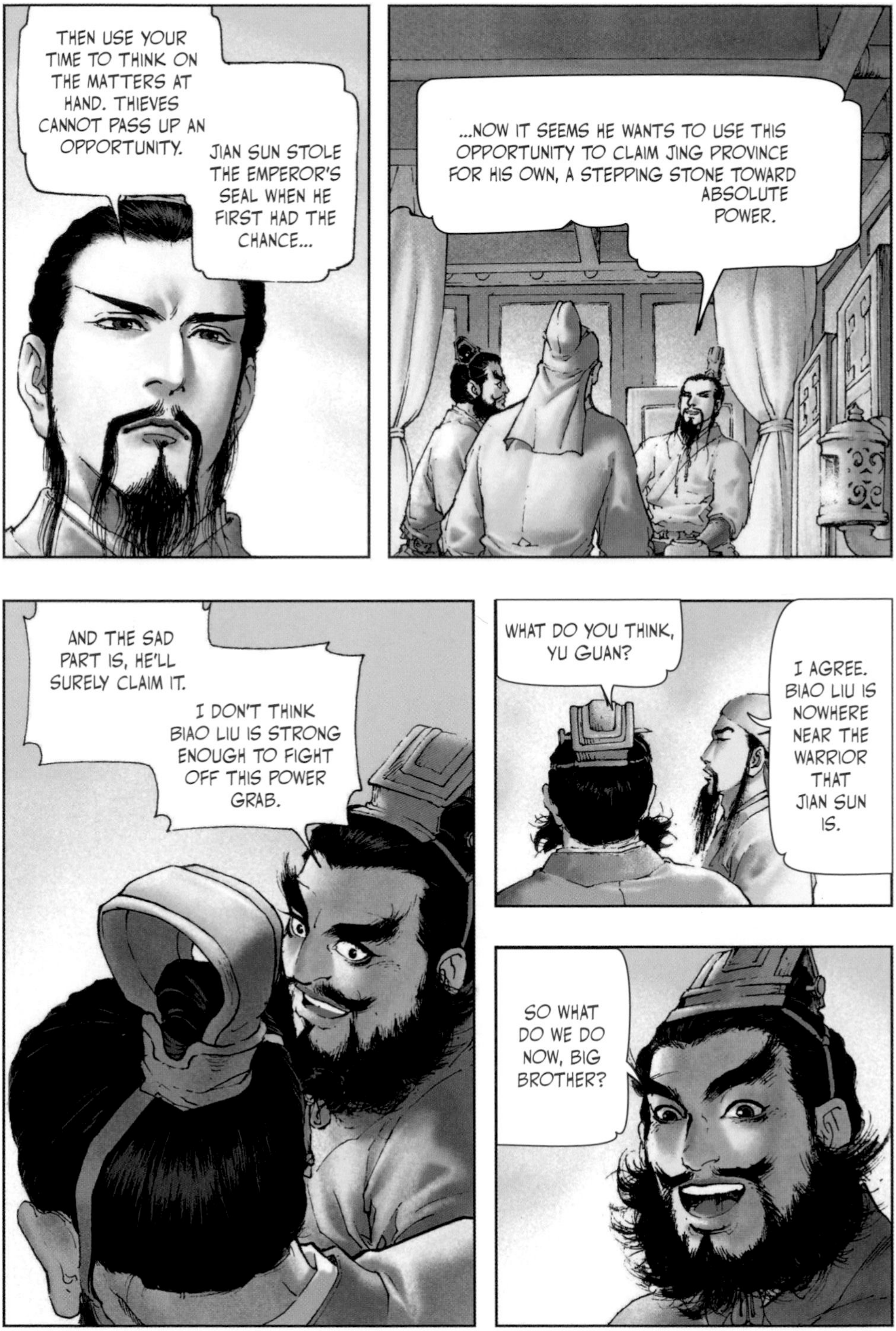
THEN USE YOUR TIME TO THINK ON THE MATTERS AT HAND. THIEVES CANNOT PASS UP AN OPPORTUNITY.
JIAN SUN STOLE THE EMPEROR'S SEAL WHEN HE FIRST HAD THE CHANCE...
...NOW IT SEEMS HE WANTS TO USE THIS OPPORTUNITY TO CLAIM JING PROVINCE FOR HIS OWN, A STEPPING STONE TOWARD ABSOLUTE POWER.
AND THE SAD PART IS, HE'LL SURELY CLAIM IT.
I DON'T THINK BIAO LIU IS STRONG ENOUGH TO FIGHT OFF THIS POWER GRAB.
WHAT DO YOU THINK, YU GUAN?
I AGREE. BIAO LIU IS NOWHERE NEAR THE WARRIOR THAT JIAN SUN IS.
SO WHAT DO WE DO NOW, BIG BROTHER?

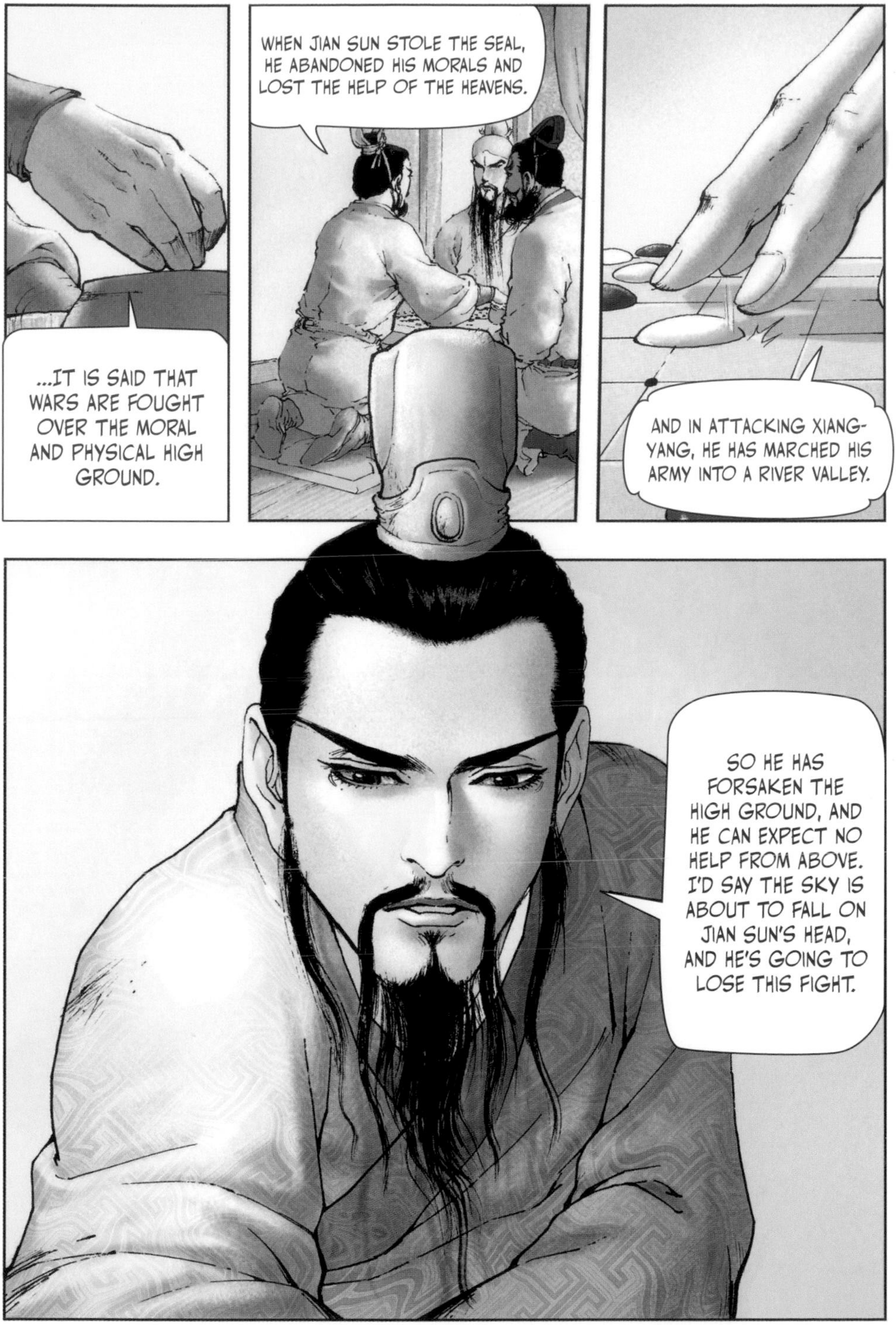
...IT IS SAID THAT WARS ARE FOUGHT OVER THE MORAL AND PHYSICAL HIGH GROUND.
WHEN JIAN SUN STOLE THE SEAL, HE ABANDONED HIS MORALS AND LOST THE HELP OF THE HEAVENS.
AND IN ATTACKING XIANG-YANG, HE HAS MARCHED HIS ARMY INTO A RIVER VALLEY.
SO HE HAS FORSAKEN THE HIGH GROUND, AND HE CAN EXPECT NO HELP FROM ABOVE. I'D SAY THE SKY IS ABOUT TO FALL ON JIAN SUN'S HEAD, AND HE'S GOING TO LOSE THIS FIGHT.

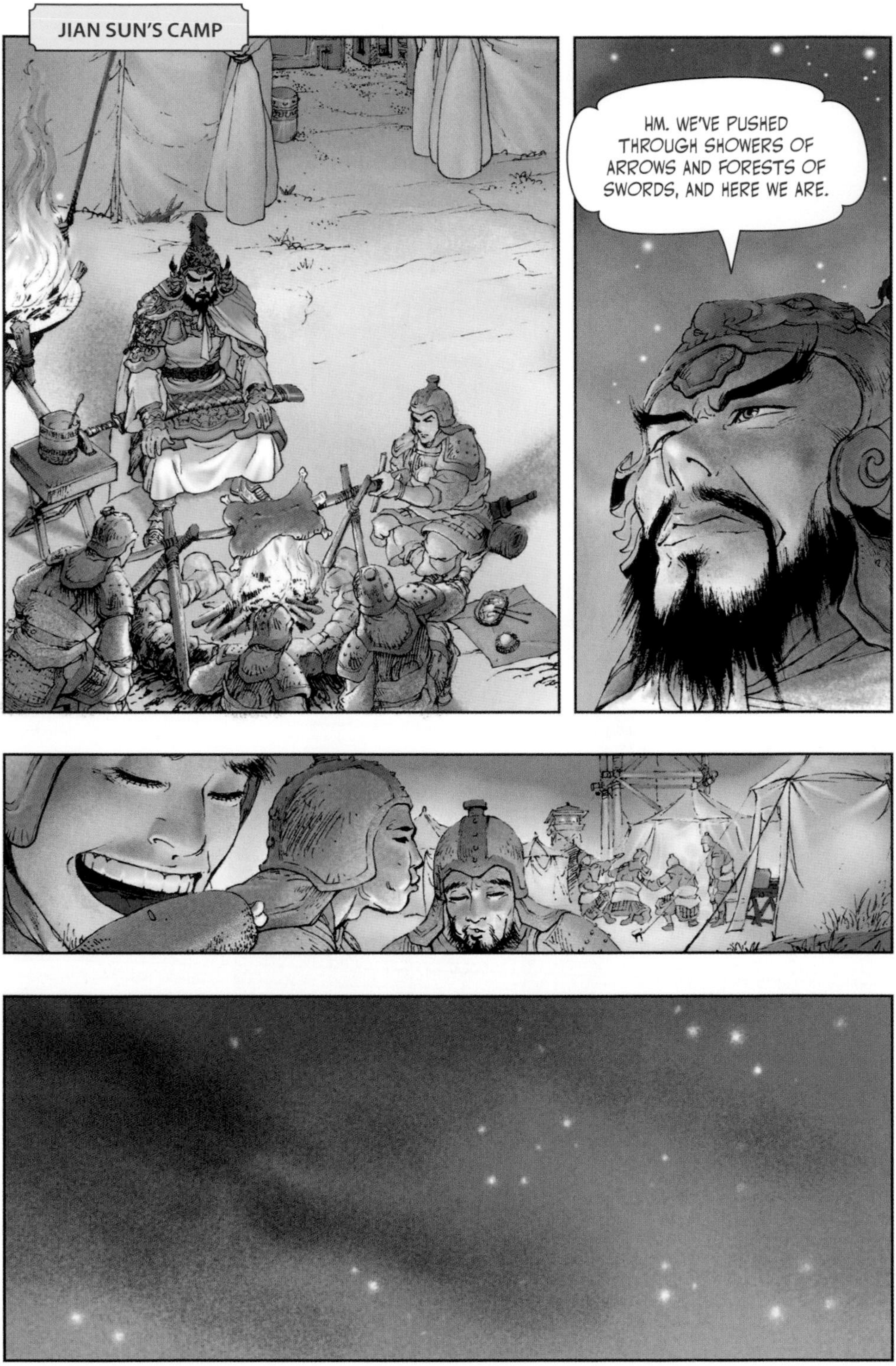
JIAN SUN'S CAMP
HM. WE'VE PUSHED THROUGH SHOWERS OF ARROWS AND FORESTS OF SWORDS, AND HERE WE ARE.

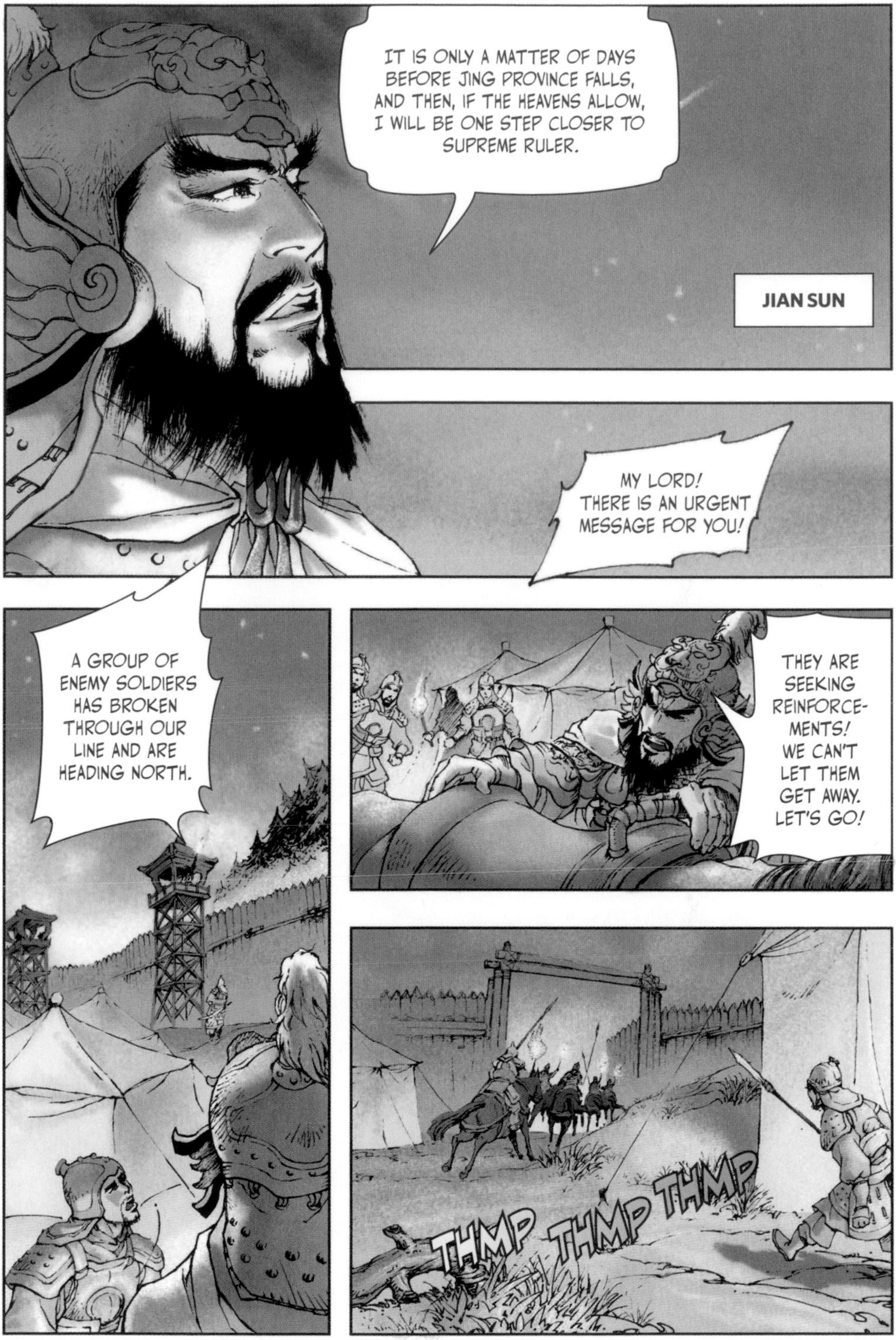
IT IS ONLY A MATTER OF DAYS BEFORE JING PROVINCE FALLS, AND THEN, IF THE HEAVENS ALLOW, I WILL BE ONE STEP CLOSER TO SUPREME RULER.
JIAN SUN
MY LORD! THERE IS AN URGENT MESSAGE FOR YOU!
A GROUP OF ENEMY SOLDIERS HAS BROKEN THROUGH OUR LINE AND ARE HEADING NORTH.
THEY ARE SEEKING REINFORCEMENTS! WE CAN'T LET THEM GET AWAY. LET'S GO!
THMP THMP THMP

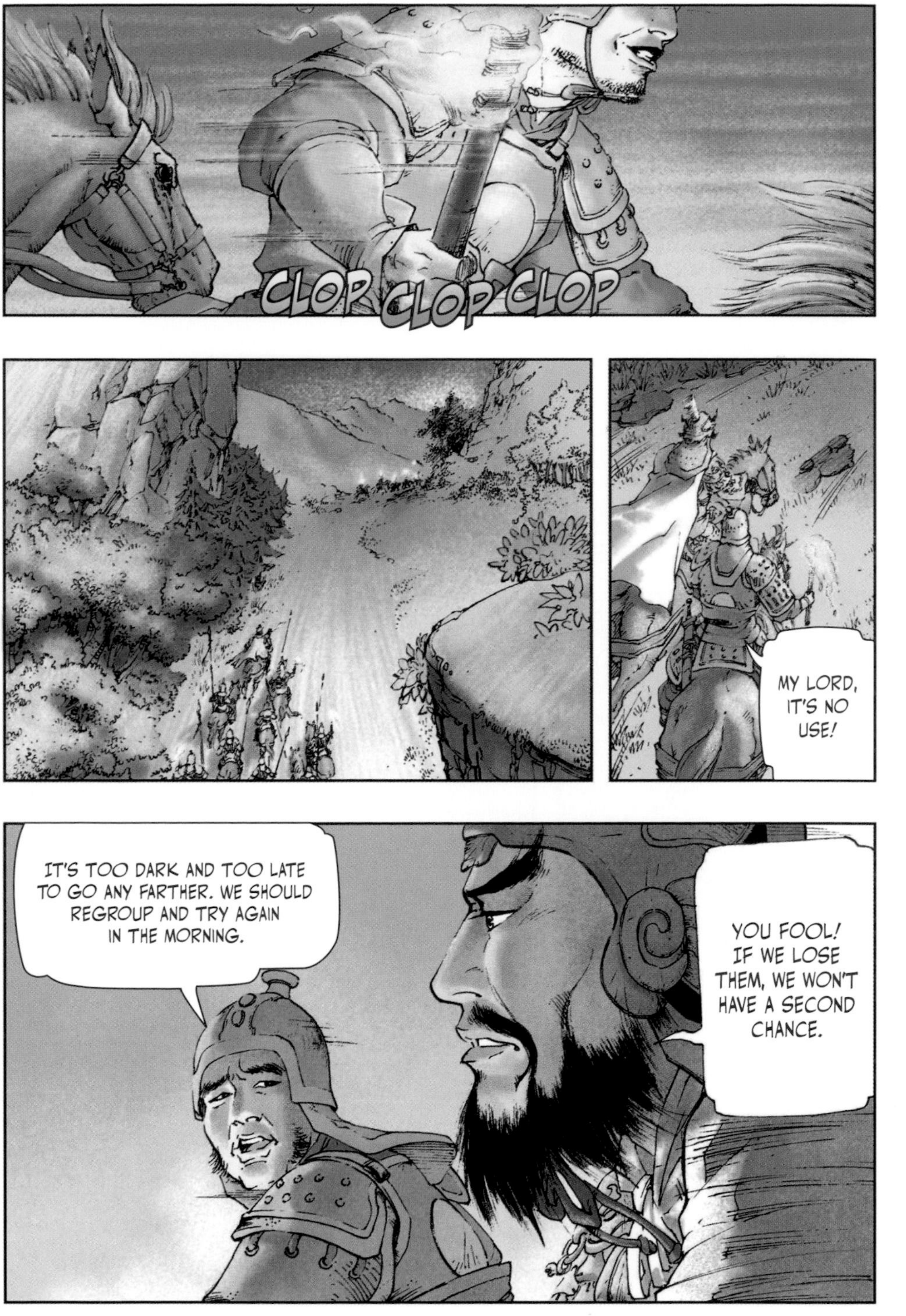
CLOP CLOP CLOP
MY LORD, IT'S NO USE!
IT'S TOO DARK AND TOO LATE TO GO ANY FARTHER. WE SHOULD REGROUP AND TRY AGAIN IN THE MORNING.
YOU FOOL! IF WE LOSE THEM, WE WON'T HAVE A SECOND CHANCE.

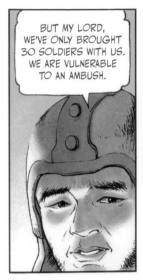

BUT MY LORD, WE'VE ONLY BROUGHT 30 SOLDIERS WITH US. WE ARE VULNERABLE TO AN AMBUSH.

HYA!

THOMP THOMP THOMP

THOMP THOMP THOMP

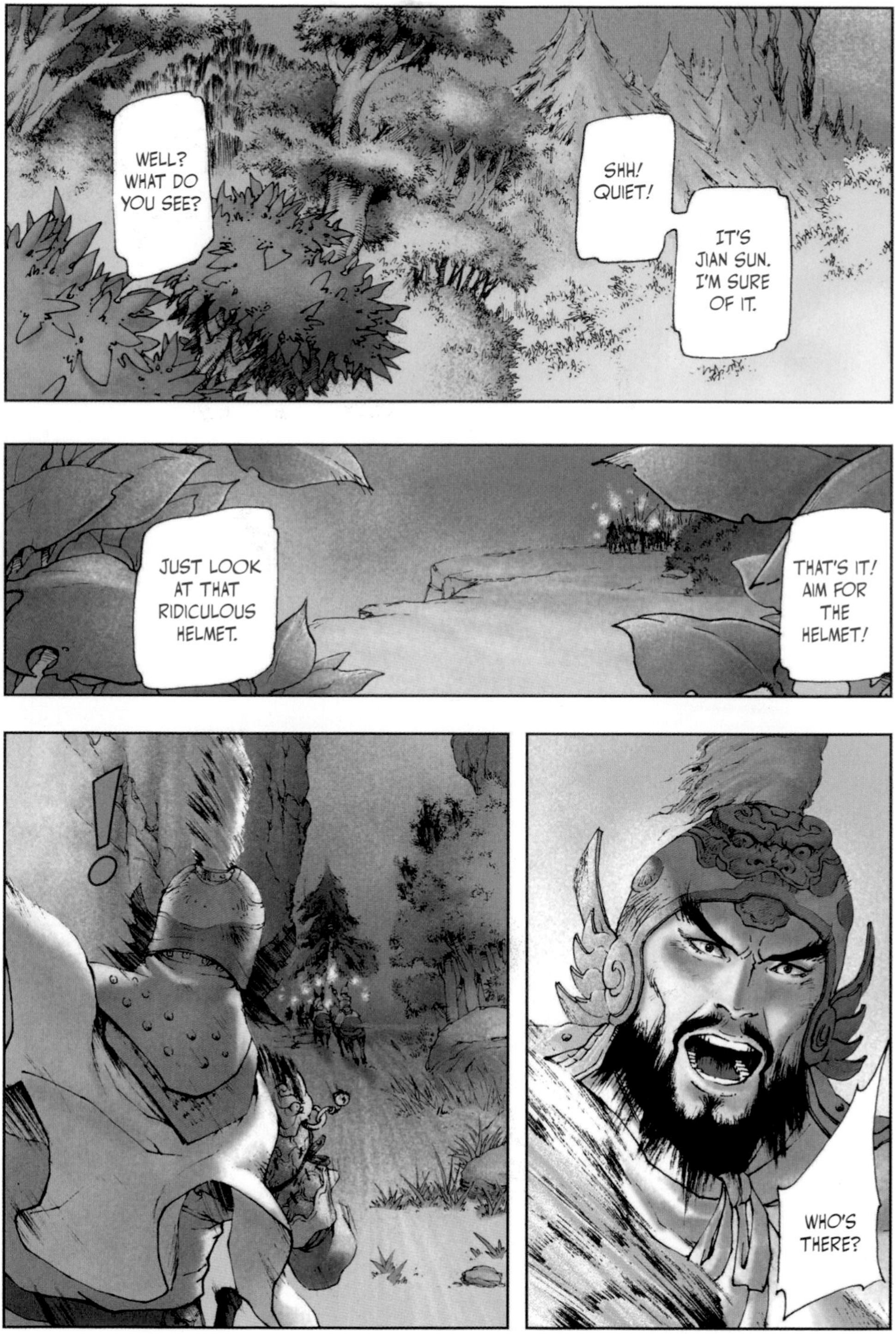
WELL? WHAT DO YOU SEE?
SHH! QUIET!
IT'S JIAN SUN. I'M SURE OF IT.
JUST LOOK AT THAT RIDICULOUS HELMET.
THAT'S IT! AIM FOR THE HELMET!
!
WHO'S THERE?

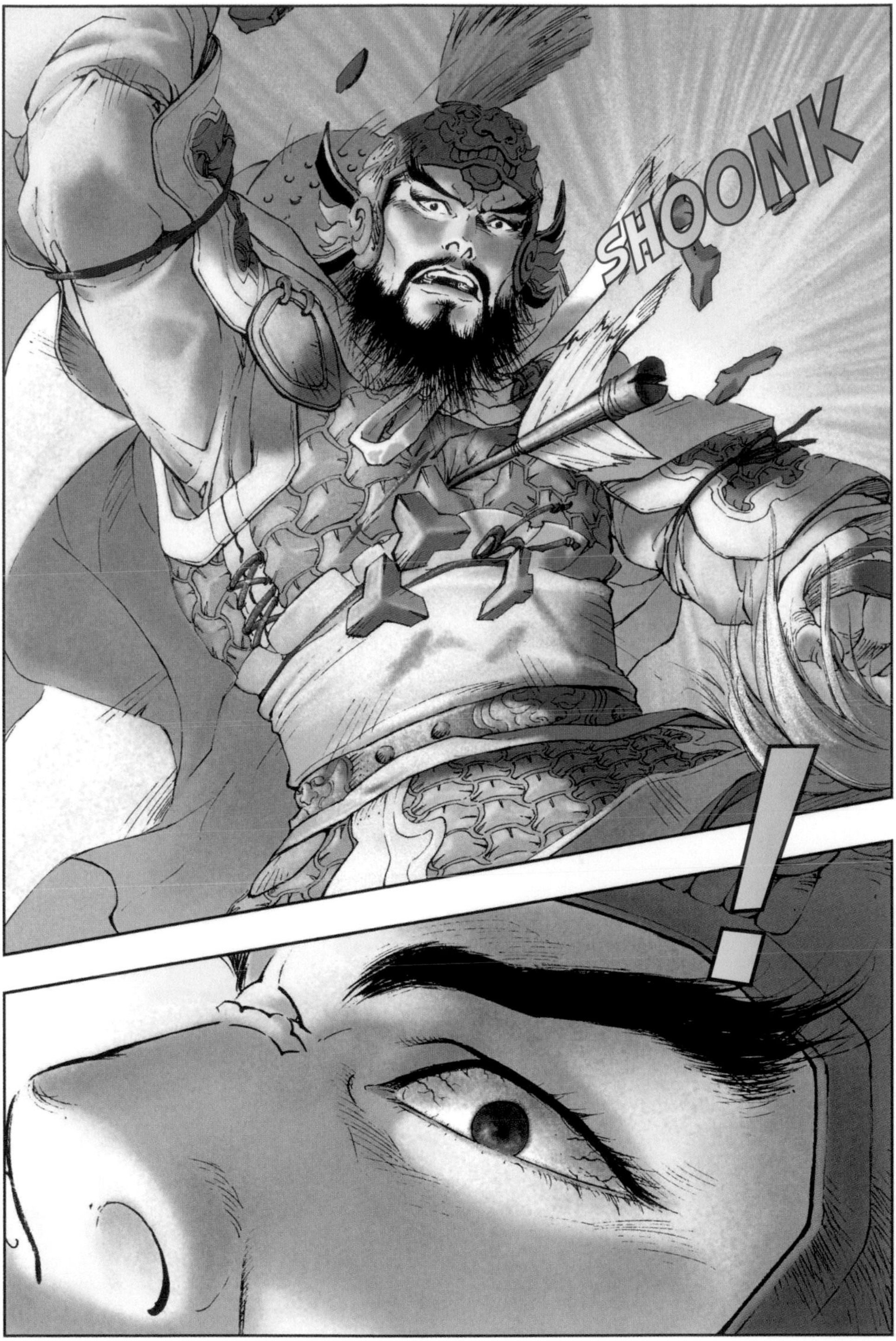
SHOONK
!

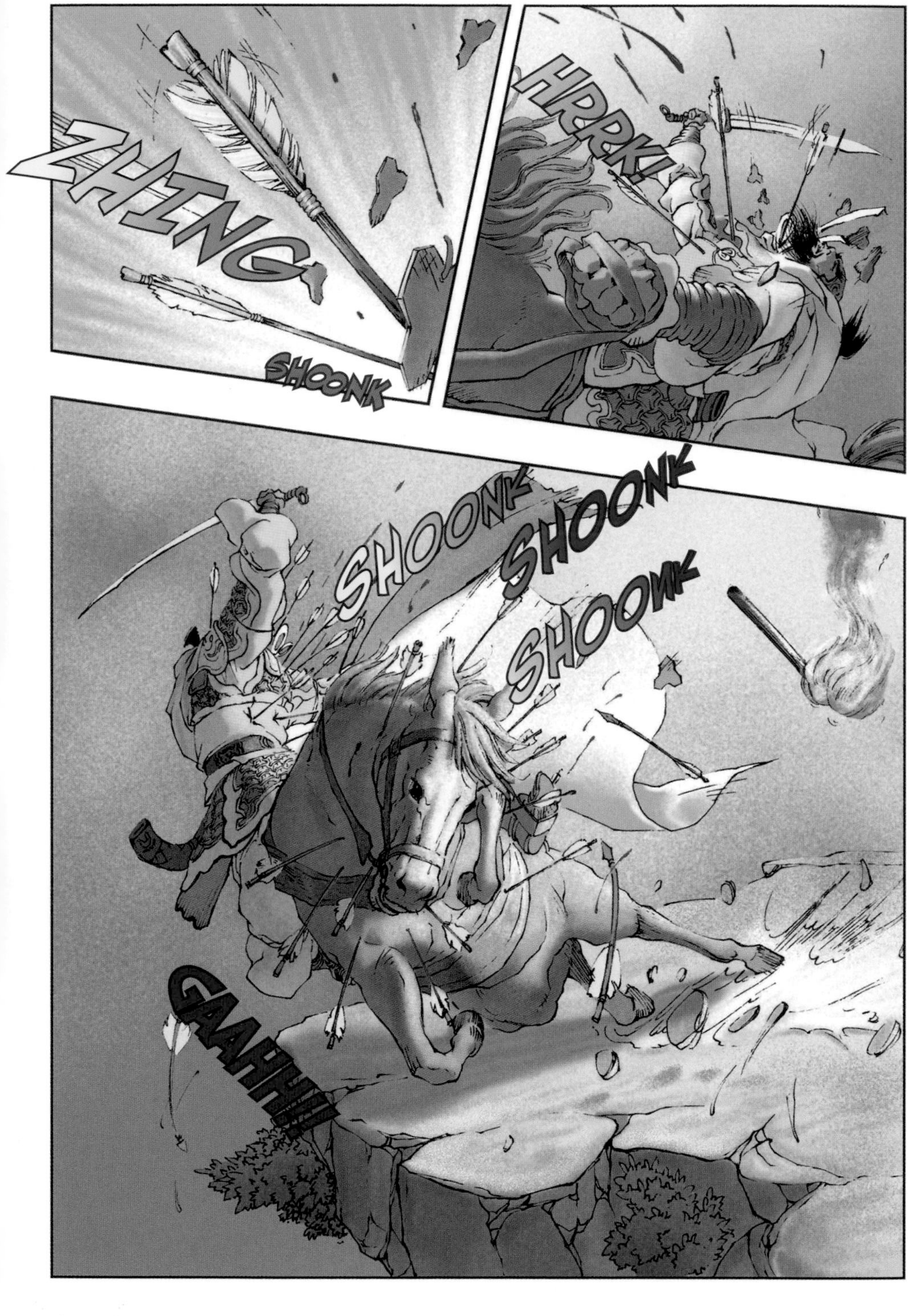
ZHING
SHOONK
HRRK!
SHOONK
SHOONK
SHOONK
GAAHH!!

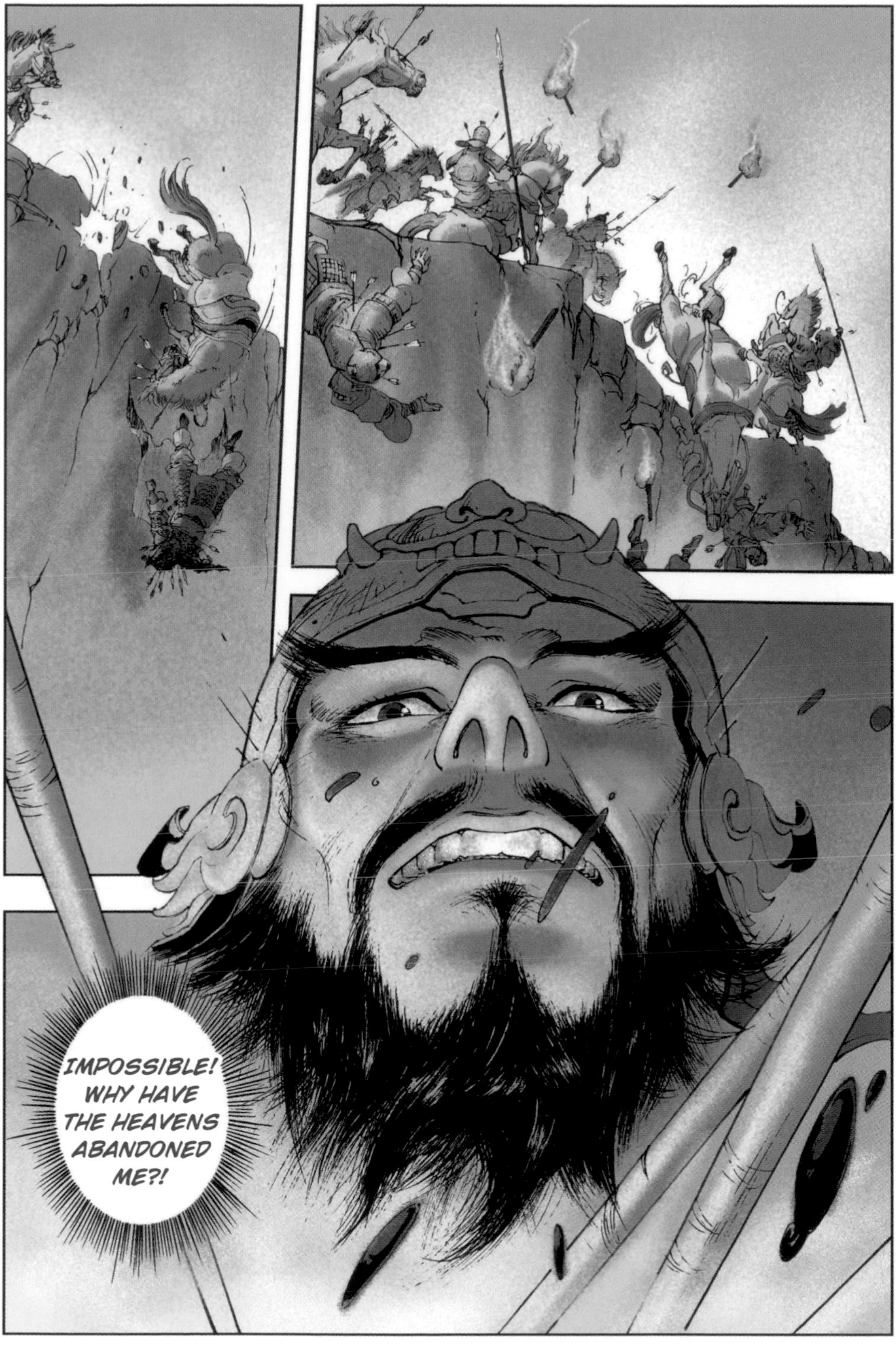
IMPOSSIBLE! WHY HAVE THE HEAVENS ABANDONED ME?!

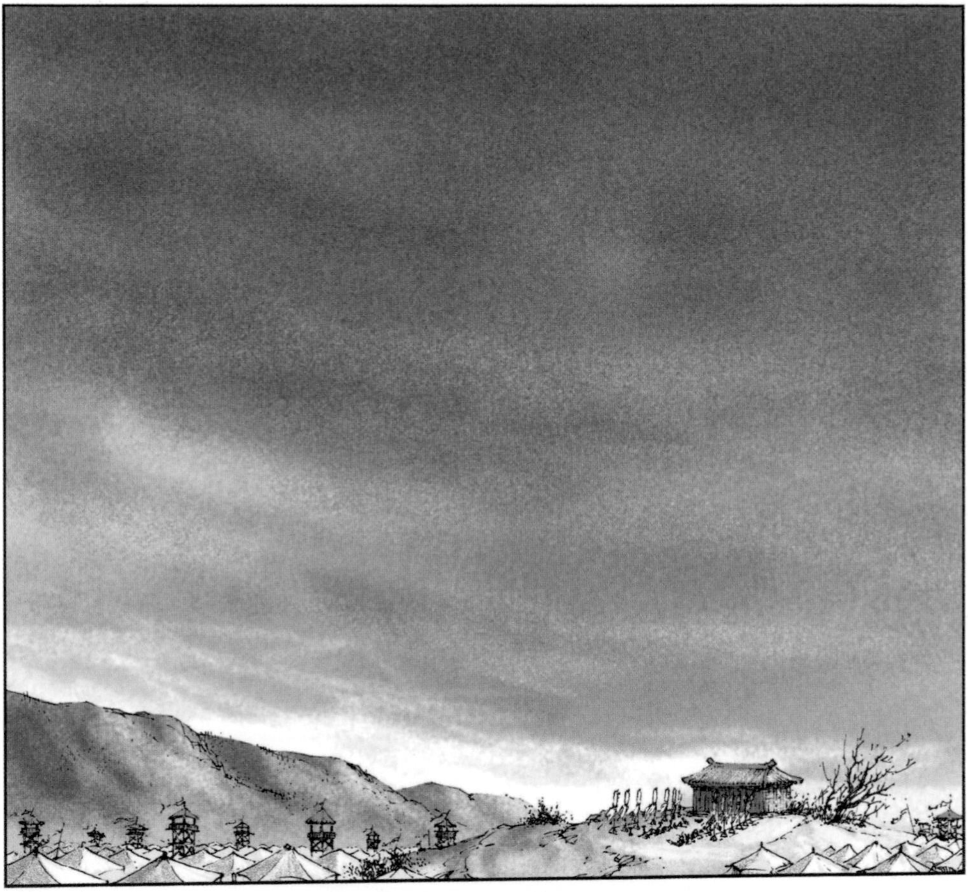

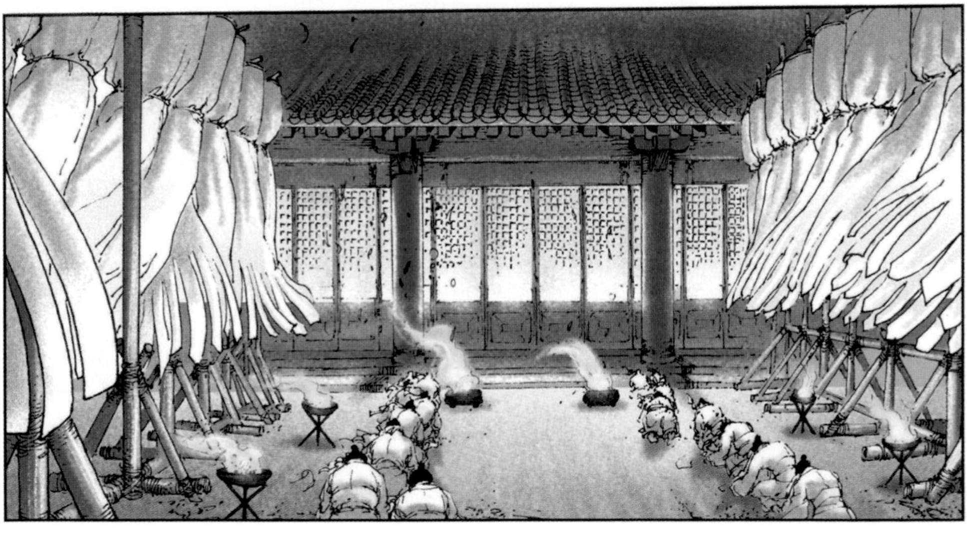

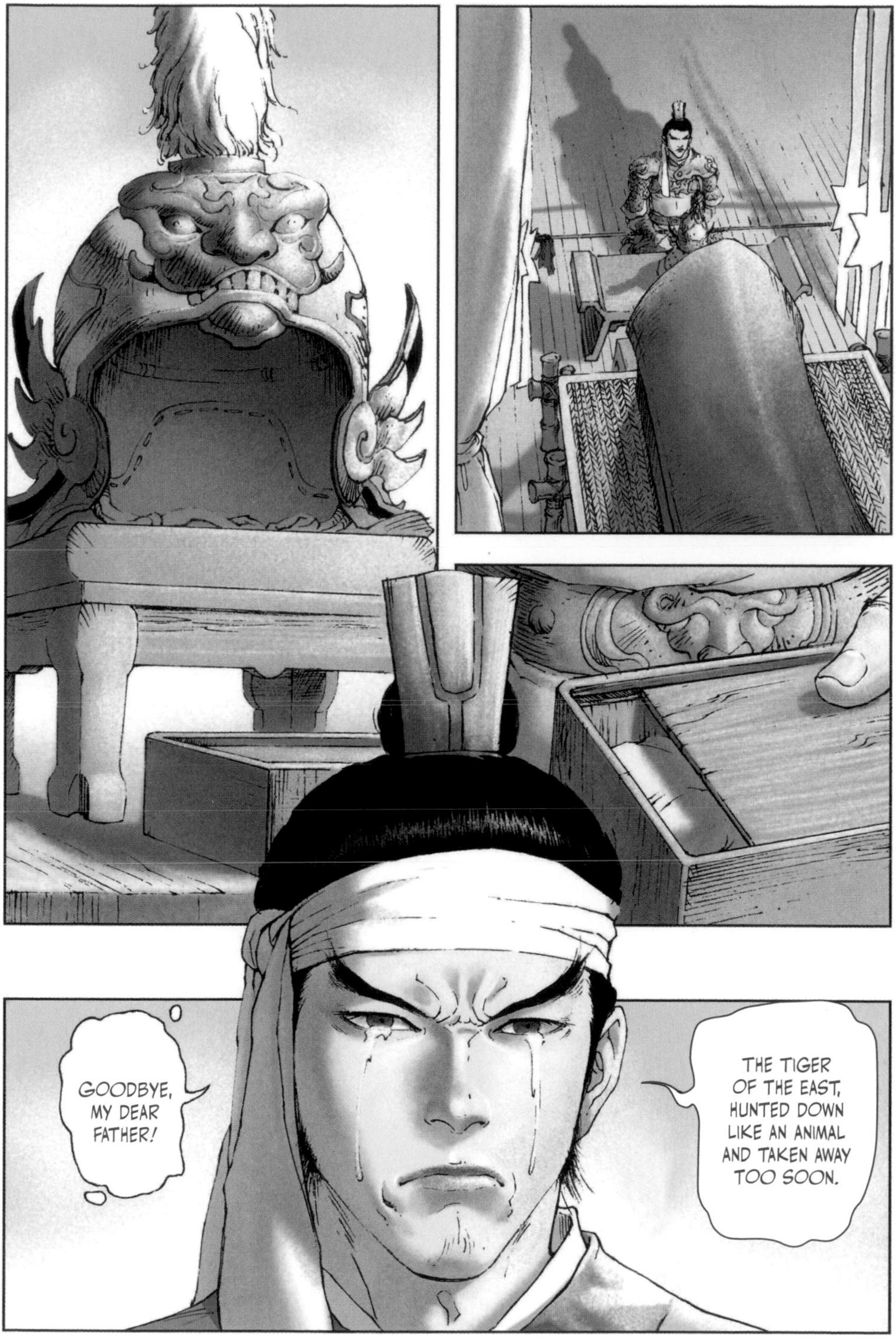
THE TIGER OF THE EAST, HUNTED DOWN LIKE AN ANIMAL AND TAKEN AWAY TOO SOON.
GOODBYE, MY DEAR FATHER!

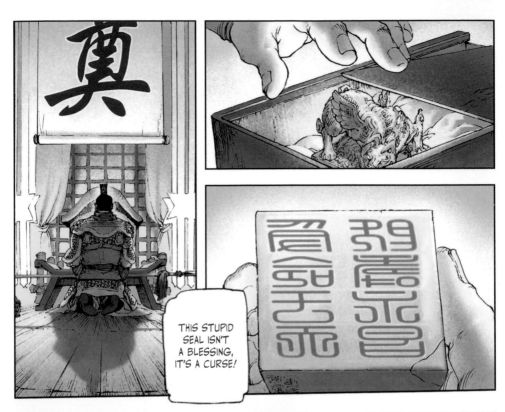

THIS STUPID SEAL ISN'T A BLESSING, IT'S A CURSE!

NOT TO WORRY, FATHER. I WILL BEAR YOUR BURDENS, HOWEVER GREAT, AND RULE IN A WAY THAT WILL MAKE YOU PROUD!

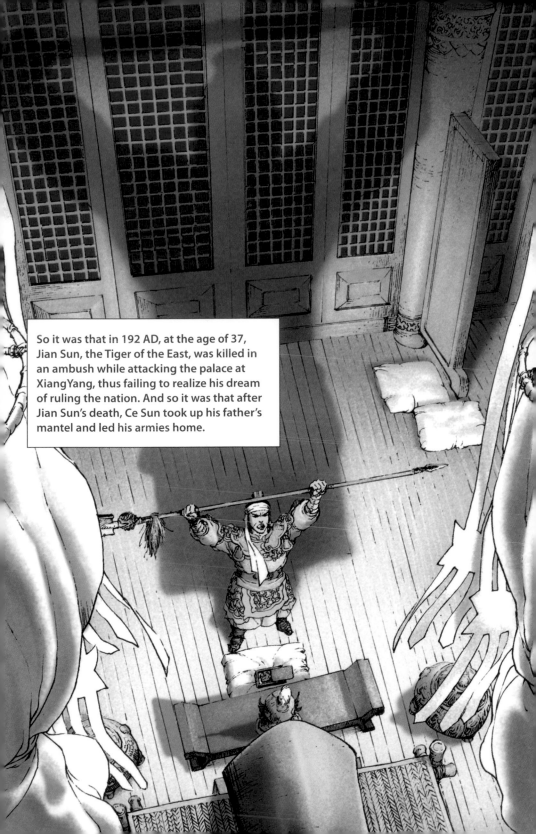

So it was that in 192 AD, at the age of 37, Jian Sun, the Tiger of the East, was killed in an ambush while attacking the palace at XiangYang, thus failing to realize his dream of ruling the nation. And so it was that after Jian Sun's death, Ce Sun took up his father's mantel and led his armies home.

Chapter 3

The Family Plot AD 192

Summary

When he learns that Jian Sun has died, Zhuo Dong is delighted and decides to celebrate by building himself a new palace and indulging in gluttony like never before. This behavior raises the suspicions of his advisors, but he maintains control by terrorizing them with violence. After a demonstration of Zhuo Dong's power results in murder, a minister named Yun Wang pledges to defeat him. Yun Wang conspires to pit Zhuo Dong against his most loyal general, Bu Lu, in a deadly contest to win the heart of a unique young woman – Yun Wang's daughter, Diao Chan.

Yun Wang's Plan

When Yun Wang pledges to destroy Zhuo Dong, he hatches a plan that is common in both classical literature and modern warfare. Using his daughter as bait, Yun Wang seeks to compromise Zhuo Dong long enough to defeat him. This strategy of having an ally infiltrate an enemy's inner circle most often intends in either blackmail or murder. But Yun Wang alters the strategy slightly; instead of using his daughter to kill Zhuo Dong, he uses her to lure Bu Lu, Zhuo Dong's most trusted and deadly ally, into a deadly contest for the young woman's affection.

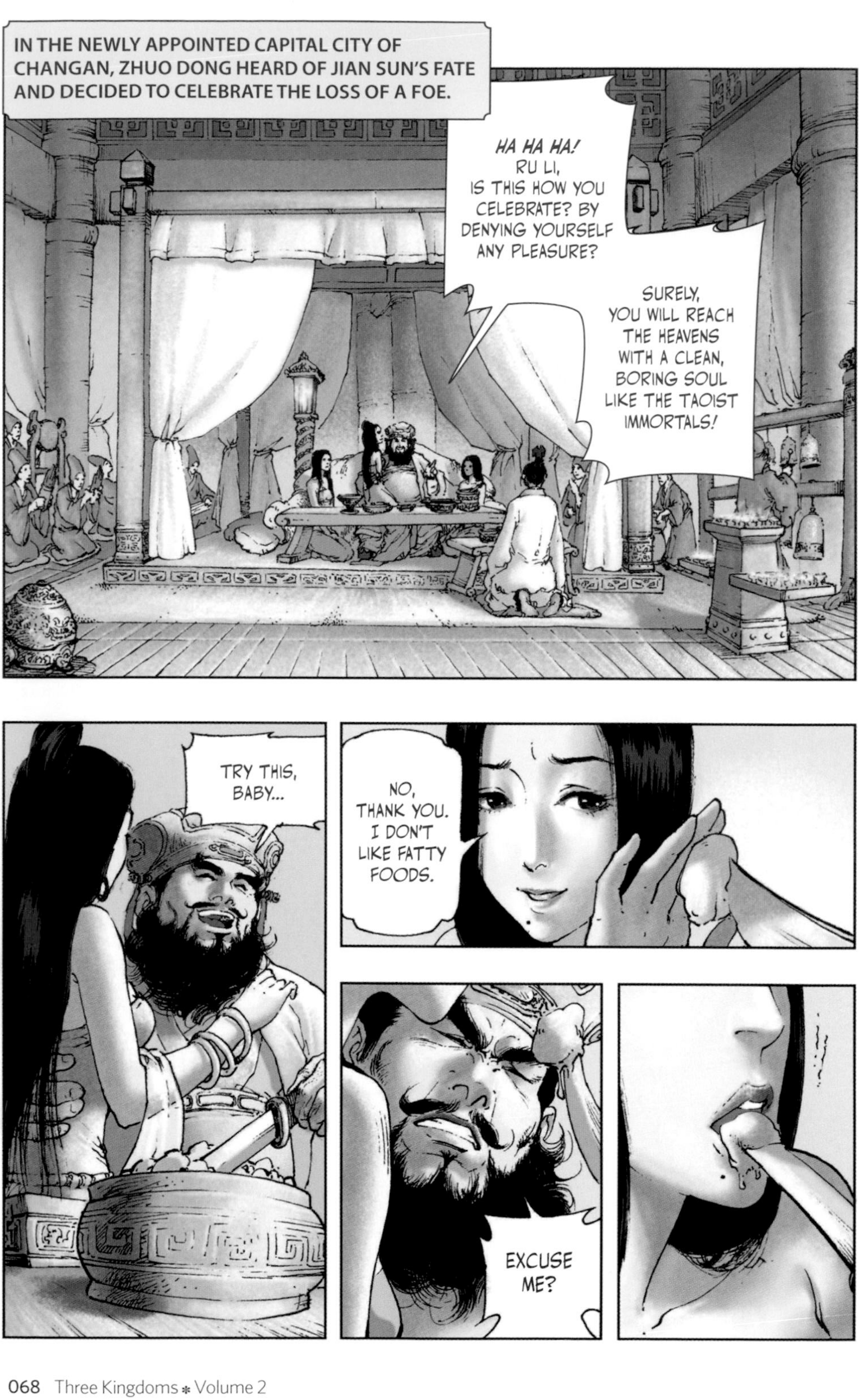
IN THE NEWLY APPOINTED CAPITAL CITY OF CHANGAN, ZHUO DONG HEARD OF JIAN SUN'S FATE AND DECIDED TO CELEBRATE THE LOSS OF A FOE.
HA HA HA! RU LI, IS THIS HOW YOU CELEBRATE? BY DENYING YOURSELF ANY PLEASURE?
SURELY, YOU WILL REACH THE HEAVENS WITH A CLEAN, BORING SOUL LIKE THE TAOIST IMMORTALS!
TRY THIS, BABY...
NO, THANK YOU. I DON'T LIKE FATTY FOODS.
EXCUSE ME?

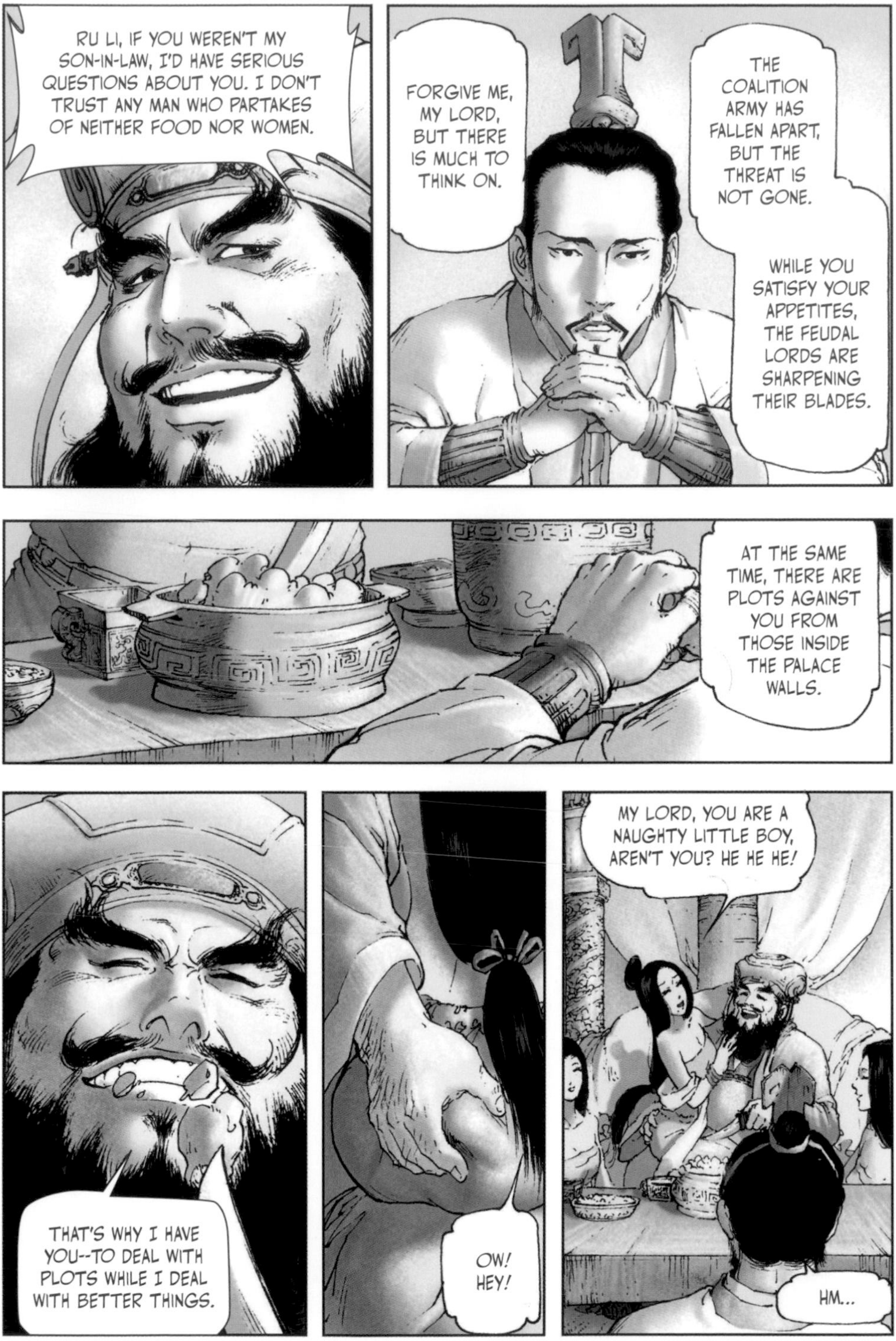
RU LI, IF YOU WEREN'T MY SON-IN-LAW, I'D HAVE SERIOUS QUESTIONS ABOUT YOU. I DON'T TRUST ANY MAN WHO PARTAKES OF NEITHER FOOD NOR WOMEN.
FORGIVE ME, MY LORD, BUT THERE IS MUCH TO THINK ON.
THE COALITION ARMY HAS FALLEN APART, BUT THE THREAT IS NOT GONE.
WHILE YOU SATISFY YOUR APPETITES, THE FEUDAL LORDS ARE SHARPENING THEIR BLADES.
AT THE SAME TIME, THERE ARE PLOTS AGAINST YOU FROM THOSE INSIDE THE PALACE WALLS.
THAT'S WHY I HAVE YOU--TO DEAL WITH PLOTS WHILE I DEAL WITH BETTER THINGS.
OW! HEY!
MY LORD, YOU ARE A NAUGHTY LITTLE BOY, AREN'T YOU? HE HE HE!
HM...

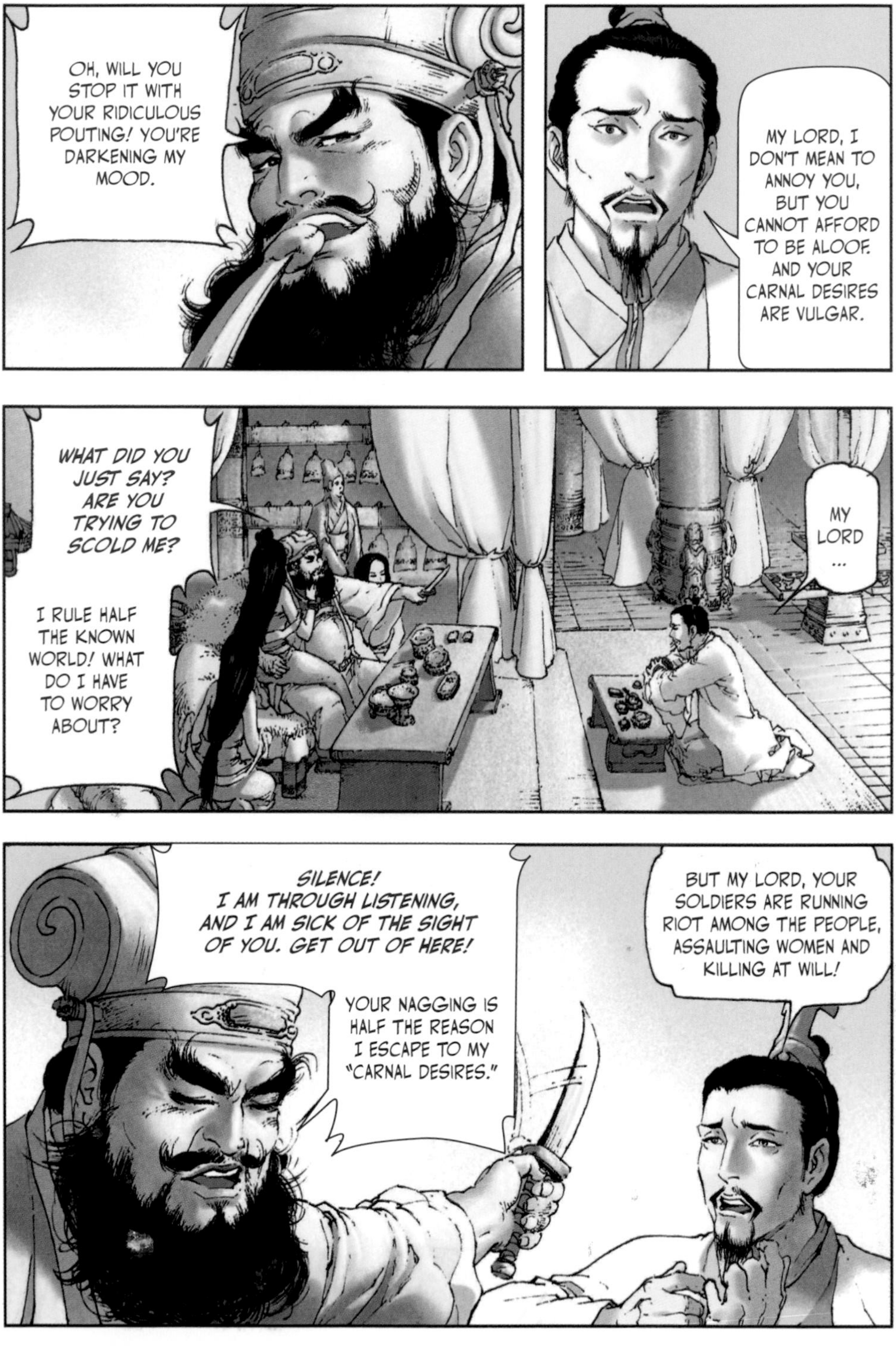
OH, WILL YOU STOP IT WITH YOUR RIDICULOUS POUTING! YOU'RE DARKENING MY MOOD.
MY LORD, I DON'T MEAN TO ANNOY YOU, BUT YOU CANNOT AFFORD TO BE ALOOF. AND YOUR CARNAL DESIRES ARE VULGAR.
WHAT DID YOU JUST SAY? ARE YOU TRYING TO SCOLD ME?
I RULE HALF THE KNOWN WORLD! WHAT DO I HAVE TO WORRY ABOUT?
MY LORD ...
BUT MY LORD, YOUR SOLDIERS ARE RUNNING RIOT AMONG THE PEOPLE, ASSAULTING WOMEN AND KILLING AT WILL!
SILENCE! I AM THROUGH LISTENING, AND I AM SICK OF THE SIGHT OF YOU. GET OUT OF HERE!
YOUR NAGGING IS HALF THE REASON I ESCAPE TO MY "CARNAL DESIRES."

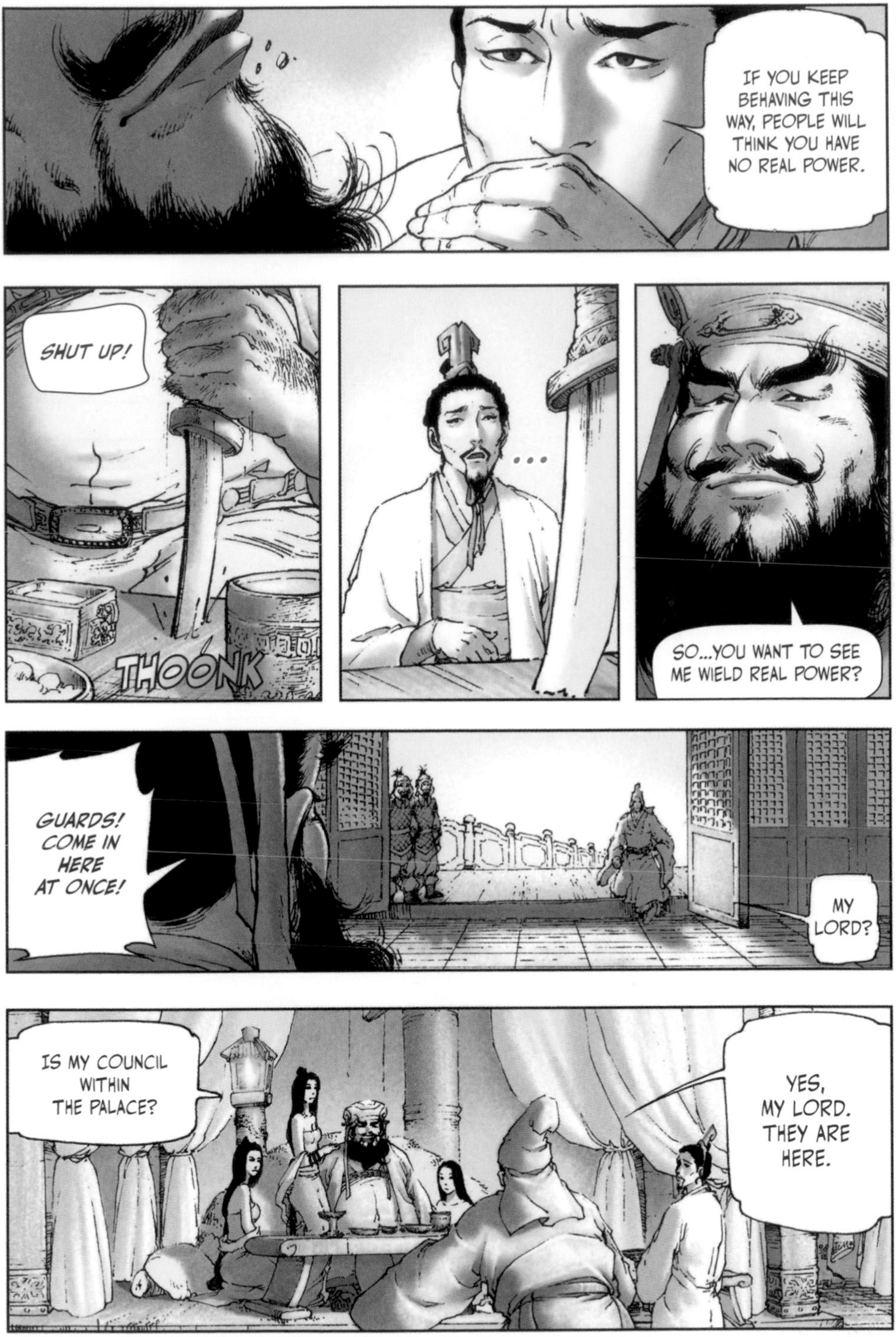
IF YOU KEEP BEHAVING THIS WAY, PEOPLE WILL THINK YOU HAVE NO REAL POWER.
SHUT UP!
THOONK
...
SO...YOU WANT TO SEE ME WIELD REAL POWER?
GUARDS! COME IN HERE AT ONCE!
MY LORD?
IS MY COUNCIL WITHIN THE PALACE?
YES, MY LORD. THEY ARE HERE.

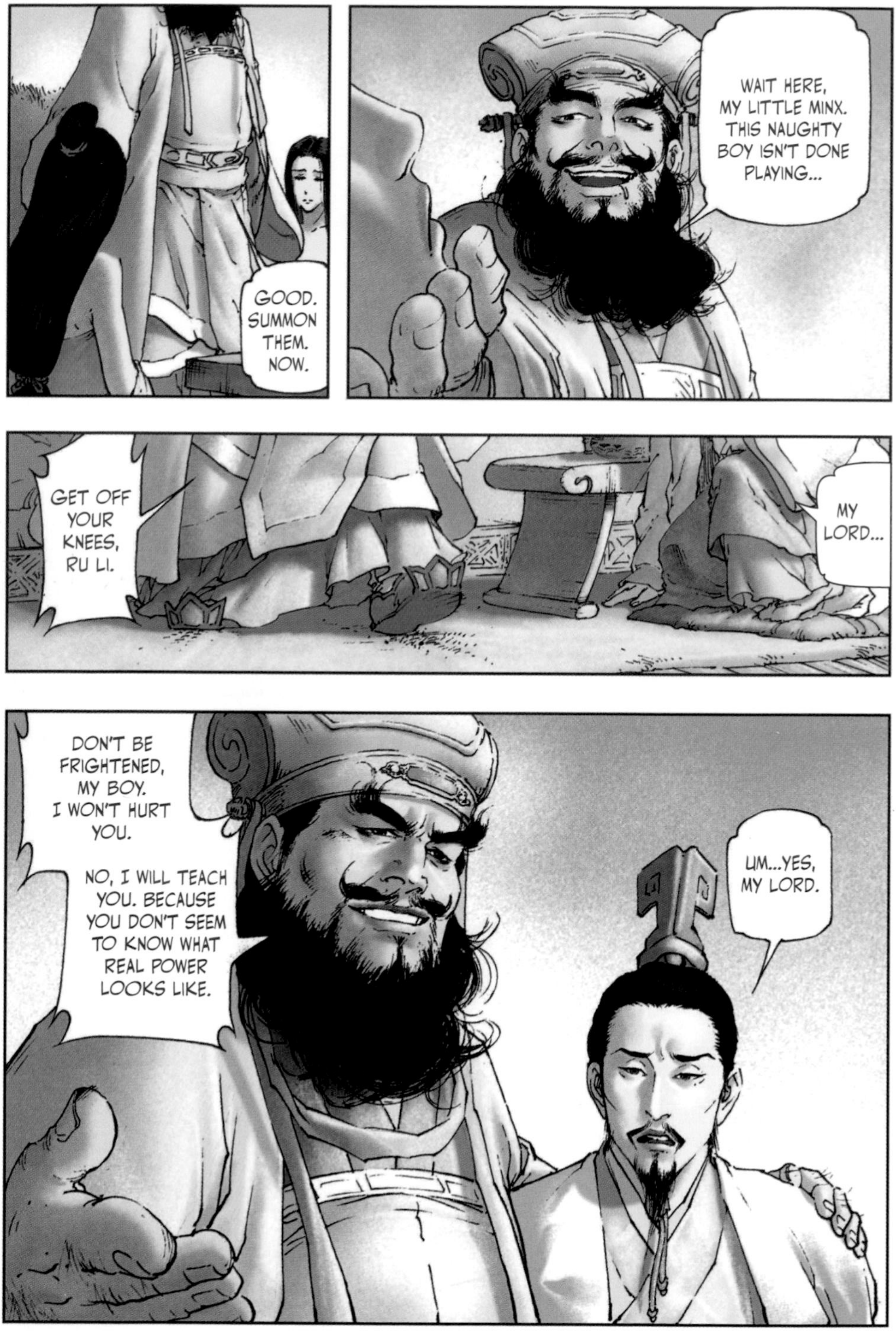
GOOD. SUMMON THEM. NOW.
WAIT HERE, MY LITTLE MINX. THIS NAUGHTY BOY ISN'T DONE PLAYING...
GET OFF YOUR KNEES, RU LI.
MY LORD...
DON'T BE FRIGHTENED, MY BOY. I WON'T HURT YOU.
NO, I WILL TEACH YOU. BECAUSE YOU DON'T SEEM TO KNOW WHAT REAL POWER LOOKS LIKE.
UM...YES, MY LORD.

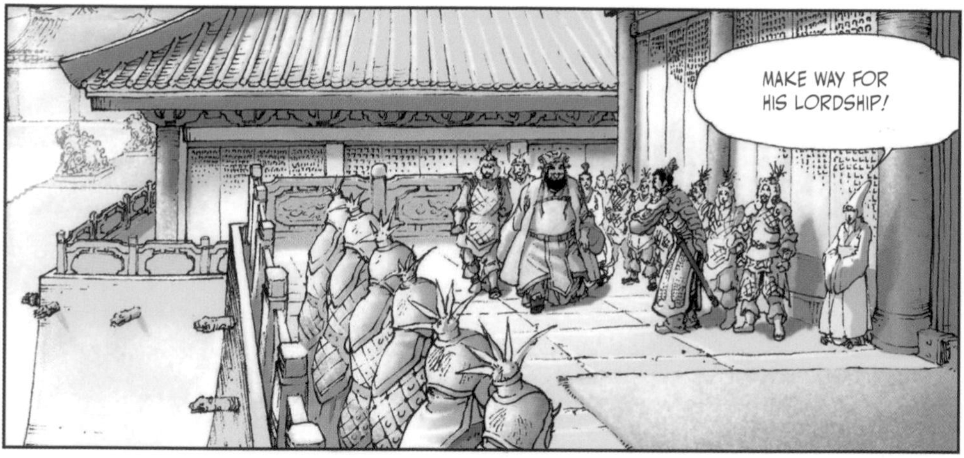
MAKE WAY FOR
HIS LORDSHIP!

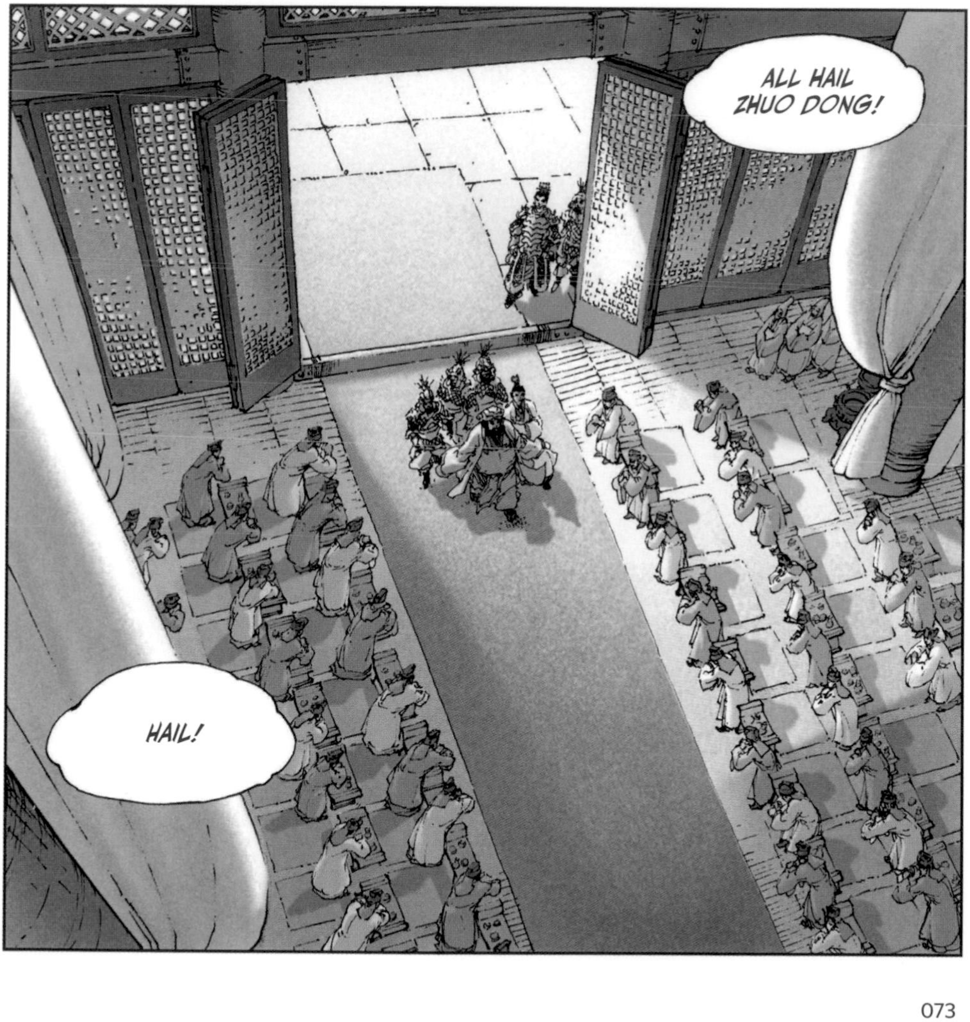
ALL HAIL
ZHUO DONG!
HAIL!

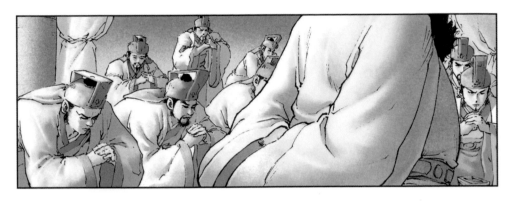

ARE ALL MEMBERS OF THE COUNCIL PRESENT?

GOOD! A TOAST, THEN...

TO REAL POWER!

FWISH

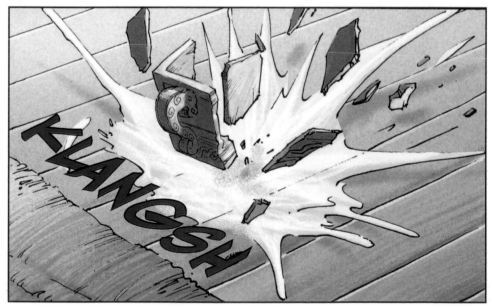

KLANGSH

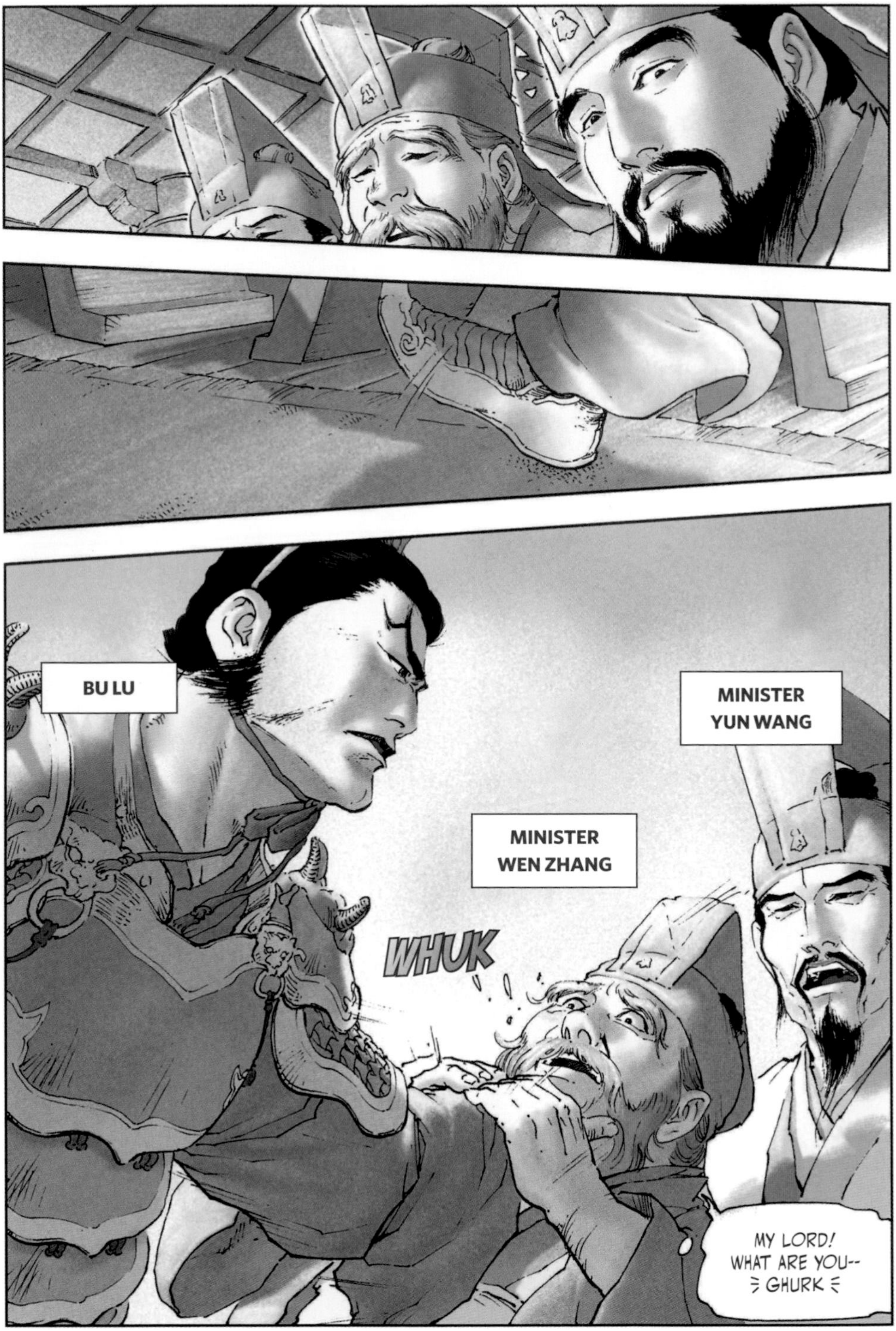
BU LU
MINISTER YUN WANG
MINISTER WEN ZHANG
WHUK
MY LORD! WHAT ARE YOU-- ≡ GHURK ≡

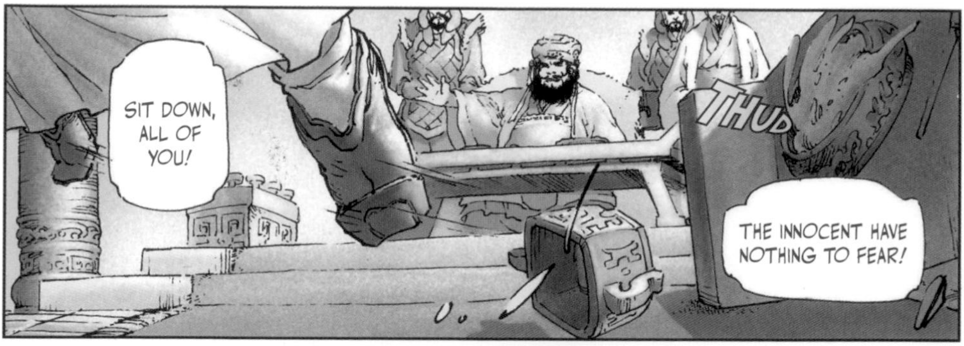
SIT DOWN, ALL OF YOU!
THUD
THE INNOCENT HAVE NOTHING TO FEAR!

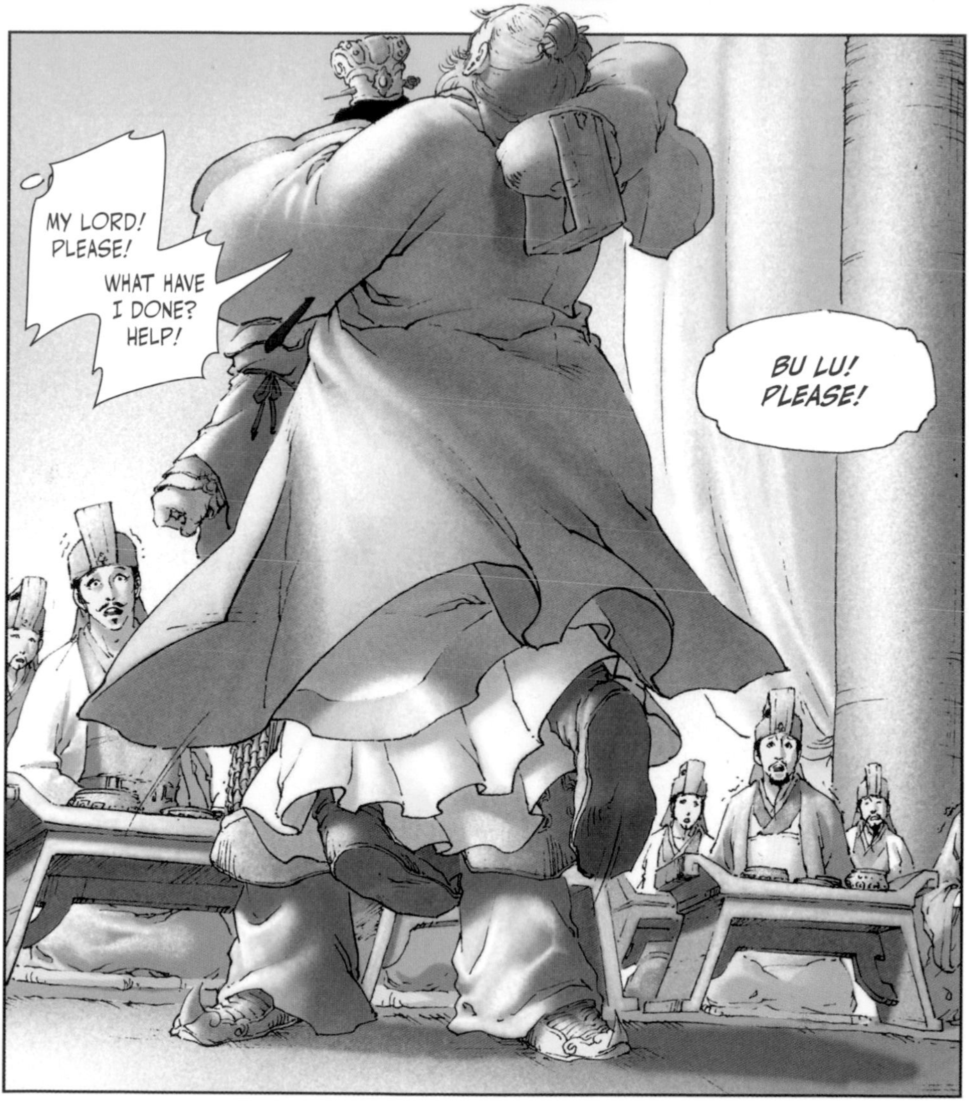
MY LORD! PLEASE!
WHAT HAVE I DONE? HELP!
BU LU! PLEASE!

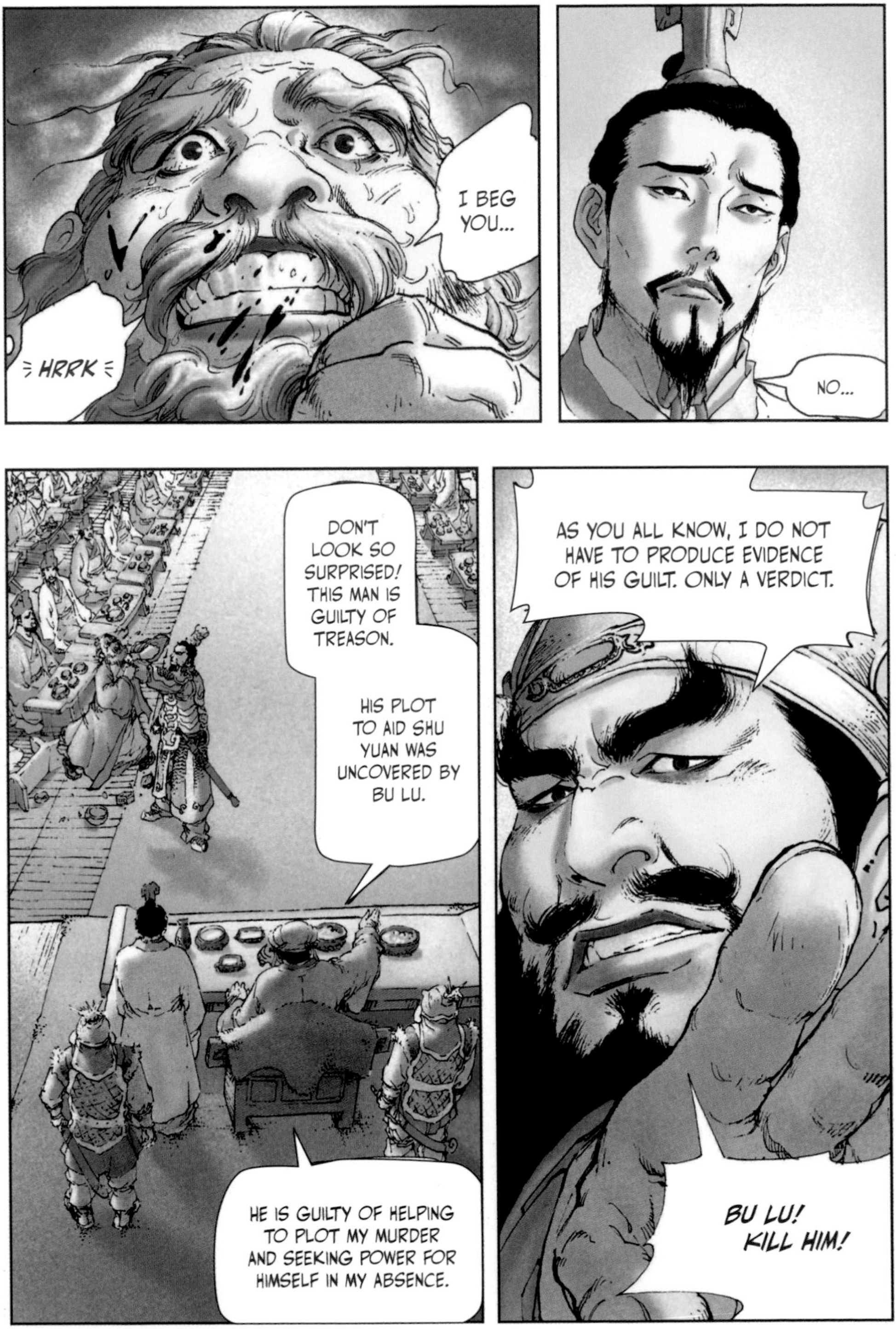
I BEG YOU...
HRRK
NO...
DON'T LOOK SO SURPRISED! THIS MAN IS GUILTY OF TREASON.
HIS PLOT TO AID SHU YUAN WAS UNCOVERED BY BU LU.
HE IS GUILTY OF HELPING TO PLOT MY MURDER AND SEEKING POWER FOR HIMSELF IN MY ABSENCE.
AS YOU ALL KNOW, I DO NOT HAVE TO PRODUCE EVIDENCE OF HIS GUILT. ONLY A VERDICT.
BU LU! KILL HIM!

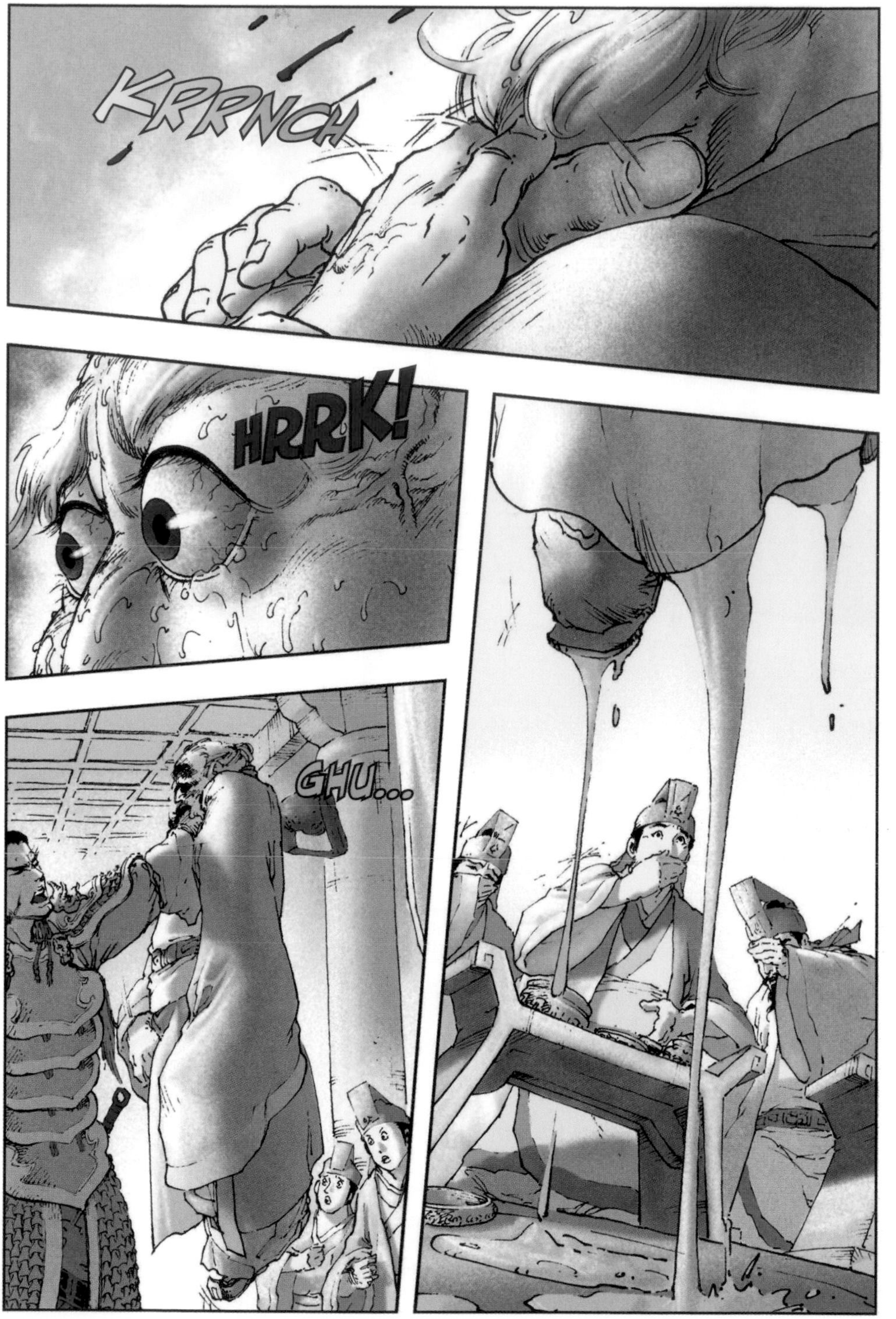
KRRNCH
HRRK!
GHU...

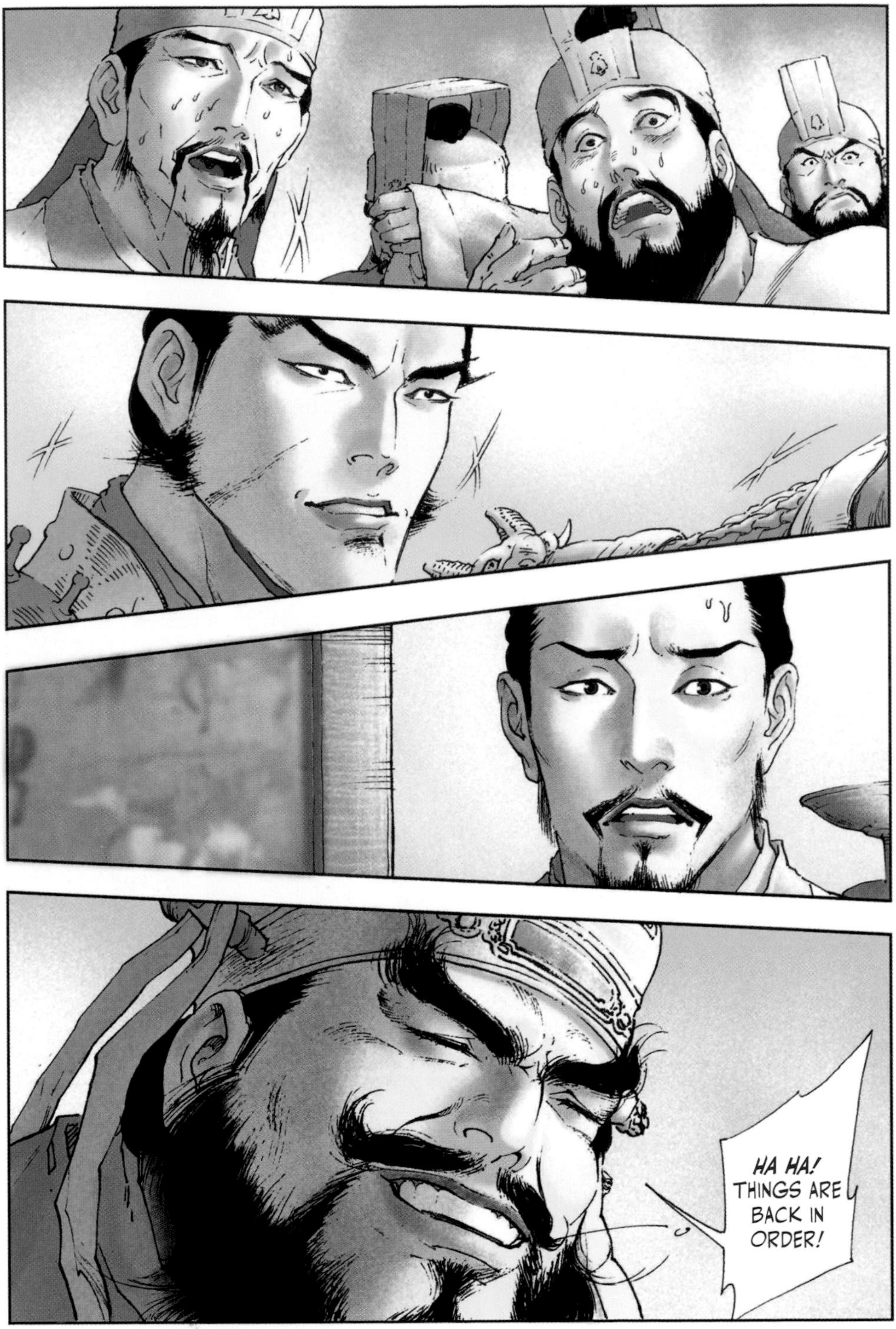
HA HA! THINGS ARE BACK IN ORDER!

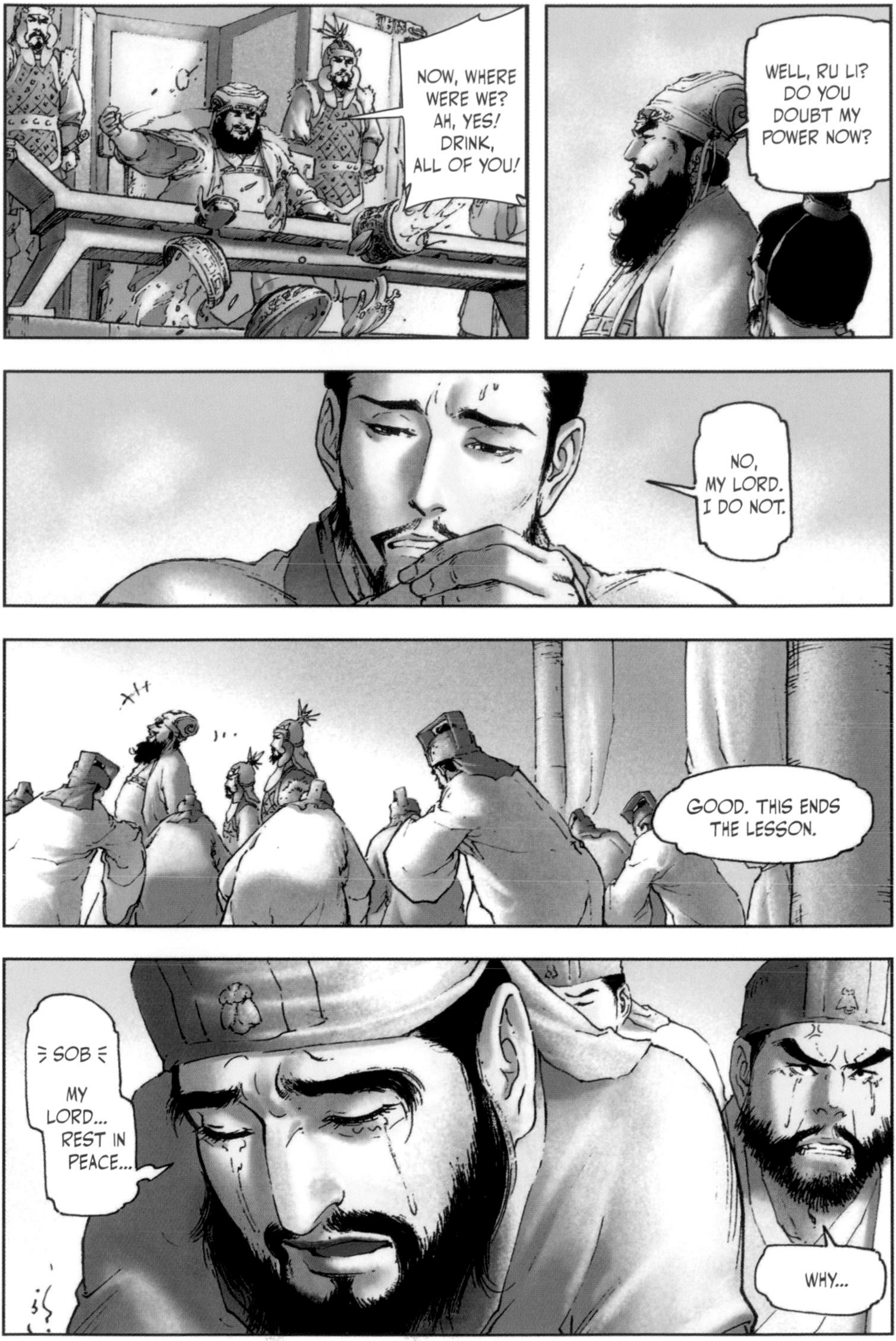
NOW, WHERE WERE WE? AH, YES! DRINK, ALL OF YOU!
WELL, RU LI? DO YOU DOUBT MY POWER NOW?
NO, MY LORD. I DO NOT.
GOOD. THIS ENDS THE LESSON.
SOB
MY LORD... REST IN PEACE...
WHY...

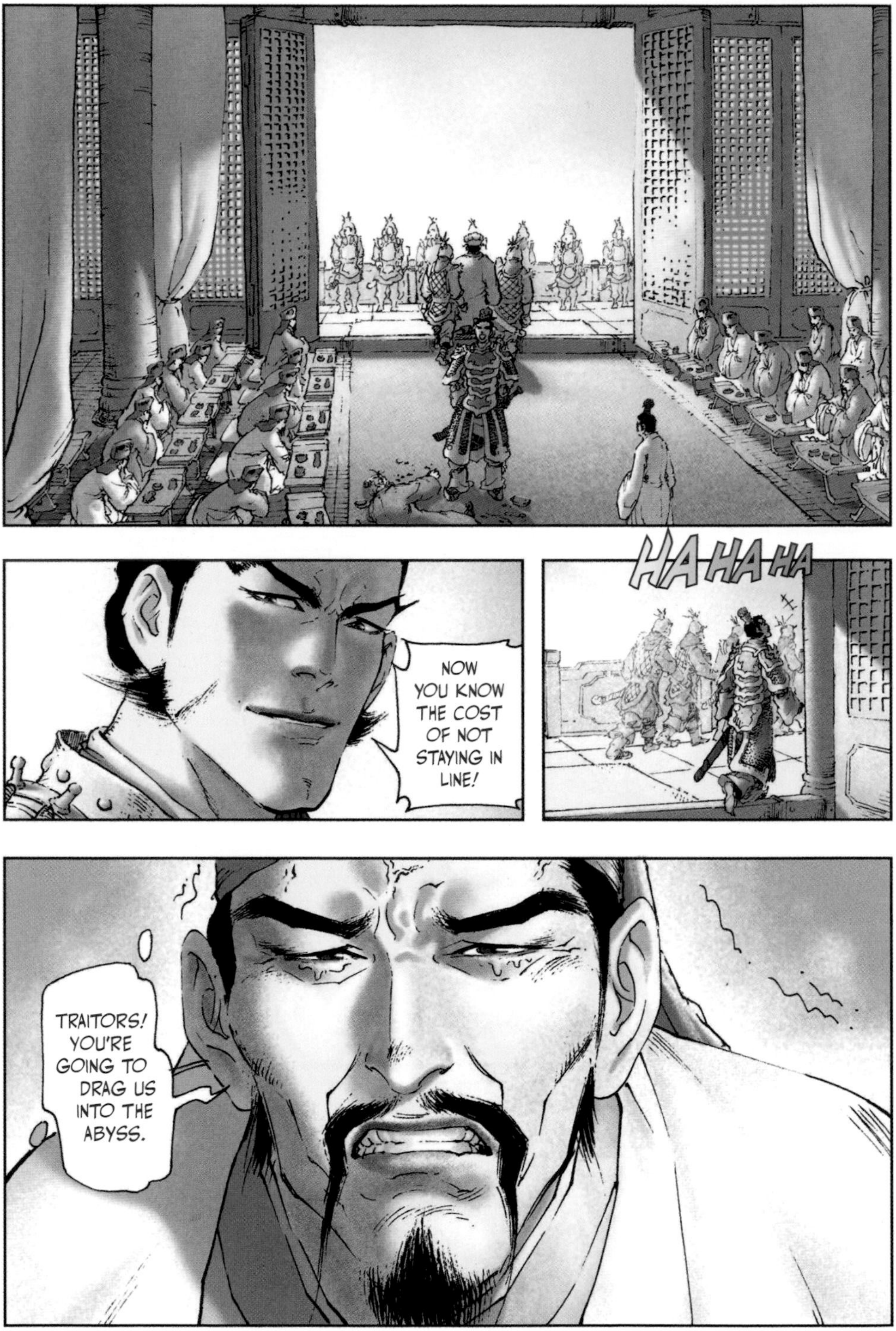
NOW YOU KNOW THE COST OF NOT STAYING IN LINE!
HA HA HA
TRAITORS! YOU'RE GOING TO DRAG US INTO THE ABYSS.

ZHUO DONG

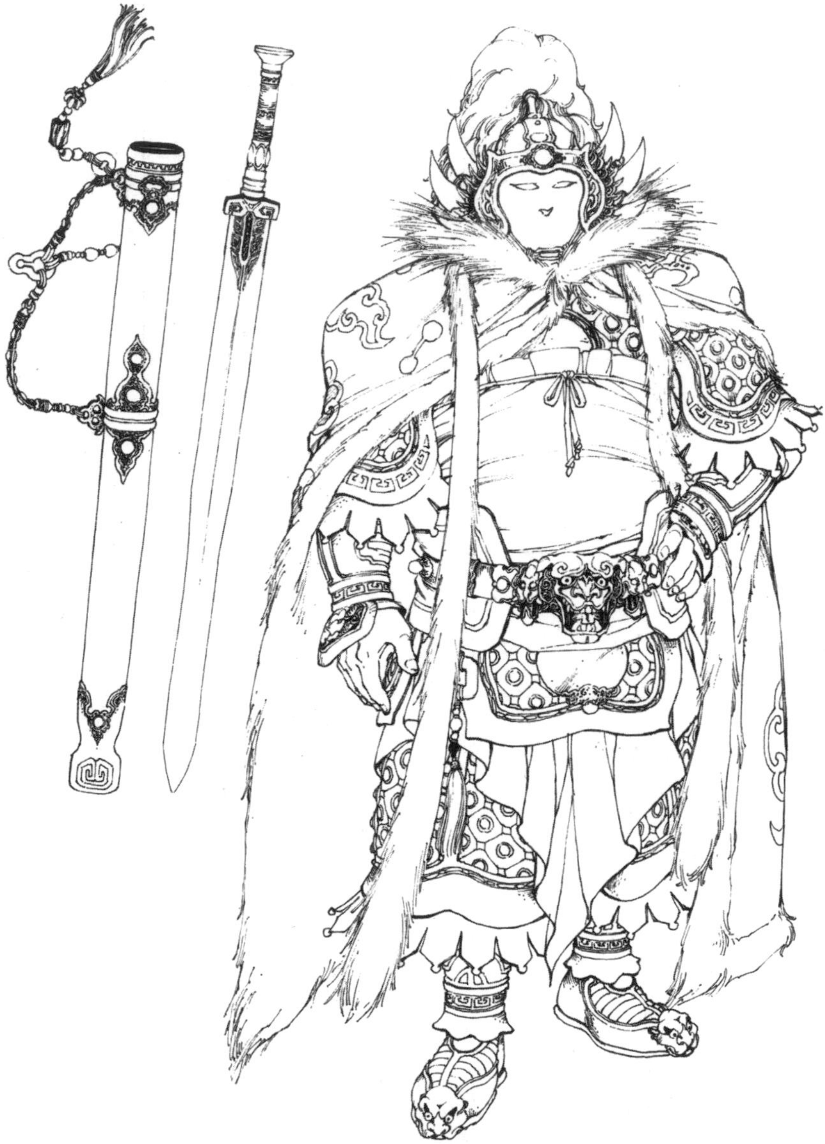

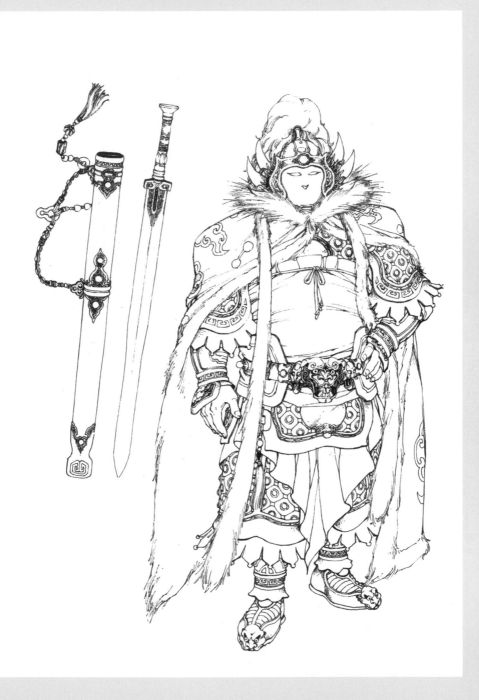

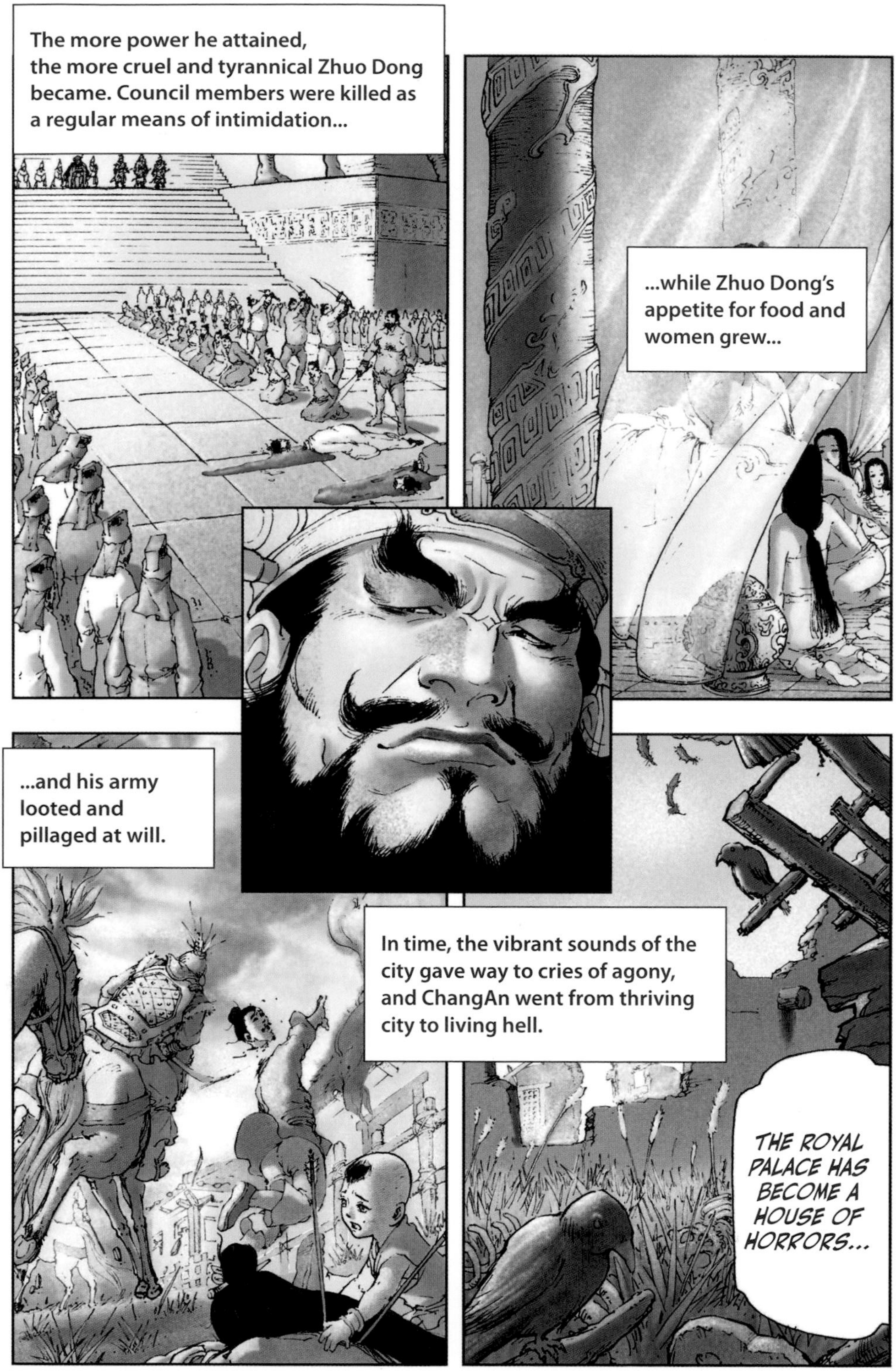
The more power he attained, the more cruel and tyrannical Zhuo Dong became. Council members were killed as a regular means of intimidation...
...while Zhuo Dong's appetite for food and women grew...
...and his army looted and pillaged at will.
In time, the vibrant sounds of the city gave way to cries of agony, and ChangAn went from thriving city to living hell.
THE ROYAL PALACE HAS BECOME A HOUSE OF HORRORS...

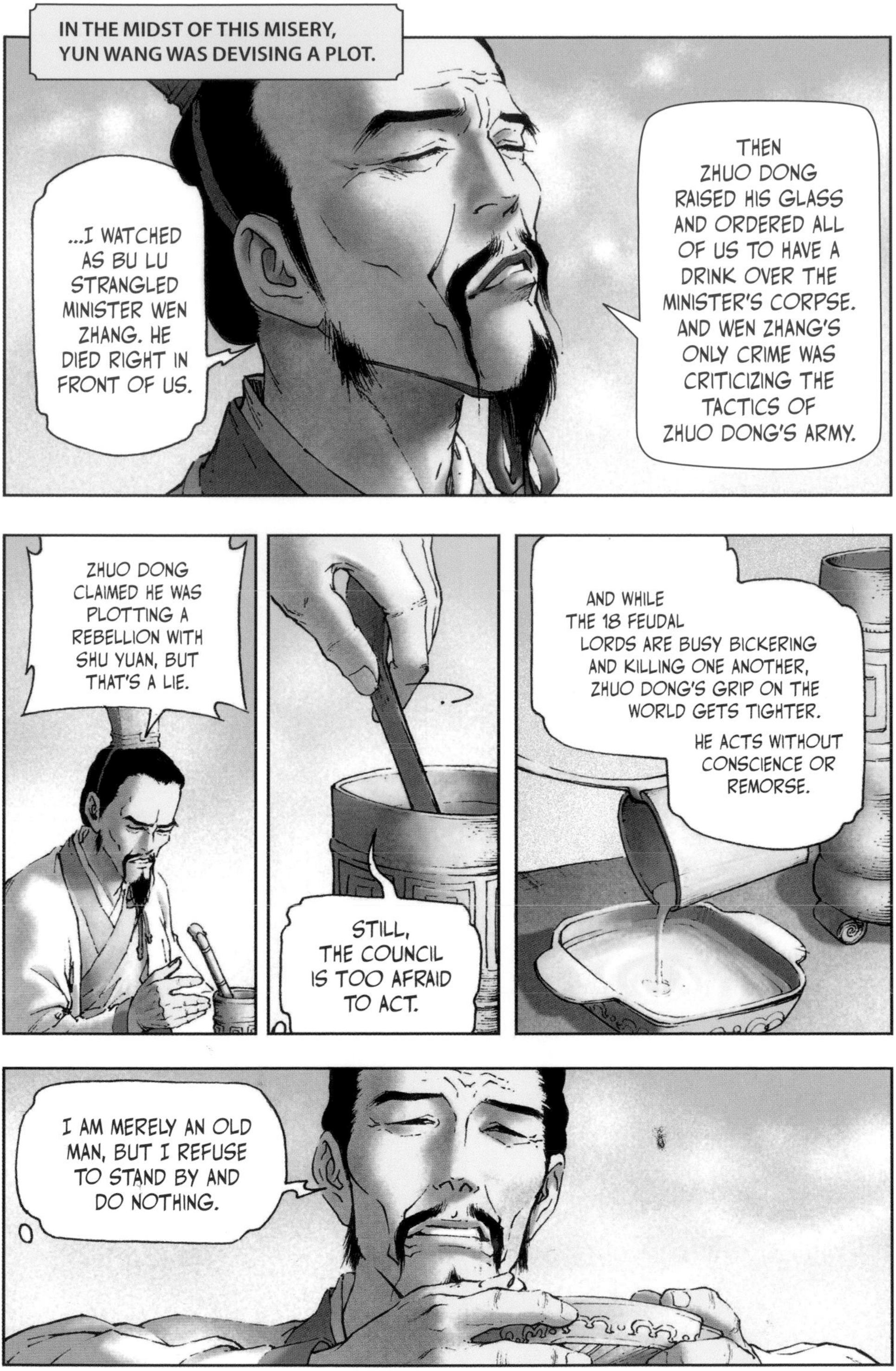
IN THE MIDST OF THIS MISERY, YUN WANG WAS DEVISING A PLOT.
...I WATCHED AS BU LU STRANGLED MINISTER WEN ZHANG. HE DIED RIGHT IN FRONT OF US.
THEN ZHUO DONG RAISED HIS GLASS AND ORDERED ALL OF US TO HAVE A DRINK OVER THE MINISTER'S CORPSE. AND WEN ZHANG'S ONLY CRIME WAS CRITICIZING THE TACTICS OF ZHUO DONG'S ARMY.
ZHUO DONG CLAIMED HE WAS PLOTTING A REBELLION WITH SHU YUAN, BUT THAT'S A LIE.
STILL, THE COUNCIL IS TOO AFRAID TO ACT.
AND WHILE THE 18 FEUDAL LORDS ARE BUSY BICKERING AND KILLING ONE ANOTHER, ZHUO DONG'S GRIP ON THE WORLD GETS TIGHTER.
HE ACTS WITHOUT CONSCIENCE OR REMORSE.
I AM MERELY AN OLD MAN, BUT I REFUSE TO STAND BY AND DO NOTHING.

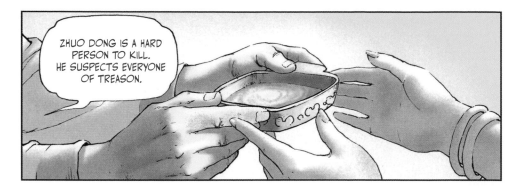

ZHUO DONG IS A HARD PERSON TO KILL. HE SUSPECTS EVERYONE OF TREASON.

BUT YOU, MY DAUGHTER – YOU CAN GET CLOSE TO HIM WITHOUT RAISING HIS SUSPICIONS.

I'M SORRY, MY CHILD. PLEASE FORGIVE YOUR FATHER FOR ASKING YOU TO DO THIS.

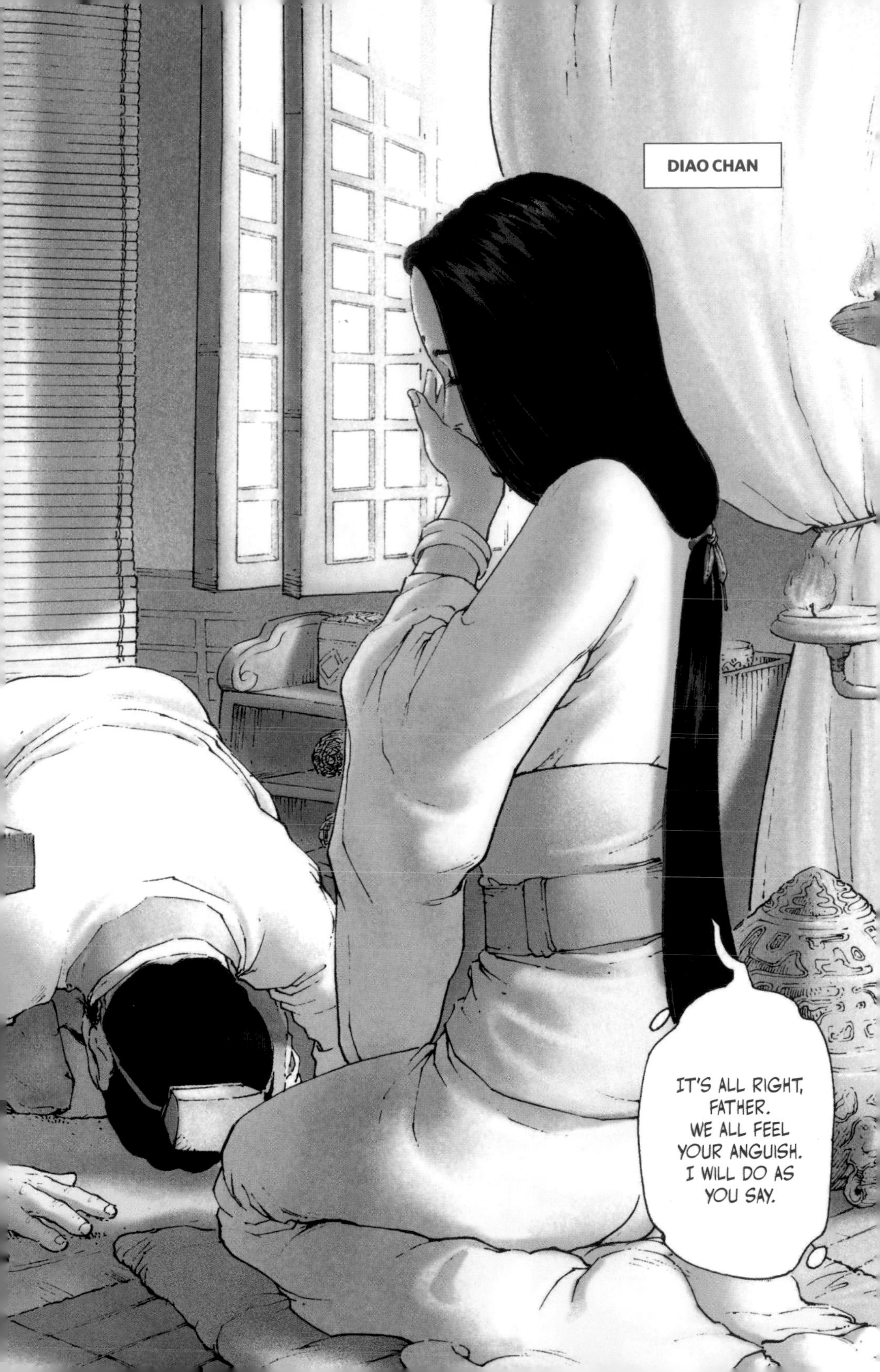
DIAO CHAN
IT'S ALL RIGHT, FATHER. WE ALL FEEL YOUR ANGUISH. I WILL DO AS YOU SAY.

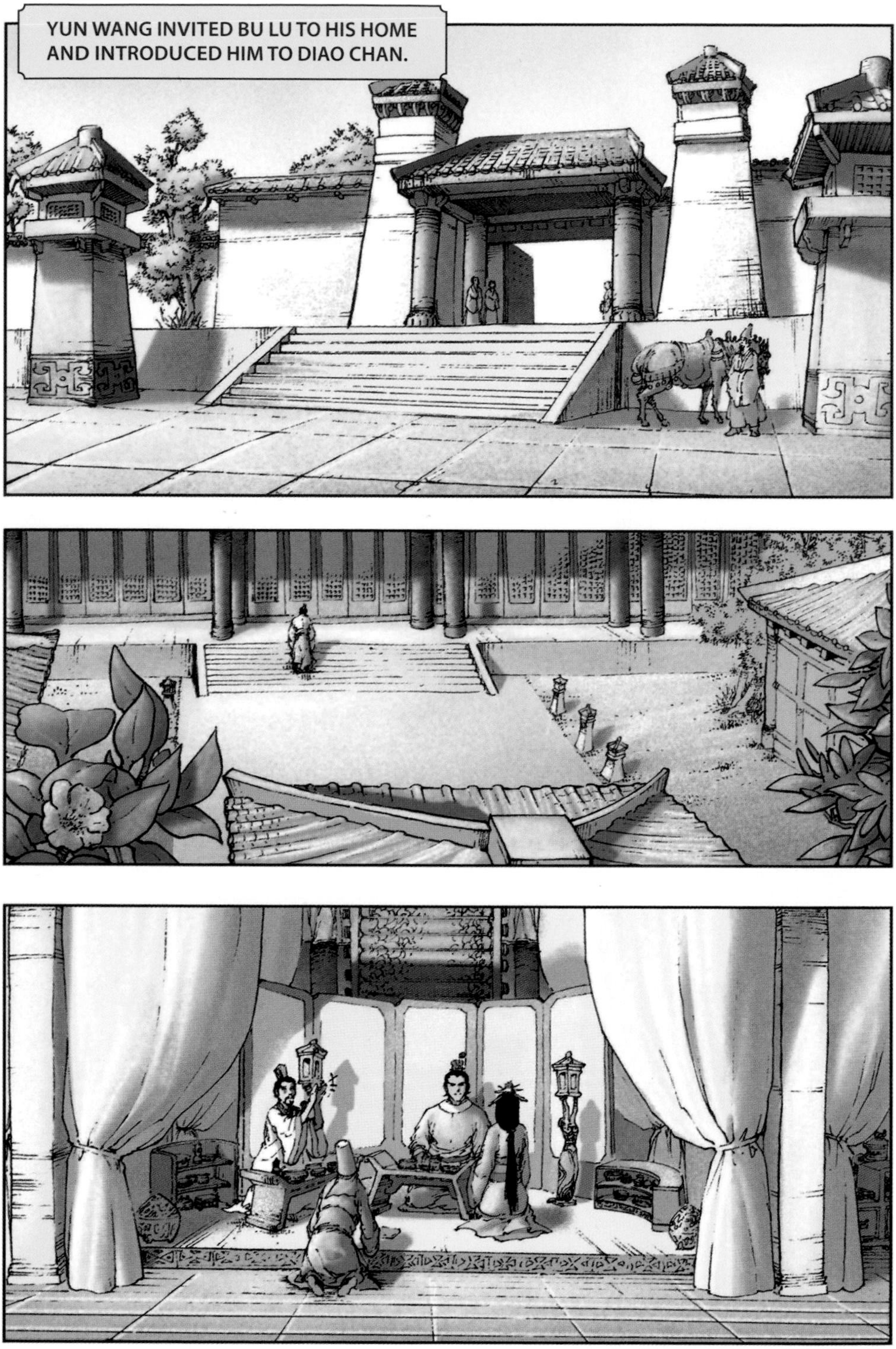
YUN WANG INVITED BU LU TO HIS HOME AND INTRODUCED HIM TO DIAO CHAN.

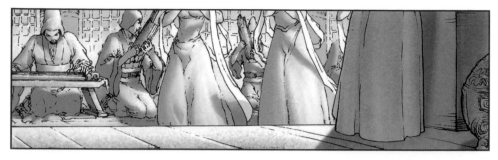

DIAO CHAN! BRING A DRINK FOR COMMANDER BU LU.

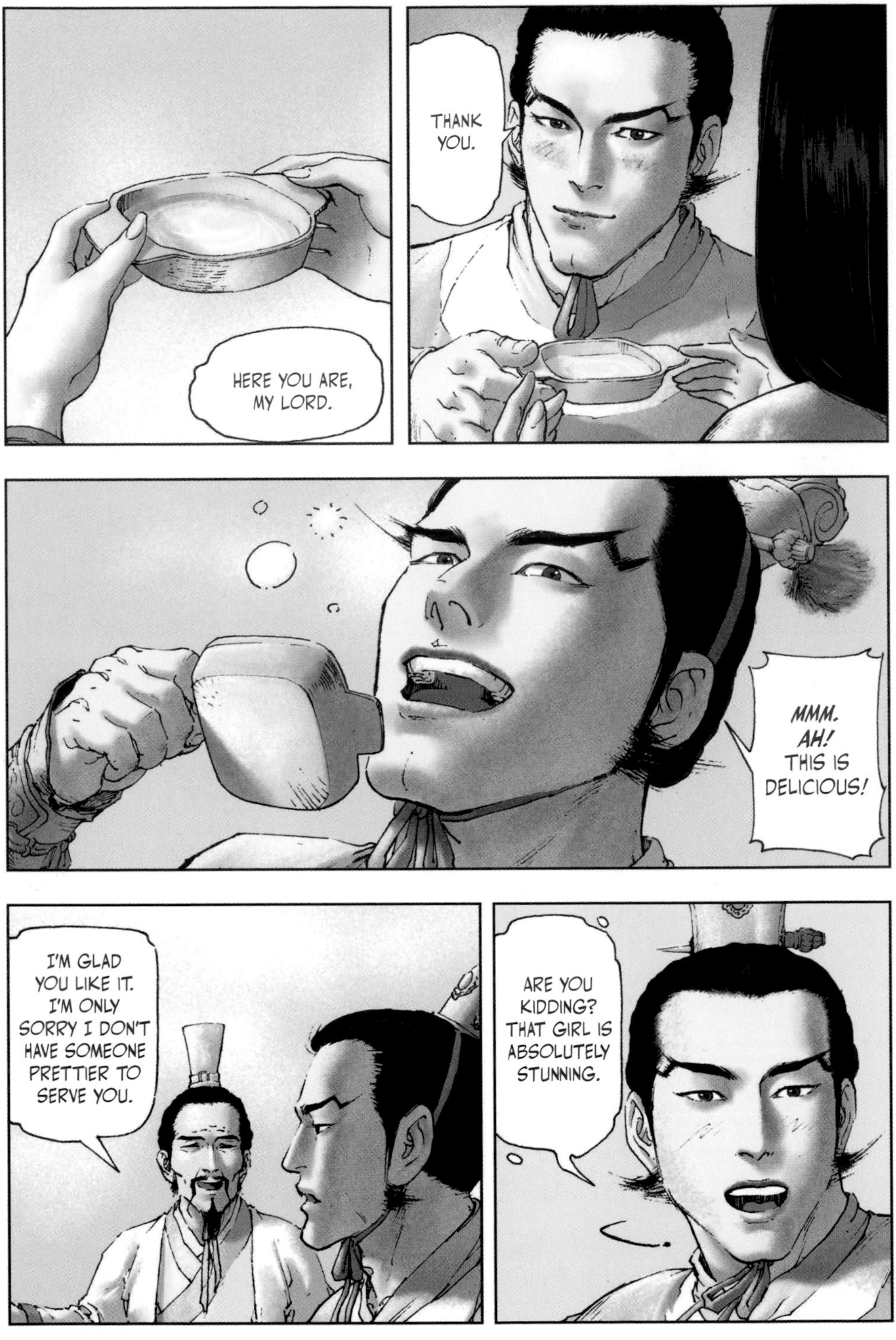
HERE YOU ARE, MY LORD.
THANK YOU.
MMM. AH! THIS IS DELICIOUS!
I'M GLAD YOU LIKE IT. I'M ONLY SORRY I DON'T HAVE SOMEONE PRETTIER TO SERVE YOU.
ARE YOU KIDDING? THAT GIRL IS ABSOLUTELY STUNNING.

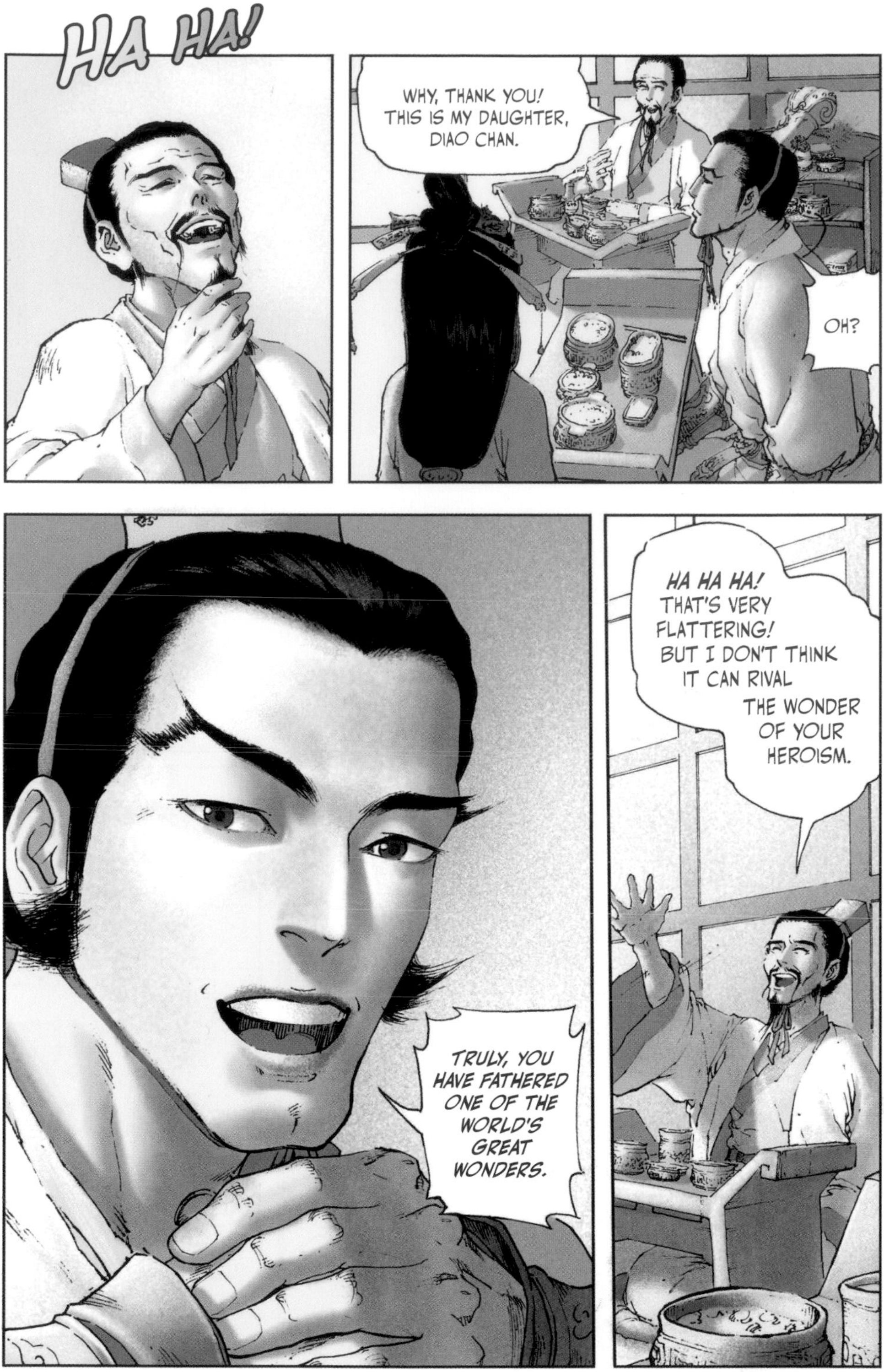
HA HA!
WHY, THANK YOU! THIS IS MY DAUGHTER, DIAO CHAN.
OH?
TRULY, YOU HAVE FATHERED ONE OF THE WORLD'S GREAT WONDERS.
HA HA HA! THAT'S VERY FLATTERING! BUT I DON'T THINK IT CAN RIVAL THE WONDER OF YOUR HEROISM.

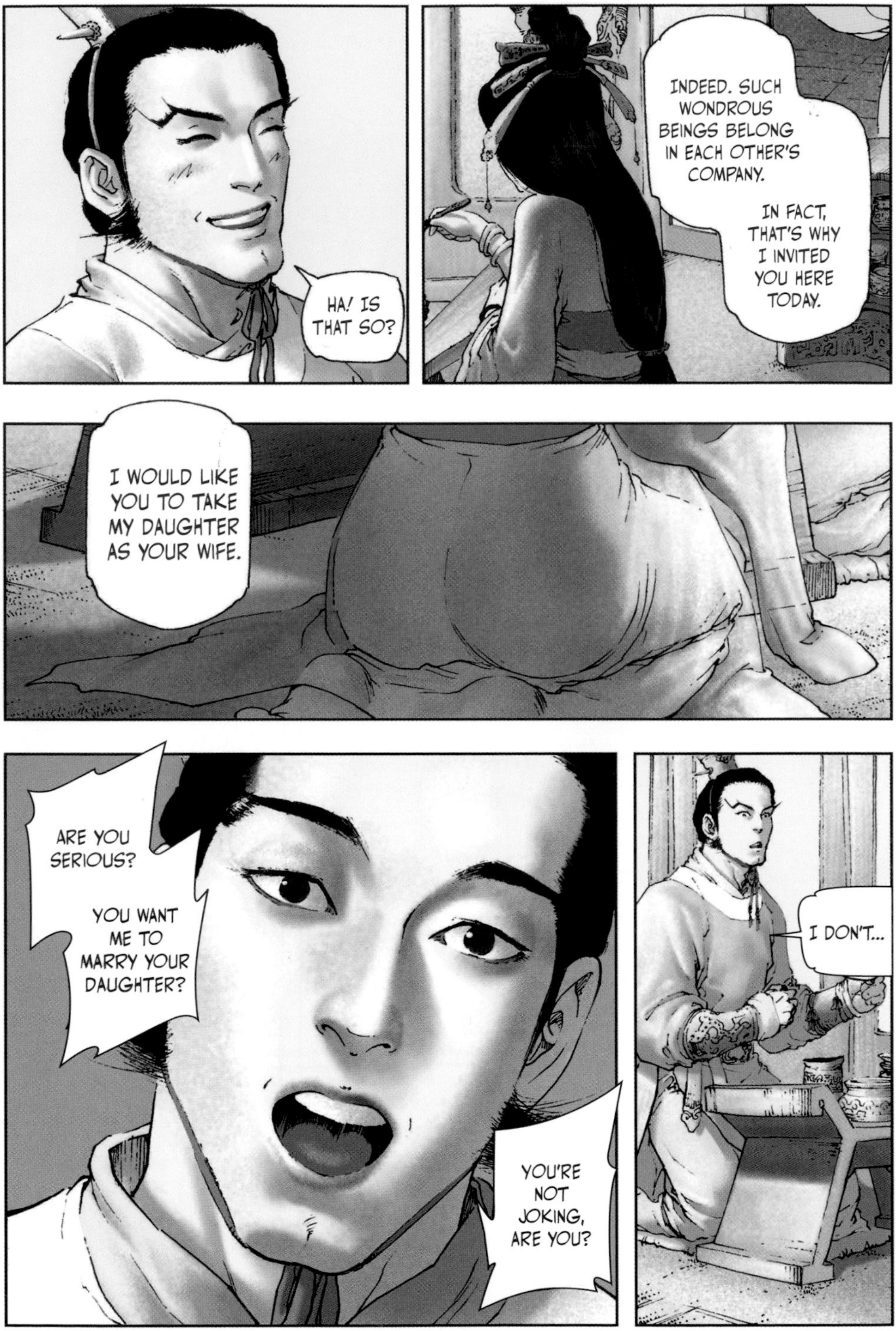
HA! IS THAT SO?
INDEED. SUCH WONDROUS BEINGS BELONG IN EACH OTHER'S COMPANY.
IN FACT, THAT'S WHY I INVITED YOU HERE TODAY.
I WOULD LIKE YOU TO TAKE MY DAUGHTER AS YOUR WIFE.
ARE YOU SERIOUS?
YOU WANT ME TO MARRY YOUR DAUGHTER?
YOU'RE NOT JOKING, ARE YOU?
I DON'T...

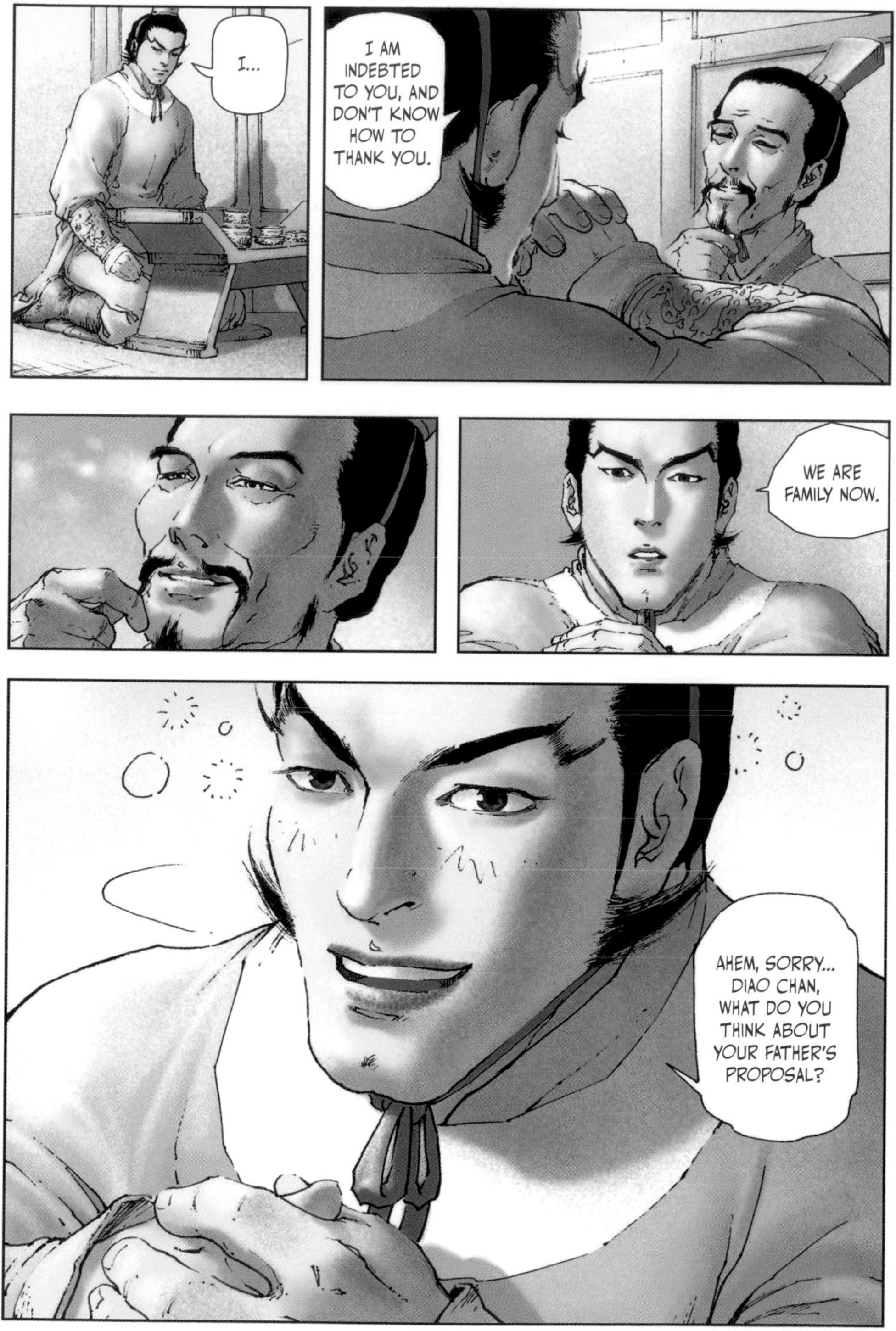
I...
I AM INDEBTED TO YOU, AND DON'T KNOW HOW TO THANK YOU.
WE ARE FAMILY NOW.
AHEM, SORRY... DIAO CHAN, WHAT DO YOU THINK ABOUT YOUR FATHER'S PROPOSAL?

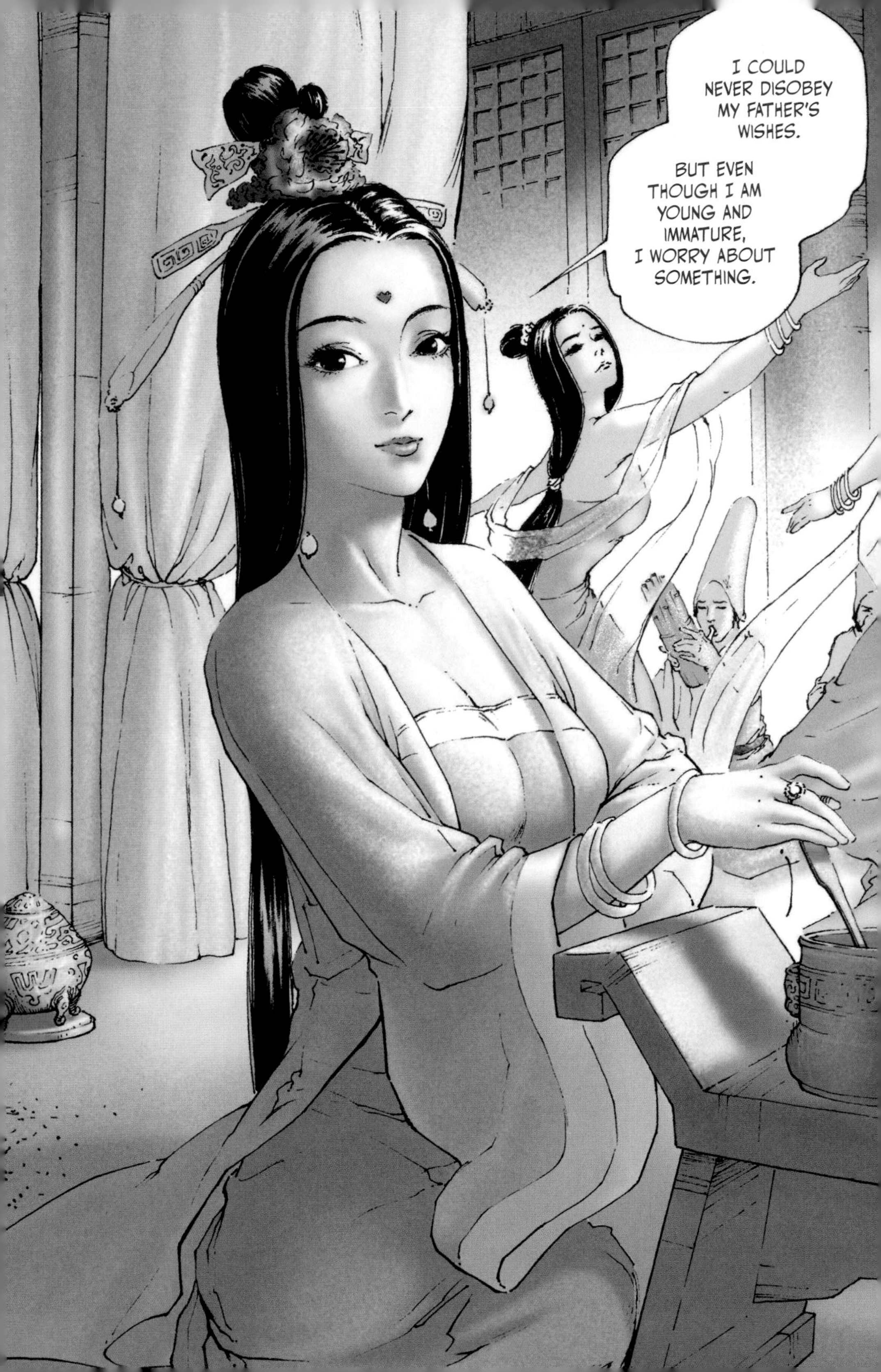
I COULD NEVER DISOBEY MY FATHER'S WISHES.
BUT EVEN THOUGH I AM YOUNG AND IMMATURE, I WORRY ABOUT SOMETHING.

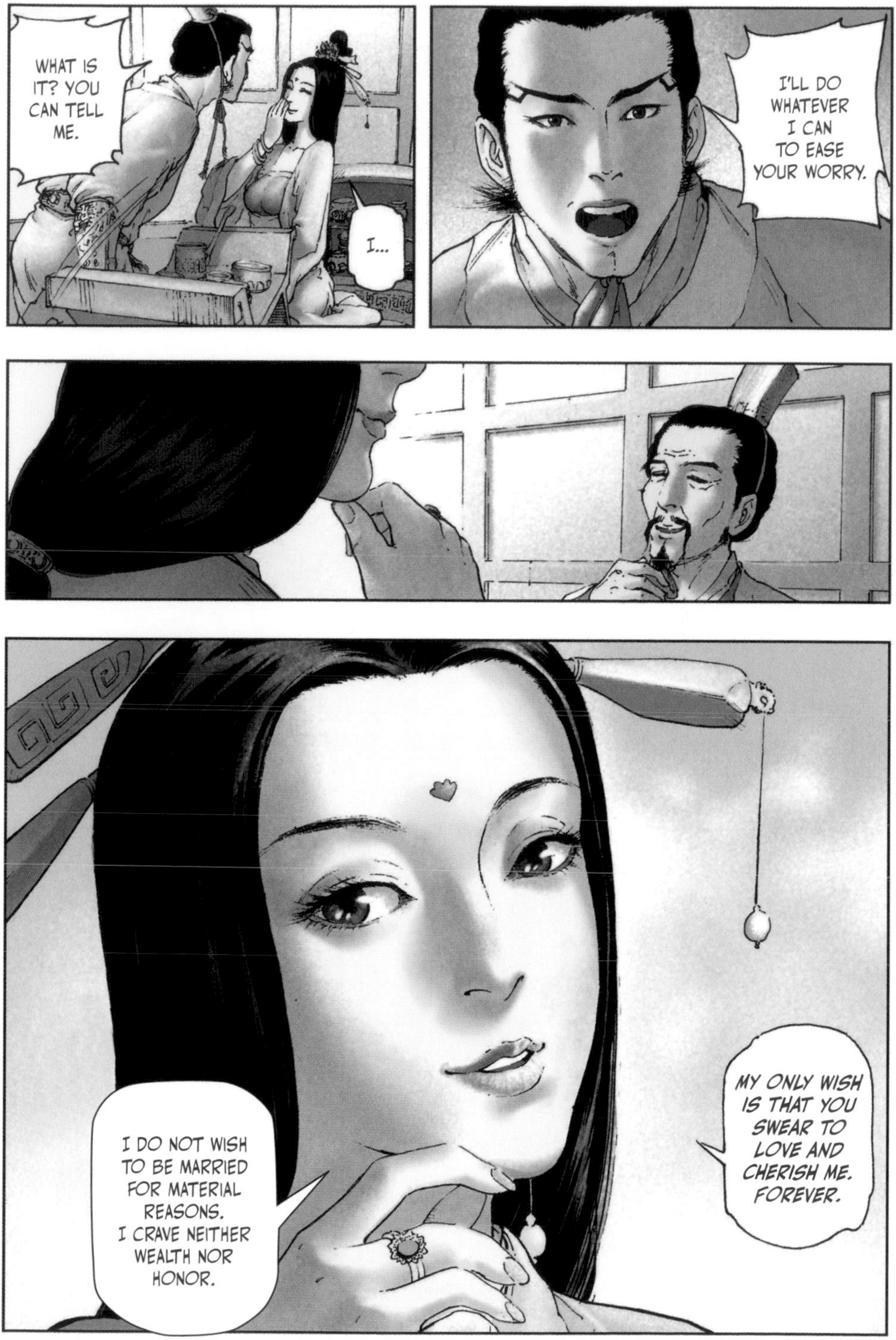
WHAT IS IT? YOU CAN TELL ME.
I...
I'LL DO WHATEVER I CAN TO EASE YOUR WORRY.
I DO NOT WISH TO BE MARRIED FOR MATERIAL REASONS. I CRAVE NEITHER WEALTH NOR HONOR.
MY ONLY WISH IS THAT YOU SWEAR TO LOVE AND CHERISH ME. FOREVER.

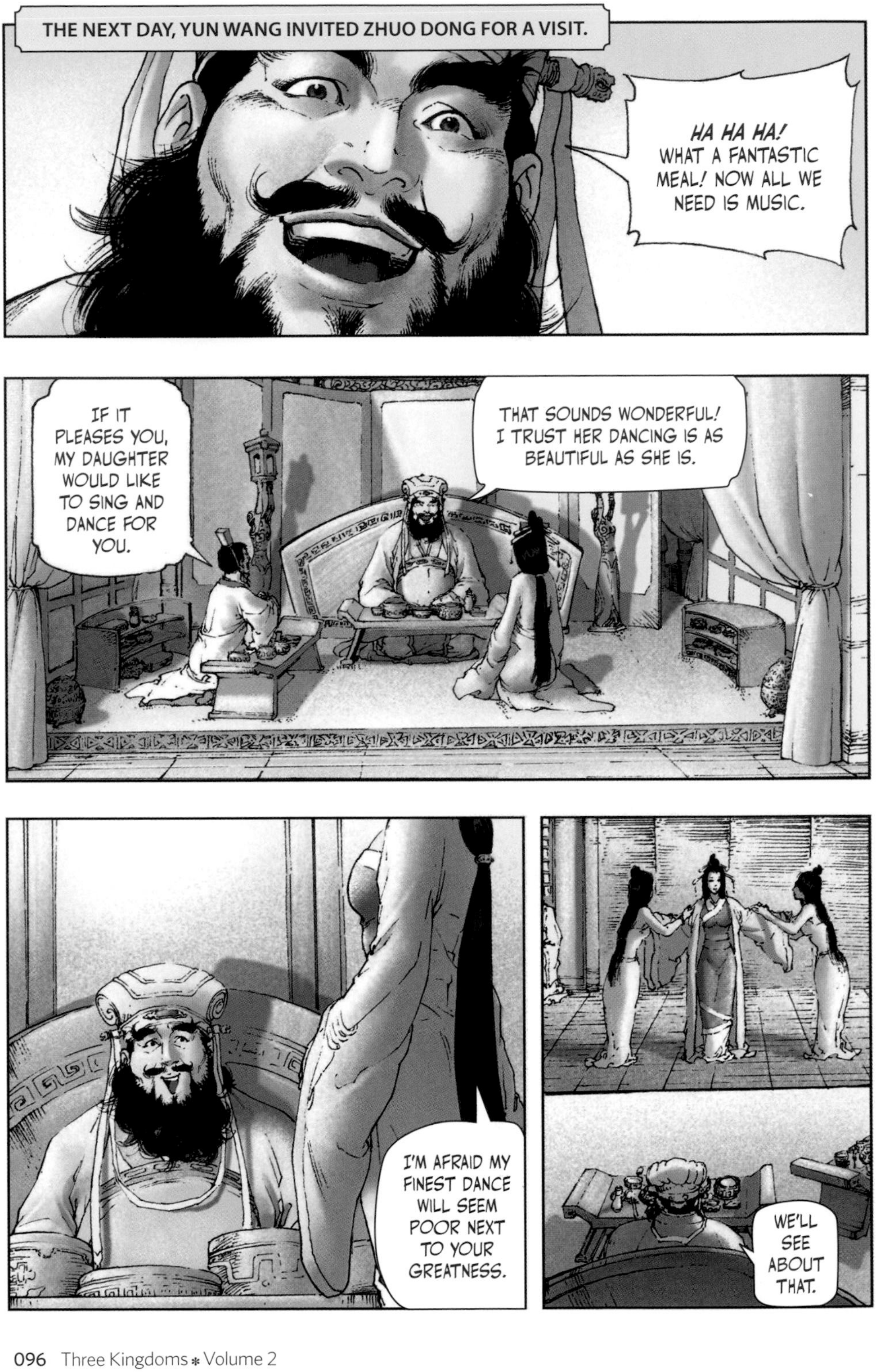
THE NEXT DAY, YUN WANG INVITED ZHUO DONG FOR A VISIT.
HA HA HA! WHAT A FANTASTIC MEAL! NOW ALL WE NEED IS MUSIC.
IF IT PLEASES YOU, MY DAUGHTER WOULD LIKE TO SING AND DANCE FOR YOU.
THAT SOUNDS WONDERFUL! I TRUST HER DANCING IS AS BEAUTIFUL AS SHE IS.
I'M AFRAID MY FINEST DANCE WILL SEEM POOR NEXT TO YOUR GREATNESS.
WE'LL SEE ABOUT THAT.

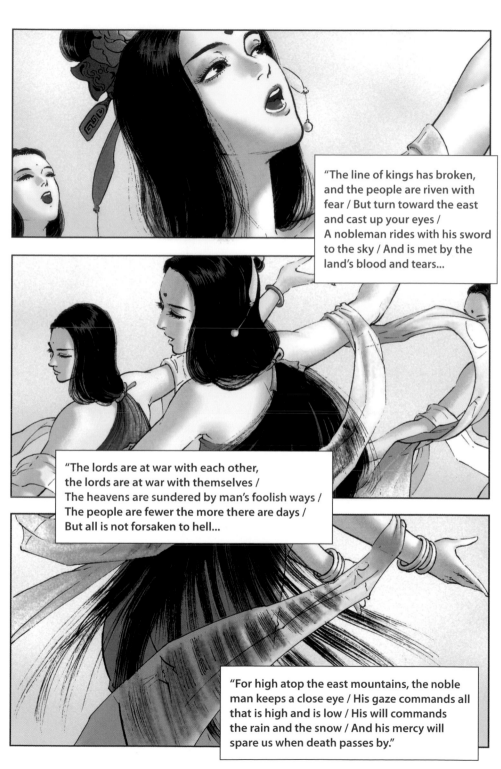

"The line of kings has broken, and the people are riven with fear / But turn toward the east and cast up your eyes / A nobleman rides with his sword to the sky / And is met by the land's blood and tears...

"The lords are at war with each other, the lords are at war with themselves / The heavens are sundered by man's foolish ways / The people are fewer the more there are days / But all is not forsaken to hell...

"For high atop the east mountains, the noble man keeps a close eye / His gaze commands all that is high and is low / His will commands the rain and the snow / And his mercy will spare us when death passes by."

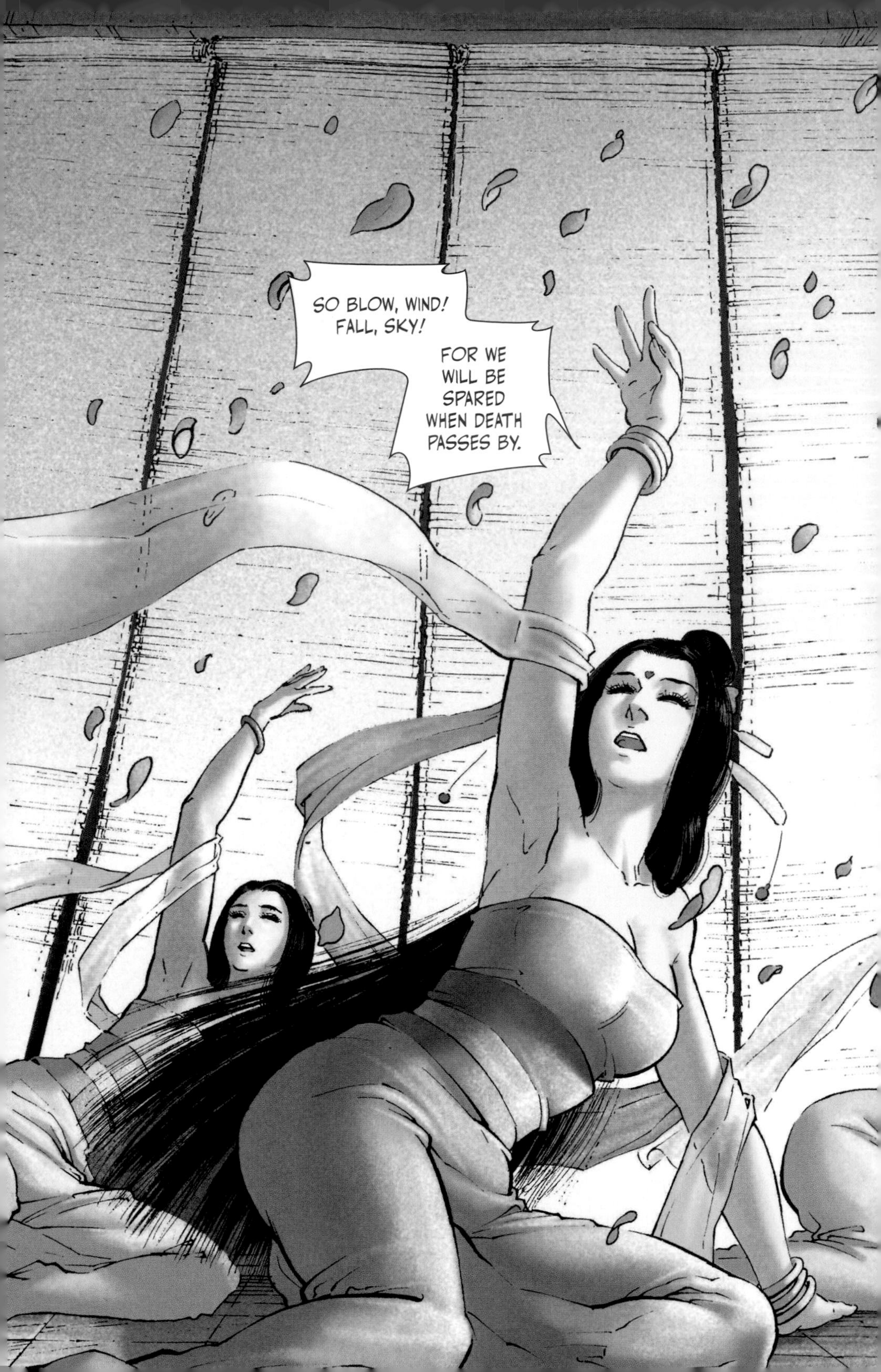
SO BLOW, WIND! FALL, SKY!
FOR WE WILL BE SPARED WHEN DEATH PASSES BY.

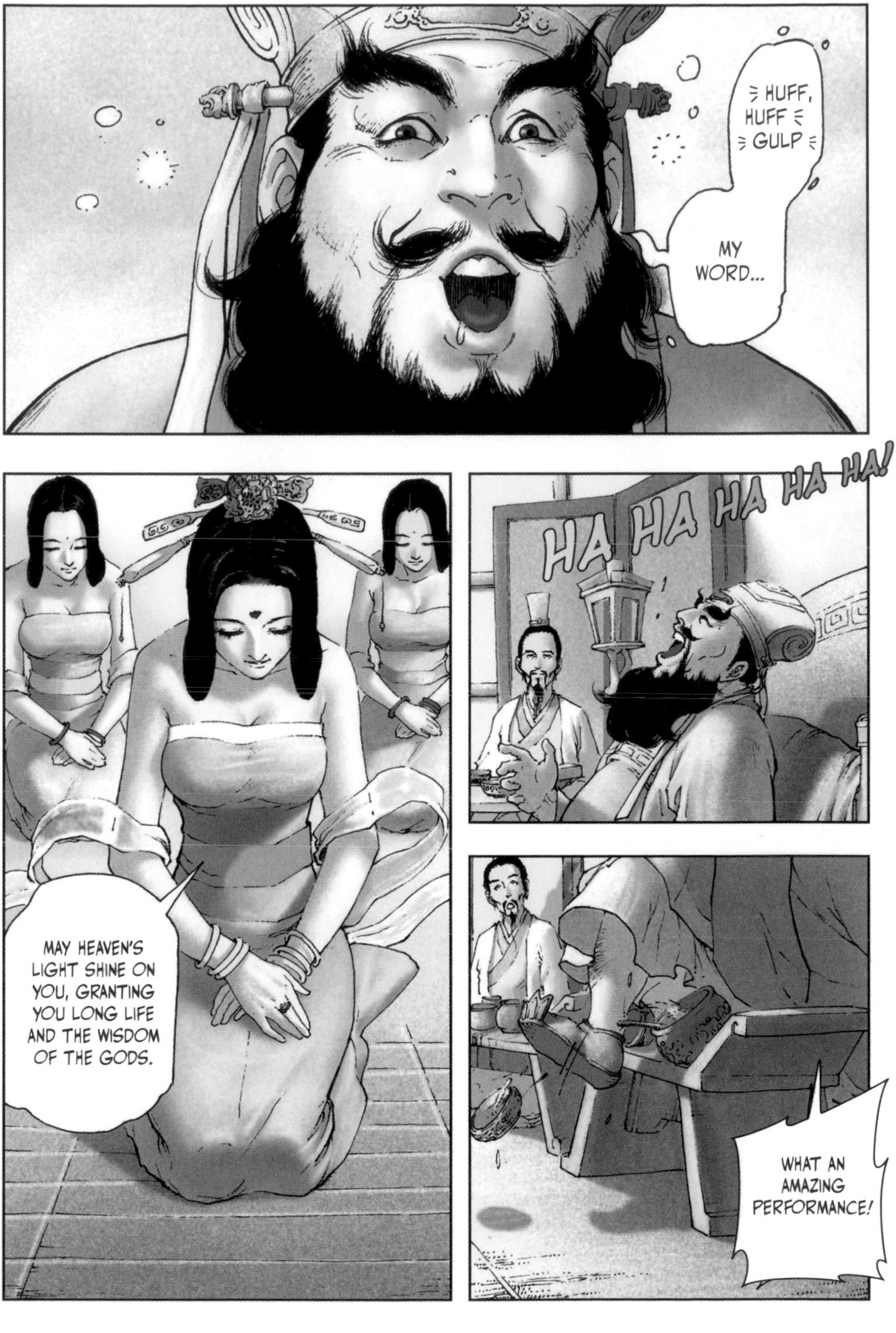
≡ HUFF, HUFF ≡ ≡ GULP ≡
MY WORD...
MAY HEAVEN'S LIGHT SHINE ON YOU, GRANTING YOU LONG LIFE AND THE WISDOM OF THE GODS.
HA HA HA HA HA!
WHAT AN AMAZING PERFORMANCE!

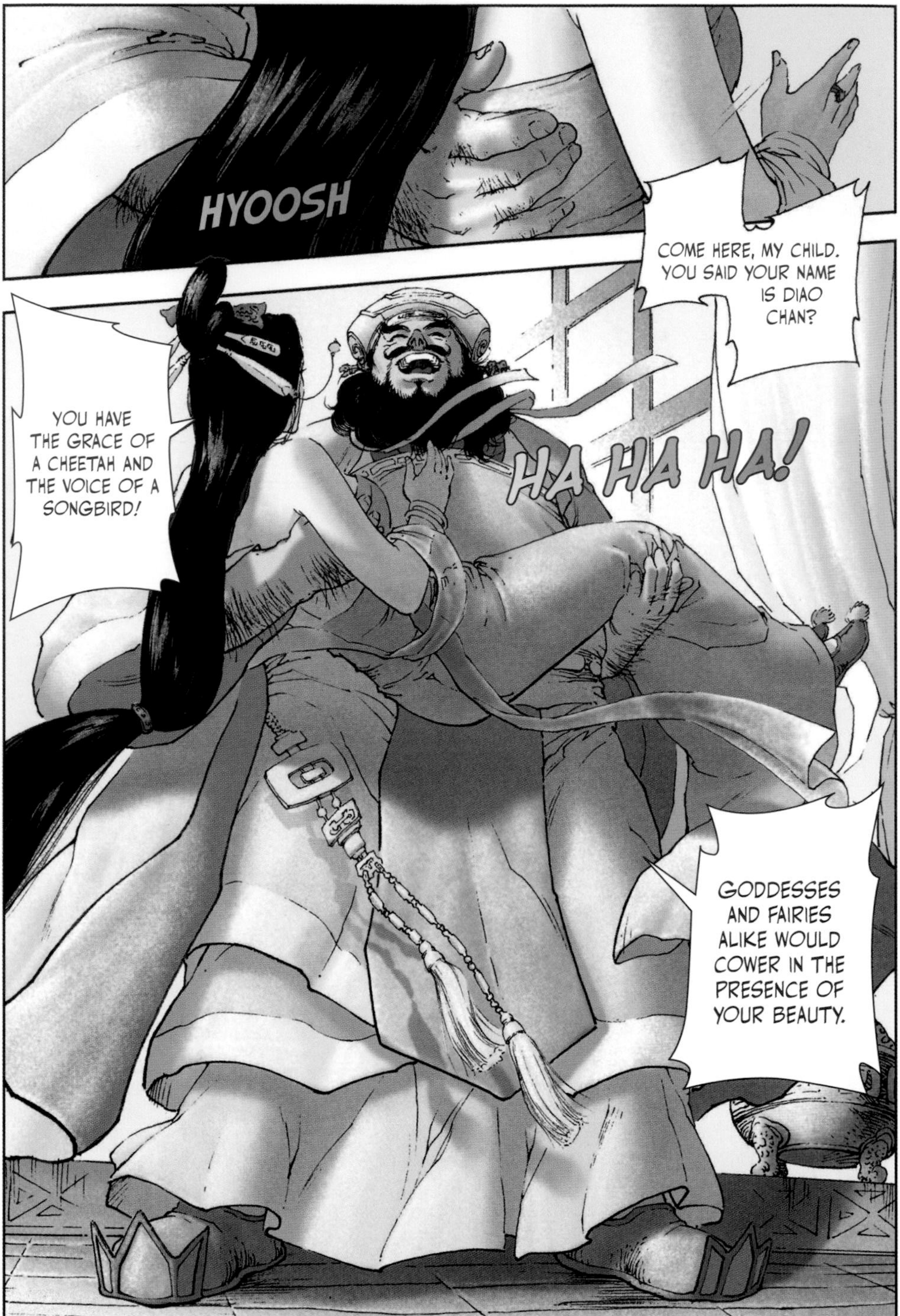
HYOOSH
COME HERE, MY CHILD. YOU SAID YOUR NAME IS DIAO CHAN?
HA HA HA!
YOU HAVE THE GRACE OF A CHEETAH AND THE VOICE OF A SONGBIRD!
GODDESSES AND FAIRIES ALIKE WOULD COWER IN THE PRESENCE OF YOUR BEAUTY.

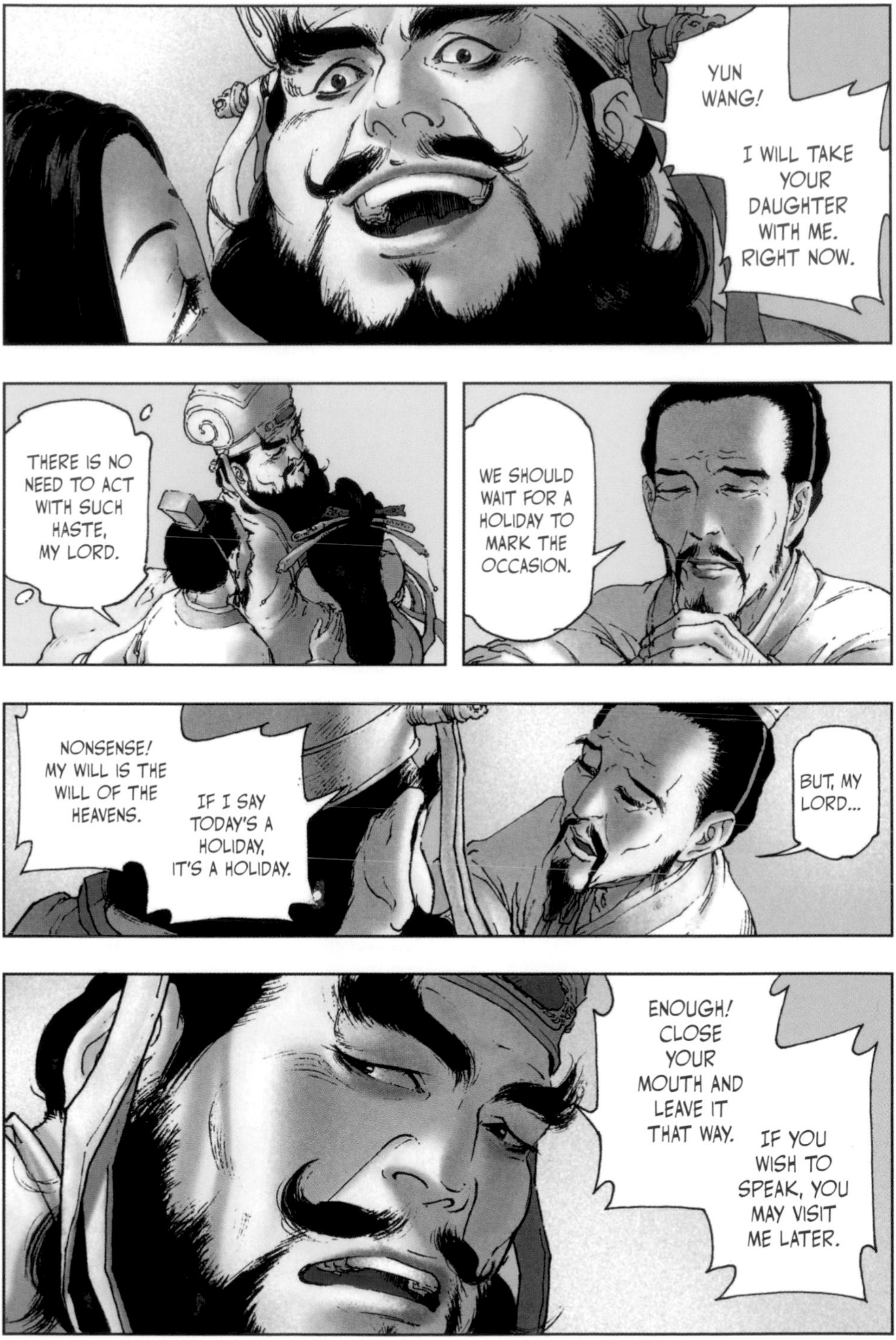
YUN WANG!
I WILL TAKE YOUR DAUGHTER WITH ME. RIGHT NOW.
THERE IS NO NEED TO ACT WITH SUCH HASTE, MY LORD.
WE SHOULD WAIT FOR A HOLIDAY TO MARK THE OCCASION.
NONSENSE! MY WILL IS THE WILL OF THE HEAVENS.
IF I SAY TODAY'S A HOLIDAY, IT'S A HOLIDAY.
BUT, MY LORD...
ENOUGH! CLOSE YOUR MOUTH AND LEAVE IT THAT WAY.
IF YOU WISH TO SPEAK, YOU MAY VISIT ME LATER.

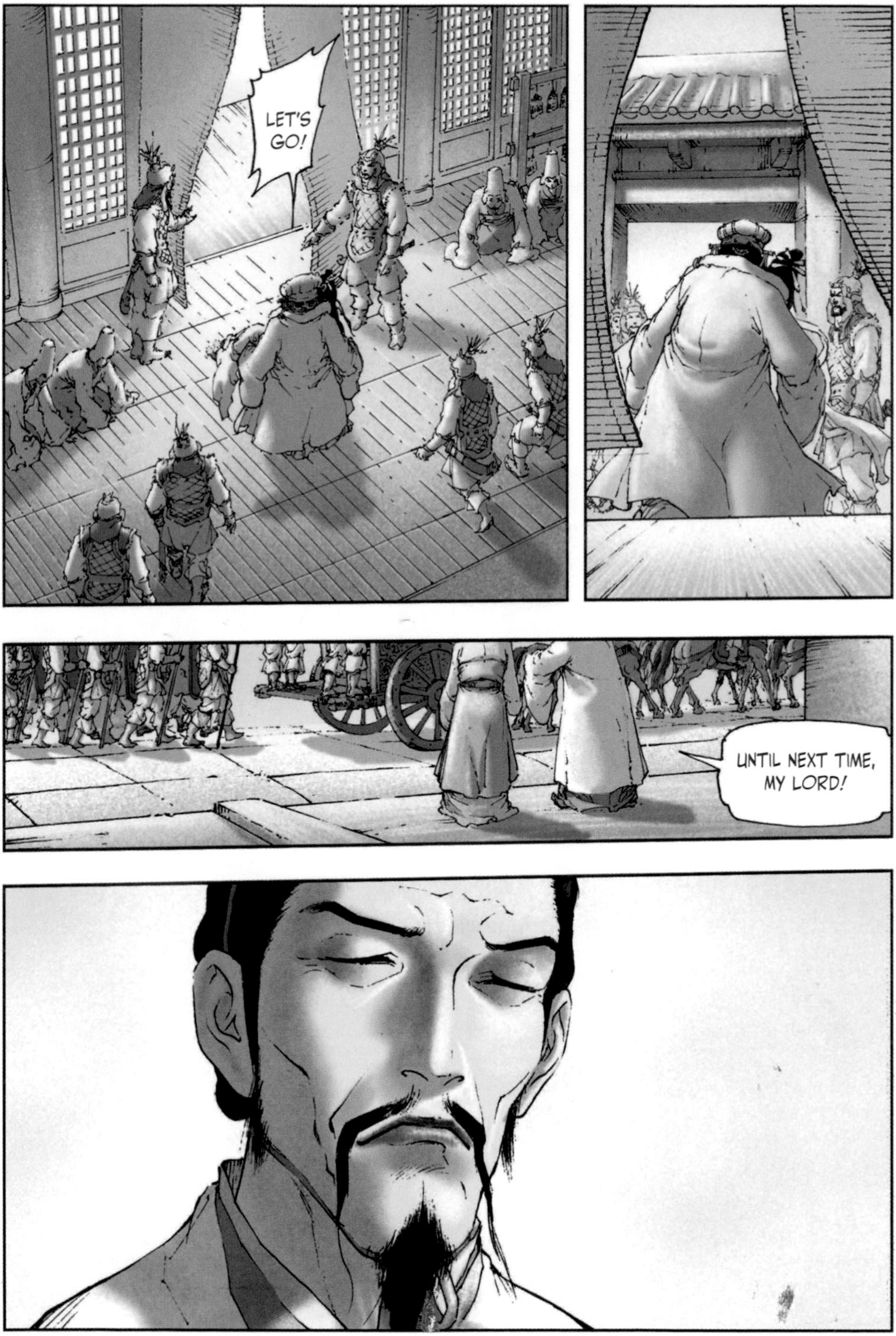
LET'S GO!
UNTIL NEXT TIME, MY LORD!

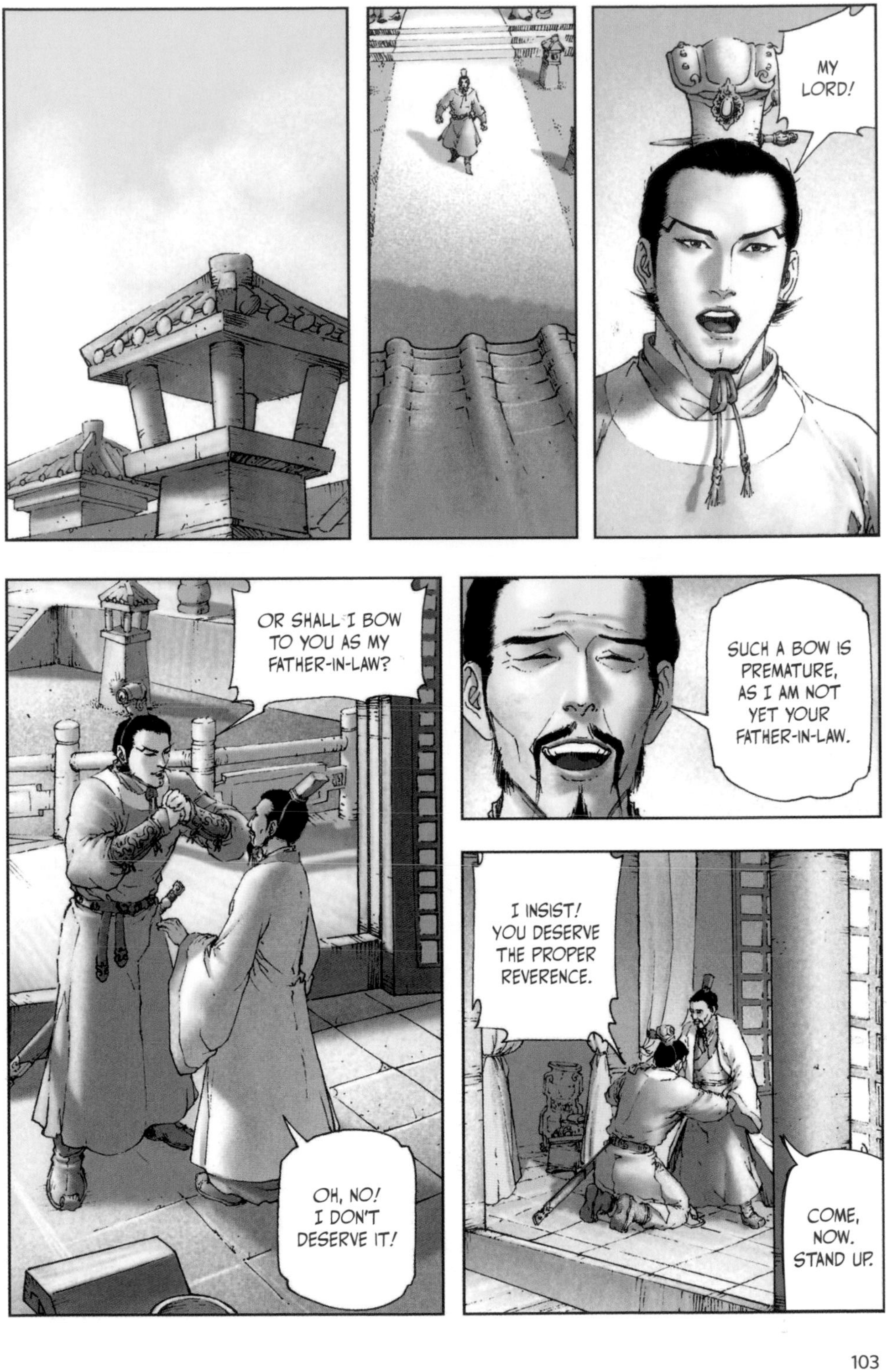
MY LORD!
OR SHALL I BOW TO YOU AS MY FATHER-IN-LAW?
SUCH A BOW IS PREMATURE, AS I AM NOT YET YOUR FATHER-IN-LAW.
OH, NO! I DON'T DESERVE IT!
I INSIST! YOU DESERVE THE PROPER REVERENCE.
COME, NOW. STAND UP.

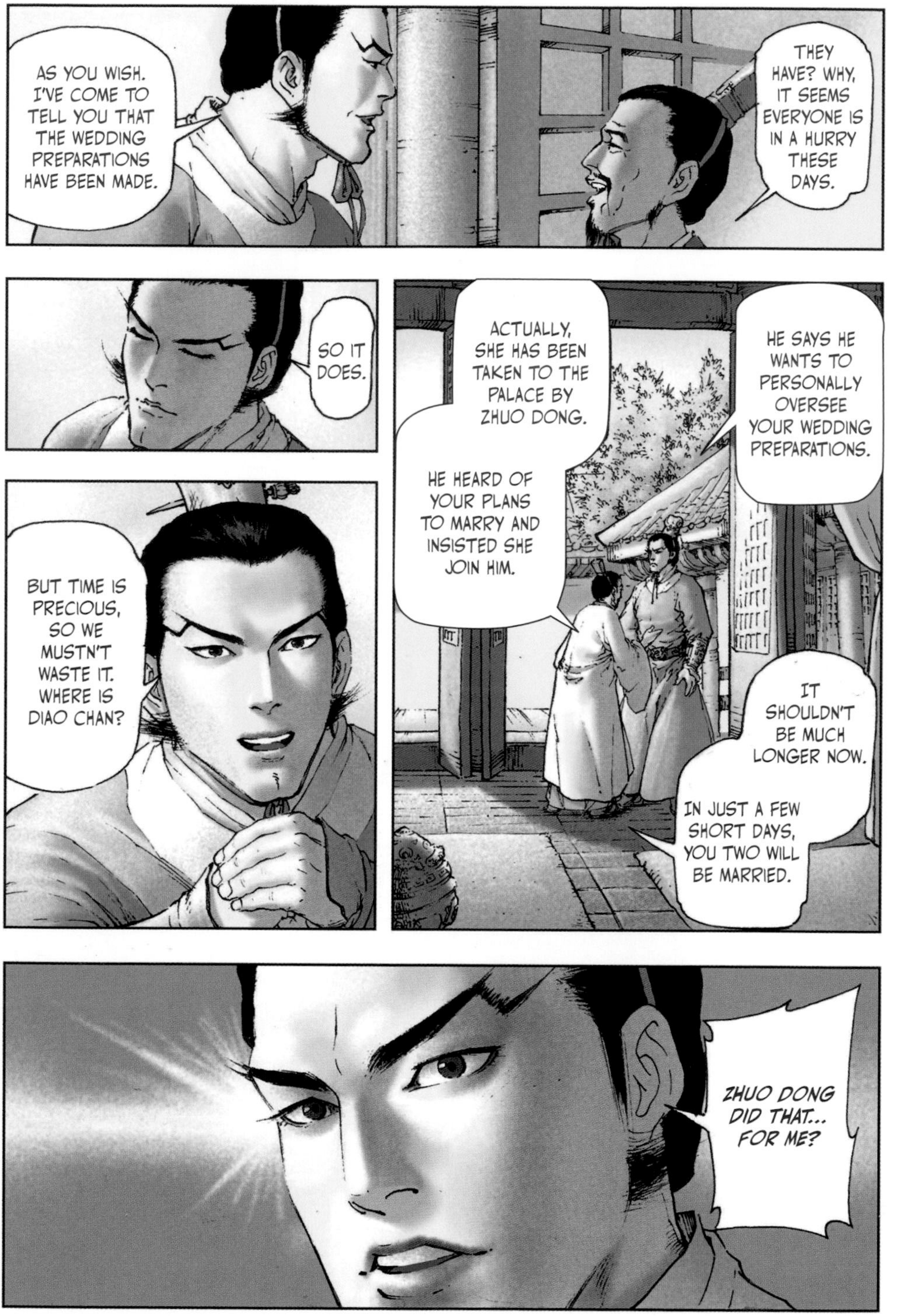
AS YOU WISH. I'VE COME TO TELL YOU THAT THE WEDDING PREPARATIONS HAVE BEEN MADE.
THEY HAVE? WHY, IT SEEMS EVERYONE IS IN A HURRY THESE DAYS.
SO IT DOES.
BUT TIME IS PRECIOUS, SO WE MUSTN'T WASTE IT. WHERE IS DIAO CHAN?
ACTUALLY, SHE HAS BEEN TAKEN TO THE PALACE BY ZHUO DONG.
HE HEARD OF YOUR PLANS TO MARRY AND INSISTED SHE JOIN HIM.
HE SAYS HE WANTS TO PERSONALLY OVERSEE YOUR WEDDING PREPARATIONS.
IT SHOULDN'T BE MUCH LONGER NOW.
IN JUST A FEW SHORT DAYS, YOU TWO WILL BE MARRIED.
ZHUO DONG DID THAT... FOR ME?

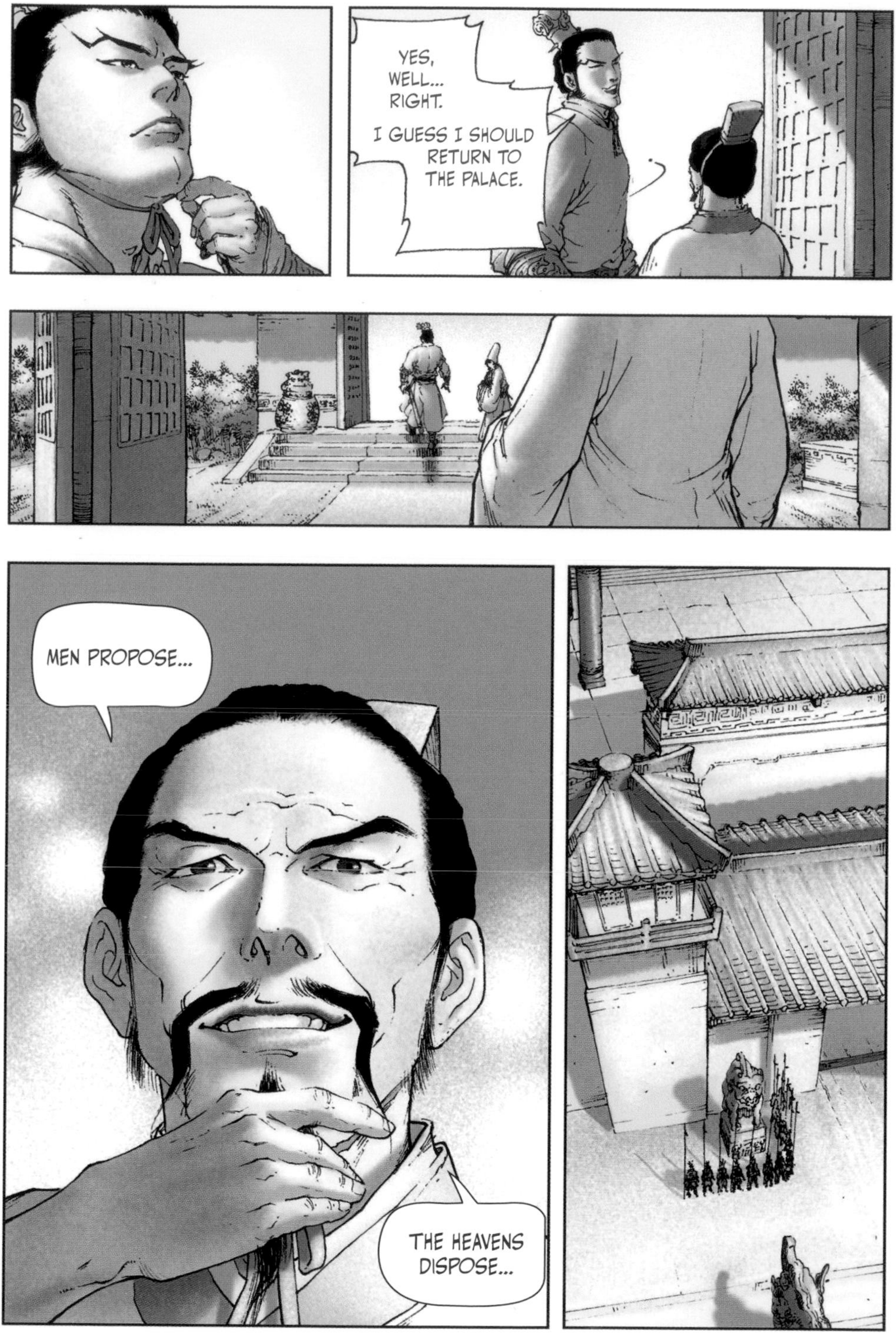
YES, WELL... RIGHT.
I GUESS I SHOULD RETURN TO THE PALACE.
MEN PROPOSE...
THE HEAVENS DISPOSE...

Chapter 4

The Battle for Diao Chan ^{AD 192}

Summary

Having been misled into believing that Zhuo Dong is both aware and enthusiastic of Bu Lu's forthcoming marriage to Diao Chan, the young general goes to Zhuo Dong's palace to check on the arrangements. Once there, he discovers that Zhuo Dong has in fact taken Diao Chan for his mistress. Bu Lu is enraged, and storms out of the castle, thus Yun Wang's plan has been put into motion. Yun Wang encounters Bu Lu outside the palace and tells him that he is Diao Chan's beloved, and that, although he is Diao Chan's beloved, he must not endanger her safety. Bu Lu goes to speak with Diao Chan, who threatens to take her life rather than live without him. Zhuo Dong finds the two of them speaking, and drives Bu Lu from the palace. Zhuo Dong wants to kill Bu Lu, but Ru Li talks him out of it. Later, Zhuo Dong wakes up from a long night of revelry to discover the emperor has handed over the crown. Zhuo Dong departs for the emperor's palace to claim the throne and is ambushed by soldiers led by Bu Lu. Zhuo Dong discovers too late that the battle for Diao Chan was a trap set by Yun Wang. He tries to explain things to Bu Lu, but it's too late.

Chain Stratagems

Chain Stratagems are one of the 36 strategic stratagems of engagement in Chinese culture. The different stratagems are to be used in matters of battle, politics, and even day-to-day interactions. Although "stratagem" sounds a lot like "strategy," the two things are different, because strategies are the blueprint for engaging an enemy, and stratagems are ruses, designed to mislead the enemy. A chain stratagem is a ruse that requires using someone or something to chain two or more enemies' fates together. When Yun Wang decides to use his daughter as bait for both Zhuo Dong and Bu Lu, he has yoked the fate of the two men by giving them a common desire. Knowing how proud and unrelenting both men are, Yun Wang knows that they would kill to have Diao Chan; thus their being chained will result in only one of them surviving. Either way, Yun Wang's objective becomes easier to attain because the number of enemies has been reduced by half.

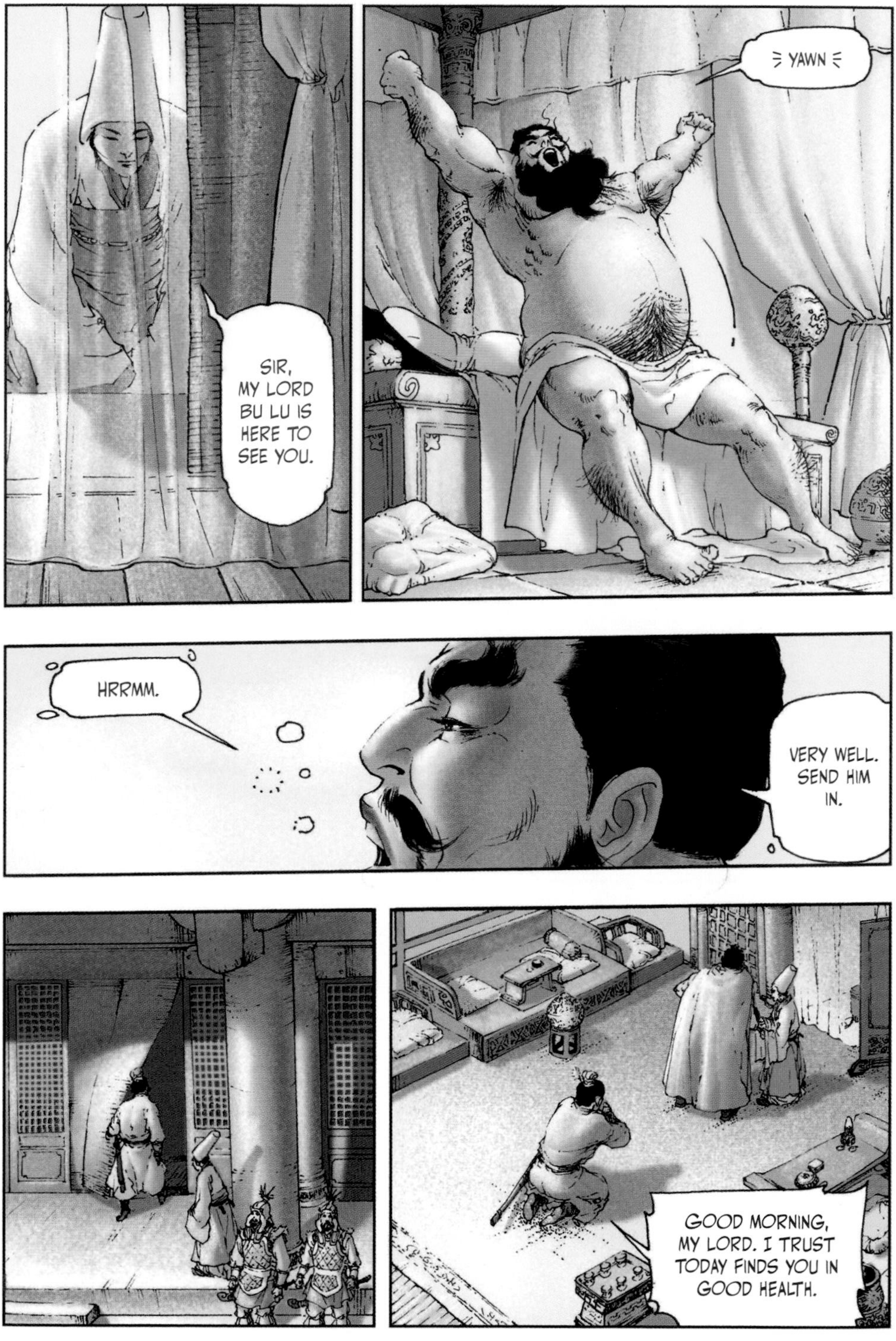
SIR, MY LORD BU LU IS HERE TO SEE YOU.
YAWN
HRRMM.
VERY WELL. SEND HIM IN.
GOOD MORNING, MY LORD. I TRUST TODAY FINDS YOU IN GOOD HEALTH.

IN FACT, IT DOES. I SLEPT MORE SOUNDLY LAST NIGHT THAN I HAVE IN AGES.

I AM GLAD TO HEAR--

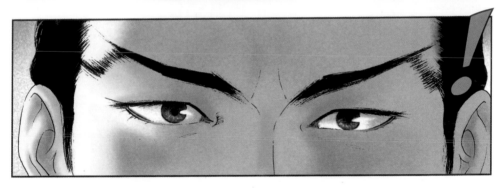

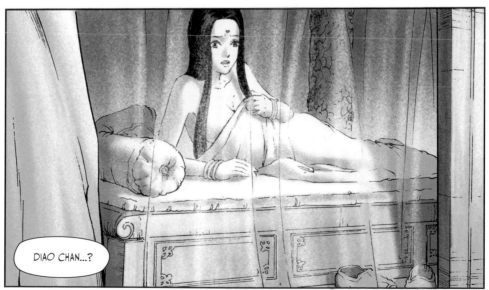

DIAO CHAN...?

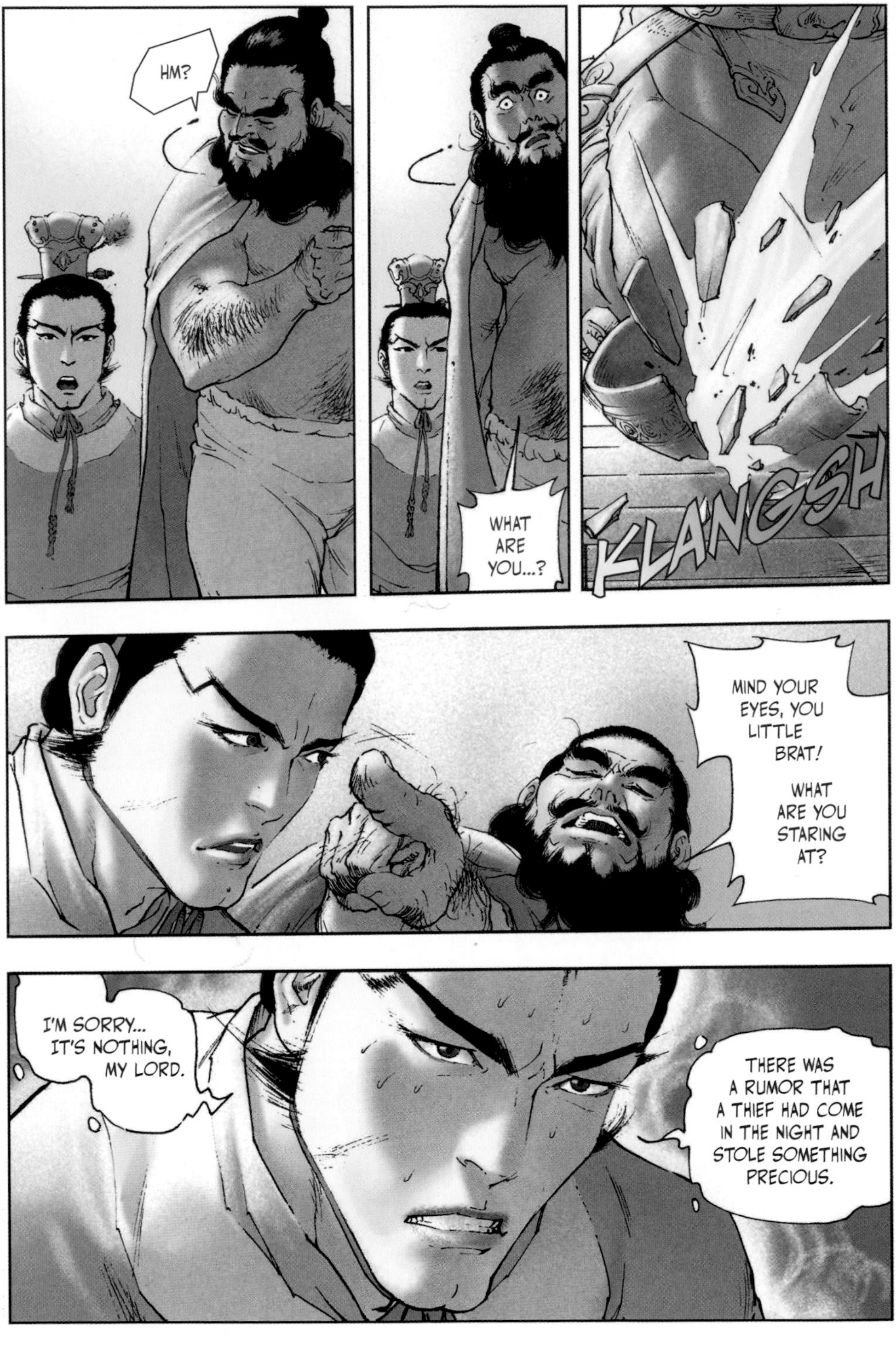
HM?
WHAT ARE YOU...?
KLANGSH
MIND YOUR EYES, YOU LITTLE BRAT!
WHAT ARE YOU STARING AT?
I'M SORRY... IT'S NOTHING, MY LORD.
THERE WAS A RUMOR THAT A THIEF HAD COME IN THE NIGHT AND STOLE SOMETHING PRECIOUS.

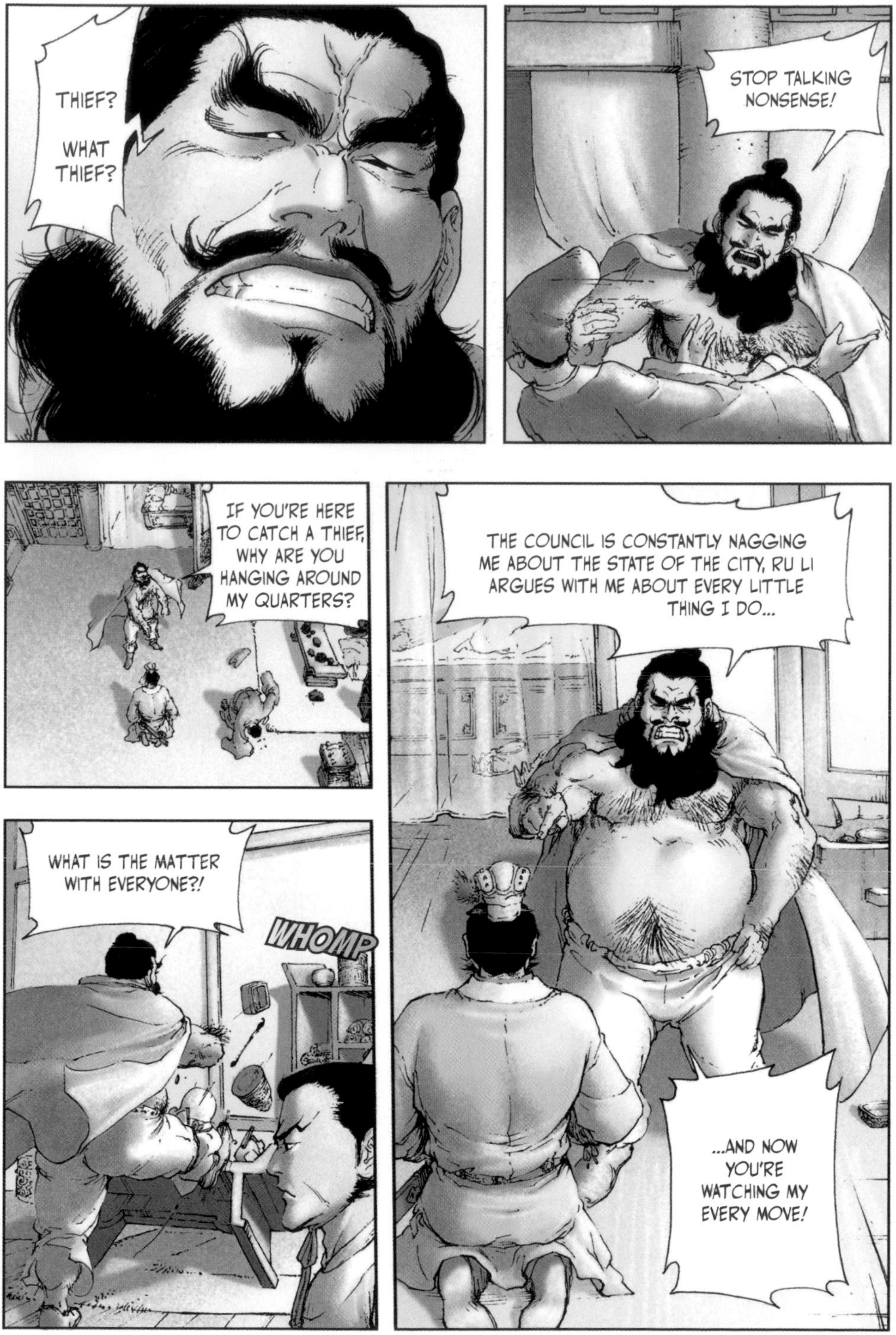
THIEF?
WHAT THIEF?
STOP TALKING NONSENSE!
IF YOU'RE HERE TO CATCH A THIEF, WHY ARE YOU HANGING AROUND MY QUARTERS?
THE COUNCIL IS CONSTANTLY NAGGING ME ABOUT THE STATE OF THE CITY, RU LI ARGUES WITH ME ABOUT EVERY LITTLE THING I DO...
...AND NOW YOU'RE WATCHING MY EVERY MOVE!
WHAT IS THE MATTER WITH EVERYONE?!
WHOMP

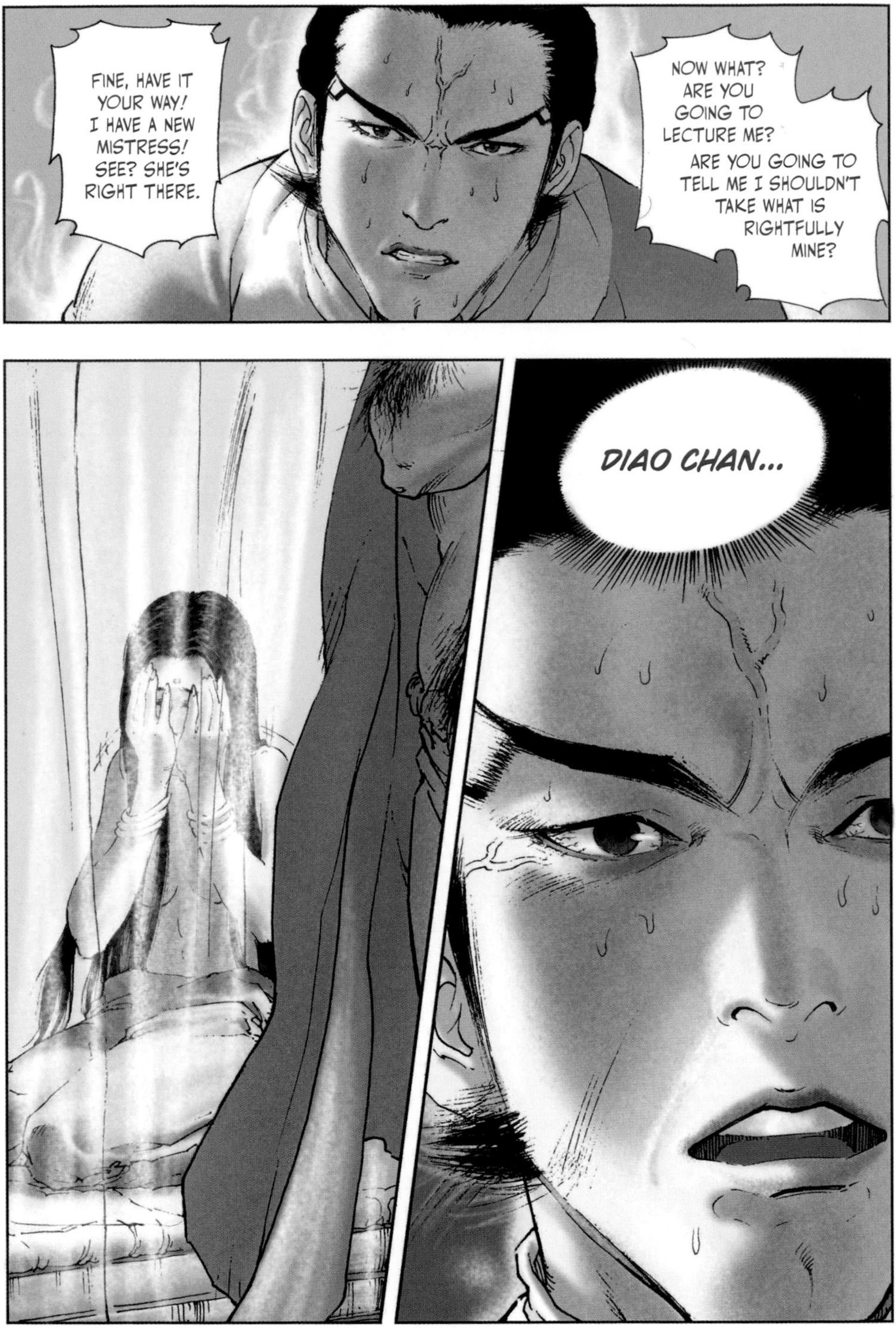
FINE, HAVE IT YOUR WAY! I HAVE A NEW MISTRESS! SEE? SHE'S RIGHT THERE.
NOW WHAT? ARE YOU GOING TO LECTURE ME?
ARE YOU GOING TO TELL ME I SHOULDN'T TAKE WHAT IS RIGHTFULLY MINE?
DIAO CHAN...

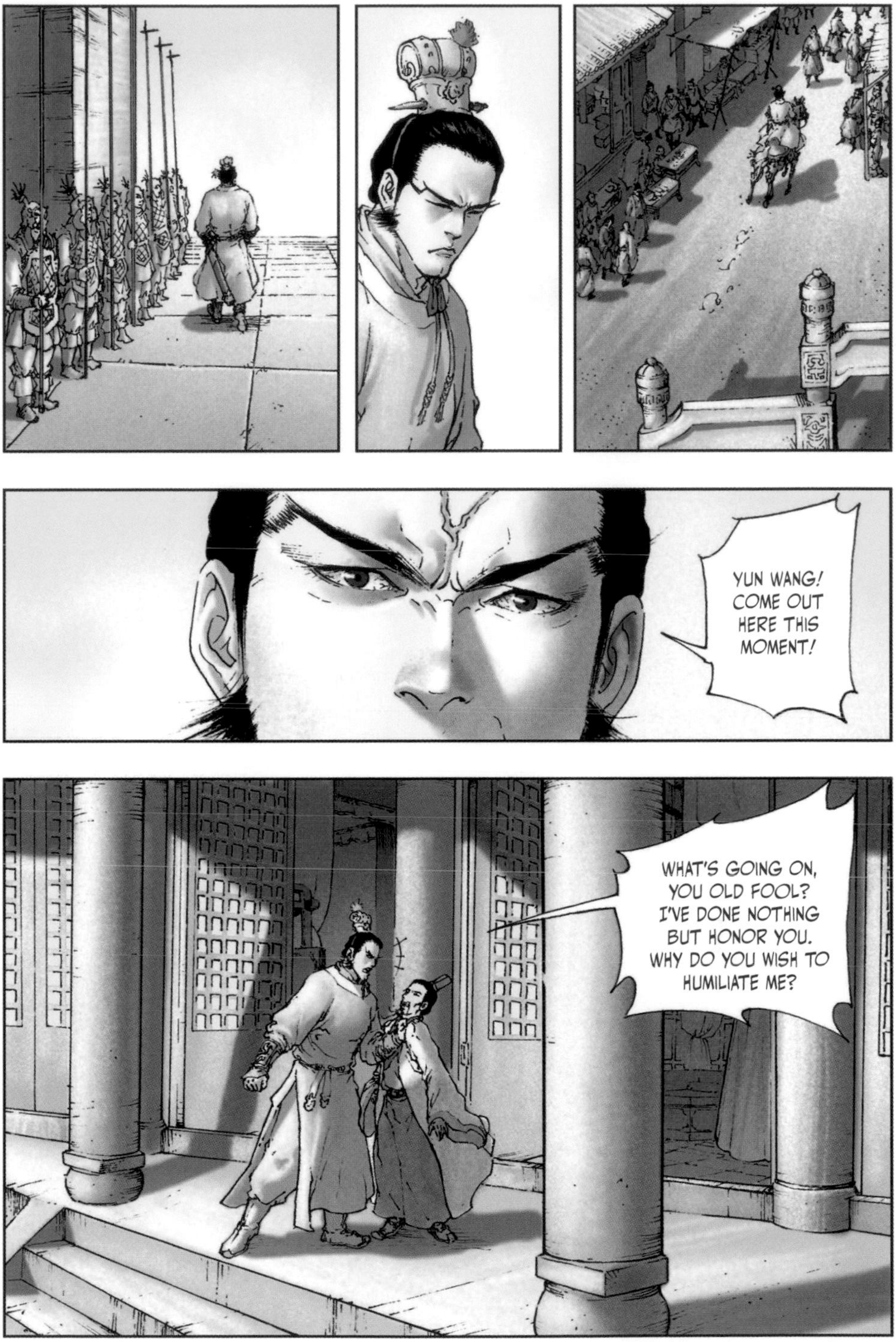
YUN WANG! COME OUT HERE THIS MOMENT!
WHAT'S GOING ON, YOU OLD FOOL? I'VE DONE NOTHING BUT HONOR YOU. WHY DO YOU WISH TO HUMILIATE ME?

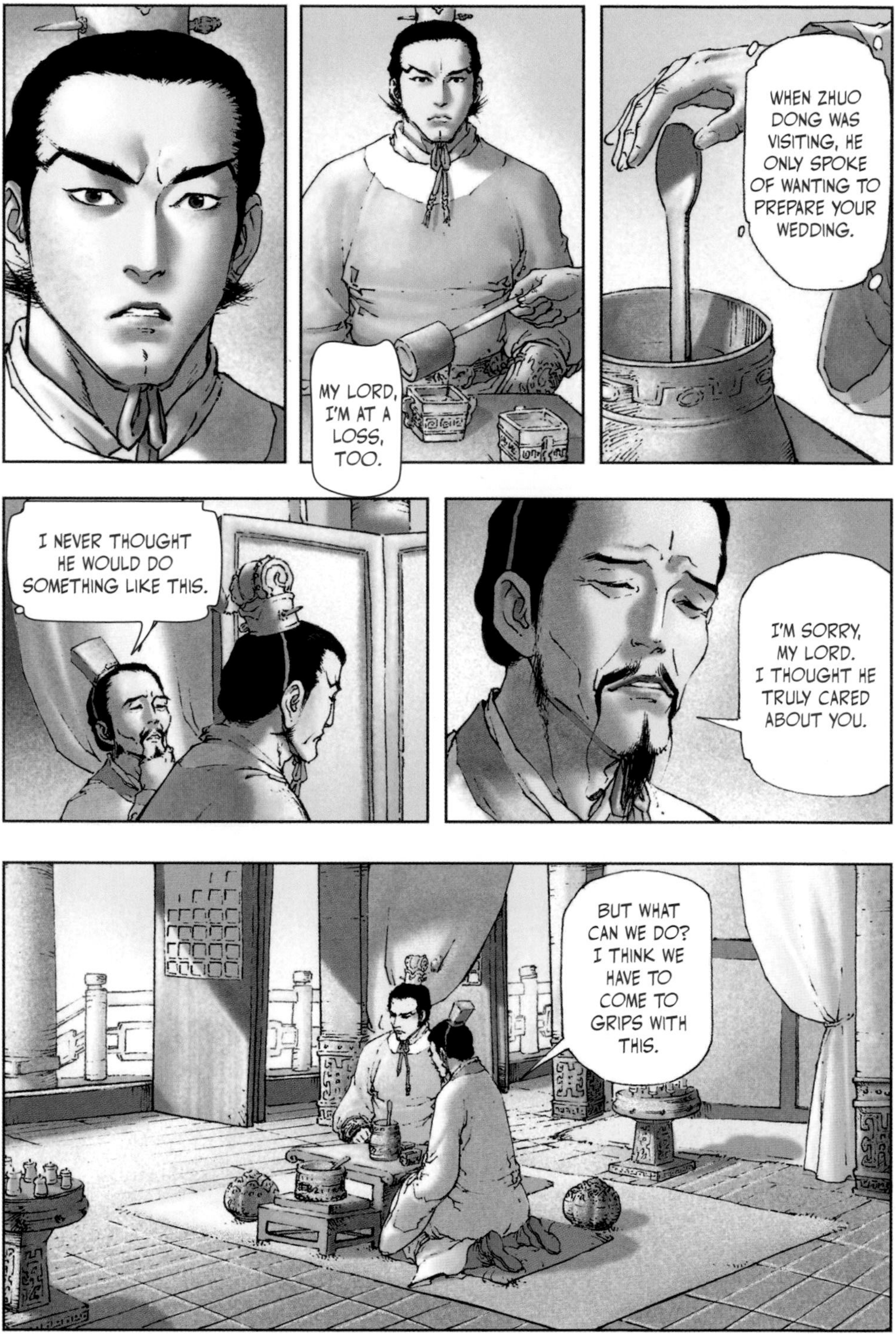
WHEN ZHUO DONG WAS VISITING, HE ONLY SPOKE OF WANTING TO PREPARE YOUR WEDDING.
MY LORD, I'M AT A LOSS, TOO.
I NEVER THOUGHT HE WOULD DO SOMETHING LIKE THIS.
I'M SORRY, MY LORD. I THOUGHT HE TRULY CARED ABOUT YOU.
BUT WHAT CAN WE DO? I THINK WE HAVE TO COME TO GRIPS WITH THIS.

ZHUO DONG IS OUR RULER, AND YOUR STEPFATHER.

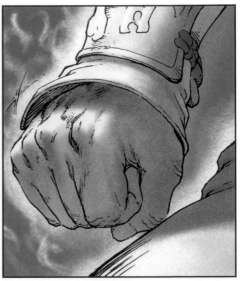

HE IS NOTHING OF THE KIND! HE IS A LIAR AND A THIEF.

ALL IS WELL ON MY END. THINGS ARE GOING EXACTLY AS EXPECTED.

THE BOARD IS SET AND THE PIECES ARE MOVING INTO PLACE.

IT WON'T BE LONG NOW.

HM...

DON'T WORRY ABOUT ME, FATHER.

THE FATE OF THE NATION HANGS IN THE BALANCE. I'M ONLY GLAD I CAN BE PUT TO USE.

OH, YES. I'LL HAVE ONE.

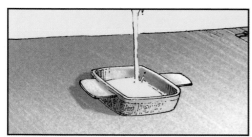

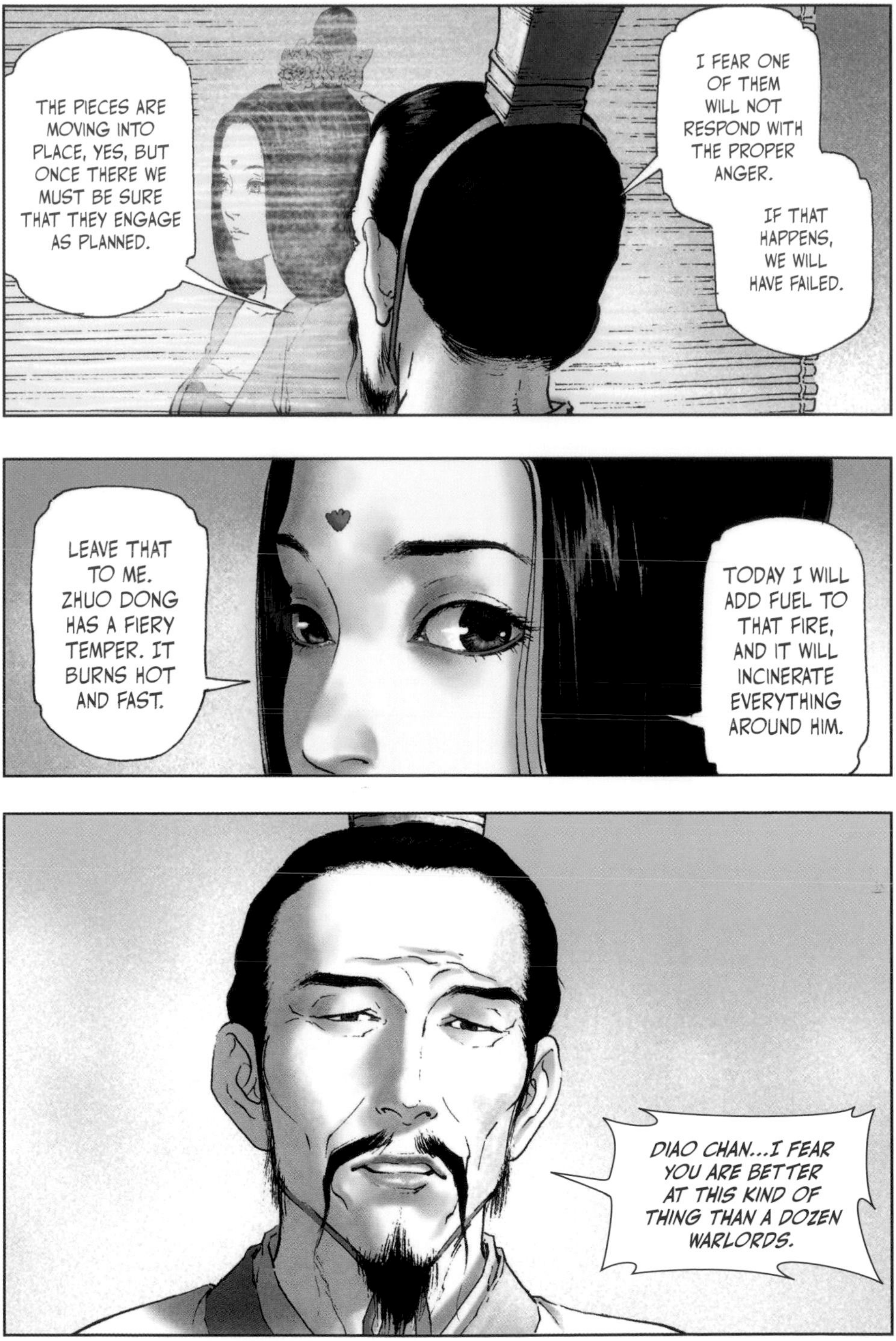
THE PIECES ARE MOVING INTO PLACE, YES, BUT ONCE THERE WE MUST BE SURE THAT THEY ENGAGE AS PLANNED.
I FEAR ONE OF THEM WILL NOT RESPOND WITH THE PROPER ANGER.
IF THAT HAPPENS, WE WILL HAVE FAILED.
LEAVE THAT TO ME. ZHUO DONG HAS A FIERY TEMPER. IT BURNS HOT AND FAST.
TODAY I WILL ADD FUEL TO THAT FIRE, AND IT WILL INCINERATE EVERYTHING AROUND HIM.
DIAO CHAN...I FEAR YOU ARE BETTER AT THIS KIND OF THING THAN A DOZEN WARLORDS.

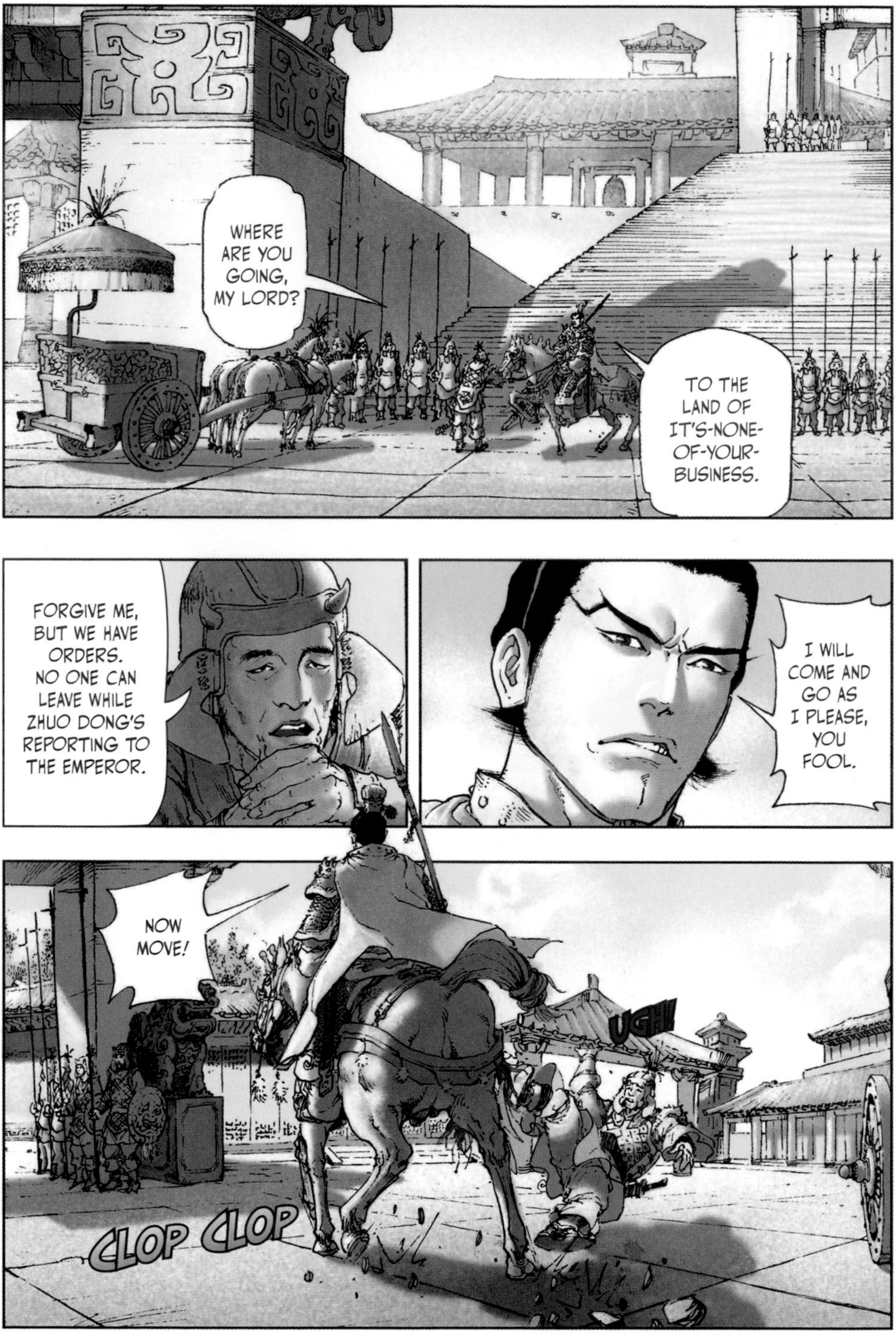
WHERE ARE YOU GOING, MY LORD?
TO THE LAND OF IT'S-NONE-OF-YOUR-BUSINESS.
FORGIVE ME, BUT WE HAVE ORDERS. NO ONE CAN LEAVE WHILE ZHUO DONG'S REPORTING TO THE EMPEROR.
I WILL COME AND GO AS I PLEASE, YOU FOOL.
NOW MOVE!
UGH!
CLOP CLOP

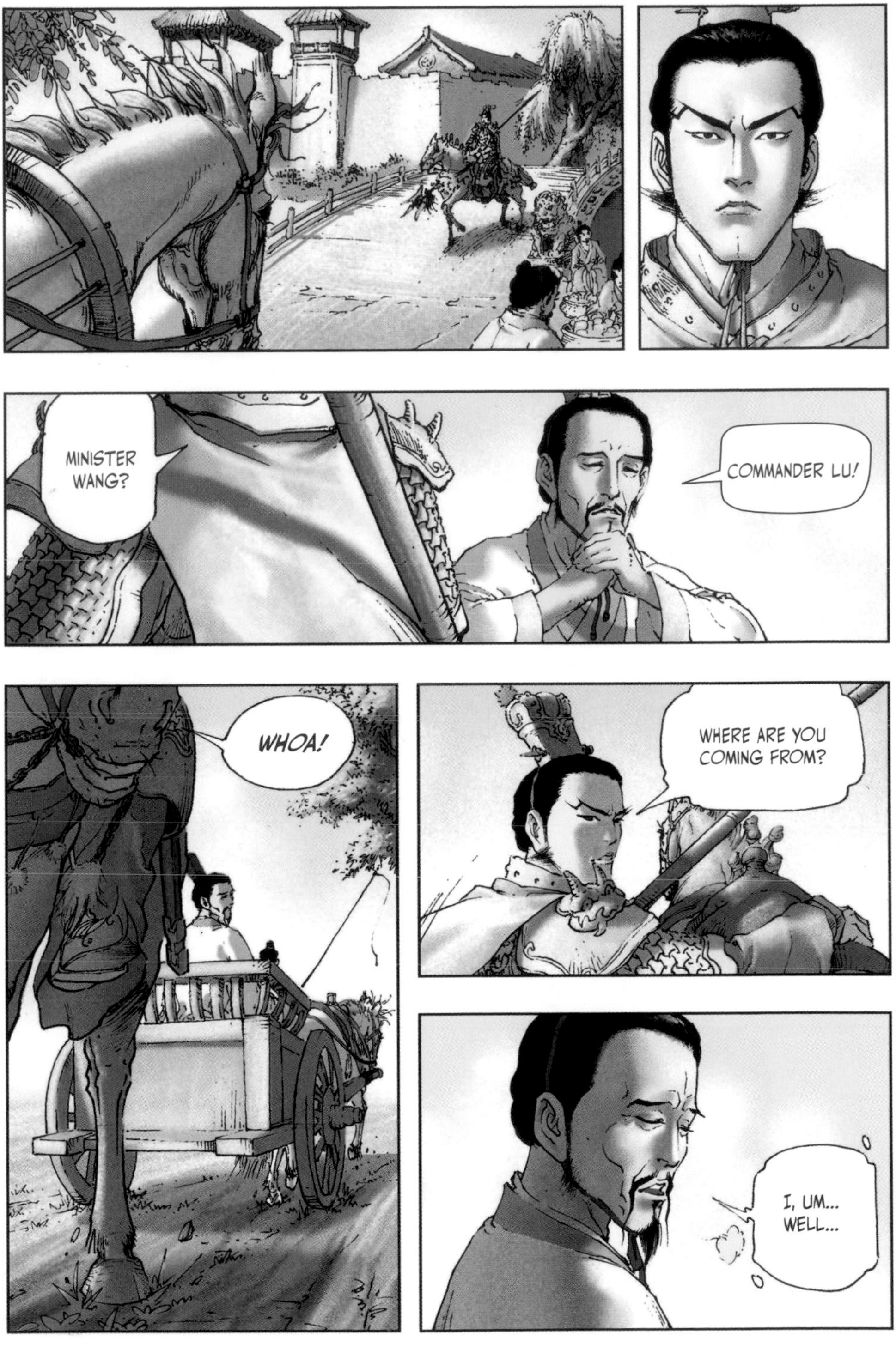
MINISTER WANG?
COMMANDER LU!
WHOA!
WHERE ARE YOU COMING FROM?
I, UM... WELL...

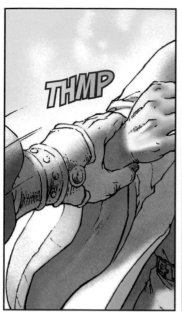

THMP

WHY DO YOU STUTTER?

WERE YOU AT THE PALACE? WAS DIAO CHAN THERE?

PLEASE, DON'T HURT ME! I'M SORRY TO TREMBLE, BUT... I DON'T KNOW WHAT TO DO.

IT'S ABOUT DIAO CHAN. I JUST SAW HER, AND SHE... I JUST CAN'T...

WHAT IS IT? WHAT'S HAPPENED TO HER?

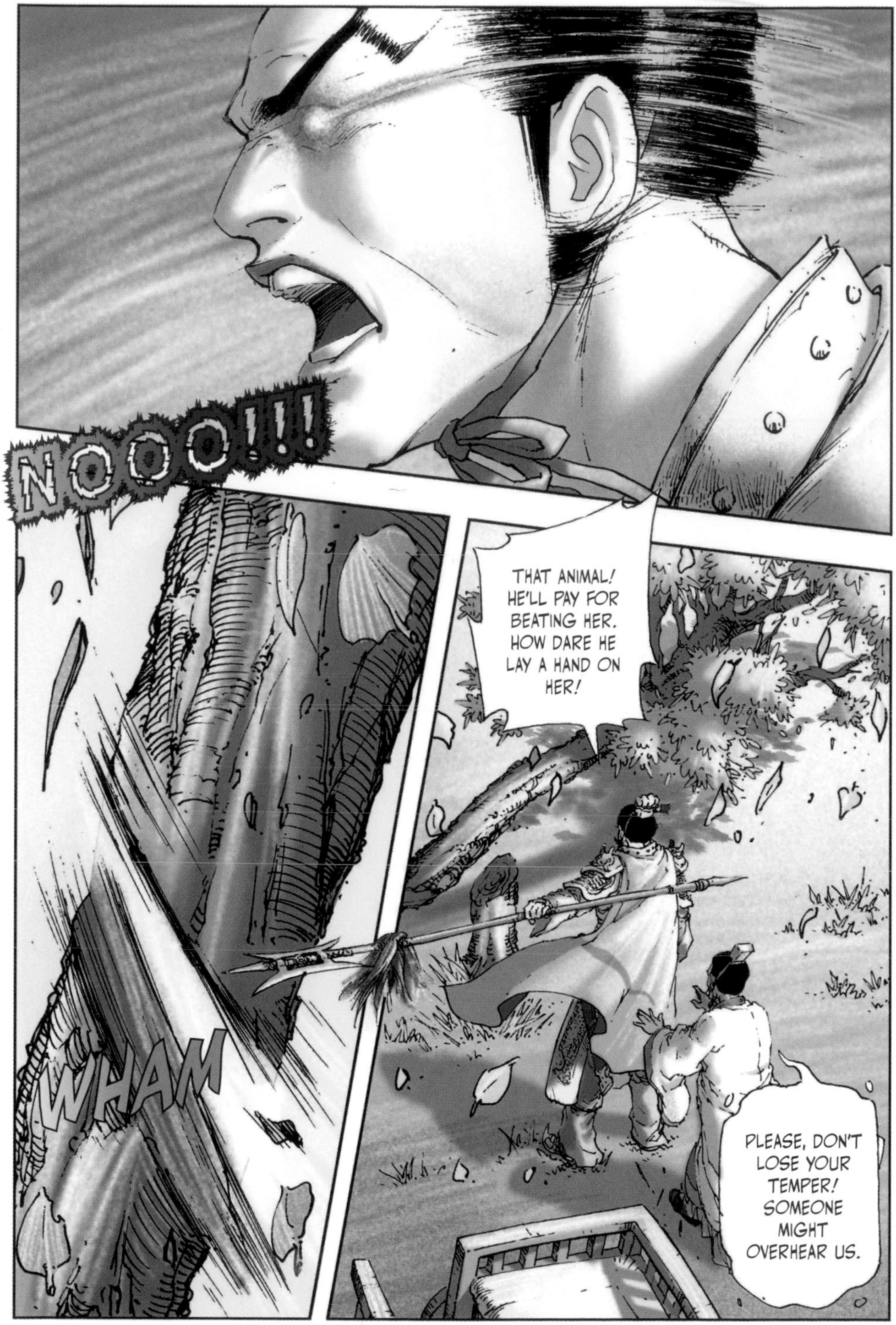
NOOO!!!
THAT ANIMAL! HE'LL PAY FOR BEATING HER. HOW DARE HE LAY A HAND ON HER!
WHAM
PLEASE, DON'T LOSE YOUR TEMPER! SOMEONE MIGHT OVERHEAR US.

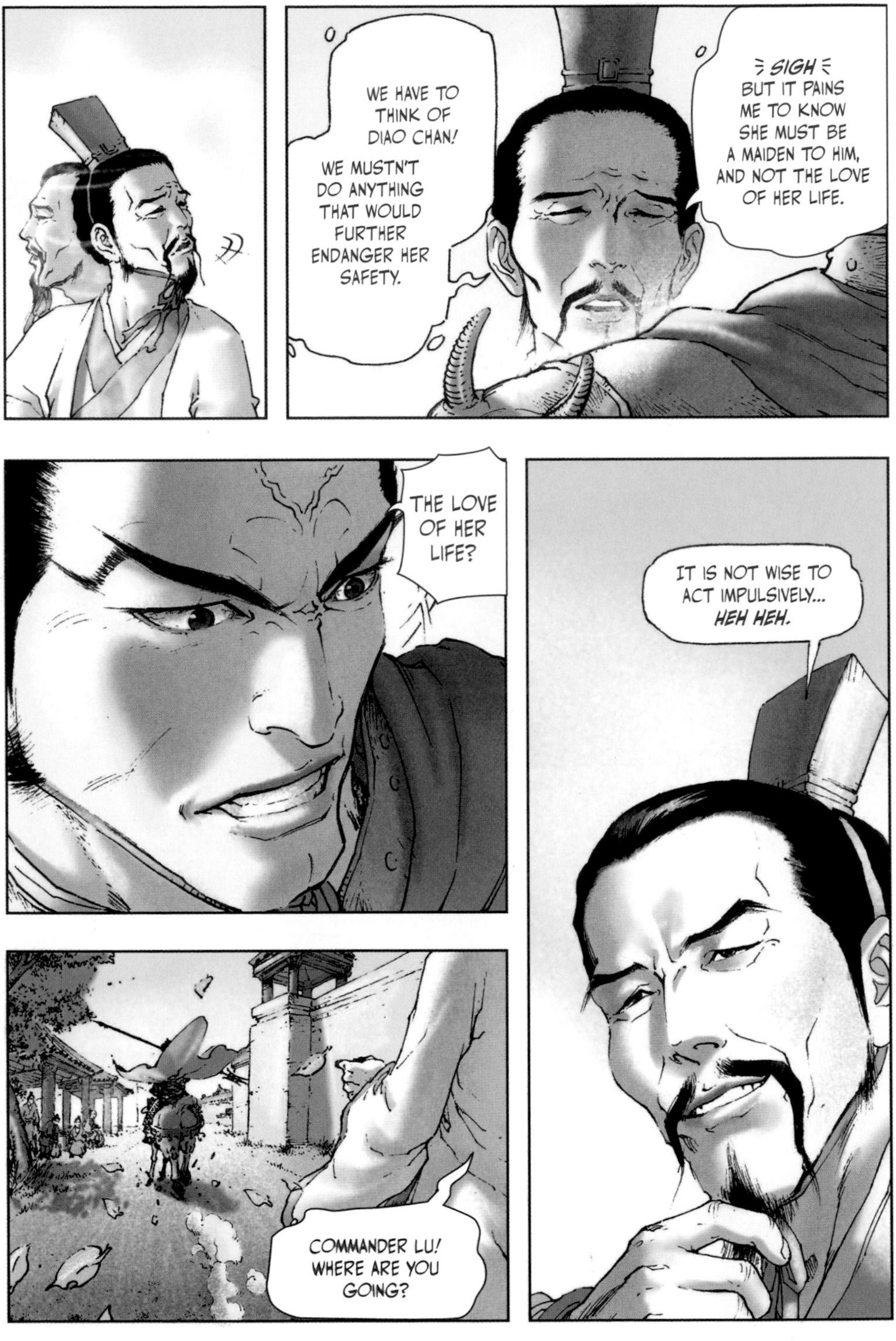
WE HAVE TO THINK OF DIAO CHAN!
WE MUSTN'T DO ANYTHING THAT WOULD FURTHER ENDANGER HER SAFETY.
SIGH
BUT IT PAINS ME TO KNOW SHE MUST BE A MAIDEN TO HIM, AND NOT THE LOVE OF HER LIFE.
THE LOVE OF HER LIFE?
IT IS NOT WISE TO ACT IMPULSIVELY... HEH HEH.
COMMANDER LU! WHERE ARE YOU GOING?

BU LU

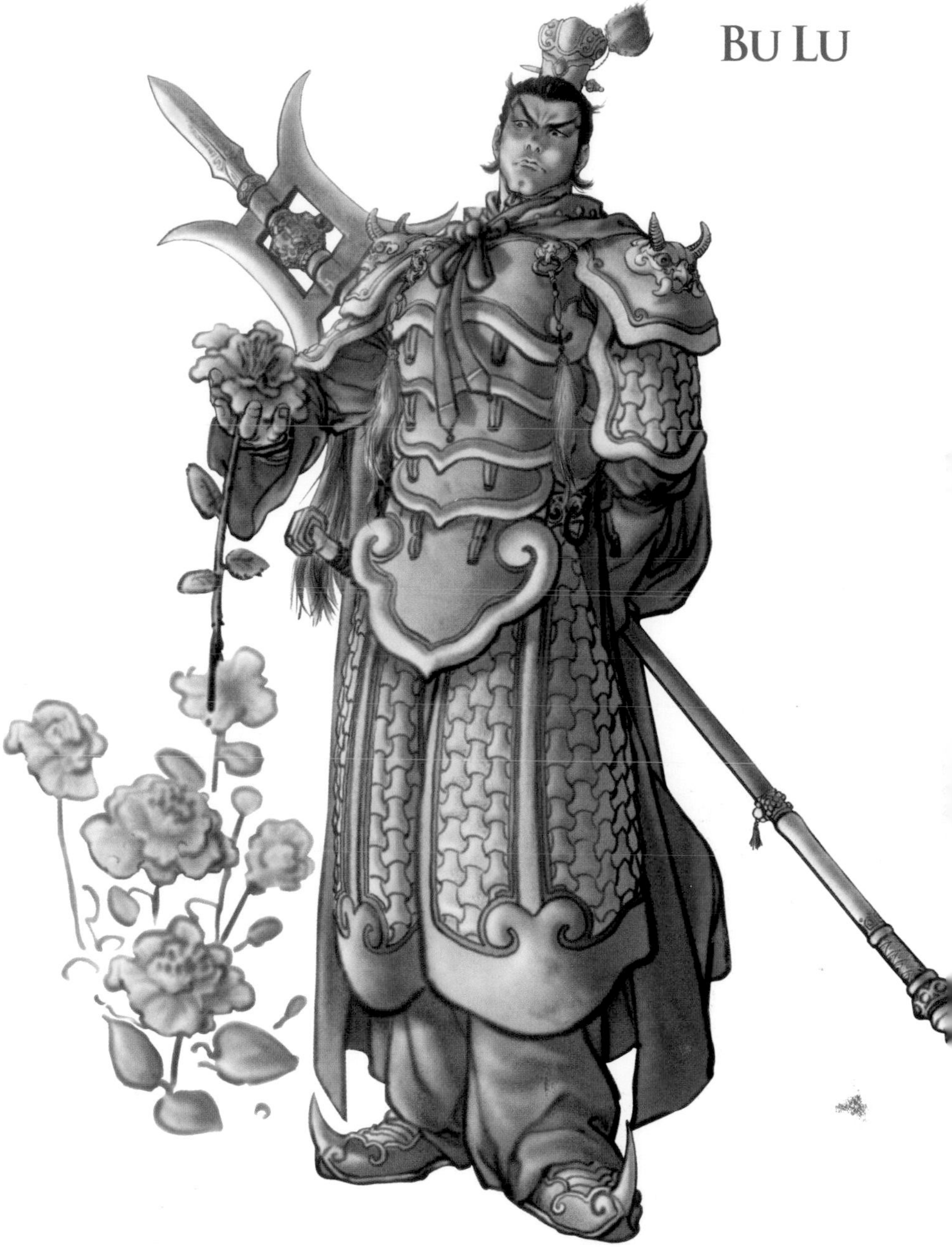

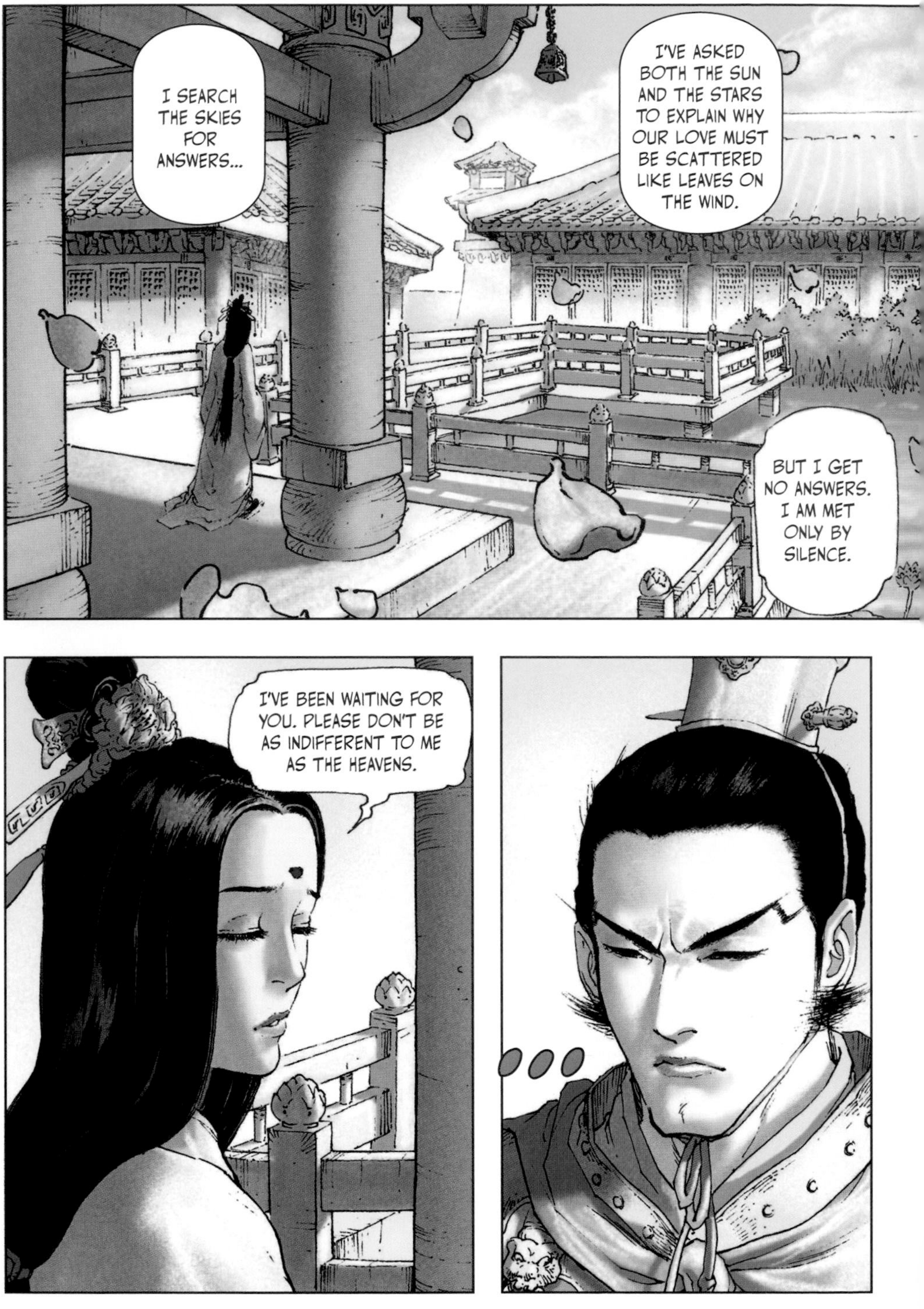
I SEARCH THE SKIES FOR ANSWERS...
I'VE ASKED BOTH THE SUN AND THE STARS TO EXPLAIN WHY OUR LOVE MUST BE SCATTERED LIKE LEAVES ON THE WIND.
BUT I GET NO ANSWERS. I AM MET ONLY BY SILENCE.
I'VE BEEN WAITING FOR YOU. PLEASE DON'T BE AS INDIFFERENT TO ME AS THE HEAVENS.

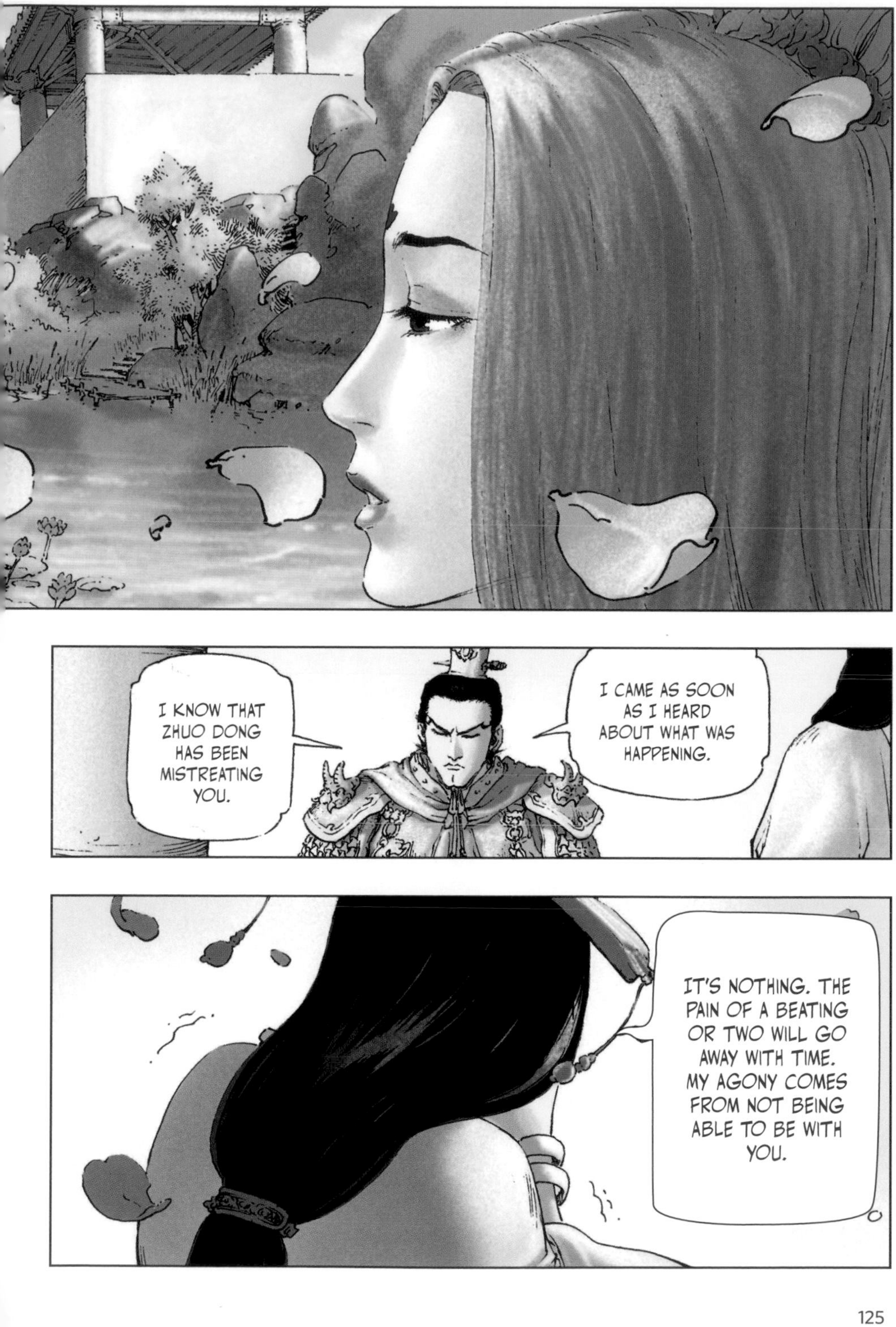

I KNOW THAT ZHUO DONG HAS BEEN MISTREATING YOU.
I CAME AS SOON AS I HEARD ABOUT WHAT WAS HAPPENING.
IT'S NOTHING. THE PAIN OF A BEATING OR TWO WILL GO AWAY WITH TIME. MY AGONY COMES FROM NOT BEING ABLE TO BE WITH YOU.

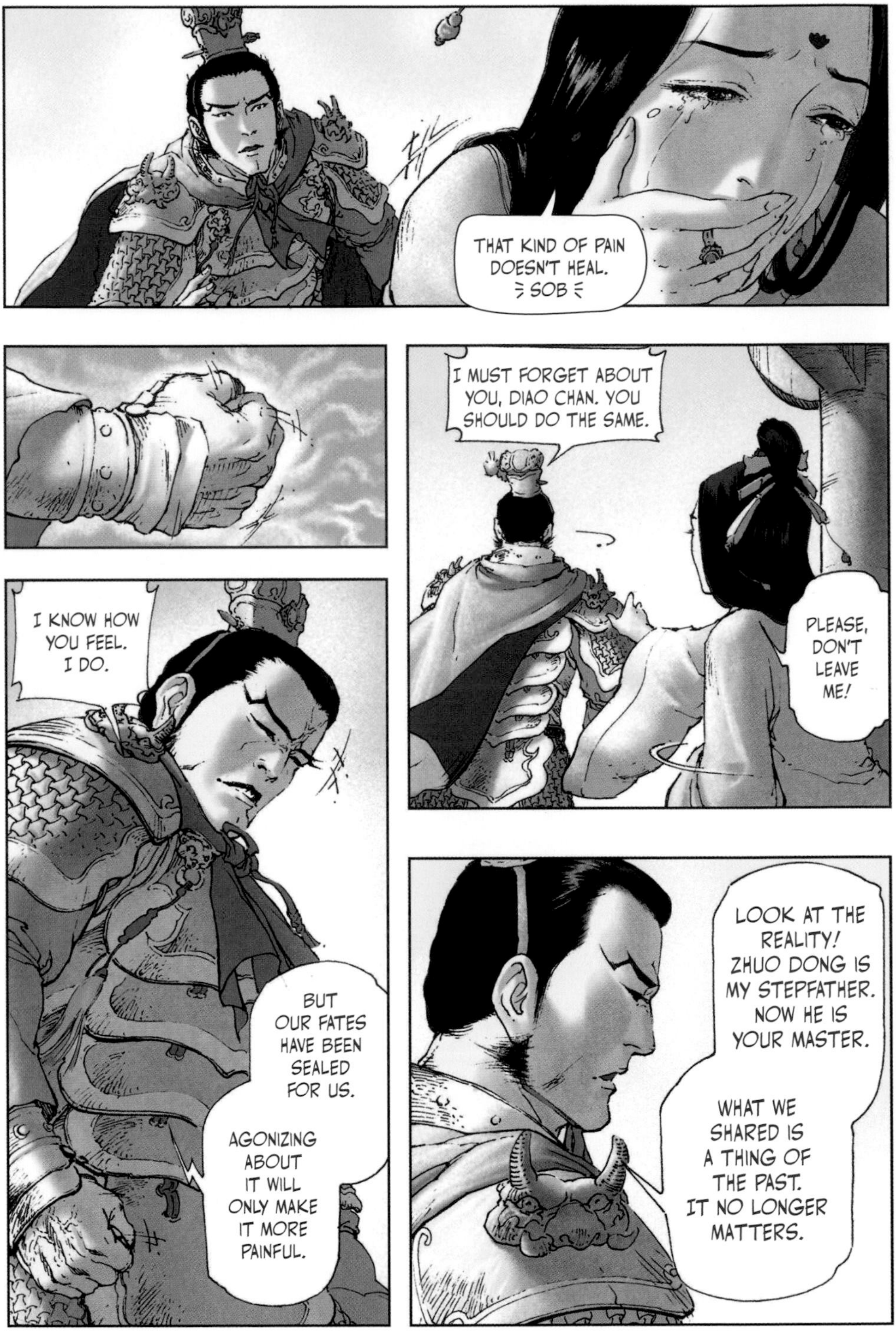
THAT KIND OF PAIN DOESN'T HEAL. ⋚ SOB ⋚
I MUST FORGET ABOUT YOU, DIAO CHAN. YOU SHOULD DO THE SAME.
PLEASE, DON'T LEAVE ME!
I KNOW HOW YOU FEEL. I DO.
BUT OUR FATES HAVE BEEN SEALED FOR US.
AGONIZING ABOUT IT WILL ONLY MAKE IT MORE PAINFUL.
LOOK AT THE REALITY! ZHUO DONG IS MY STEPFATHER. NOW HE IS YOUR MASTER.
WHAT WE SHARED IS A THING OF THE PAST. IT NO LONGER MATTERS.

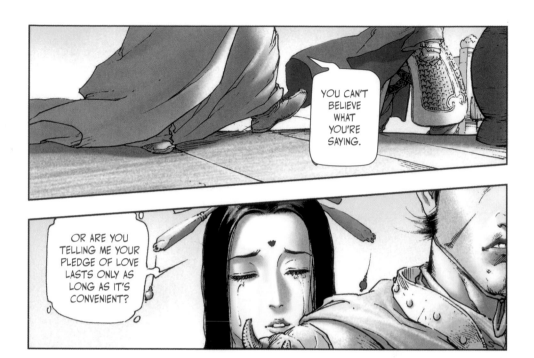

YOU CAN'T BELIEVE WHAT YOU'RE SAYING.

OR ARE YOU TELLING ME YOUR PLEDGE OF LOVE LASTS ONLY AS LONG AS IT'S CONVENIENT?

MAYBE IT'S BECAUSE I'M YOUNG, BUT I BELIEVE PROMISING TO LOVE SOMEONE FOREVER MEANS YOU LOVE HER THROUGH ANYTHING.

ARE YOU BANISHING ME TO YOUR PAST BECAUSE I'VE SLEPT WITH ZHUO DONG?

IS THAT HOW YOUR LOVE WORKS?

OF COURSE NOT.

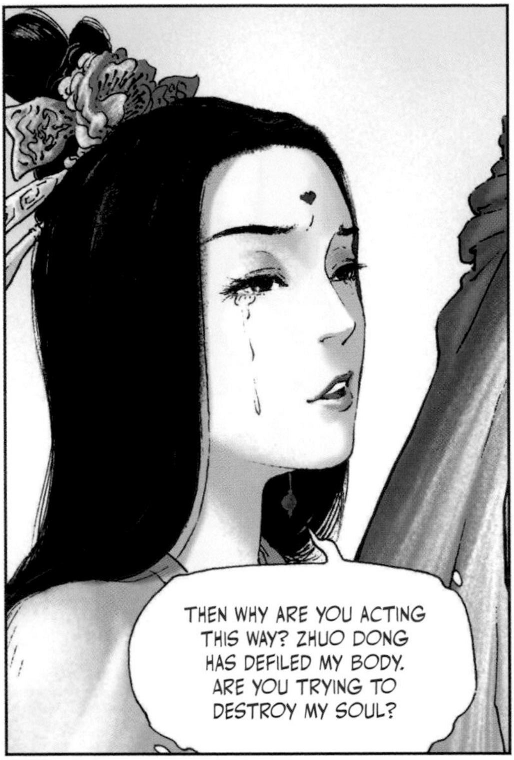
THEN WHY ARE YOU ACTING THIS WAY? ZHUO DONG HAS DEFILED MY BODY. ARE YOU TRYING TO DESTROY MY SOUL?

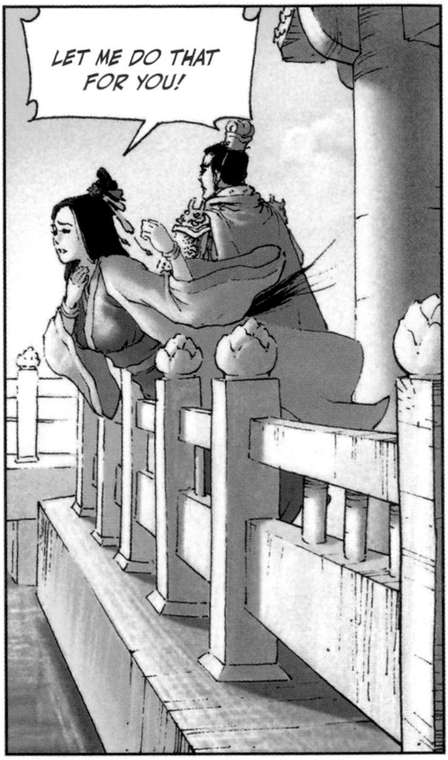
LET ME DO THAT FOR YOU!

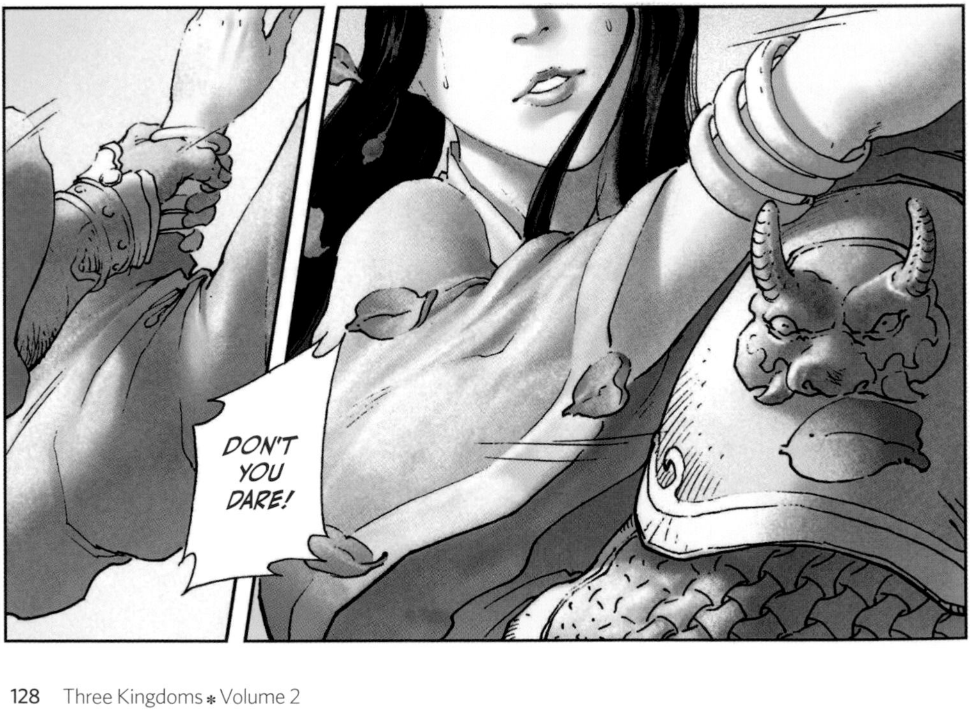
DON'T YOU DARE!

WHAT DO YOU THINK YOU'RE DOING?

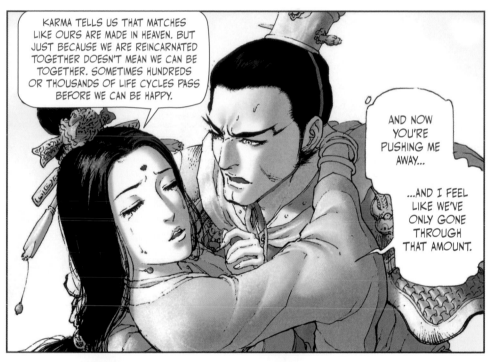

KARMA TELLS US THAT MATCHES LIKE OURS ARE MADE IN HEAVEN. BUT JUST BECAUSE WE ARE REINCARNATED TOGETHER DOESN'T MEAN WE CAN BE TOGETHER. SOMETIMES HUNDREDS OR THOUSANDS OF LIFE CYCLES PASS BEFORE WE CAN BE HAPPY.

AND NOW YOU'RE PUSHING ME AWAY...

...AND I FEEL LIKE WE'VE ONLY GONE THROUGH THAT AMOUNT.

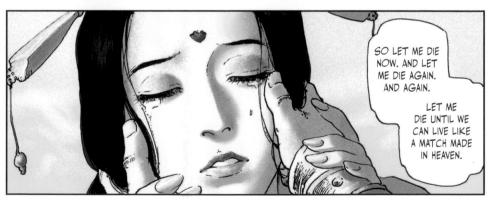

SO LET ME DIE NOW. AND LET ME DIE AGAIN. AND AGAIN.

LET ME DIE UNTIL WE CAN LIVE LIKE A MATCH MADE IN HEAVEN.

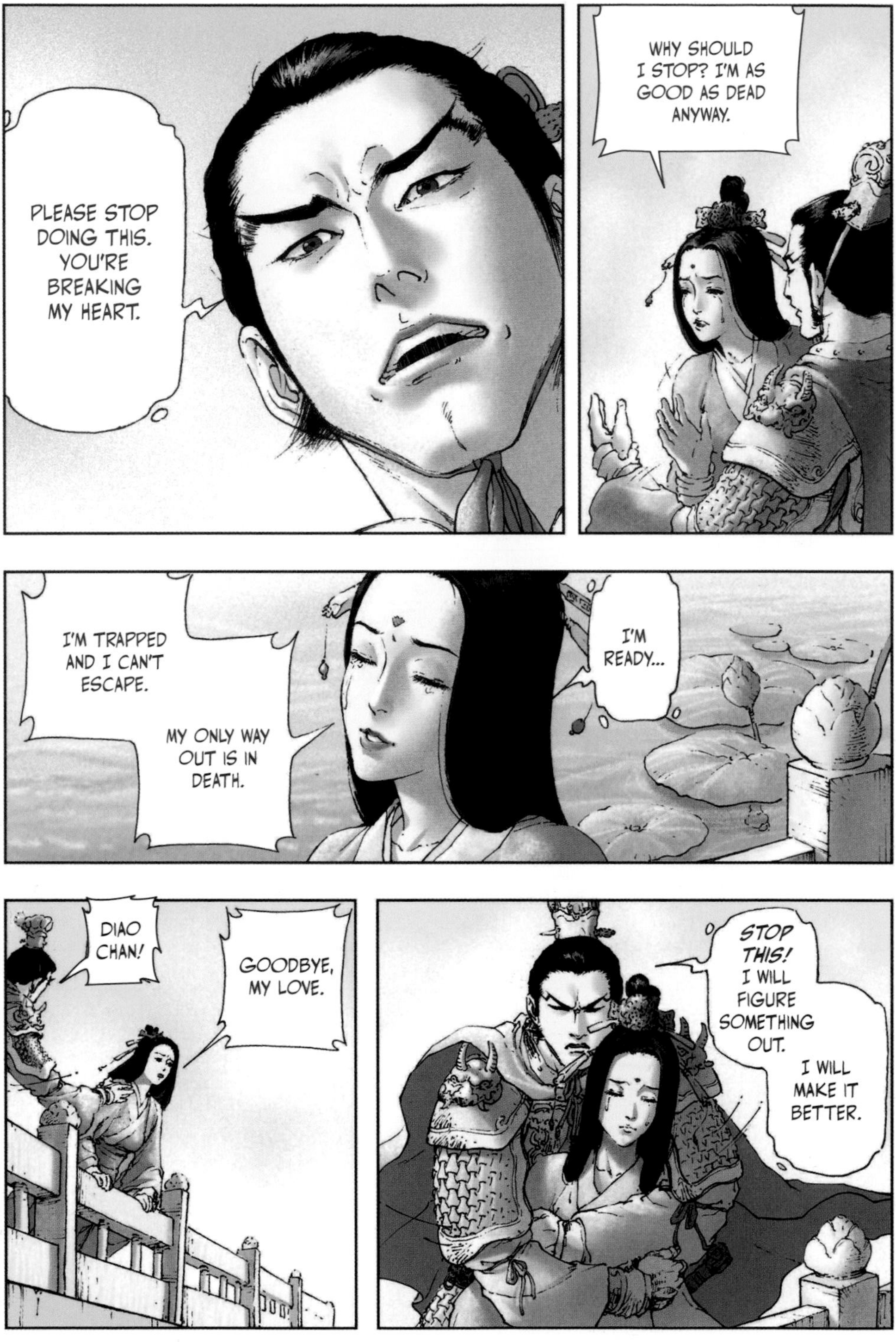
PLEASE STOP DOING THIS. YOU'RE BREAKING MY HEART.
WHY SHOULD I STOP? I'M AS GOOD AS DEAD ANYWAY.
I'M TRAPPED AND I CAN'T ESCAPE.
MY ONLY WAY OUT IS IN DEATH.
I'M READY...
DIAO CHAN!
GOODBYE, MY LOVE.
STOP THIS! I WILL FIGURE SOMETHING OUT.
I WILL MAKE IT BETTER.

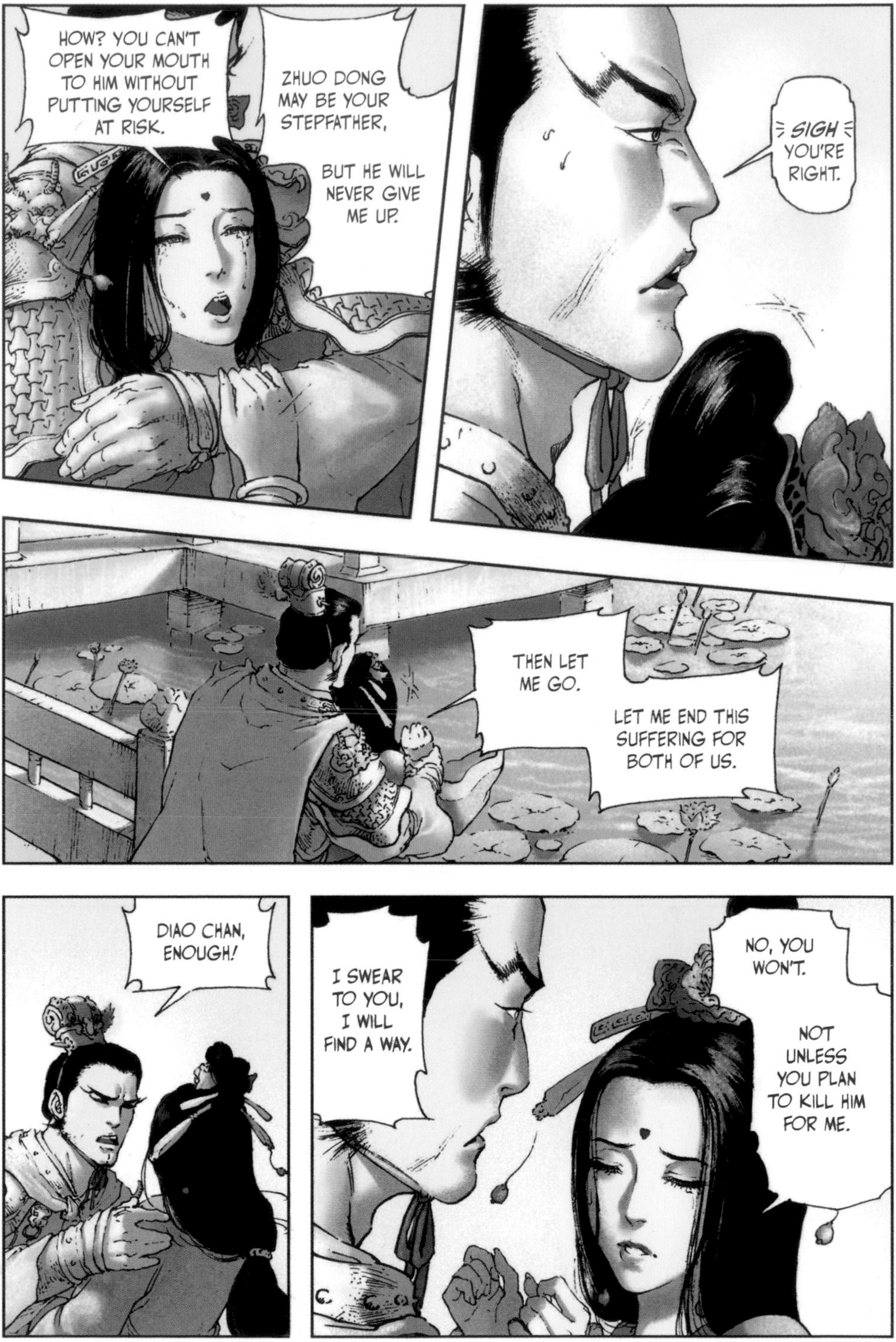
HOW? YOU CAN'T OPEN YOUR MOUTH TO HIM WITHOUT PUTTING YOURSELF AT RISK.
ZHUO DONG MAY BE YOUR STEPFATHER,
BUT HE WILL NEVER GIVE ME UP.
SIGH YOU'RE RIGHT.
THEN LET ME GO.
LET ME END THIS SUFFERING FOR BOTH OF US.
DIAO CHAN, ENOUGH!
I SWEAR TO YOU, I WILL FIND A WAY.
NO, YOU WON'T.
NOT UNLESS YOU PLAN TO KILL HIM FOR ME.

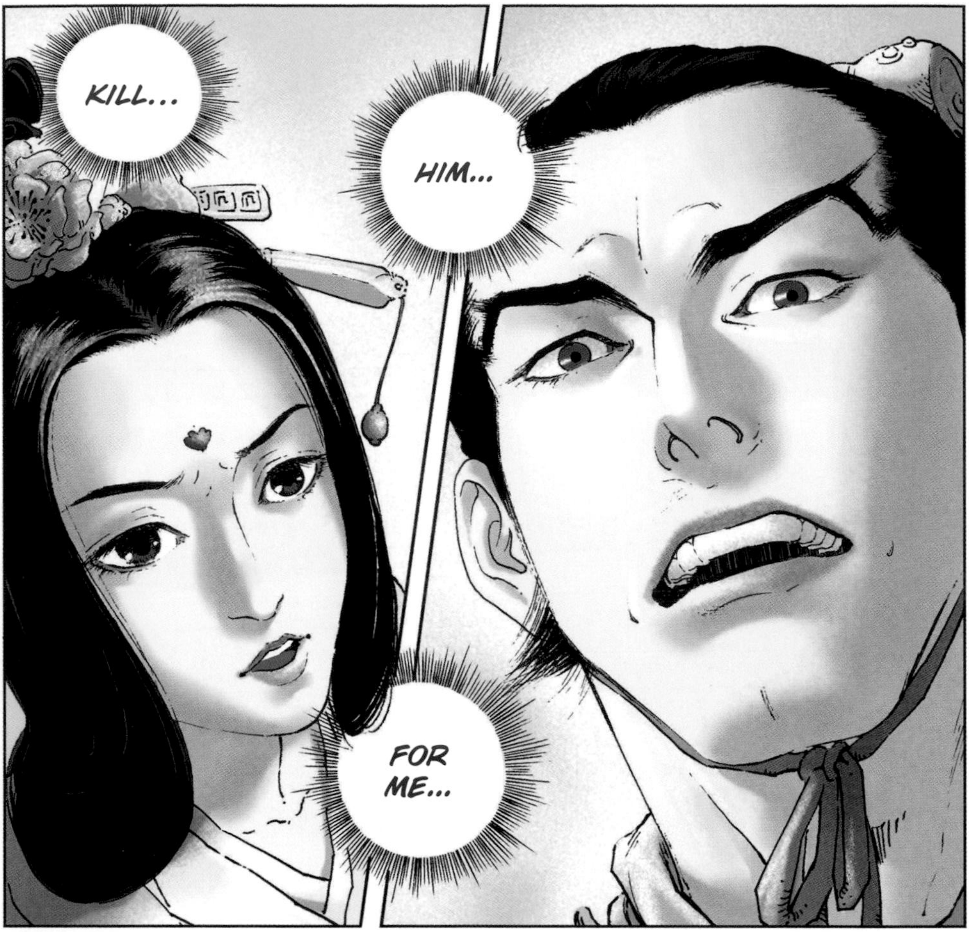
KILL...
HIM...
FOR ME...

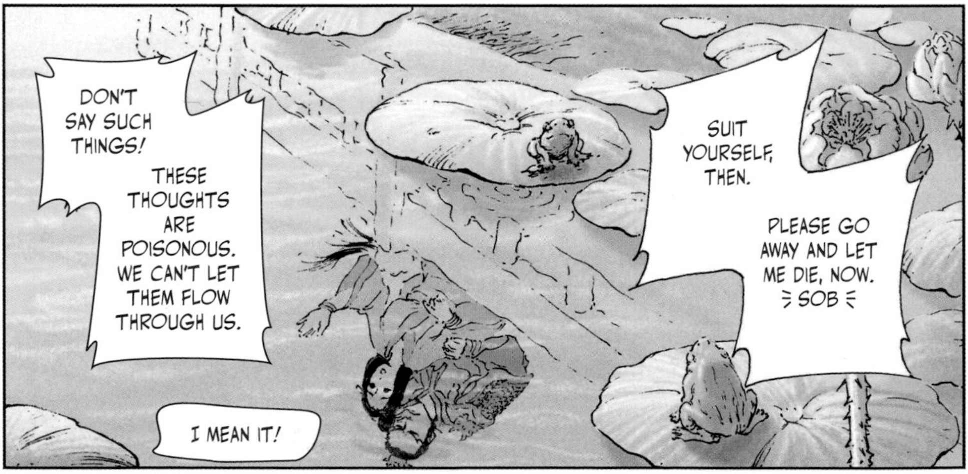
DON'T SAY SUCH THINGS!
THESE THOUGHTS ARE POISONOUS. WE CAN'T LET THEM FLOW THROUGH US.
I MEAN IT!
SUIT YOURSELF, THEN.
PLEASE GO AWAY AND LET ME DIE, NOW. SOB

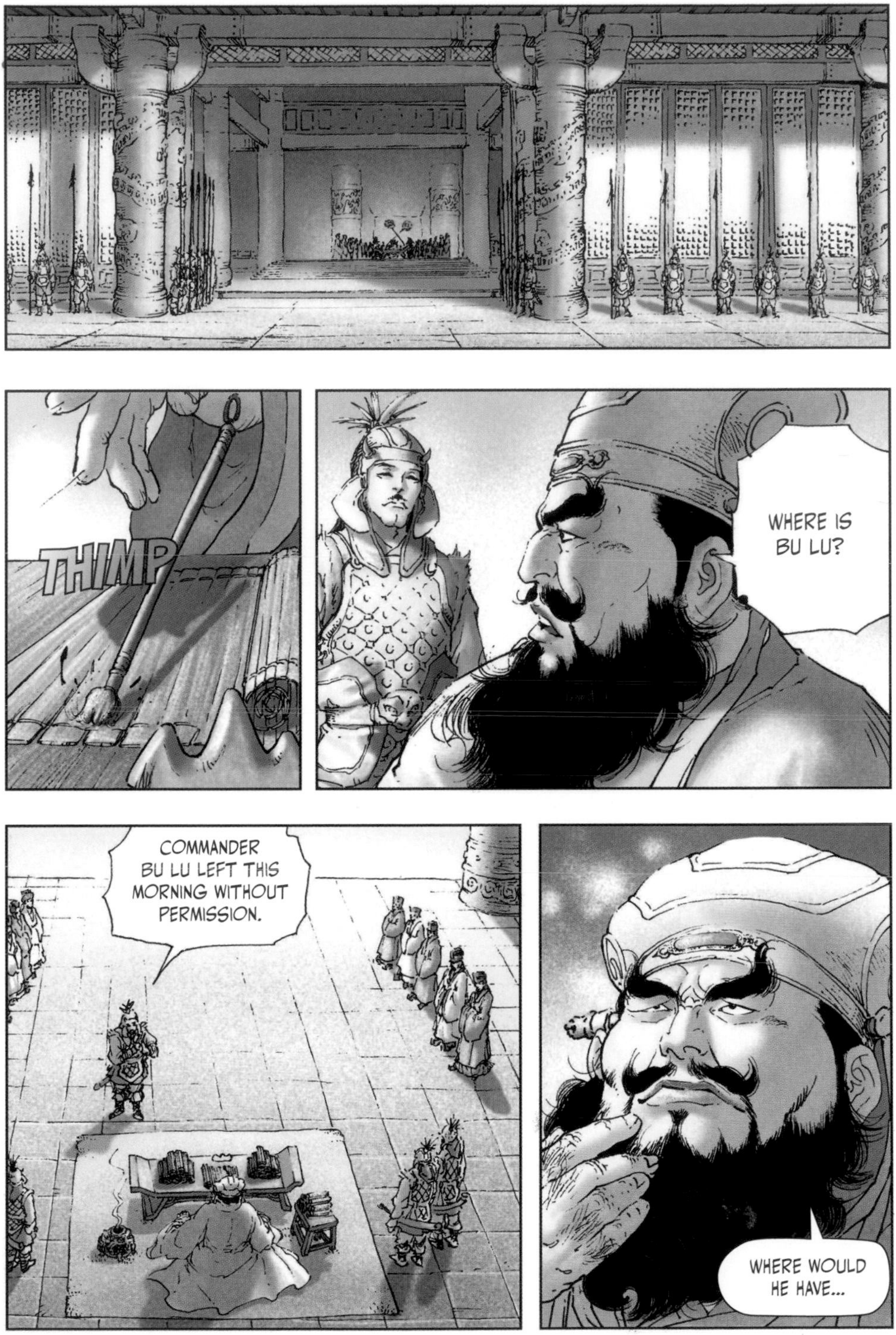
THIMP
WHERE IS BU LU?
COMMANDER BU LU LEFT THIS MORNING WITHOUT PERMISSION.
WHERE WOULD HE HAVE...

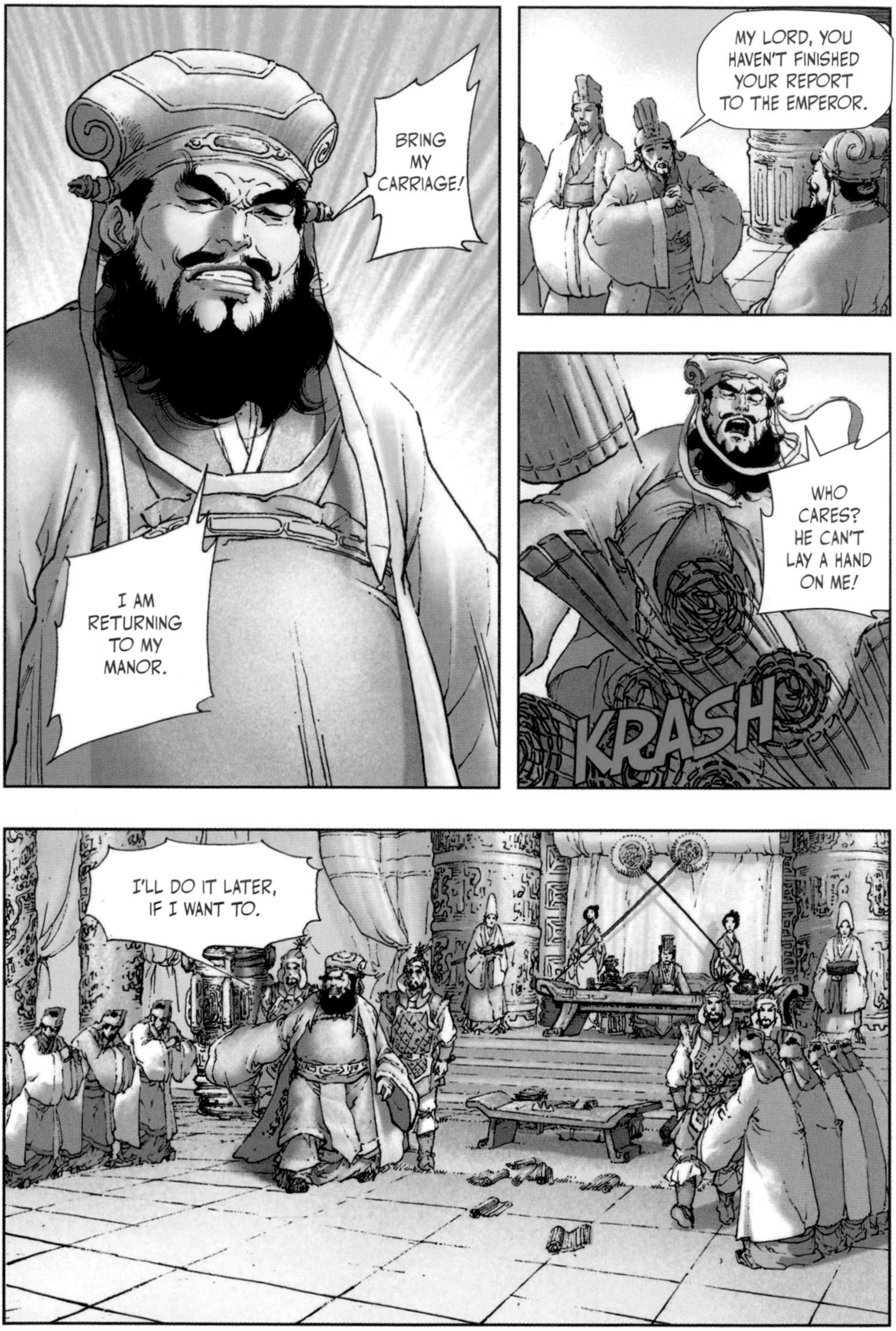
BRING MY CARRIAGE!
I AM RETURNING TO MY MANOR.
MY LORD, YOU HAVEN'T FINISHED YOUR REPORT TO THE EMPEROR.
WHO CARES? HE CAN'T LAY A HAND ON ME!
KRASH
I'LL DO IT LATER, IF I WANT TO.

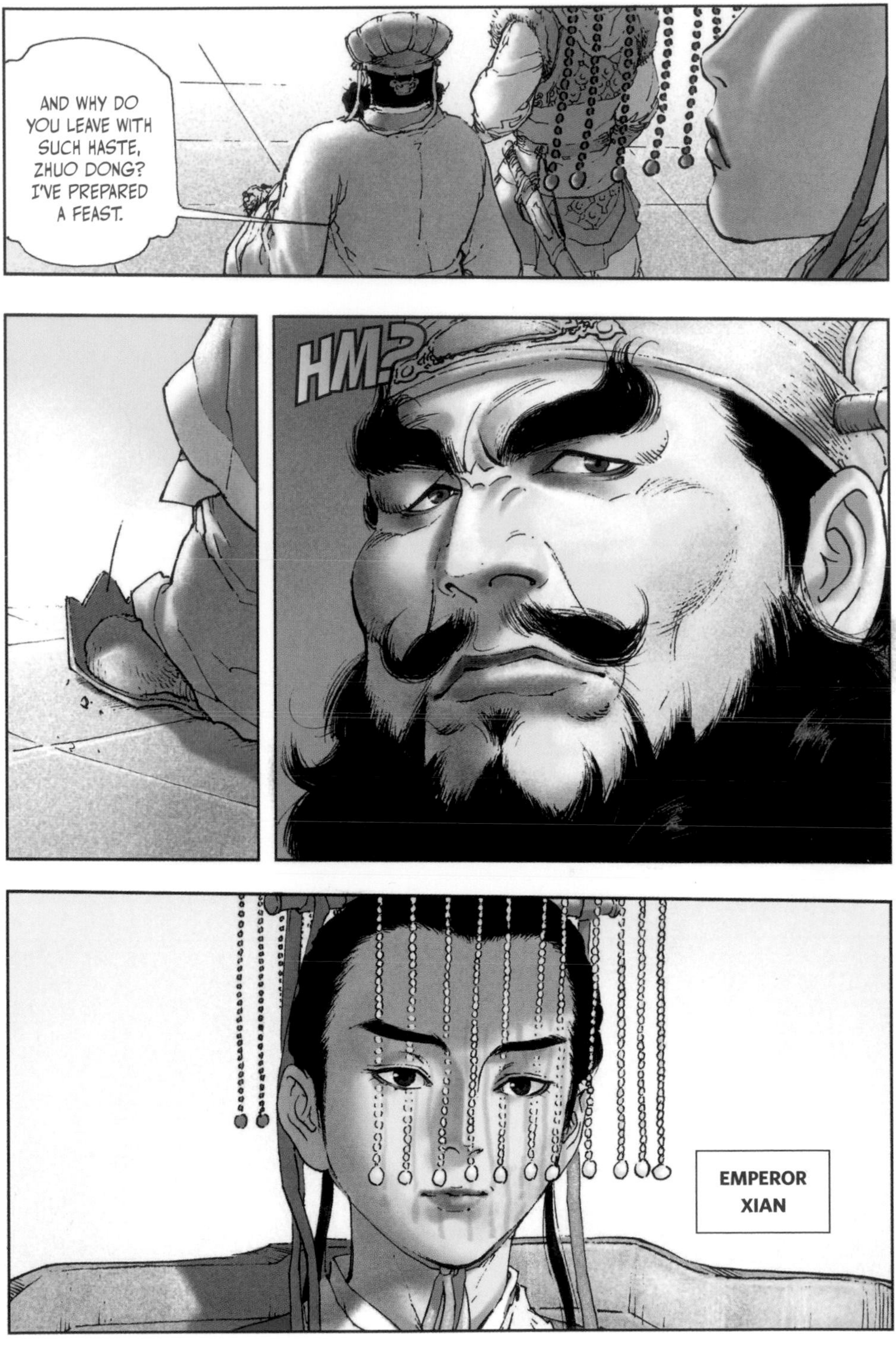
AND WHY DO YOU LEAVE WITH SUCH HASTE, ZHUO DONG? I'VE PREPARED A FEAST.
HM?
EMPEROR XIAN

IT WILL HAVE TO WAIT.

SAVE IT FOR NEXT TIME.

WHERE IS BU LU?

HE'S IN THE COURTYARD, MY LORD, AWAITING YOUR RETURN.

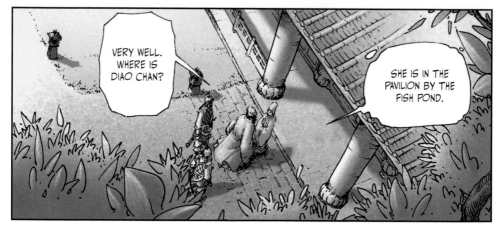

VERY WELL. WHERE IS DIAO CHAN?

SHE IS IN THE PAVILION BY THE FISH POND.

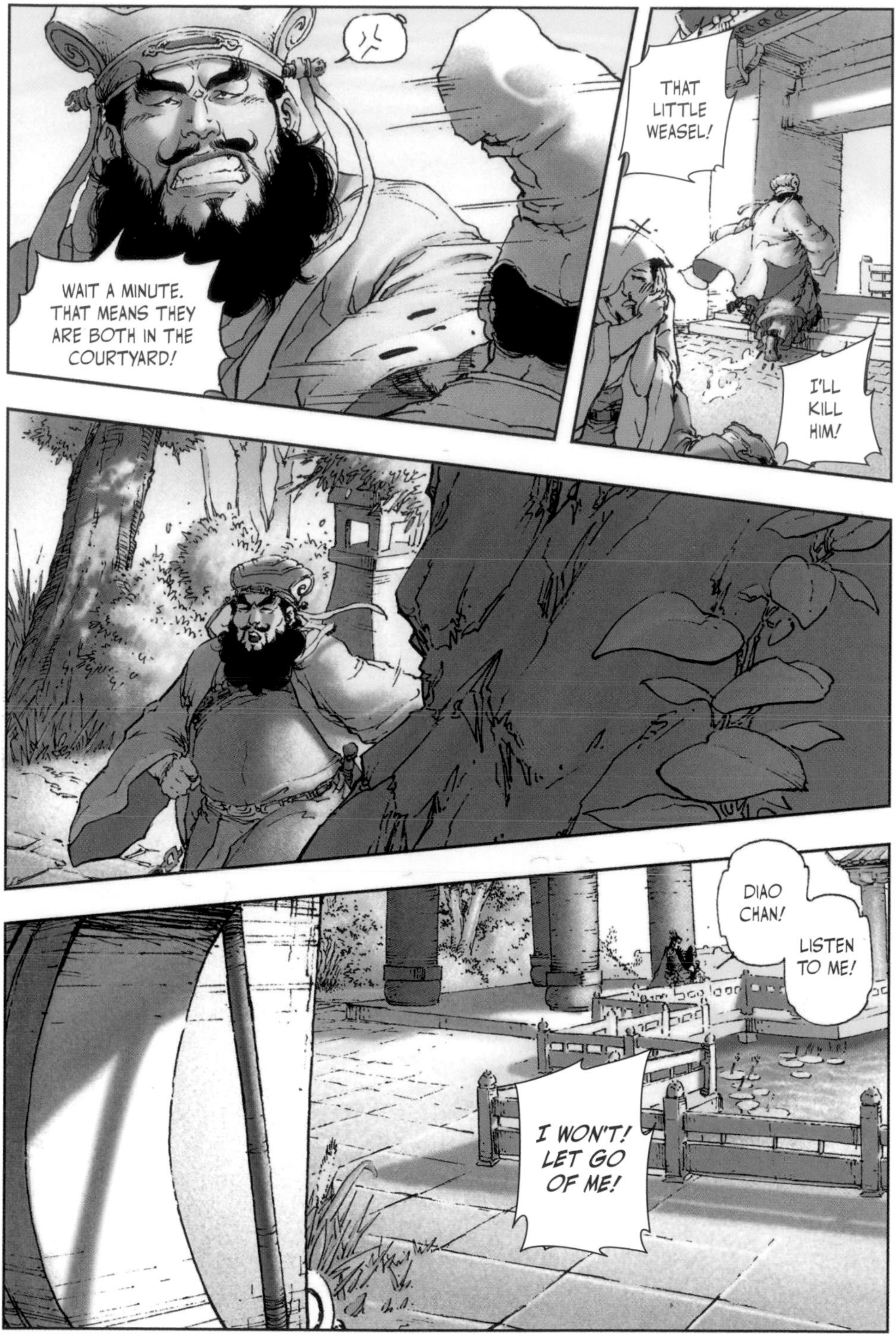

WAIT A MINUTE. THAT MEANS THEY ARE BOTH IN THE COURTYARD!
THAT LITTLE WEASEL!
I'LL KILL HIM!
DIAO CHAN!
LISTEN TO ME!
I WON'T! LET GO OF ME!

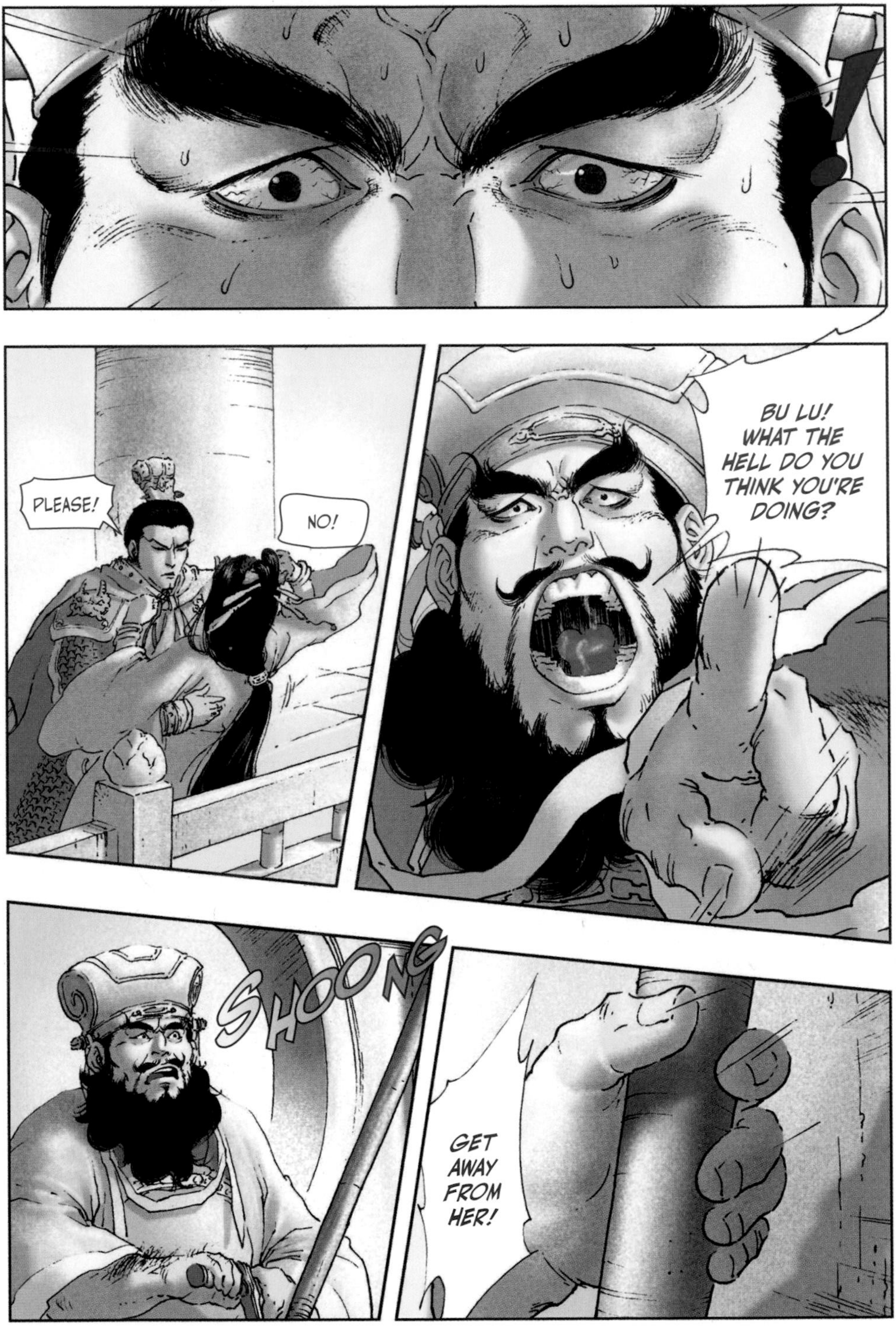
PLEASE!
NO!
BU LU! WHAT THE HELL DO YOU THINK YOU'RE DOING?
SHOONG
GET AWAY FROM HER!

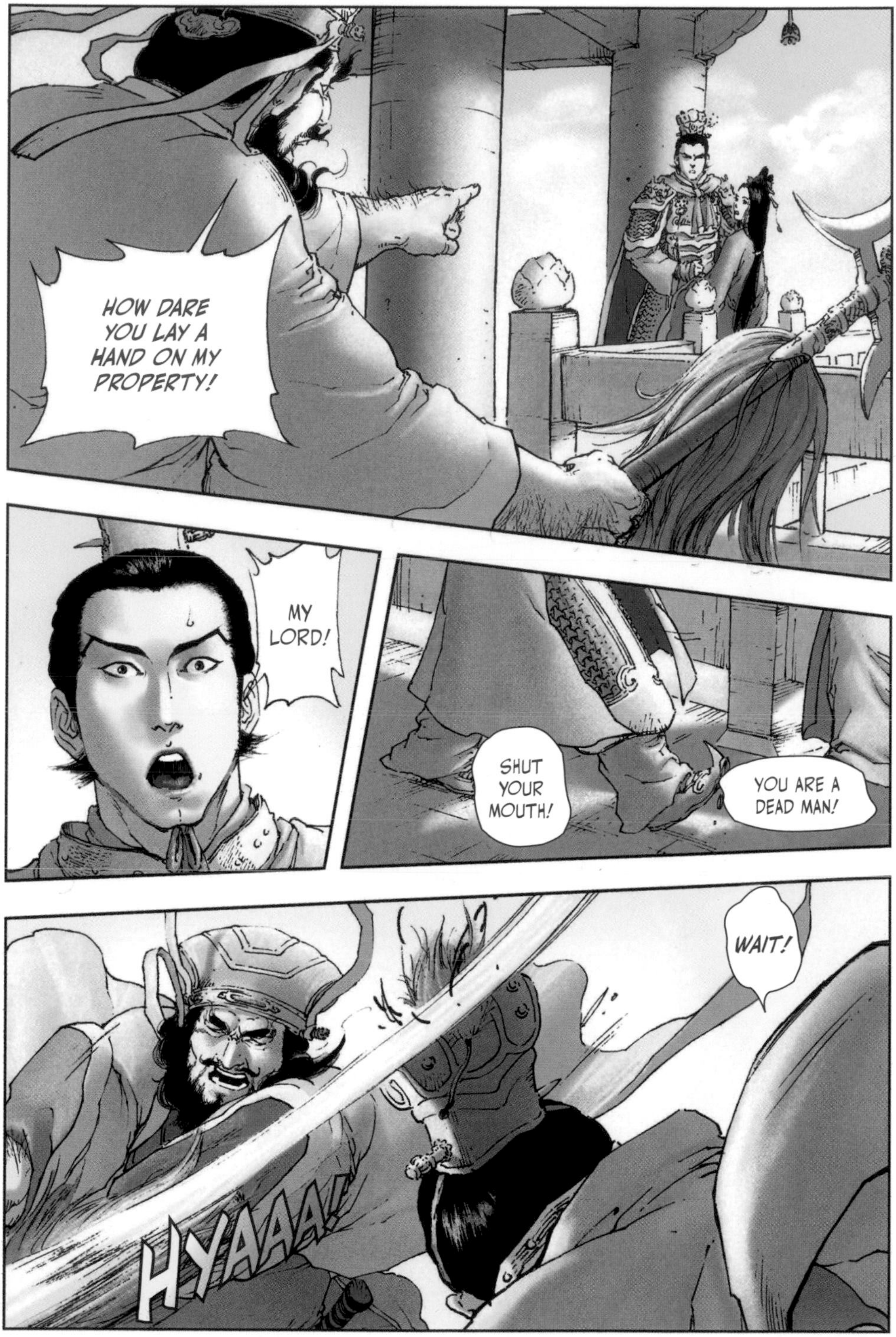
HOW DARE YOU LAY A HAND ON MY PROPERTY!
MY LORD!
SHUT YOUR MOUTH!
YOU ARE A DEAD MAN!
WAIT!
HYAAA!

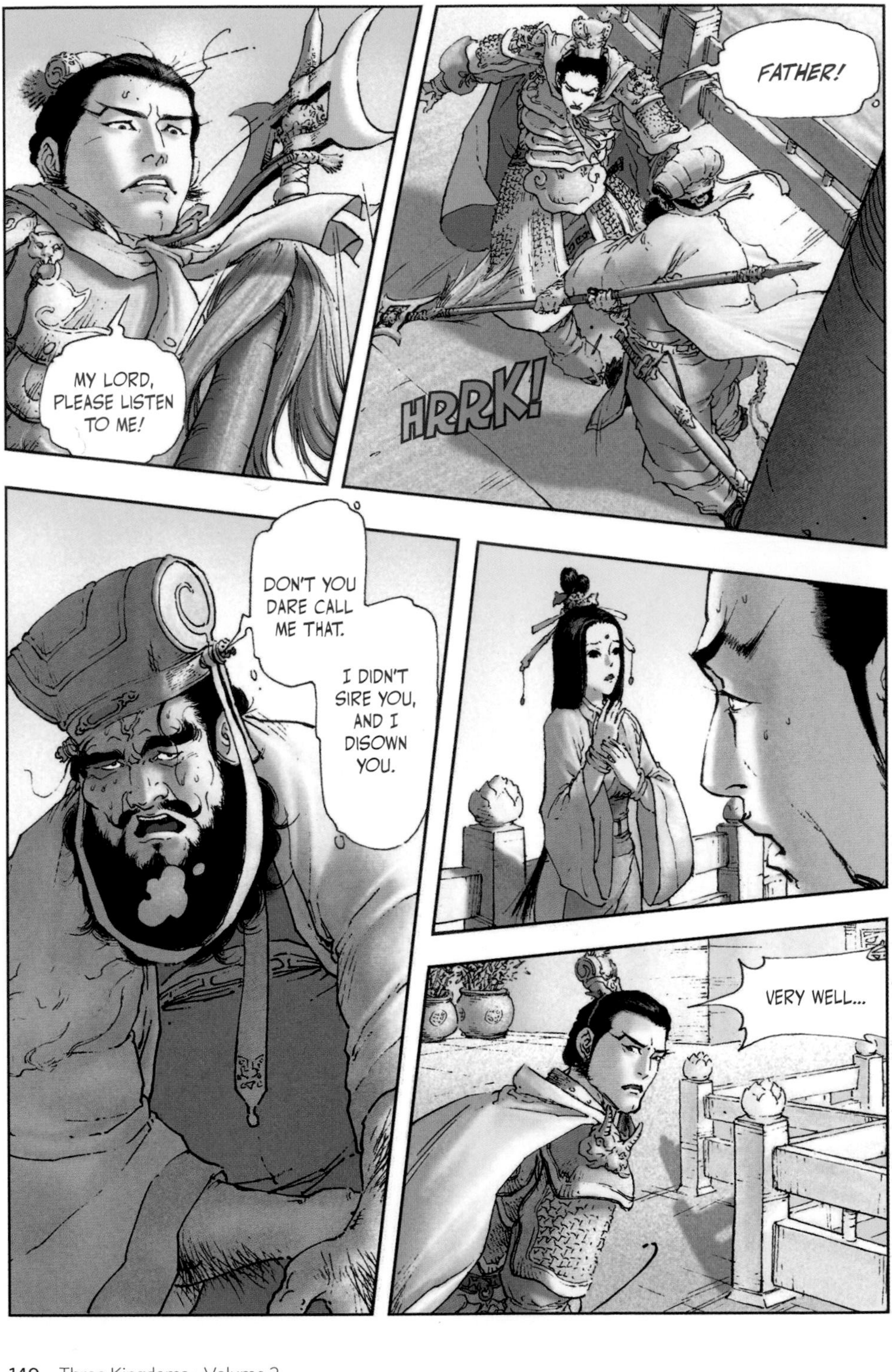
MY LORD, PLEASE LISTEN TO ME!
FATHER!
HRRK!
DON'T YOU DARE CALL ME THAT.
I DIDN'T SIRE YOU, AND I DISOWN YOU.
VERY WELL...

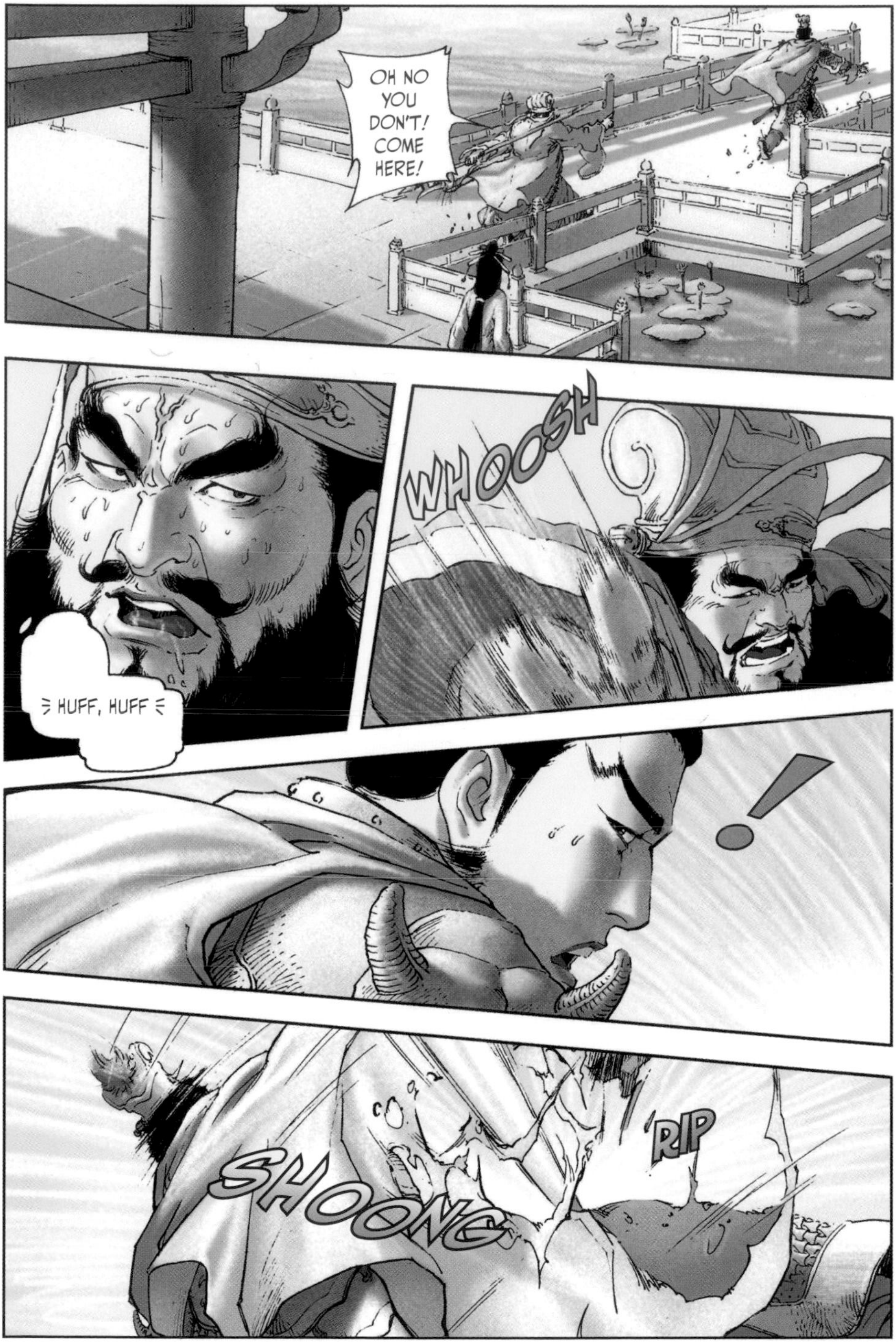
OH NO YOU DON'T! COME HERE!
WHOOSH
HUFF, HUFF
!
SHOONG
RIP

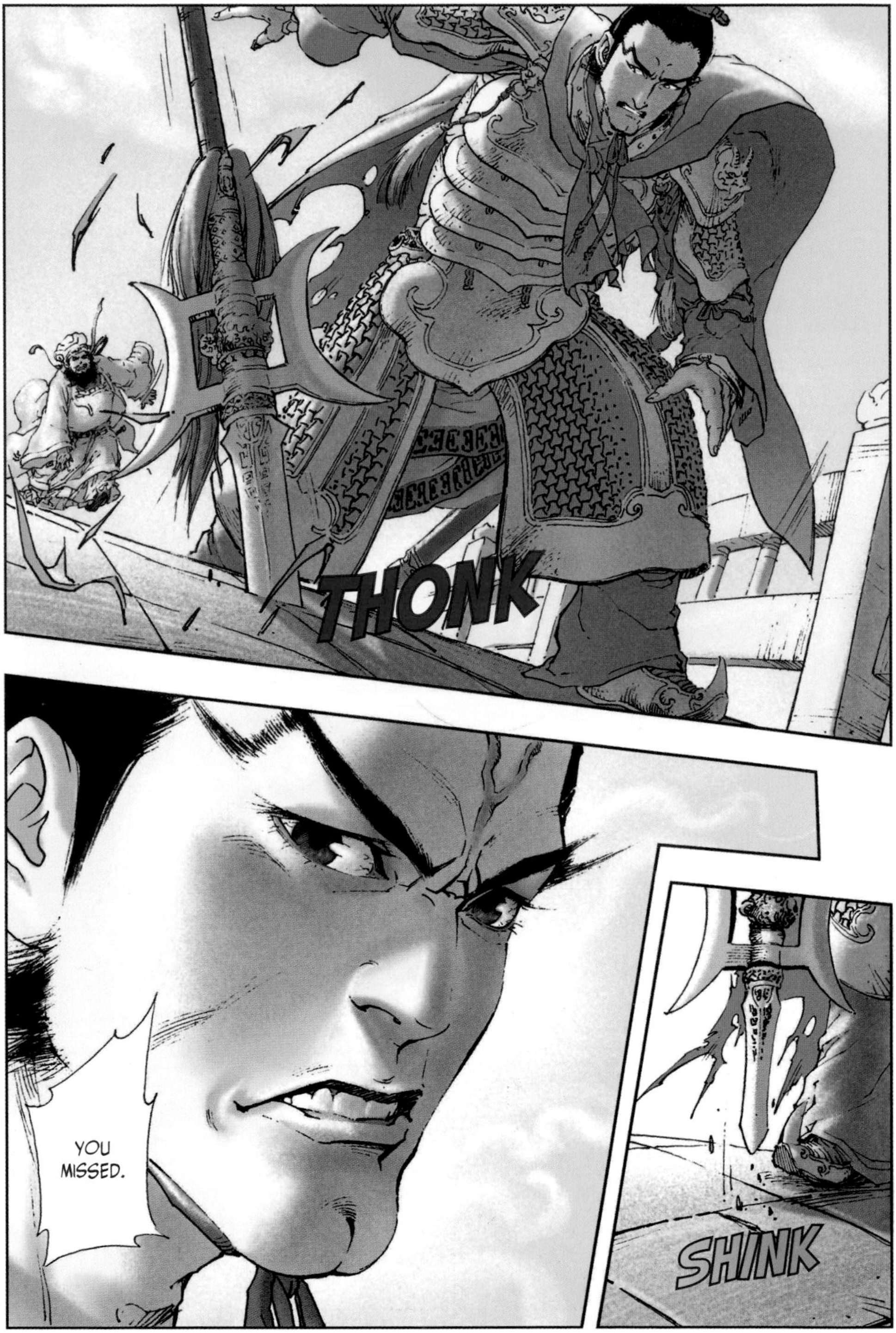
THONK
YOU MISSED.
SHINK

COME BACK HERE!

NOBODY GLARES AT ME LIKE THAT AND LIVES!

I WILL TEACH YOU TO RESPECT MY THINGS!

SHING

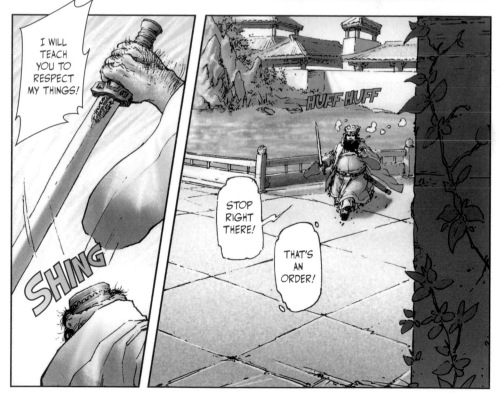

HUFF HUFF

STOP RIGHT THERE!

THAT'S AN ORDER!

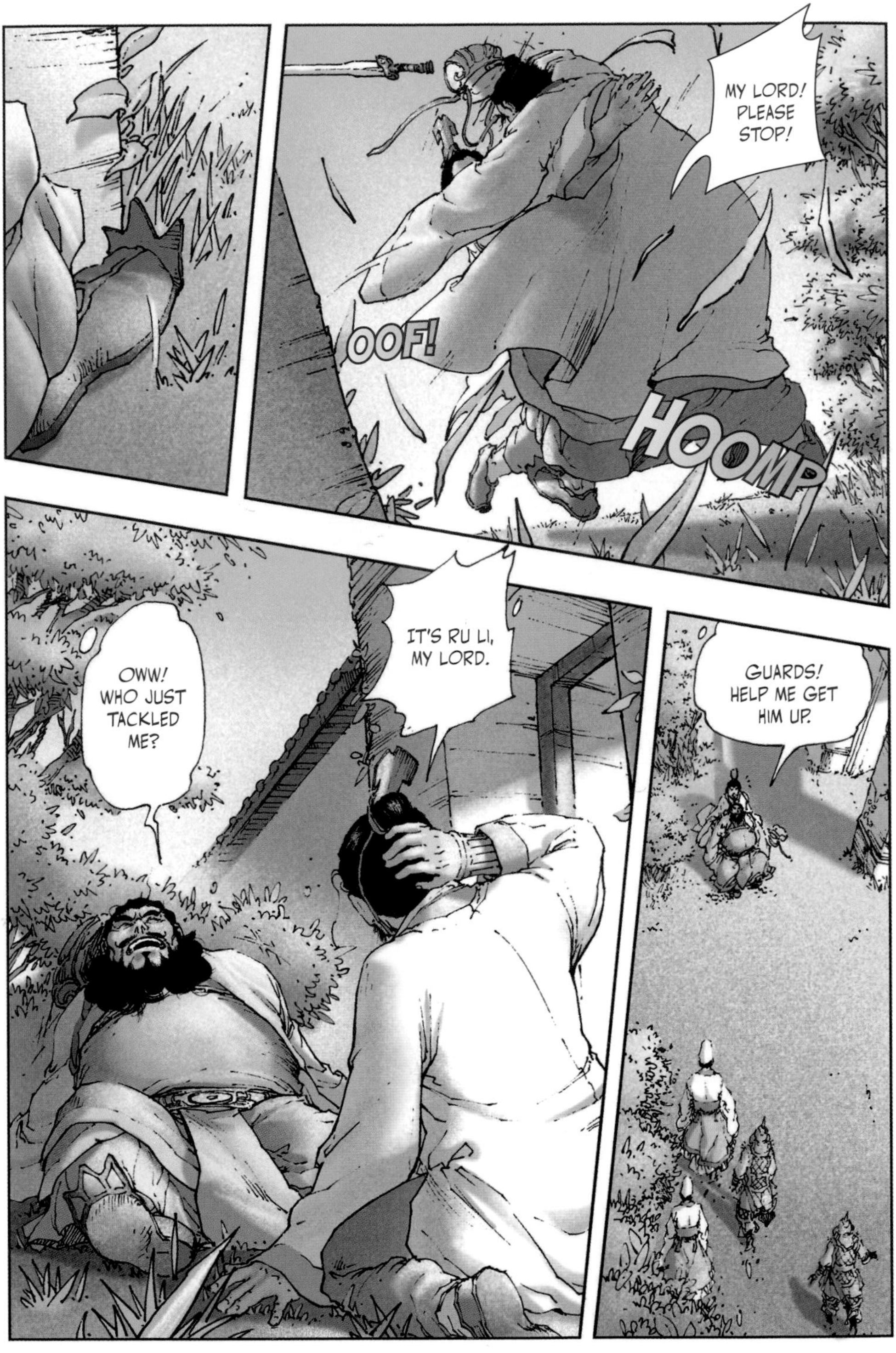
MY LORD! PLEASE STOP!
OOF!
HOOMP
OWW! WHO JUST TACKLED ME?
IT'S RU LI, MY LORD.
GUARDS! HELP ME GET HIM UP.

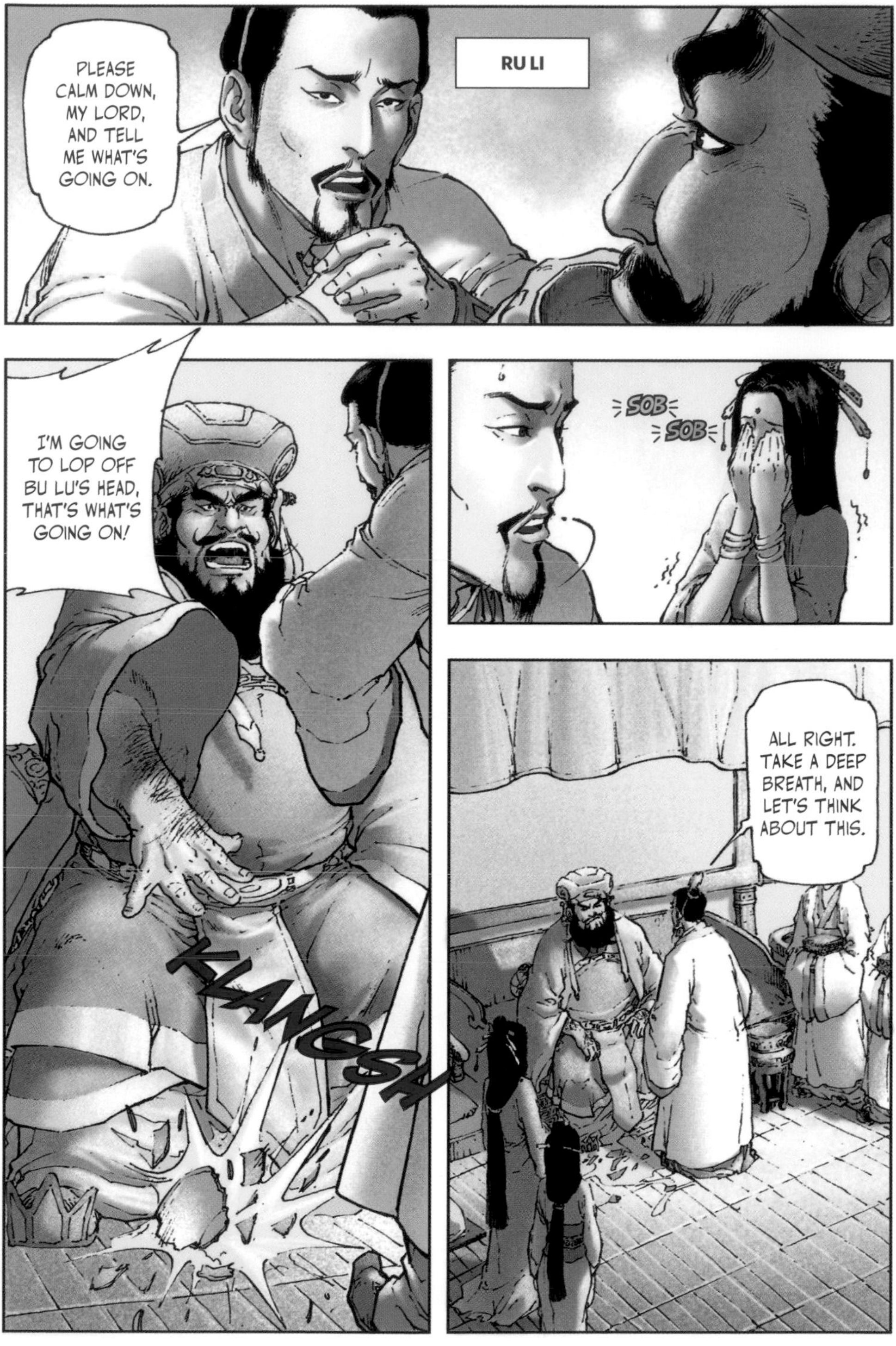
RU LI
PLEASE CALM DOWN, MY LORD, AND TELL ME WHAT'S GOING ON.
I'M GOING TO LOP OFF BU LU'S HEAD, THAT'S WHAT'S GOING ON!
KLANGSH
SOB SOB
ALL RIGHT. TAKE A DEEP BREATH, AND LET'S THINK ABOUT THIS.

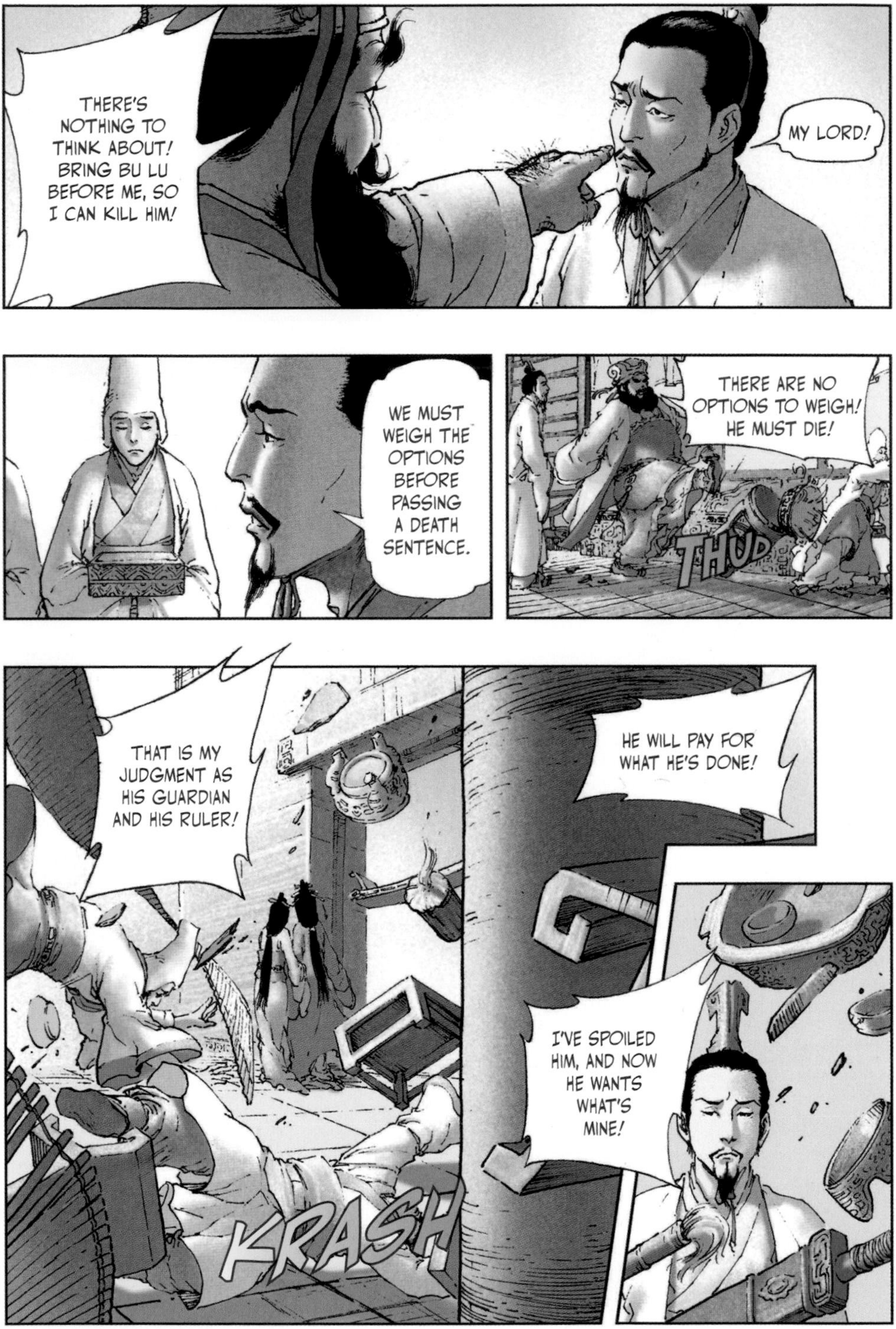
THERE'S NOTHING TO THINK ABOUT! BRING BU LU BEFORE ME, SO I CAN KILL HIM!
MY LORD!
WE MUST WEIGH THE OPTIONS BEFORE PASSING A DEATH SENTENCE.
THERE ARE NO OPTIONS TO WEIGH! HE MUST DIE!
THUD
THAT IS MY JUDGMENT AS HIS GUARDIAN AND HIS RULER!
HE WILL PAY FOR WHAT HE'S DONE!
I'VE SPOILED HIM, AND NOW HE WANTS WHAT'S MINE!
KRASH

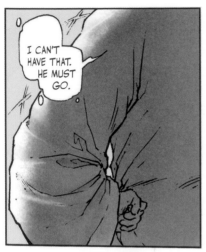

I CAN'T HAVE THAT. HE MUST GO.

MY LORD, BU LU MAY BE GUILTY OF COVETING WHAT'S YOURS,

BUT HE'S PROTECTED YOU FROM REBELLION ALMOST BY HIMSELF.

IF YOU KILL BU LU, YOU WILL HAVE TO FIGHT ALL FUTURE BATTLES ALONE.

WHAT ARE YOU SUGGESTING? THAT I CAN'T PROTECT MYSELF?

NO MY LORD, BUT YOU MUST KEEP AN EYE ON THE FUTURE.

BU LU IS A CRUCIAL ALLY, AND HE STILL HAS AN IMPORTANT ROLE TO PLAY.

BUT HE HAS OPENLY TRIED TO STEAL MY MISTRESS! WHO'S TO SAY THAT TOMORROW HE WON'T TRY TO STEAL MY THRONE?

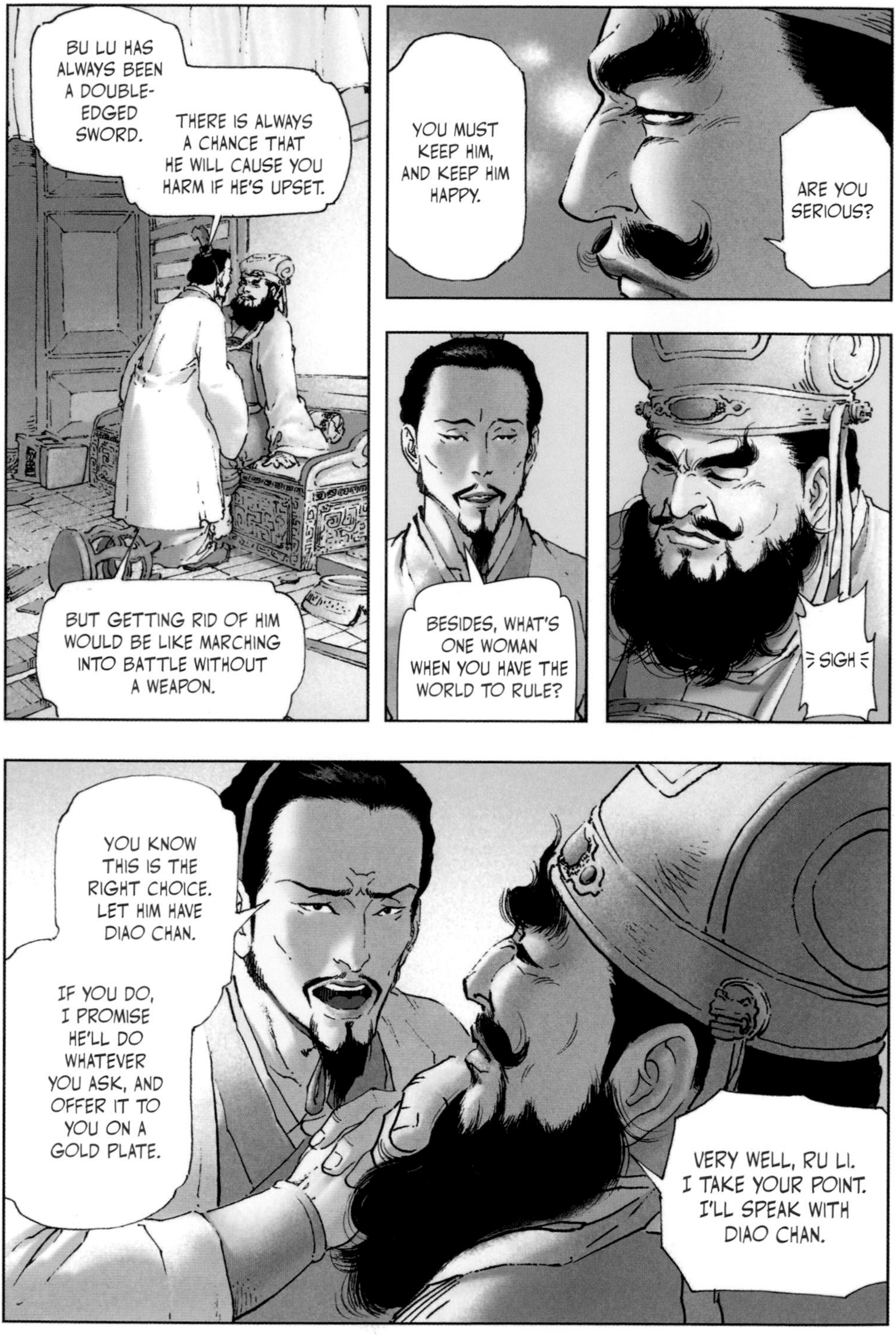
BU LU HAS ALWAYS BEEN A DOUBLE-EDGED SWORD.
THERE IS ALWAYS A CHANCE THAT HE WILL CAUSE YOU HARM IF HE'S UPSET.
BUT GETTING RID OF HIM WOULD BE LIKE MARCHING INTO BATTLE WITHOUT A WEAPON.
YOU MUST KEEP HIM, AND KEEP HIM HAPPY.
ARE YOU SERIOUS?
BESIDES, WHAT'S ONE WOMAN WHEN YOU HAVE THE WORLD TO RULE?
SIGH
YOU KNOW THIS IS THE RIGHT CHOICE. LET HIM HAVE DIAO CHAN.
IF YOU DO, I PROMISE HE'LL DO WHATEVER YOU ASK, AND OFFER IT TO YOU ON A GOLD PLATE.
VERY WELL, RU LI. I TAKE YOUR POINT. I'LL SPEAK WITH DIAO CHAN.

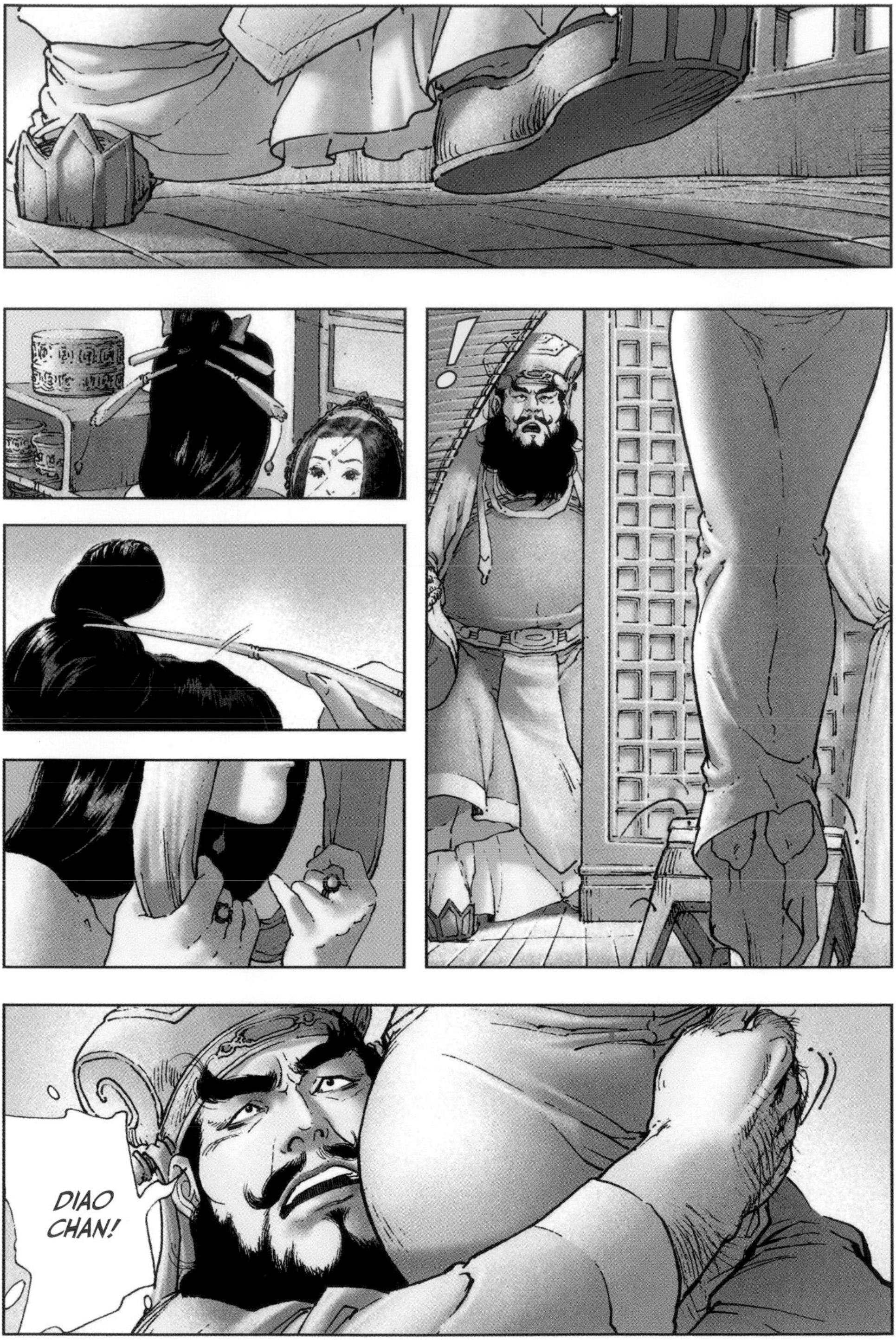
!
DIAO CHAN!

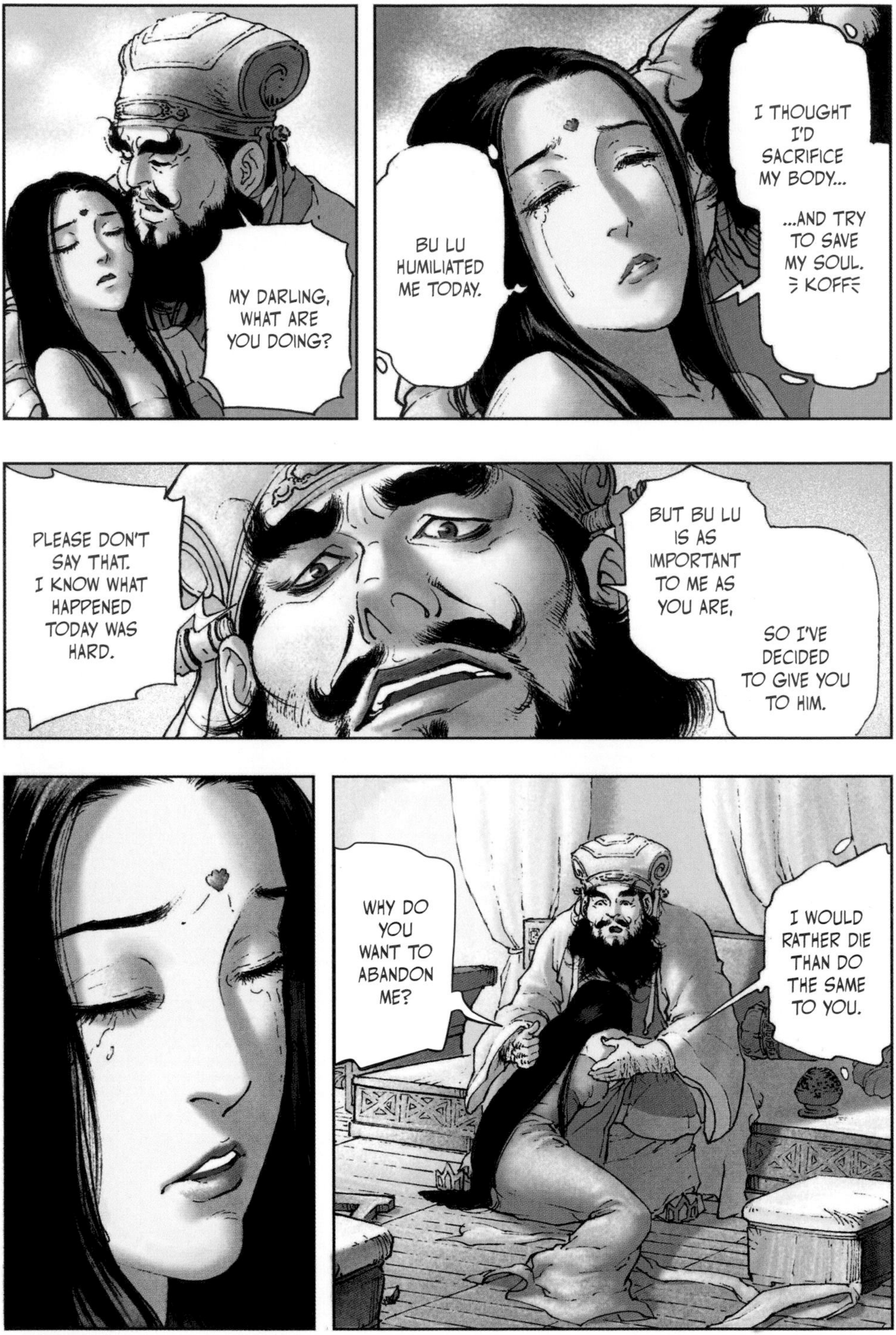
MY DARLING, WHAT ARE YOU DOING?
BU LU HUMILIATED ME TODAY.
I THOUGHT I'D SACRIFICE MY BODY...
...AND TRY TO SAVE MY SOUL.
KOFF
PLEASE DON'T SAY THAT. I KNOW WHAT HAPPENED TODAY WAS HARD.
BUT BU LU IS AS IMPORTANT TO ME AS YOU ARE,
SO I'VE DECIDED TO GIVE YOU TO HIM.
WHY DO YOU WANT TO ABANDON ME?
I WOULD RATHER DIE THAN DO THE SAME TO YOU.

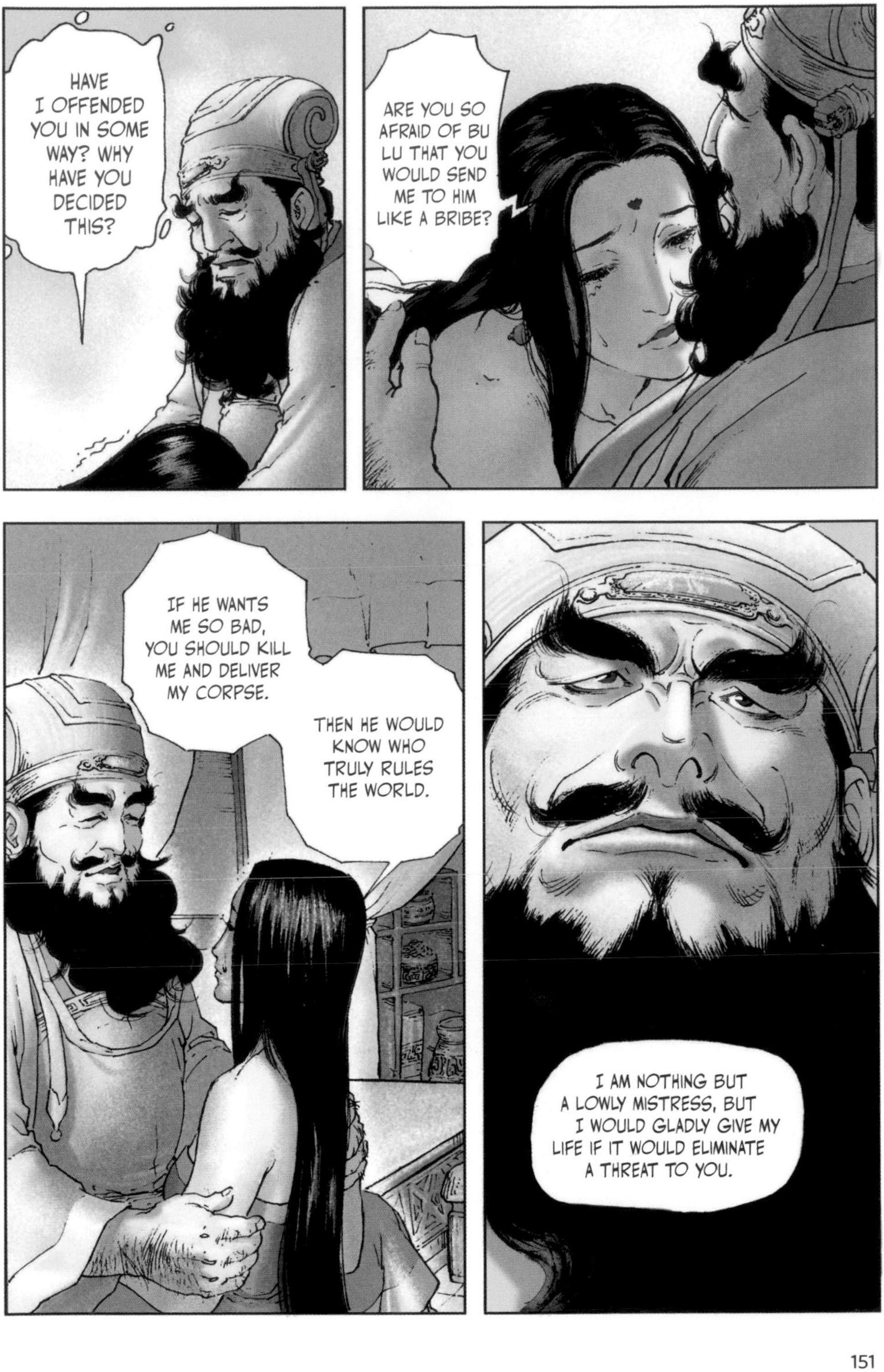
HAVE I OFFENDED YOU IN SOME WAY? WHY HAVE YOU DECIDED THIS?
ARE YOU SO AFRAID OF BU LU THAT YOU WOULD SEND ME TO HIM LIKE A BRIBE?
IF HE WANTS ME SO BAD, YOU SHOULD KILL ME AND DELIVER MY CORPSE.
THEN HE WOULD KNOW WHO TRULY RULES THE WORLD.
I AM NOTHING BUT A LOWLY MISTRESS, BUT I WOULD GLADLY GIVE MY LIFE IF IT WOULD ELIMINATE A THREAT TO YOU.

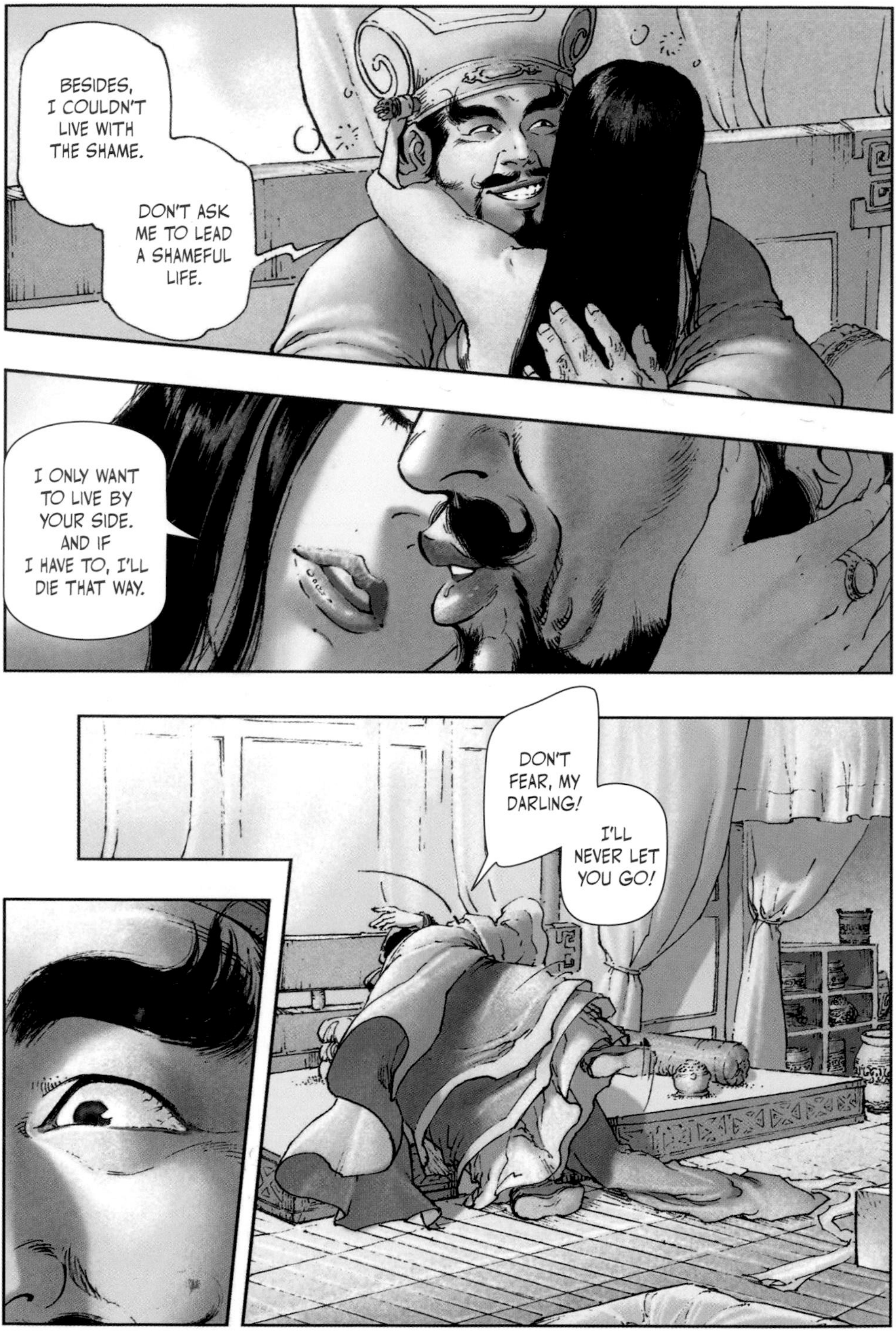
BESIDES, I COULDN'T LIVE WITH THE SHAME.
DON'T ASK ME TO LEAD A SHAMEFUL LIFE.
I ONLY WANT TO LIVE BY YOUR SIDE. AND IF I HAVE TO, I'LL DIE THAT WAY.
DON'T FEAR, MY DARLING!
I'LL NEVER LET YOU GO!

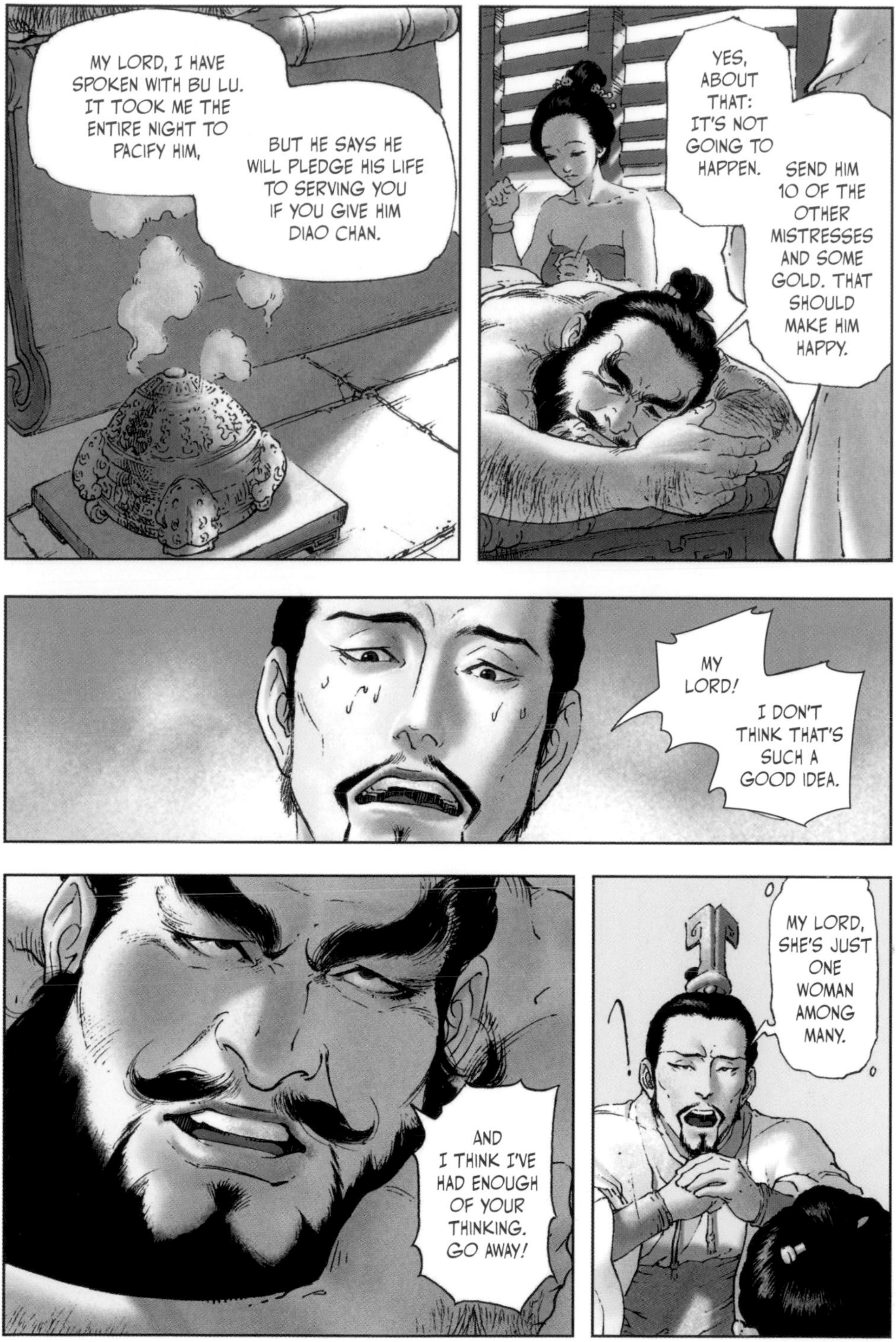
MY LORD, I HAVE SPOKEN WITH BU LU. IT TOOK ME THE ENTIRE NIGHT TO PACIFY HIM,
BUT HE SAYS HE WILL PLEDGE HIS LIFE TO SERVING YOU IF YOU GIVE HIM DIAO CHAN.
YES, ABOUT THAT: IT'S NOT GOING TO HAPPEN.
SEND HIM 10 OF THE OTHER MISTRESSES AND SOME GOLD. THAT SHOULD MAKE HIM HAPPY.
MY LORD!
I DON'T THINK THAT'S SUCH A GOOD IDEA.
MY LORD, SHE'S JUST ONE WOMAN AMONG MANY.
AND I THINK I'VE HAD ENOUGH OF YOUR THINKING. GO AWAY!

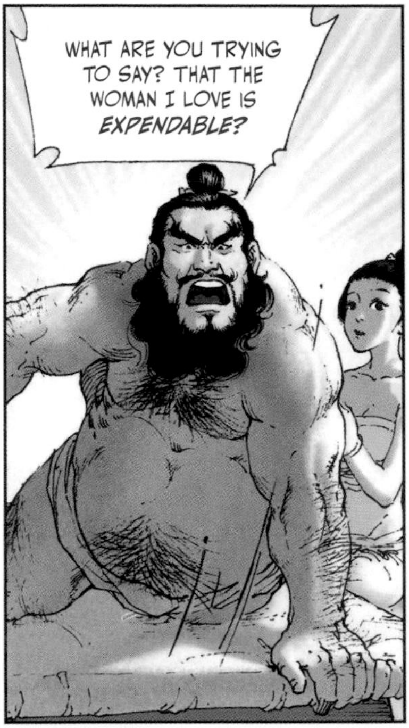
WHAT ARE YOU TRYING TO SAY? THAT THE WOMAN I LOVE IS *EXPENDABLE?*

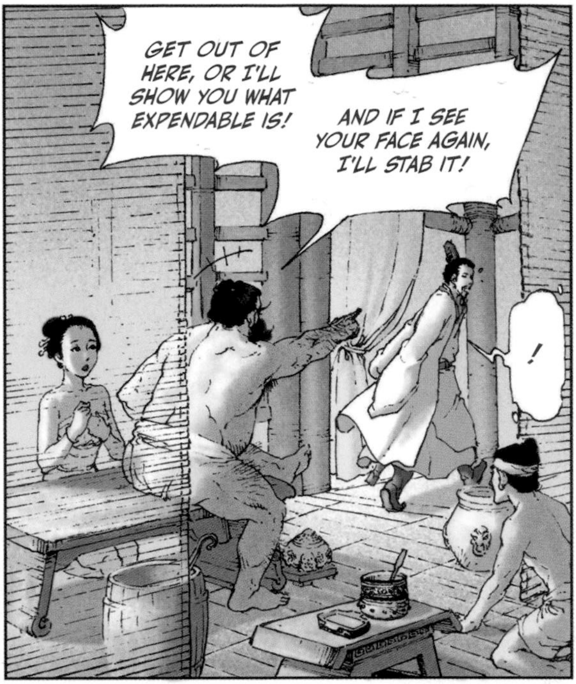
GET OUT OF HERE, OR I'LL SHOW YOU WHAT EXPENDABLE IS!
AND IF I SEE YOUR FACE AGAIN, I'LL STAB IT!
!

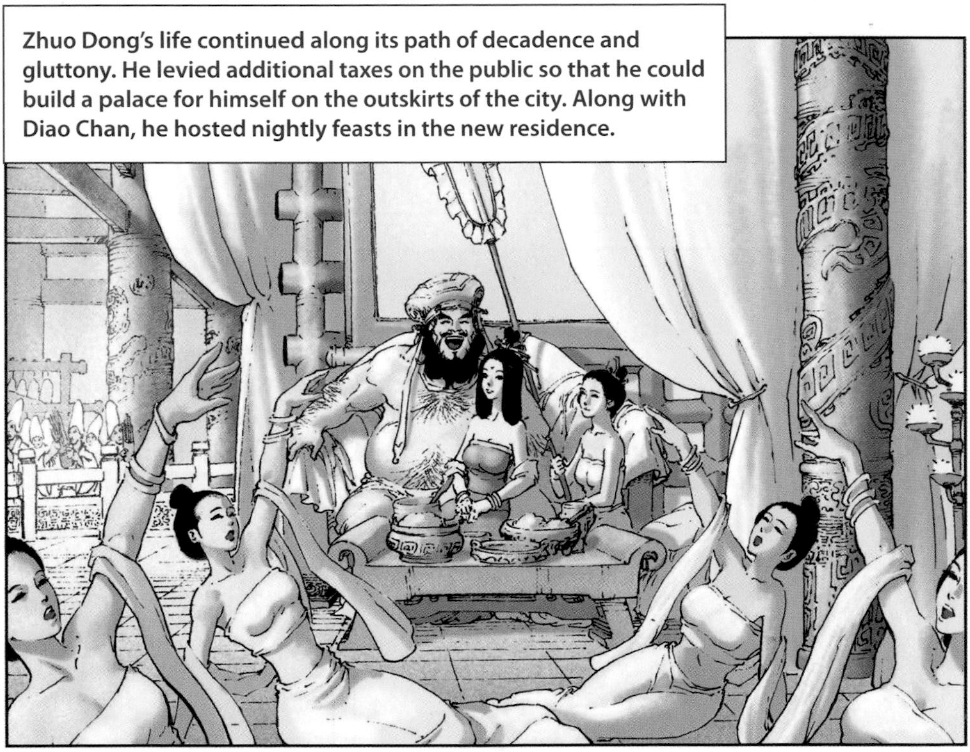
Zhuo Dong's life continued along its path of decadence and gluttony. He levied additional taxes on the public so that he could build a palace for himself on the outskirts of the city. Along with Diao Chan, he hosted nightly feasts in the new residence.

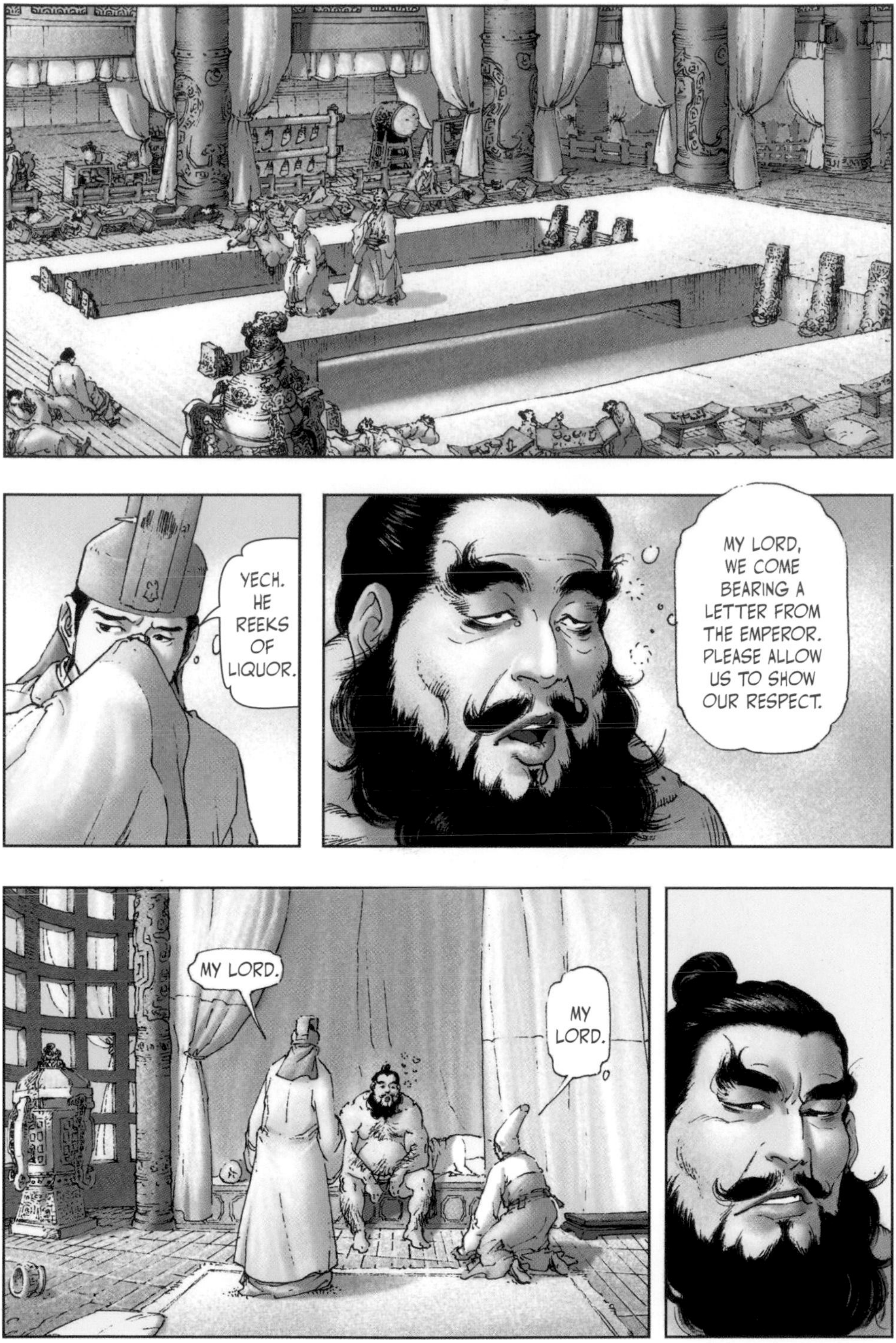
YECH. HE REEKS OF LIQUOR.
MY LORD, WE COME BEARING A LETTER FROM THE EMPEROR. PLEASE ALLOW US TO SHOW OUR RESPECT.
MY LORD.
MY LORD.

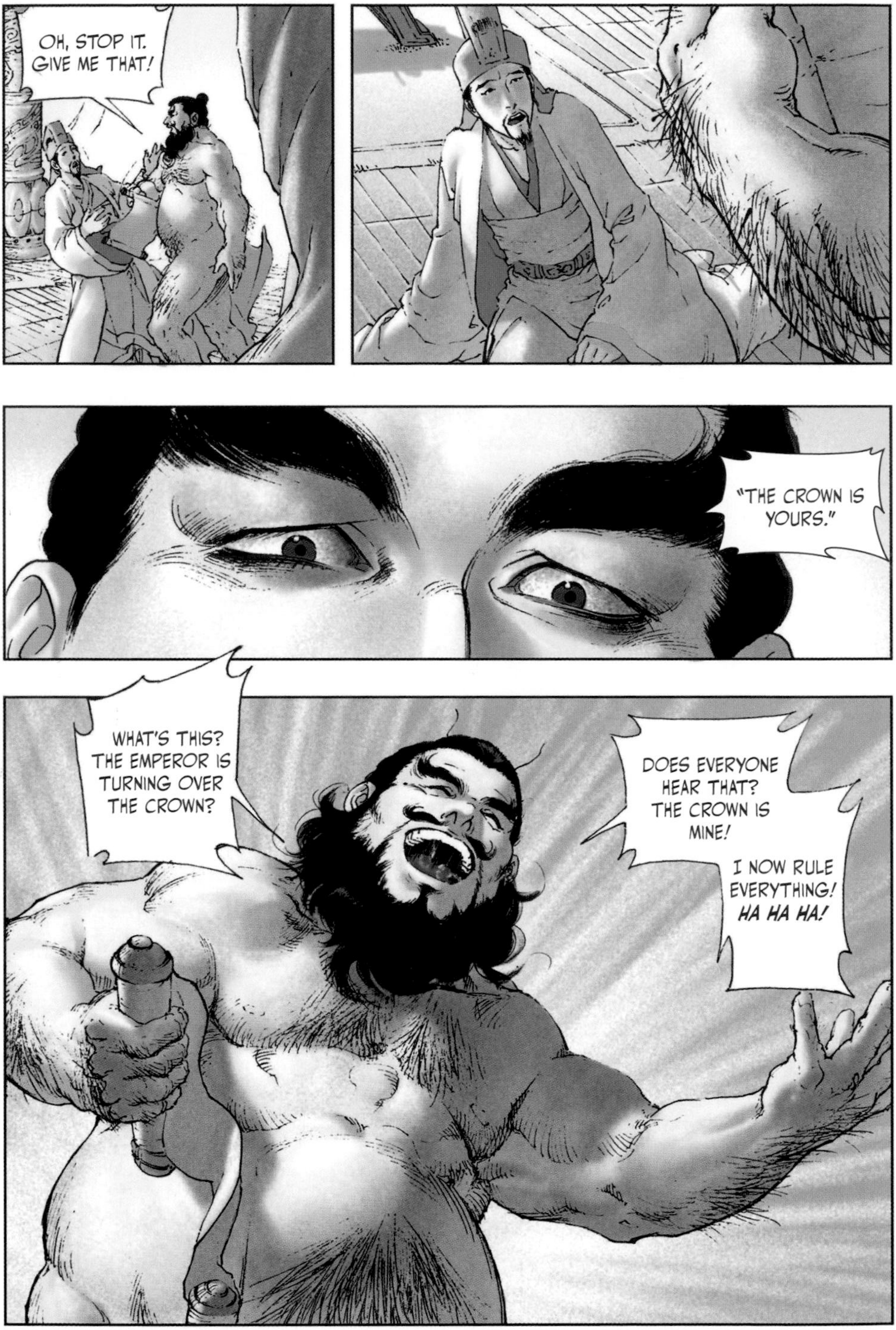
OH, STOP IT. GIVE ME THAT!
"THE CROWN IS YOURS."
WHAT'S THIS? THE EMPEROR IS TURNING OVER THE CROWN?
DOES EVERYONE HEAR THAT? THE CROWN IS MINE!
I NOW RULE EVERYTHING! ***HA HA HA!***

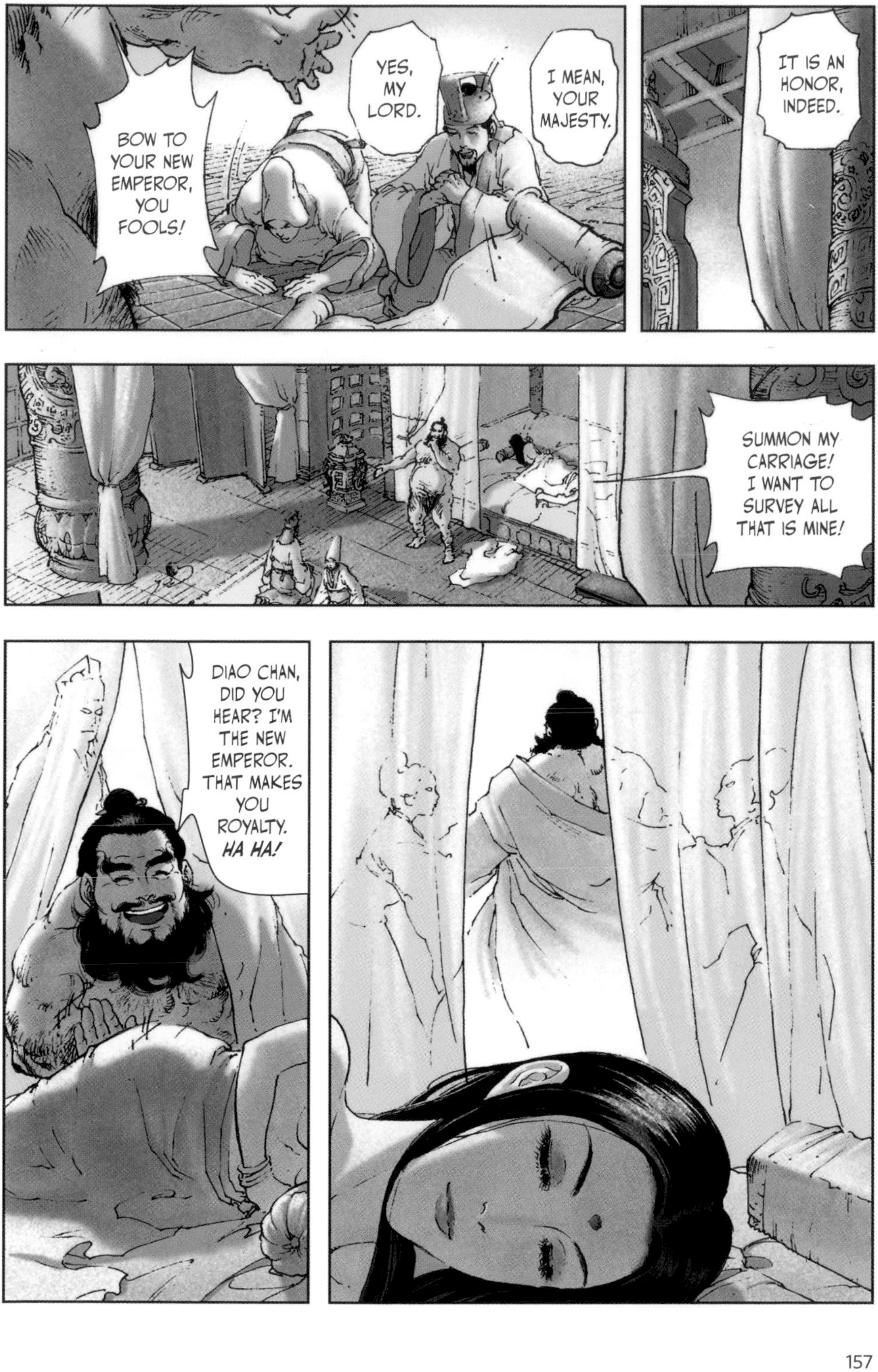
BOW TO YOUR NEW EMPEROR, YOU FOOLS!
YES, MY LORD.
I MEAN, YOUR MAJESTY.
IT IS AN HONOR, INDEED.
SUMMON MY CARRIAGE! I WANT TO SURVEY ALL THAT IS MINE!
DIAO CHAN, DID YOU HEAR? I'M THE NEW EMPEROR. THAT MAKES YOU ROYALTY. *HA HA!*

MEANWHILE, AT THE HOME OF ZHUO DONG'S FAMILY

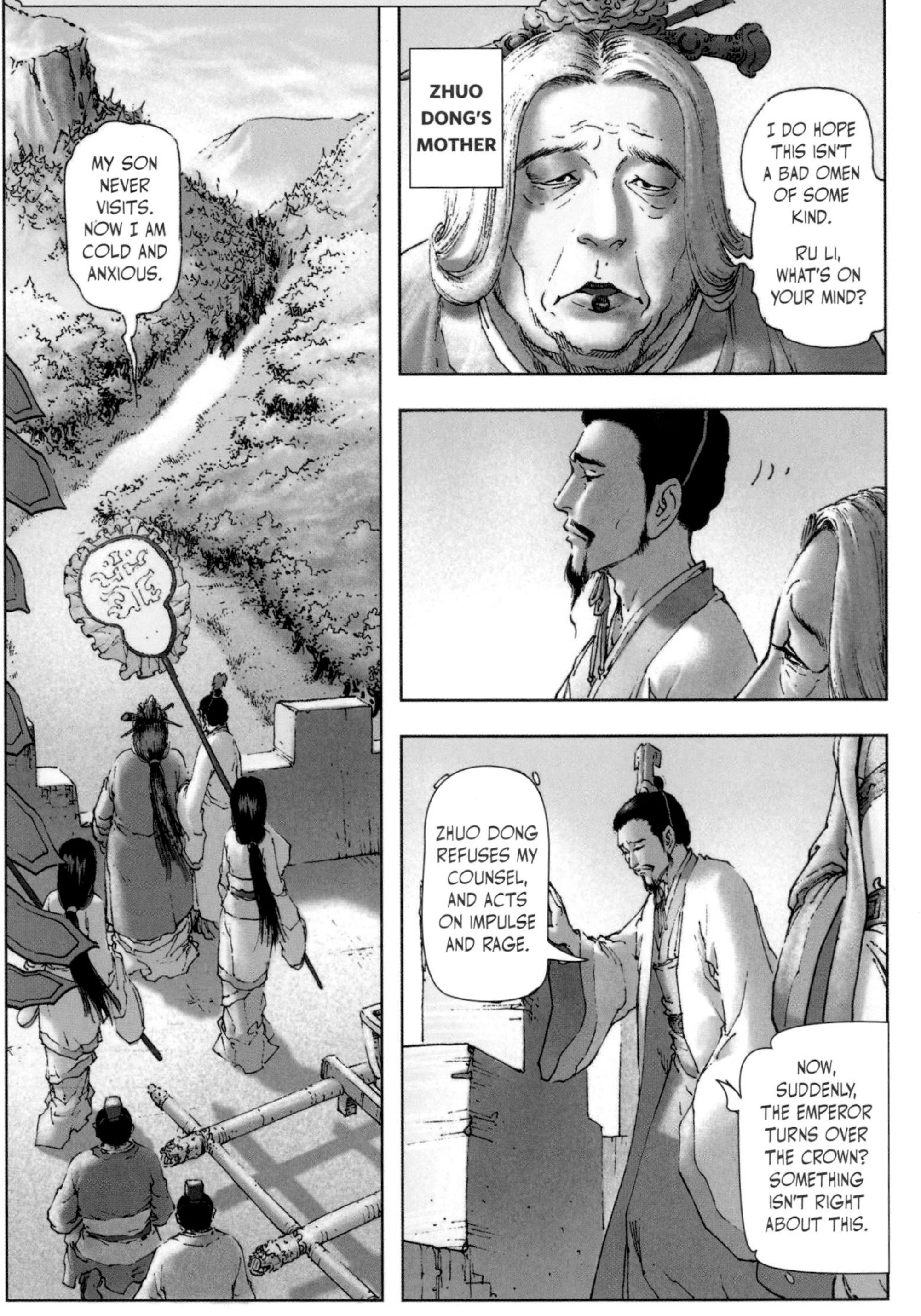
MY SON NEVER VISITS. NOW I AM COLD AND ANXIOUS.
ZHUO DONG'S MOTHER
I DO HOPE THIS ISN'T A BAD OMEN OF SOME KIND.
RU LI, WHAT'S ON YOUR MIND?
ZHUO DONG REFUSES MY COUNSEL, AND ACTS ON IMPULSE AND RAGE.
NOW, SUDDENLY, THE EMPEROR TURNS OVER THE CROWN? SOMETHING ISN'T RIGHT ABOUT THIS.

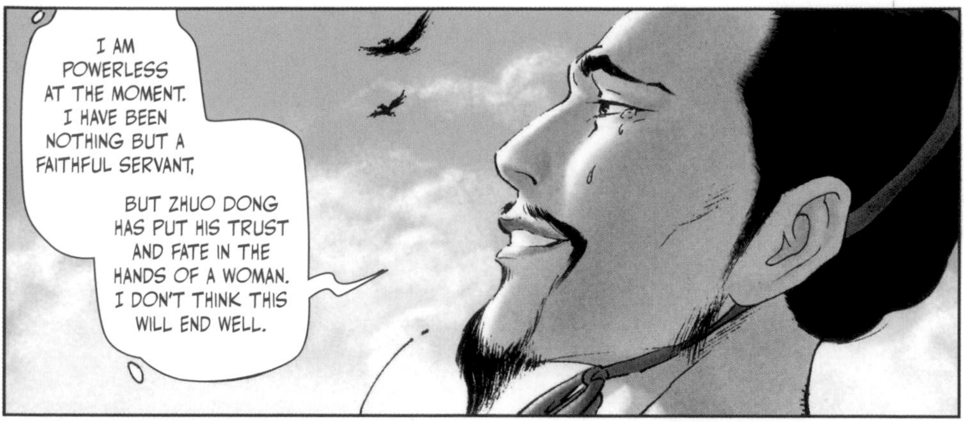
I AM POWERLESS AT THE MOMENT. I HAVE BEEN NOTHING BUT A FAITHFUL SERVANT,
BUT ZHUO DONG HAS PUT HIS TRUST AND FATE IN THE HANDS OF A WOMAN. I DON'T THINK THIS WILL END WELL.

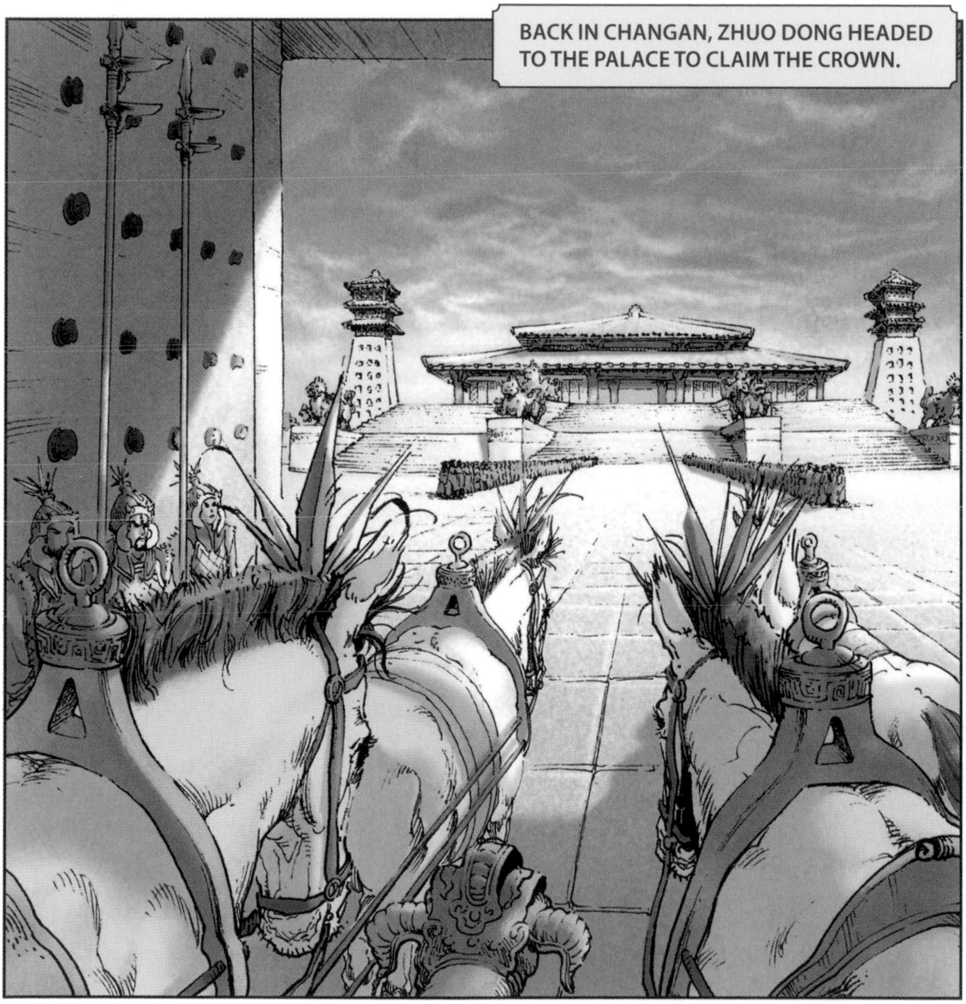
BACK IN CHANGAN, ZHUO DONG HEADED TO THE PALACE TO CLAIM THE CROWN.

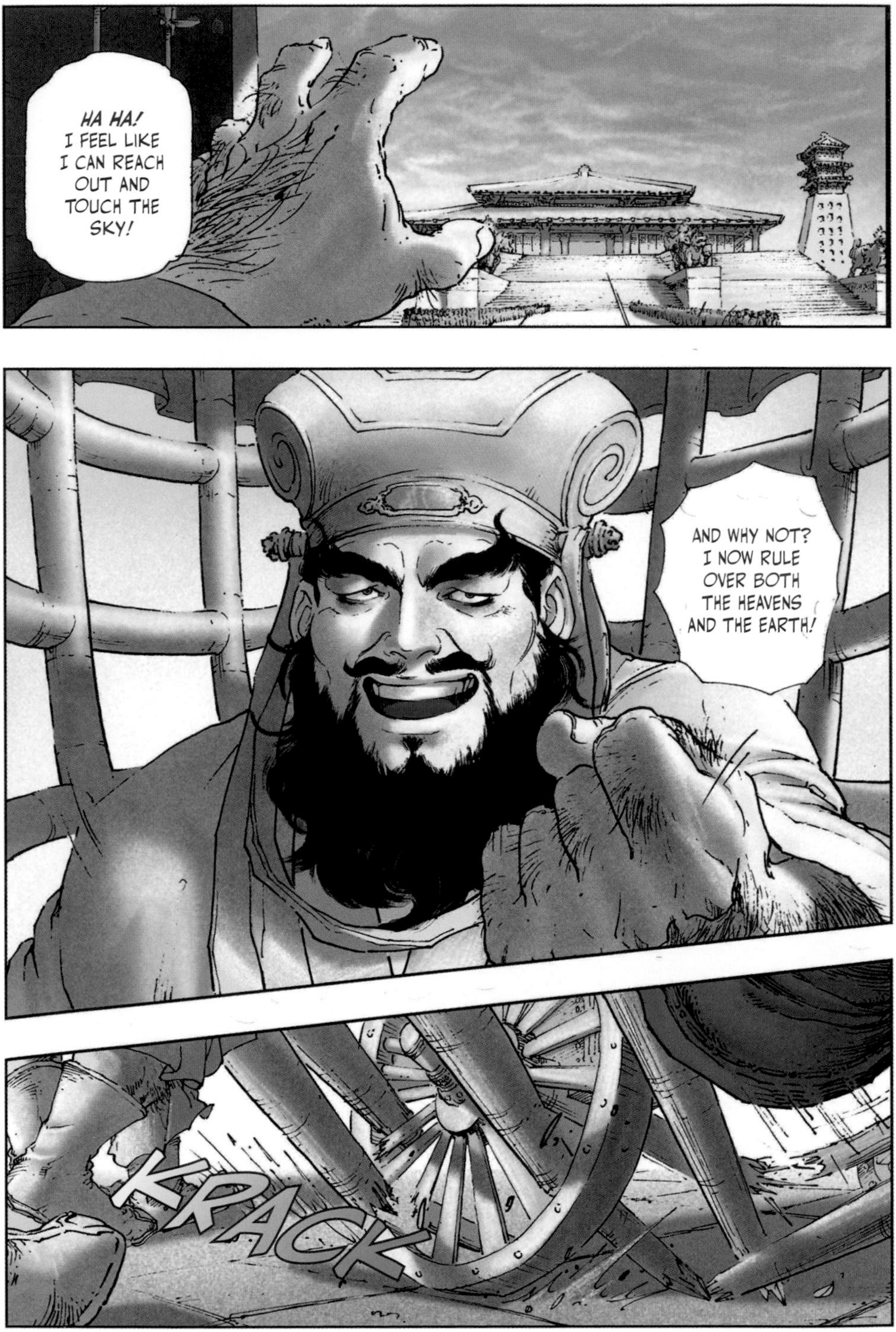
HA HA!
I FEEL LIKE I CAN REACH OUT AND TOUCH THE SKY!
AND WHY NOT? I NOW RULE OVER BOTH THE HEAVENS AND THE EARTH!
KRACK

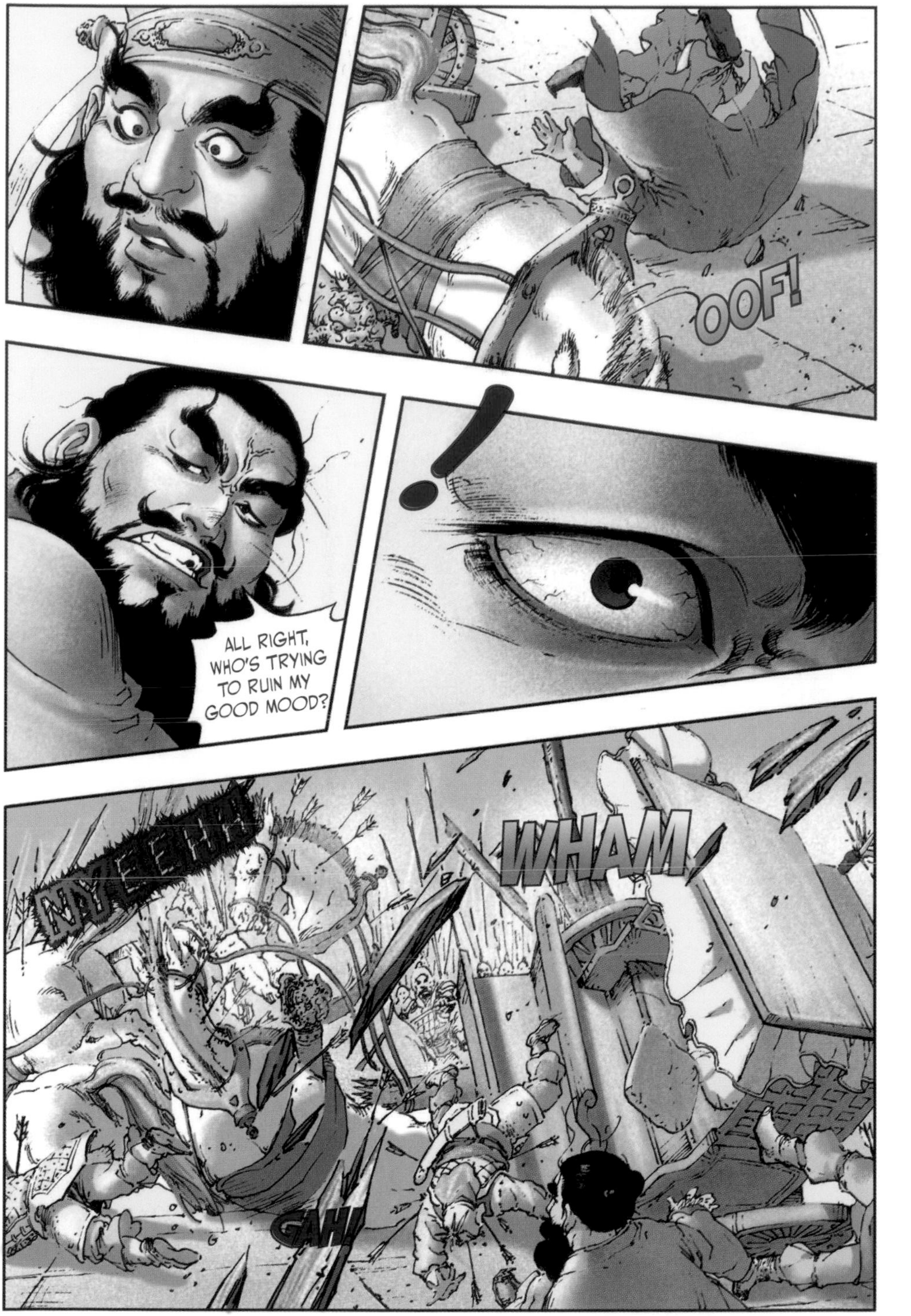
OOF!
ALL RIGHT, WHO'S TRYING TO RUIN MY GOOD MOOD?
!
NYEEHH
WHAM
GAH

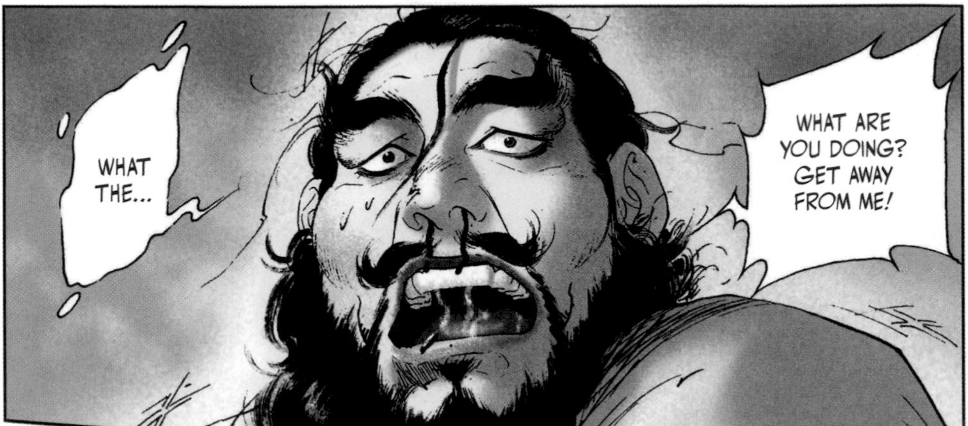
WHAT ARE YOU DOING? GET AWAY FROM ME!
WHAT THE...

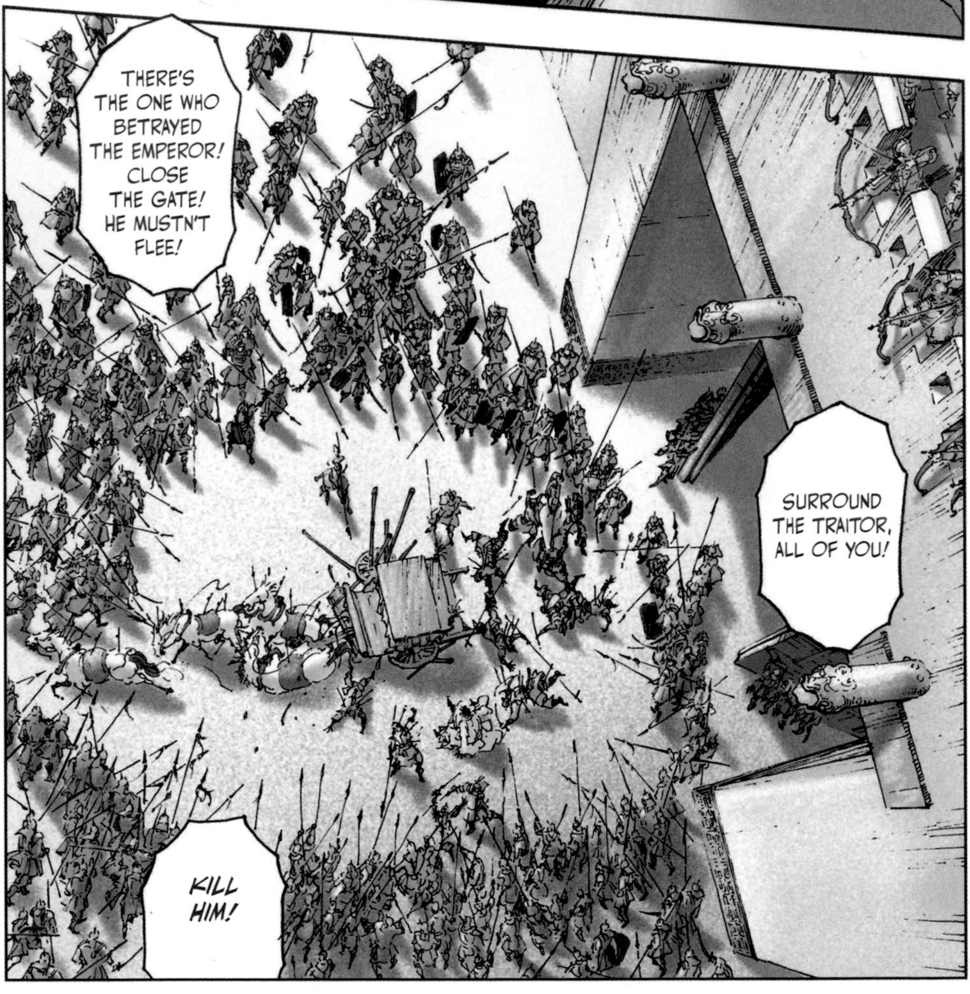
THERE'S THE ONE WHO BETRAYED THE EMPEROR! CLOSE THE GATE! HE MUSTN'T FLEE!
SURROUND THE TRAITOR, ALL OF YOU!
KILL HIM!

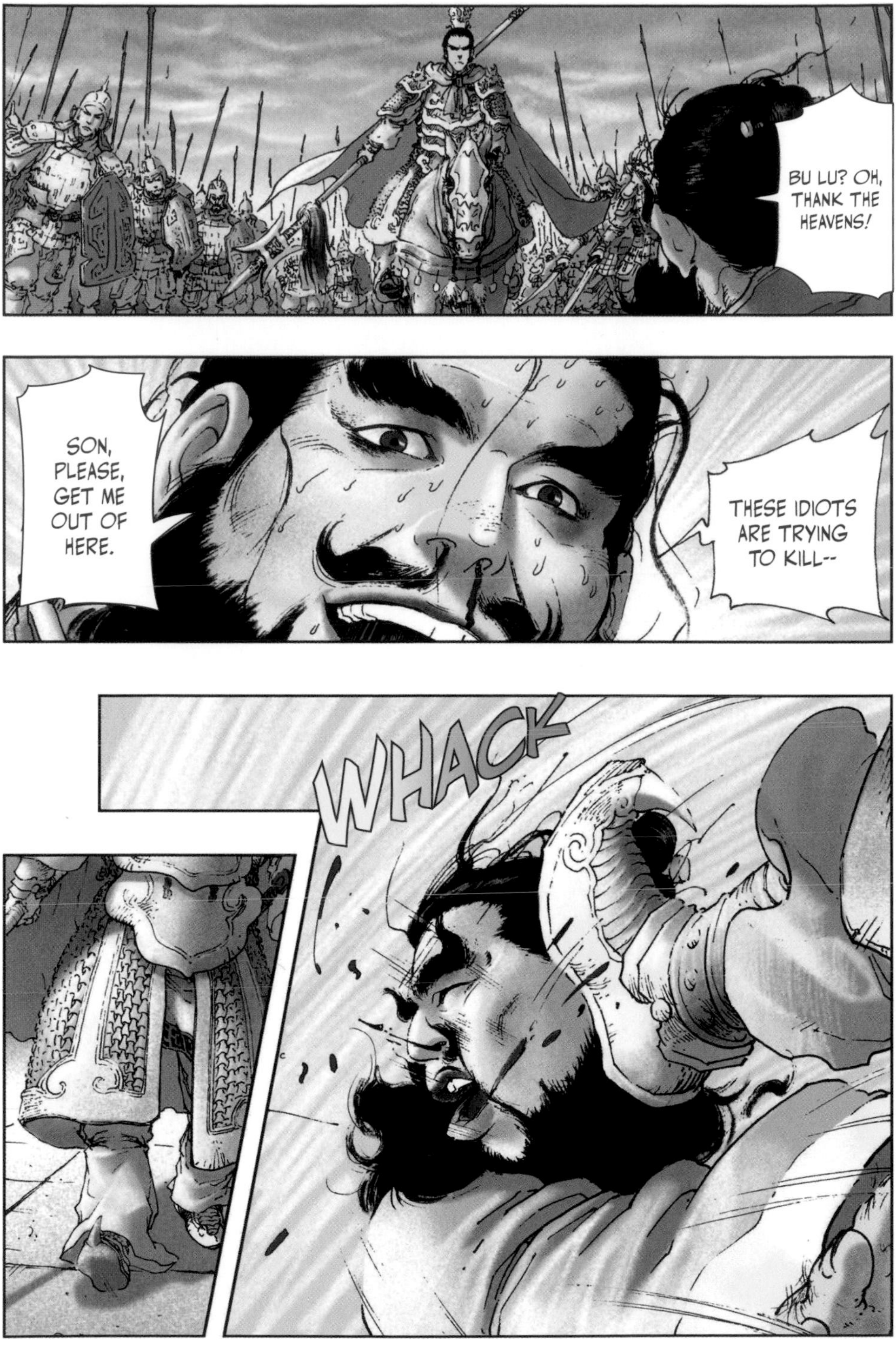
BU LU? OH, THANK THE HEAVENS!
SON, PLEASE, GET ME OUT OF HERE.
THESE IDIOTS ARE TRYING TO KILL--
WHACK

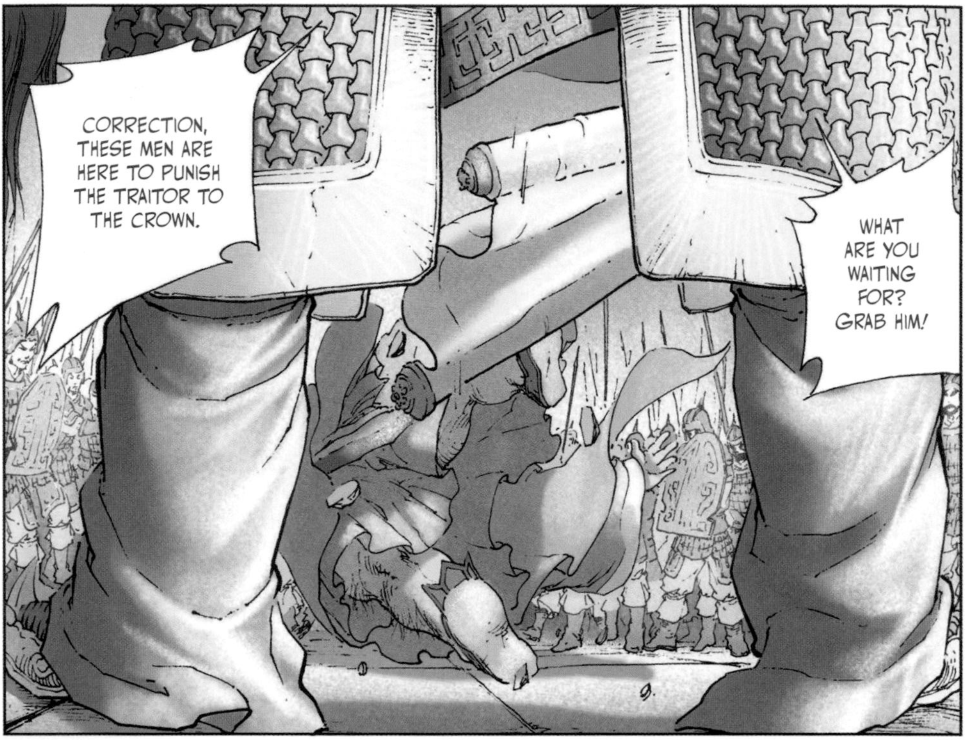
CORRECTION, THESE MEN ARE HERE TO PUNISH THE TRAITOR TO THE CROWN.
WHAT ARE YOU WAITING FOR? GRAB HIM!

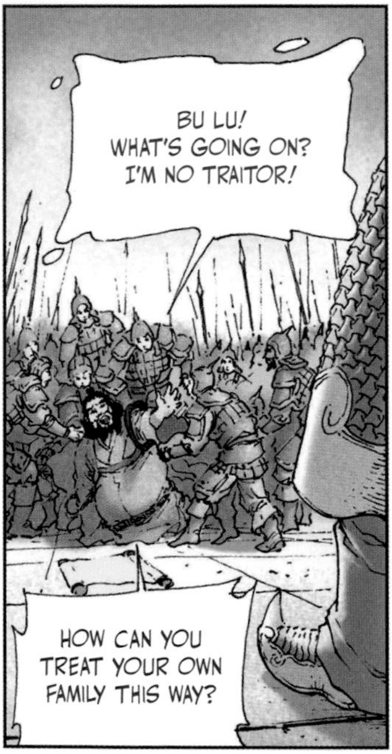
BU LU! WHAT'S GOING ON? I'M NO TRAITOR!
HOW CAN YOU TREAT YOUR OWN FAMILY THIS WAY?

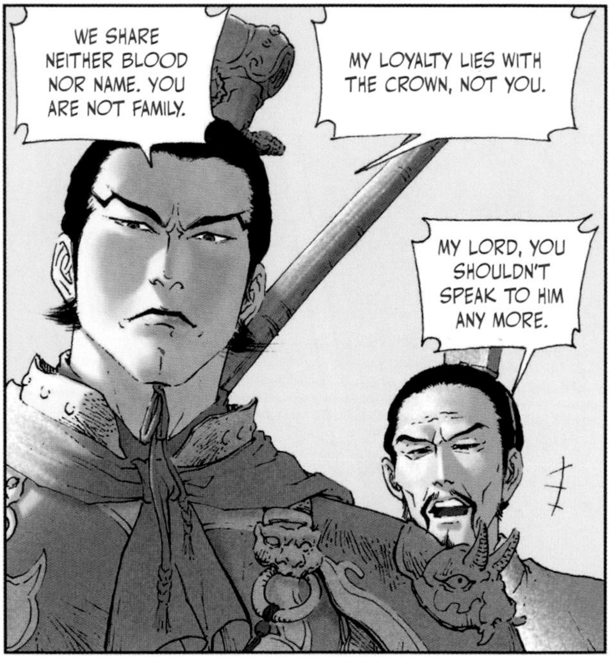
WE SHARE NEITHER BLOOD NOR NAME. YOU ARE NOT FAMILY.
MY LOYALTY LIES WITH THE CROWN, NOT YOU.
MY LORD, YOU SHOULDN'T SPEAK TO HIM ANY MORE.

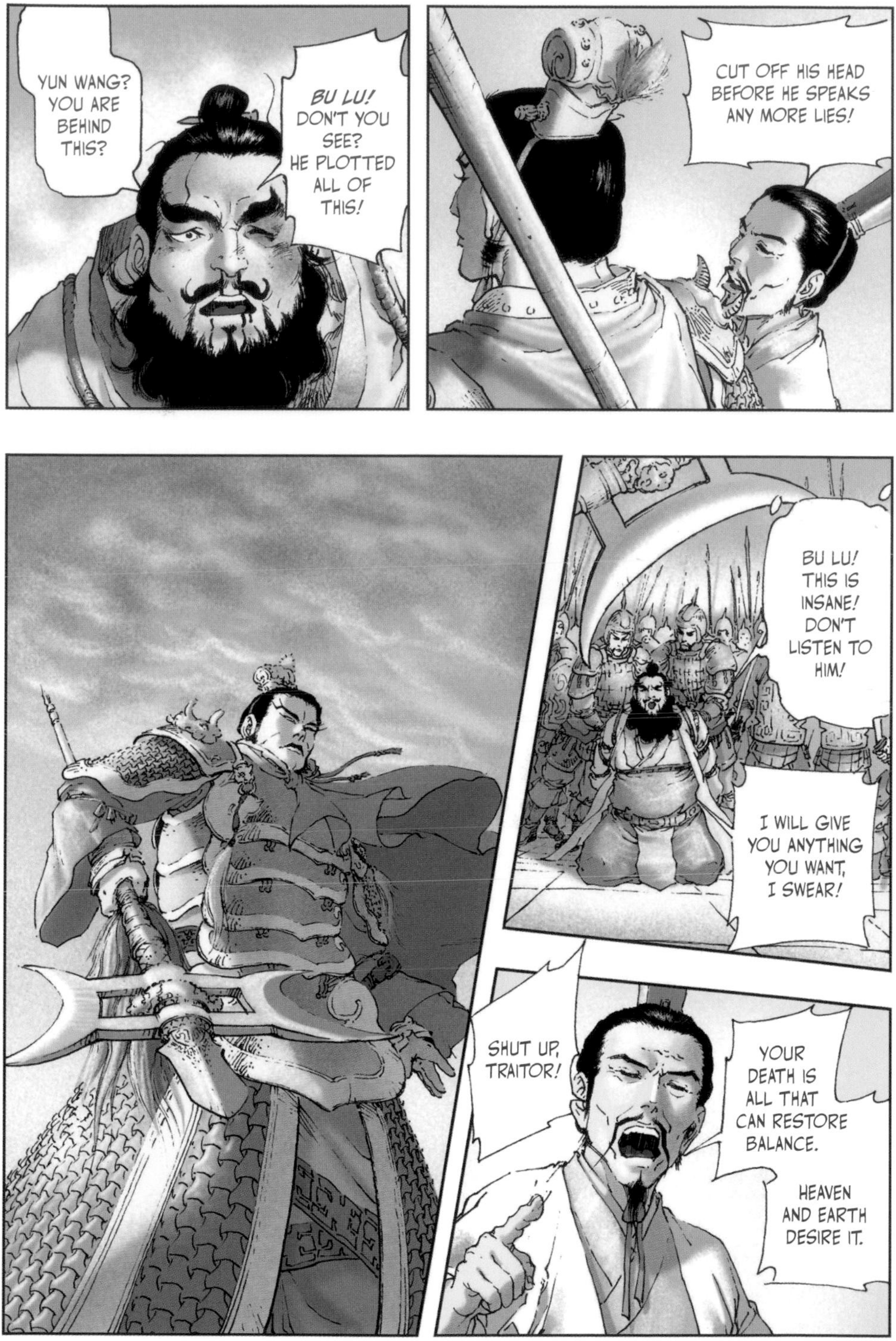
YUN WANG? YOU ARE BEHIND THIS?
BU LU! DON'T YOU SEE? HE PLOTTED ALL OF THIS!
CUT OFF HIS HEAD BEFORE HE SPEAKS ANY MORE LIES!
BU LU! THIS IS INSANE! DON'T LISTEN TO HIM!
I WILL GIVE YOU ANYTHING YOU WANT, I SWEAR!
SHUT UP, TRAITOR!
YOUR DEATH IS ALL THAT CAN RESTORE BALANCE.
HEAVEN AND EARTH DESIRE IT.

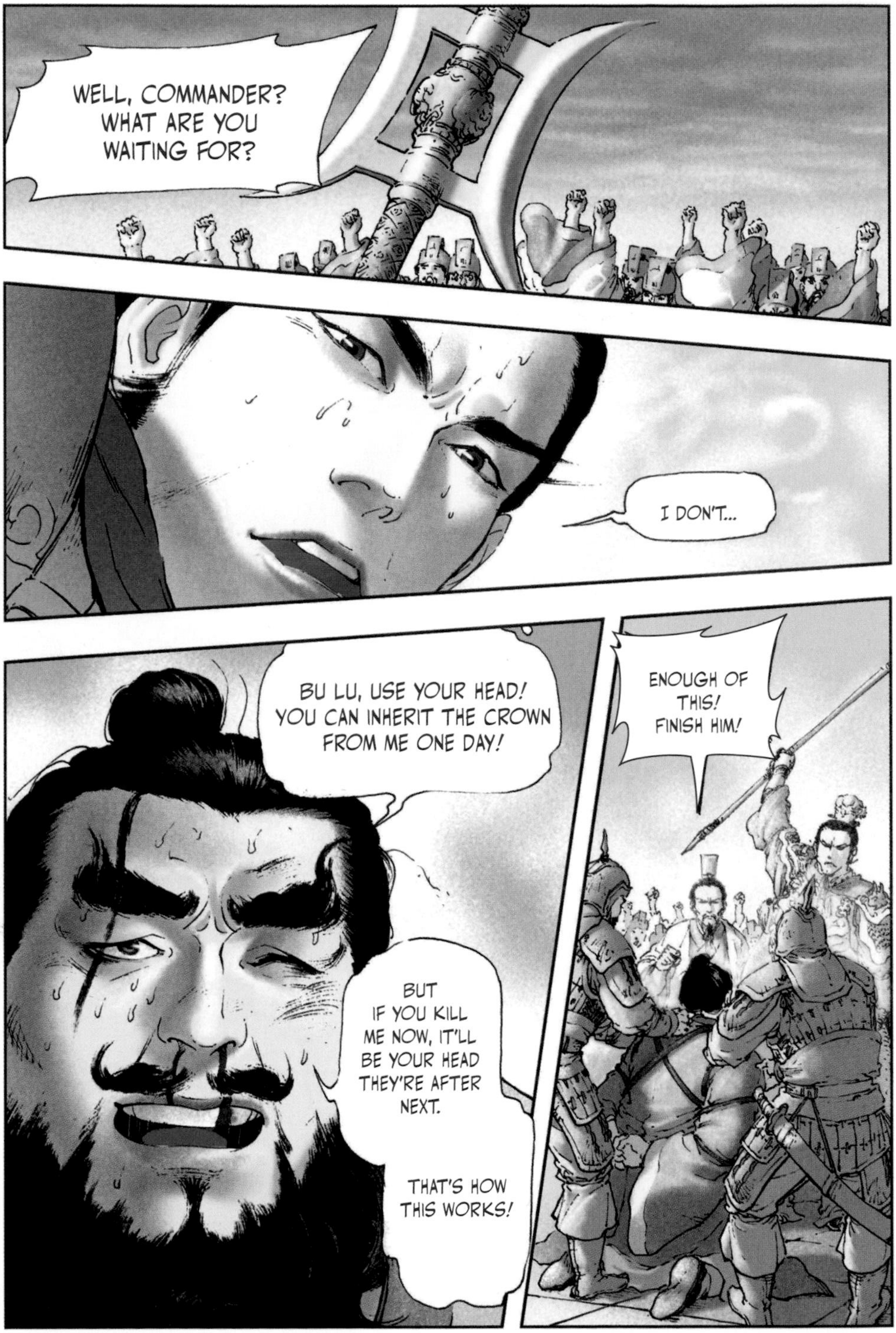
WELL, COMMANDER? WHAT ARE YOU WAITING FOR?
I DON'T...
BU LU, USE YOUR HEAD! YOU CAN INHERIT THE CROWN FROM ME ONE DAY!
BUT IF YOU KILL ME NOW, IT'LL BE YOUR HEAD THEY'RE AFTER NEXT.
THAT'S HOW THIS WORKS!
ENOUGH OF THIS! FINISH HIM!

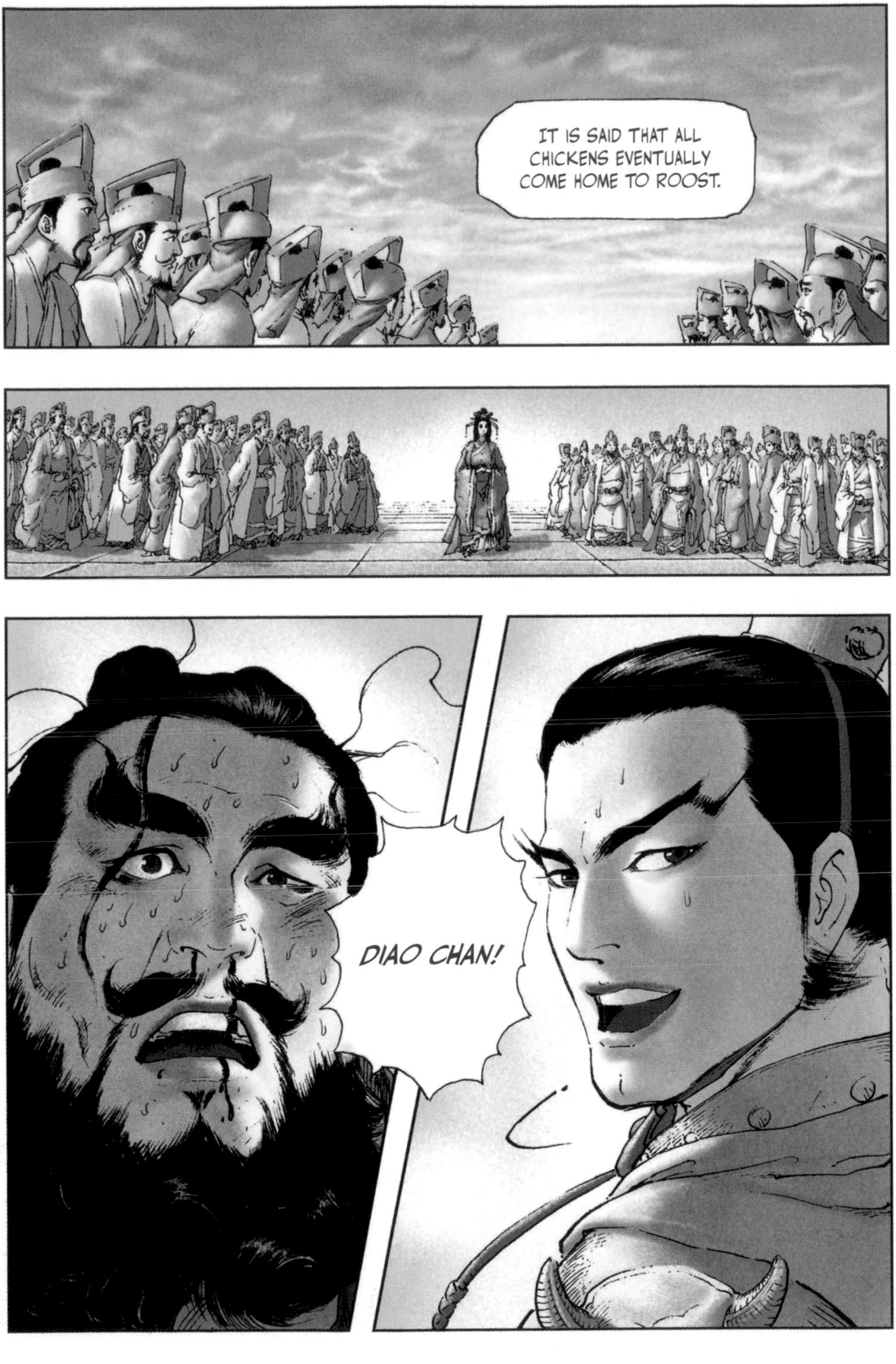
IT IS SAID THAT ALL CHICKENS EVENTUALLY COME HOME TO ROOST.
DIAO CHAN!

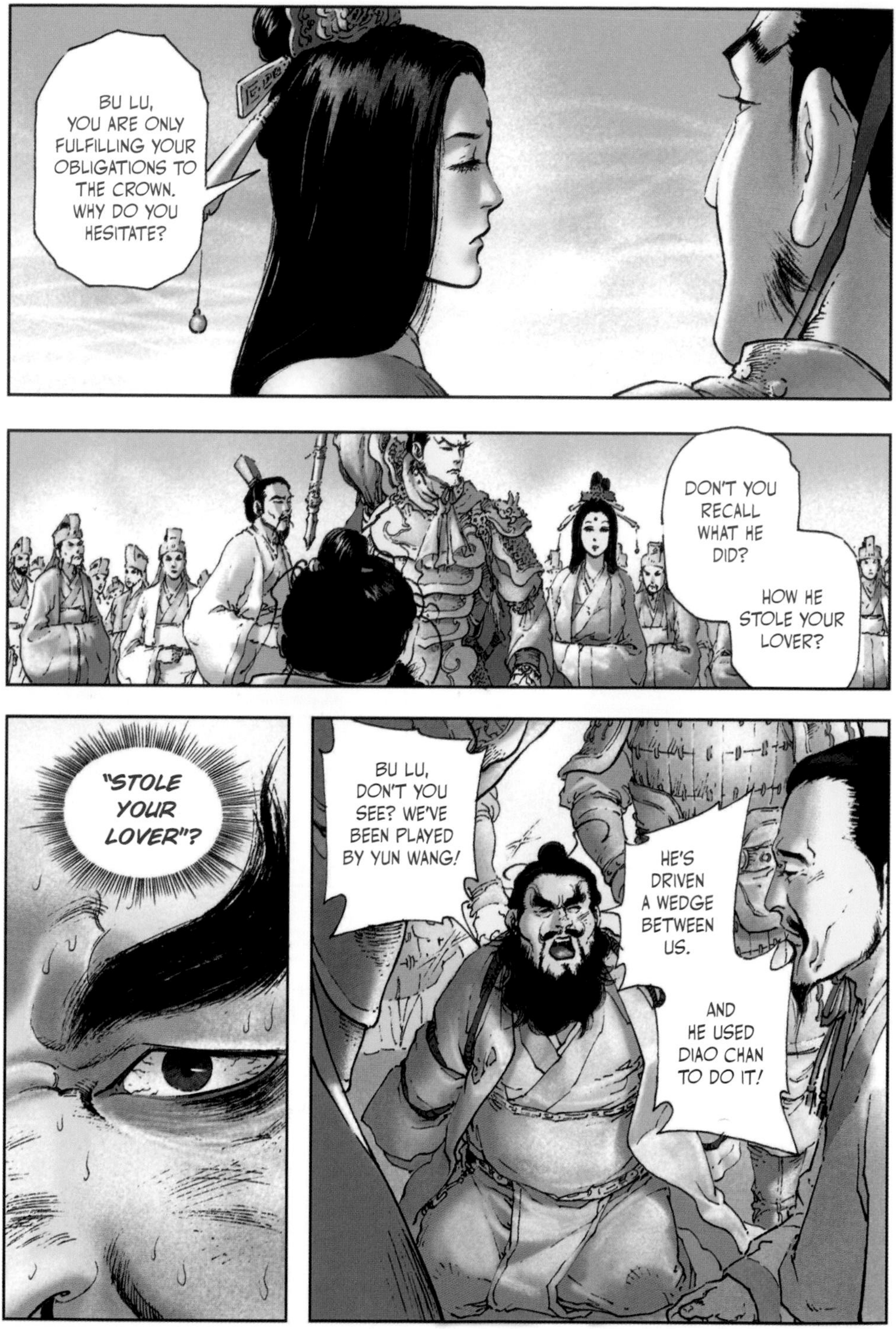
BU LU, YOU ARE ONLY FULFILLING YOUR OBLIGATIONS TO THE CROWN. WHY DO YOU HESITATE?
DON'T YOU RECALL WHAT HE DID?
HOW HE STOLE YOUR LOVER?
"STOLE YOUR LOVER"?
BU LU, DON'T YOU SEE? WE'VE BEEN PLAYED BY YUN WANG!
HE'S DRIVEN A WEDGE BETWEEN US.
AND HE USED DIAO CHAN TO DO IT!

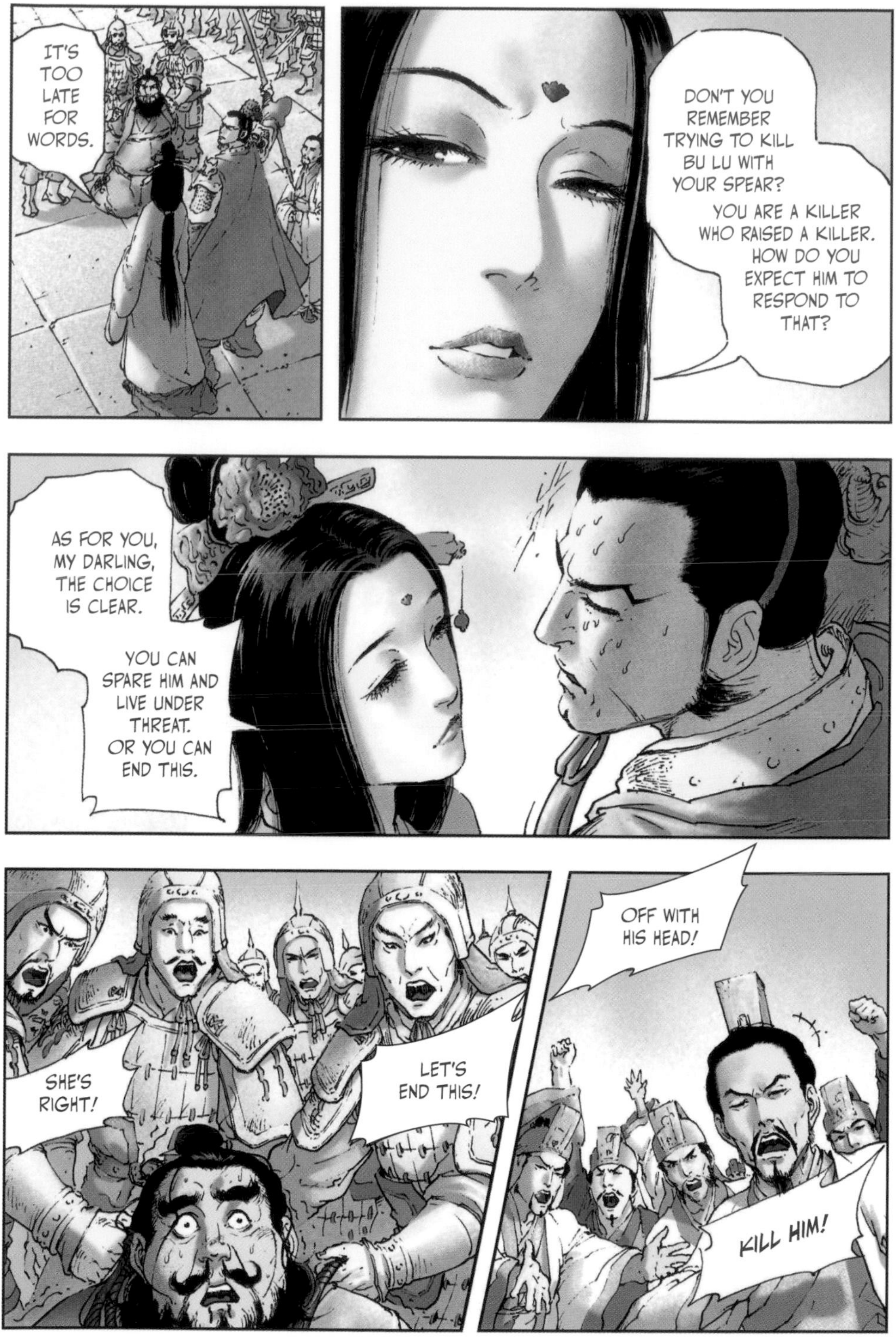
IT'S TOO LATE FOR WORDS.
DON'T YOU REMEMBER TRYING TO KILL BU LU WITH YOUR SPEAR?
YOU ARE A KILLER WHO RAISED A KILLER. HOW DO YOU EXPECT HIM TO RESPOND TO THAT?
AS FOR YOU, MY DARLING, THE CHOICE IS CLEAR.
YOU CAN SPARE HIM AND LIVE UNDER THREAT. OR YOU CAN END THIS.
SHE'S RIGHT!
LET'S END THIS!
OFF WITH HIS HEAD!
KILL HIM!

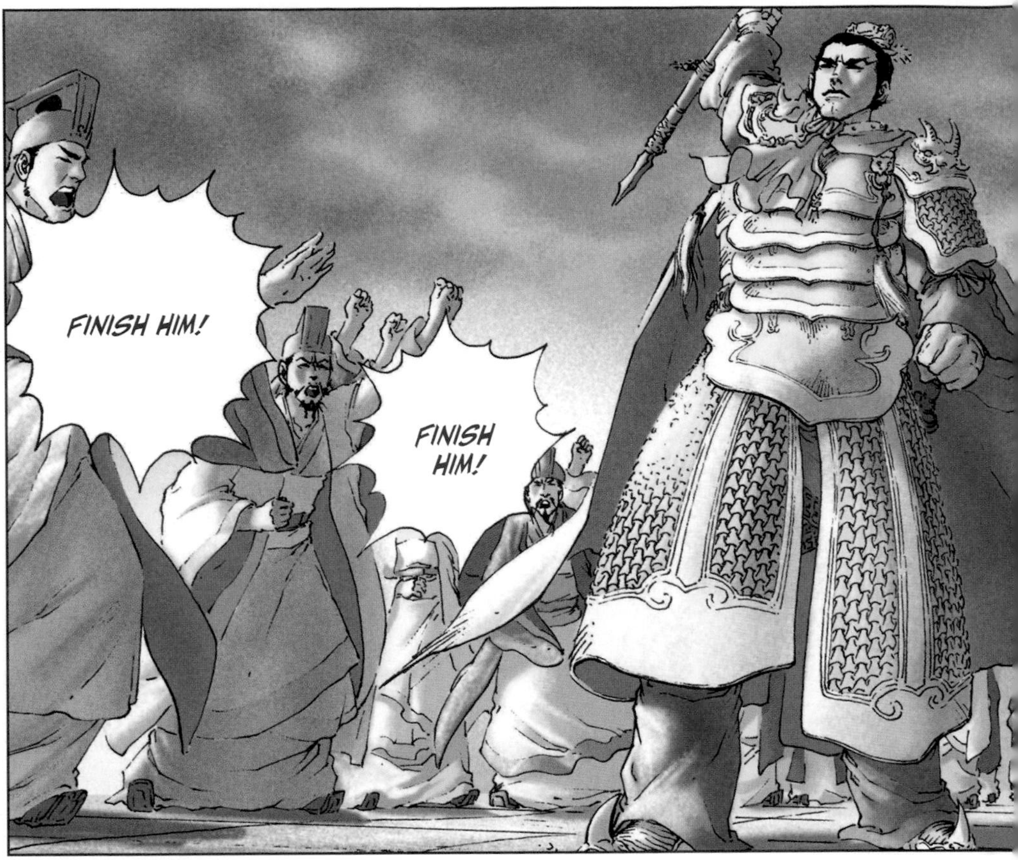
FINISH HIM!
FINISH HIM!

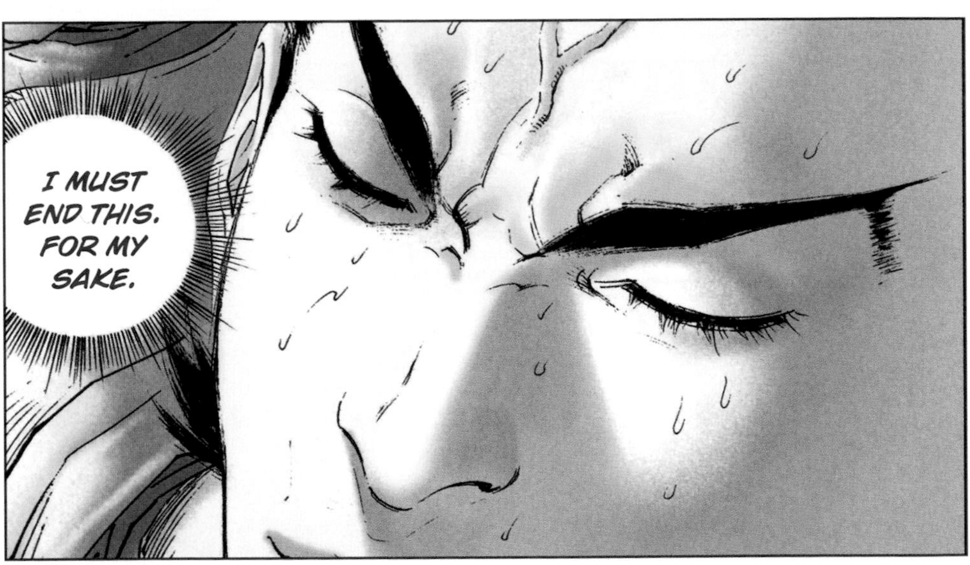
I MUST END THIS. FOR MY SAKE.

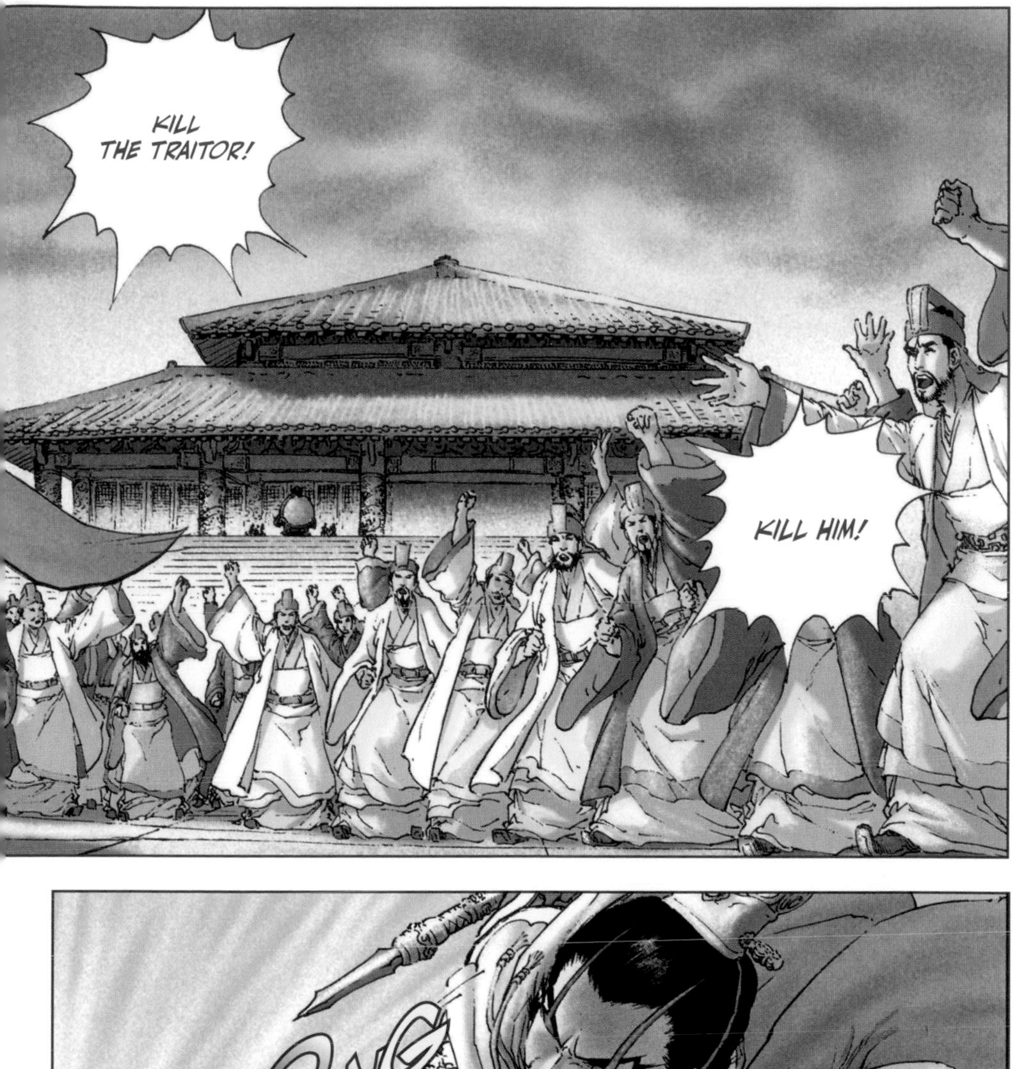
KILL
THE TRAITOR!
KILL HIM!

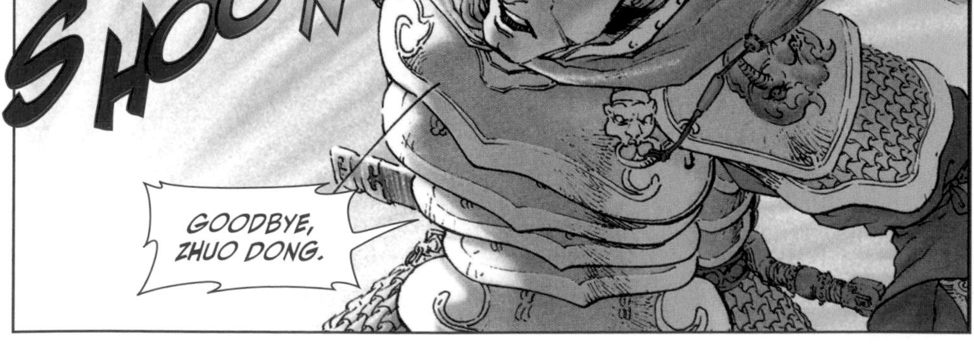
SHOONG
GOODBYE,
ZHUO DONG.

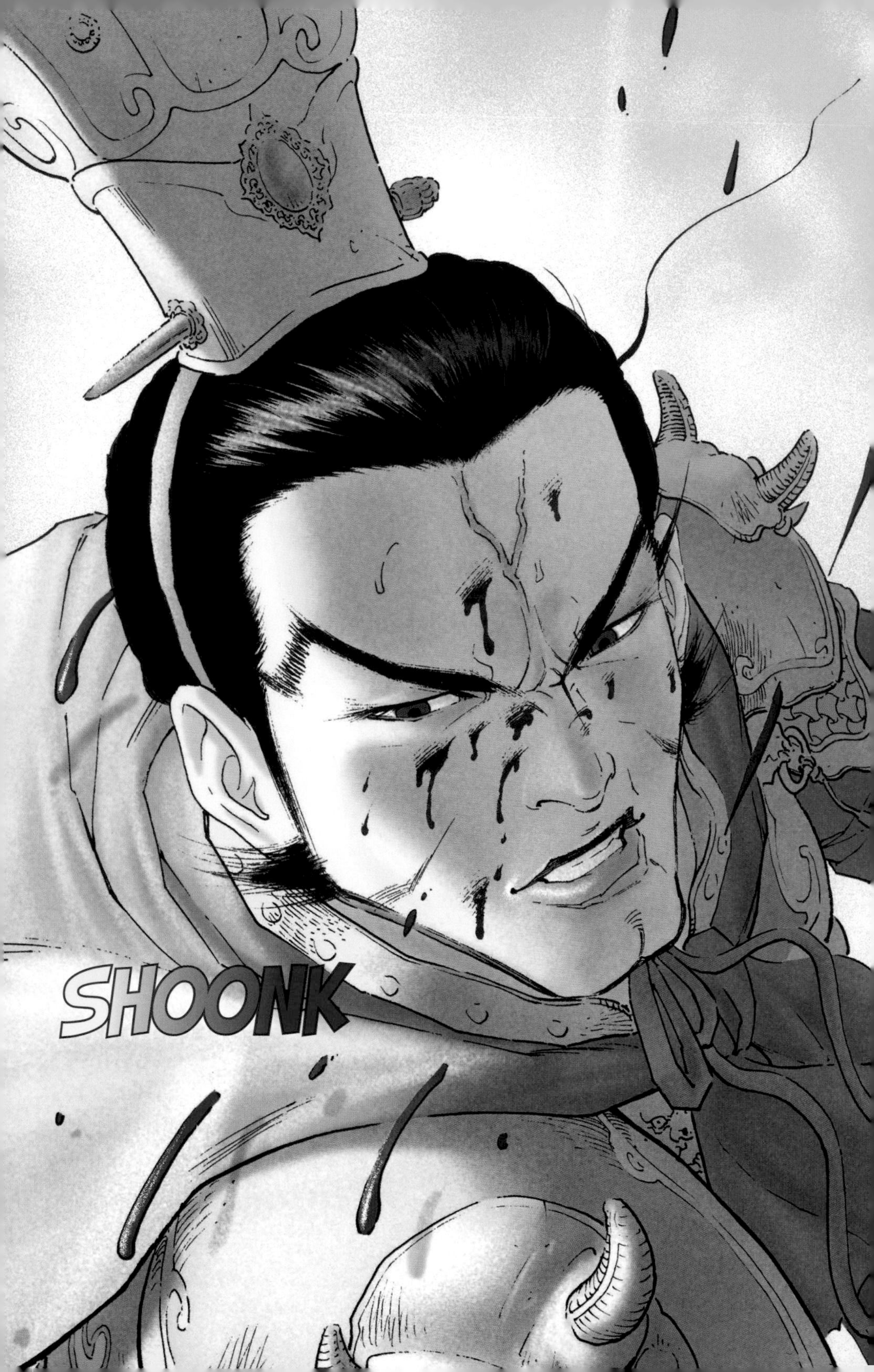
SHOONK

THE TIMELESS WORLD OF THREE KINGDOMS

Three Kingdoms is the story of a decades-long civil war that engulfed China during the first three centuries AD. Because it is the story of war, it is also a study of power: what it is, how it is won, how it is lost, and, most important, how it can corrupt a person's sense of self to the point where they feel invincible, thus precipitating a shameful undoing. There is a long tradition in both Eastern and Western culture of literary characters coming into power through a combination of strength, cunning, and ruthlessness only to be undone at the height of their powers when an adversary plots to exploit a flaw common to powerful characters: that even though they can exercise power in profound ways, sparing and taking life at will, they are often powerless to resist the covetous, jealous power of the heart. Yun Wang understands this shortcoming, and uses his foster daughter, Diao Chan, to lure Zhuo Dong and Bu Lu into a winner-take-all death match.

A similar scenario unfolds in Shakespeare's Othello. In the play, Iago orchestrates Othello's downfall by using Desdemona to arouse his murderous jealousy. By suggesting time and again that Desdemona is betraying Othello with his friend Cassio, Iago successfully exploits the very thing that Othello's power gives him an excess of: vanity. To be betrayed by his wife and his best friend is more than the ultimately fragile ego of Othello can bear. Of course, in Shakespeare's tragedy Othello's murderous rage befalls Desdemona, not Cassio, but we can see a similar scenario unfolding in the story of Bu Lu, Zhuo Dong, Diao Chan, and Yun Wang. When Yun Wang decides to fight back against the tyrannical rule of Zhuo Dong and Bu Lu, he astutely determines that a woman would be the most successful way of exploiting their respective vulnerabilities. Bu Lu, the legendary and much-feared warrior, would never believe that another person could have power over his emotions, and Zhuo Dong, the greedy zealot who has usurped the power of the emperor, cannot fathom the notion of there being someone or something he cannot possess. The two men are perhaps the most powerful in China, yet the very things that drove them to attain power also make them acutely susceptible to schemes like Yun Wang's.

To properly portray the notion of power, it is necessary

to understand more than just how it was attained or the wisdom or cruelty with which it is exercised. It is also important to display the ways in which power can disguise weakness in even the most seemingly invincible people, and how those weaknesses can be exploited. Of course, it's also important to understand that the more power you have, the more enemies you gain.

Legends from China THREE KINGDOMS

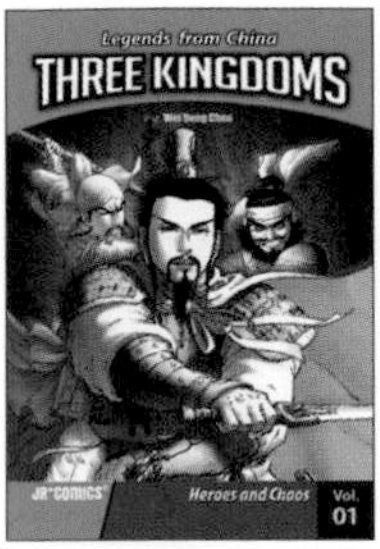
Legends from China
THREE KINGDOMS
JR COMICS
Heroes and Chaos
Vol. 01
Vol. 01

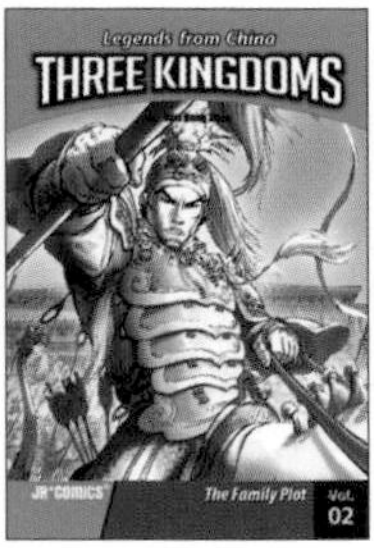
Legends from China
THREE KINGDOMS
JR COMICS
The Family Plot
Vol. 02
Vol. 02

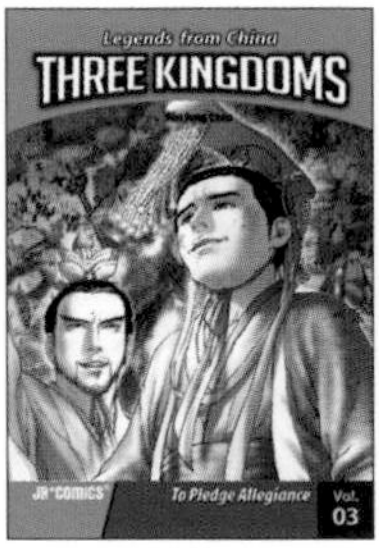
Legends from China
THREE KINGDOMS
JR COMICS
To Pledge Allegiance
Vol. 03
Vol. 03

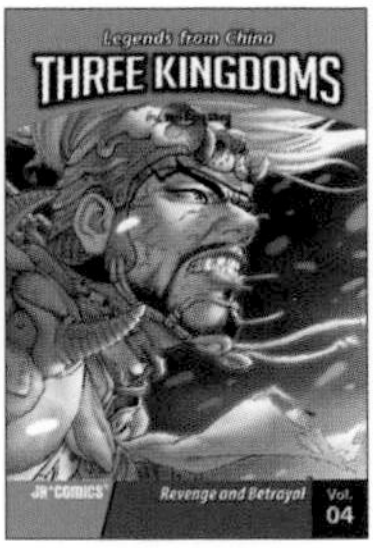
Legends from China
THREE KINGDOMS
JR COMICS
Revenge and Betrayal
Vol. 04
Vol. 04

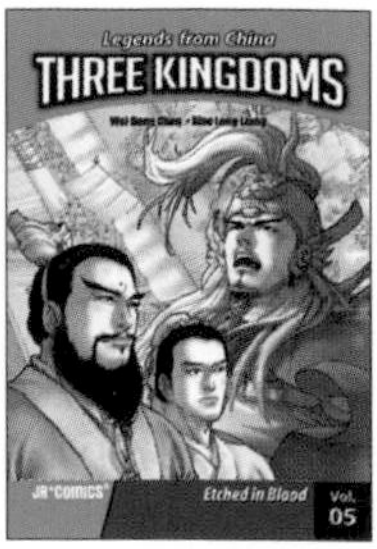
Legends from China
THREE KINGDOMS
JR COMICS
Etched in Blood
Vol. 05
Vol. 05

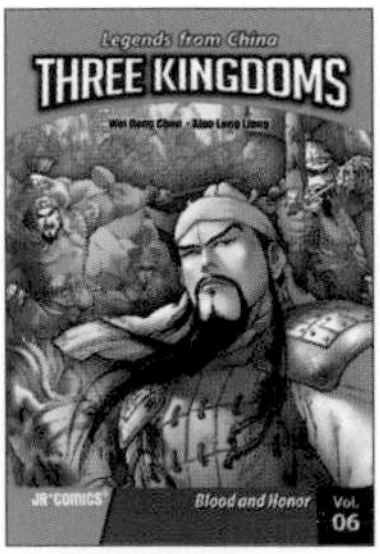
Legends from China
THREE KINGDOMS
JR COMICS
Blood and Honor
Vol. 06
Vol. 06

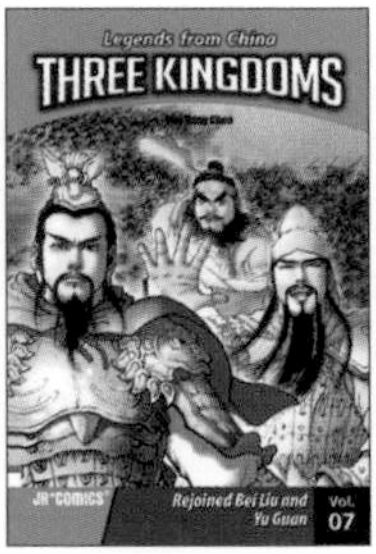
Legends from China
THREE KINGDOMS
JR COMICS
Rejoined Bei Liu and Yu Guan
Vol. 07
Vol. 07

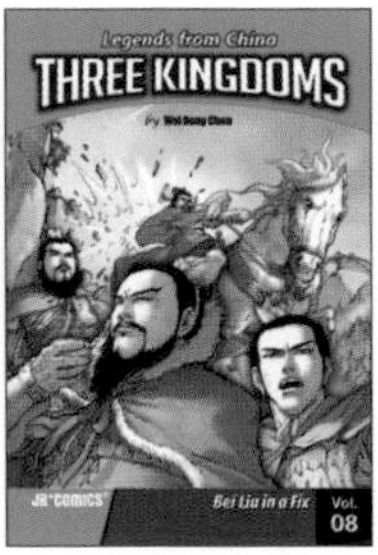
Legends from China
THREE KINGDOMS
JR COMICS
Bei Liu in a Fix
Vol. 08
Vol. 08

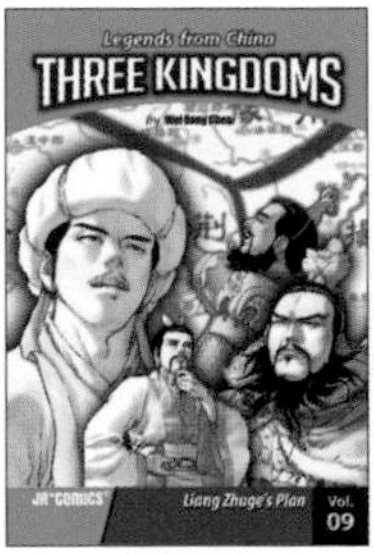
Legends from China
THREE KINGDOMS
JR COMICS
Liang Zhuge's Plan
Vol. 09
Vol. 09

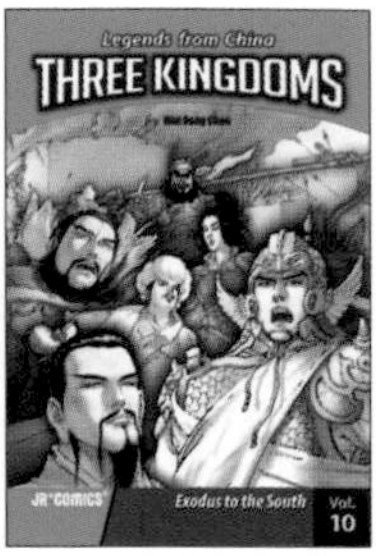
Legends from China
THREE KINGDOMS
JR COMICS
Exodus to the South
Vol. 10
Vol. 10

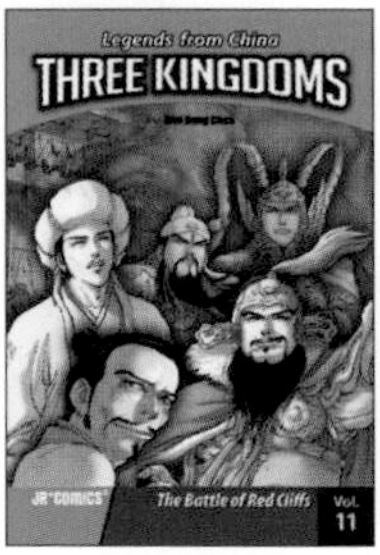
Legends from China
THREE KINGDOMS
JR COMICS
The Battle of Red Cliffs
Vol. 11
Vol. 11

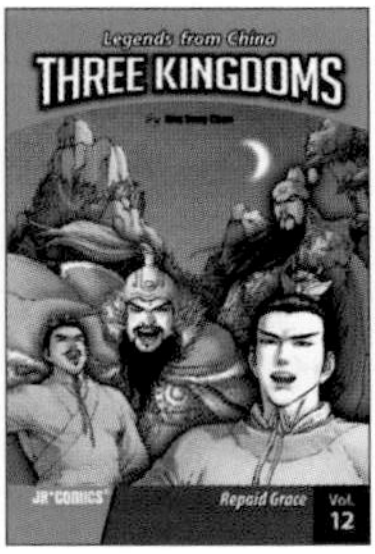
Legends from China
THREE KINGDOMS
JR COMICS
Repaid Grace
Vol. 12
Vol. 12

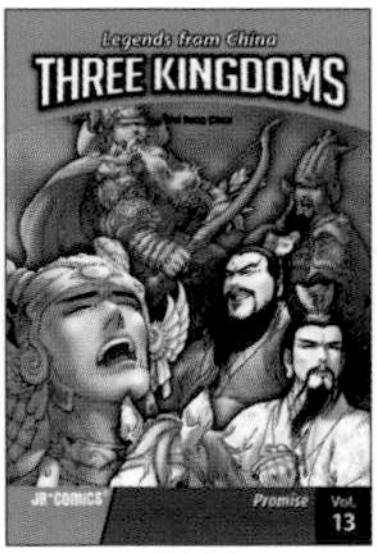
Legends from China
THREE KINGDOMS
JR COMICS
Promise
Vol. 13
Vol. 13

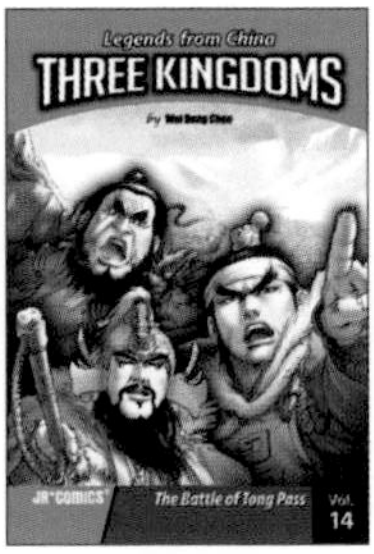
Legends from China
THREE KINGDOMS
JR COMICS
The Battle of Tong Pass
Vol. 14
Vol. 14

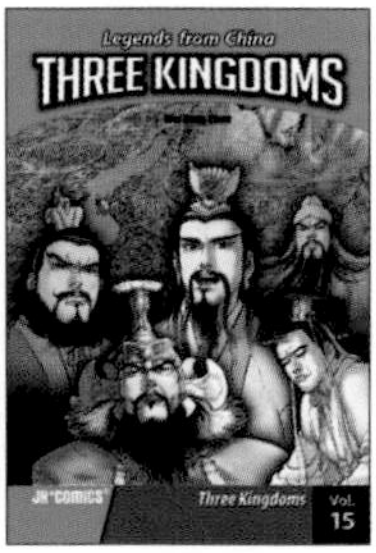
Legends from China
THREE KINGDOMS
JR COMICS
Three Kingdoms
Vol. 15
Vol. 15

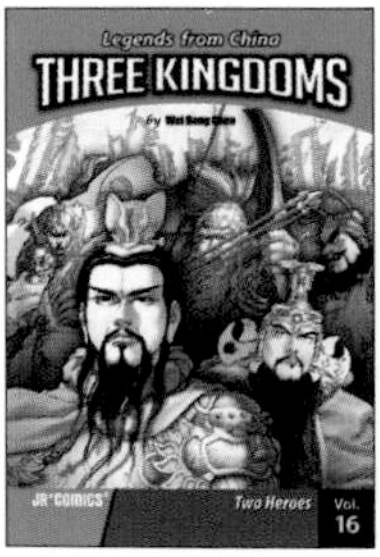
Legends from China
THREE KINGDOMS
JR COMICS
Two Heroes
Vol. 16
Vol. 16

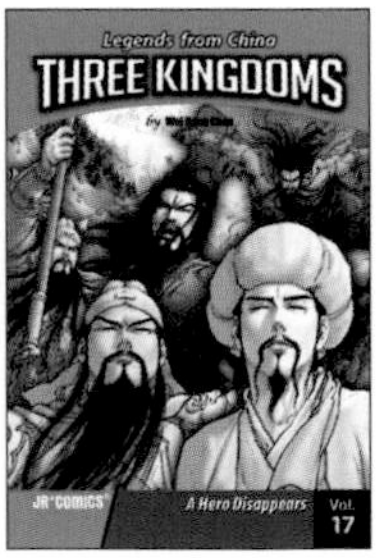
Legends from China
THREE KINGDOMS
JR COMICS
A Hero Disappears
Vol. 17
Vol. 17

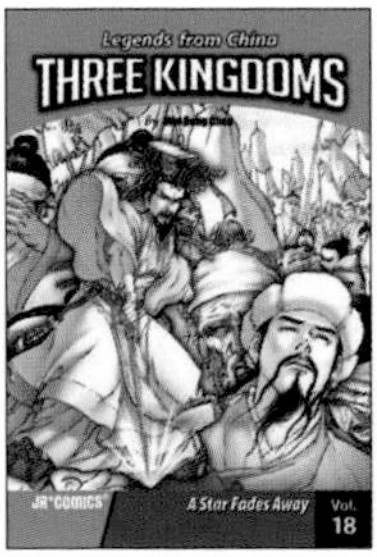
Legends from China
THREE KINGDOMS
JR COMICS
A Star Fades Away
Vol. 18
Vol. 18

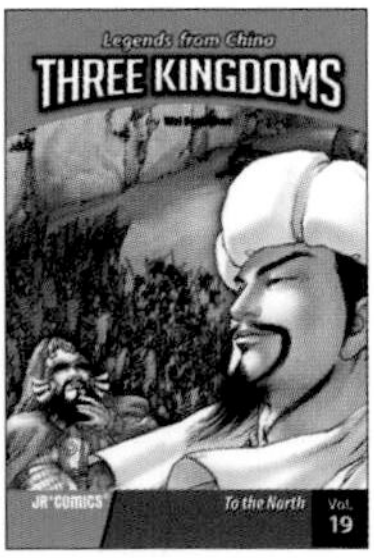
Legends from China
THREE KINGDOMS
JR COMICS
To the North
Vol. 19
Vol. 19

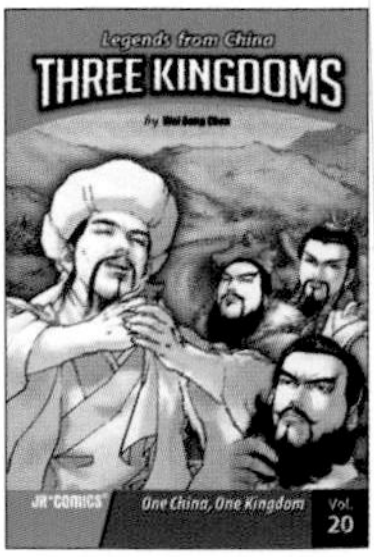
Legends from China
THREE KINGDOMS
JR COMICS
One China, One Kingdom
Vol. 20
Vol. 20